YA PIKE

DATE DUE

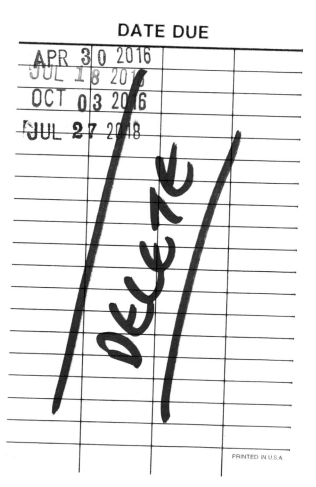

STRANGE GIRL

STRANGE GIRL

CHRISTOPHER PIKE

Simon Pulse

NEW YORK LONDON TORONTO SYDNEY NEW DELHI

SIMON PULSE

An imprint of Simon & Schuster Children's Publishing Division

1230 Avenue of the Americas, New York, New York 10020

This Simon Pulse edition November 2015

Text copyright © 2015 by Christopher Pike

Cover photograph copyright © 2015 by Ebru Sidar/Trevillion Images

All rights reserved, including the right of reproduction in whole or in part in any form.

SIMON PULSE and colophon are registered trademarks of Simon & Schuster, Inc.

For information about special discounts for bulk purchases, please contact Simon & Schuster Special Sales at 1-866-506-1949 or business@simonandschuster.com.

The Simon & Schuster Speakers Bureau can bring authors to your live event. For more information or to book an event contact the Simon & Schuster Speakers Bureau at 1-866-248-3049 or visit our website at www.simonspeakers.com.

Cover designed by Regina Flath

Interior designed by Hilary Zarycky

The text of this book was set in Adobe Garamond Pro.

Manufactured in the United States of America

2 4 6 8 10 9 7 5 3 1

The Library of Congress has cataloged the paperback edition as follows:

Pike, Christopher, 1955–, author.

Strange girl / by Christopher Pike. — First Simon Pulse paperback edition.

p. cm.

Summary: Told from the perspective of a seventeen-year-old boy in love with a mysterious girl who seems to have an unearthly ability to heal, but the ability carries quite a cost.

[1. Love—Fiction. 2. Supernatural—Fiction. 3. Healers—Fiction. 4. Goddesses—Fiction.]

I. Title.

PZ7.P626St 2015   [Fic]—dc23   2015012476

ISBN 978-1-4814-5059-1 (hc)

ISBN 978-1-4814-5058-4 (pbk)

ISBN 978-1-4814-5060-7 (eBook)

For Abir, who told me to write this story

CHAPTER ONE

I STILL GET ASKED ABOUT AJA, WHERE SHE CAME from, what it was like to be her friend, to actually date her, whether the stories about her were true, and who—or what—I really thought she was.

The last question makes me smile, probably because I understand it's hard to talk about Aja without sounding like a nut. That's what I try telling people who want to know about her. She was a mystery, a genuine enigma, in a world that has more trouble each day believing in such things. And now that she's gone, I think she'll forever remain a mystery.

At least to those who loved her.

And to those who feared her.

My name's Fred Allen, and I was a seventeen-year-old senior in high school when I met Aja. I was heading home on a hot Friday afternoon after a boring two weeks of classes when I spotted her sitting in the park across the street from campus. I'd like to say I saw something special about her from the start but I'd be lying, although later I wondered if she might have been kind of strange.

There was a perfectly fine bench five feet off to her left but instead of sitting on it like a normal person she was kneeling in the grass and plucking at a few scrawny daisies, while occasionally looking up at Elder High's sweaty student body as they poured into the side streets or else cut across the park toward their homes.

The sweat was because of the humidity. From June until October, it hovered around 90 percent. But the stickiness was usually vanquished by a brief autumn that blew by in a month or less, and was replaced by bitter winter winds that were so cold they'd bite your ass off—even if you had the bad taste to wear long underwear to school, which only the principal and the teachers did.

I suppose it could have been worse. Elder could have been located in North Dakota instead of South Dakota. Our northern neighbors were something of a mystery to most of us. I mean, it's not like anyone went to vacation up there. All we really knew about them was that they were always lobbying to change their name to just plain "Dakota." For some reason they thought that would make their state sound more inviting. Go figure.

Anyway, the thing that struck me about Aja at the start, besides her love of grass and daisies, was that she stared at many of the students who walked by. She didn't smile at them, didn't say hi or bat her long lashes or anything seductive like that. She just looked straight at them, which probably made most of them feel uncomfortable. I noticed the majority looked away as they strode by.

I mentioned her long lashes, and yeah, I did happen to notice she was pretty. Not beautiful in the usual social-media way, but an easy eight or nine on Fred Allen's relatively generous scale of one to ten. Even at a distance of a hundred yards I could see her hair was dark brown, shiny, and that her skin was the same color as my favorite ice cream—Häagen-Dazs Coffee.

Yet I didn't equate her with ice cream because I wanted to take a bite out of her or anything gross like that. It's not like I felt some mad rush of seventeen-year-old hormones and experienced first love for the twentieth time. I just sort of, you know, noticed that she looked nice, very nice, and that her long lashes framed a pair of large, dark eyes that were, sadly, not looking anywhere in my direction.

That was it; that was my first impression of Aja. Oh, there

was one other thing. I did happen to notice that she had on a simple white dress that didn't quite reach to her knees. The thing that struck me about the dress was—not that it was filthy—it looked like it could have used a wash.

Introduction to Aja complete. I went home and didn't give her more than a few hours of thought all weekend. And no, honestly, my fantasies were not a hundred percent sexual. I mainly wondered why a girl her age, if she was new to town, wasn't going to school. It was just a thought. Elder High, *my* school, was the only one in town for someone our age.

Monday morning I heard about Aja from my best friend, Janet Shell, five minutes before our first period, calculus, started. I was taking calculus because it was an AP class and my parents were obsessed that I ace as many hard classes as possible so I'd go to college and not grow up to be as miserable as they were.

That was sort of a joke in our household but, unfortunately, it was mostly true. My dad sold new and used cars at a Toyota dealership in a neighboring town of ours, Balen, which actually had a multiplex where the speaker system didn't sound like a jukebox and there was a generous selection of eight movies. Unlike Elder's sole theater, where you had to wear 3-D glasses just to keep from squinting at the sagging screen.

My mom also worked in Balen as an executive secretary for a boss that couldn't have spelled her job title. My parents were both smart, and they loved each other, I think, but when I asked why they hadn't moved away from Elder—like, say, before I was born—they just told me to pass the salt. What I mean is, the way they fell silent whenever I asked about their past made me feel like I was somehow rubbing salt in old wounds. I joke about it now—a bad habit, I still joke about most things—but it did worry me that they weren't happy.

Janet Shell, on the other hand, was super happy, or else she knew how to act the part, which according to her was all that mattered. She was taking calculus because she was smart and loved math. But she was cool, too. For example, although a straight-A student, she intended to get a C in calculus simply because she didn't want to get elected our class valedictorian.

Besides hating the spotlight, Janet knew if she was required to give a speech to us graduating seniors, there was no way she'd be able to resist telling us that virtually our whole class would still be living in Elder when our ten- and twenty-year high school reunions rolled around—her way of saying that the majority of us were destined to be losers.

"Have you seen the new girl yet?" Janet asked before Mr. Simon showed up his usual five minutes late. We'd had him as our math teacher three years running. The guy came into class reeking of pot almost every morning until Halloween rolled around, when he'd switch over to some kind of mysterious blue pill—Janet swore it was the stimulant Adderall—and lecture us on three chapters a week instead of his normal three pages.

Naturally, Janet's question about the "new girl" piqued my interest. I'd been looking for her since I'd arrived at school. Still, I acted cool.

"Nope," I said, adding a shrug.

"Bullshit. You must have seen her. You just blushed."

"I don't know what you're talking about."

Janet looked me over. "Her name's Aja—*A-J-A*. It's pronounced like Asia but with more of a *J* sound. She's a total fox, super exotic-looking. She just moved here from a remote village in Brazil. Everyone's talking about her but I hear she's not talking much. The word is—she's not stuck-up, just quiet." Janet paused. "What do you think? Want to ask her out?"

"How about I meet her first, then decide?" I said.

"Okay. But I think with this one you're going to have to act fast. She's no Nicole. You can't wait two years to get up your nerve. She'll go quick."

I felt a stab of pain that Janet had so carelessly brought up Nicole but hid it. "What makes you so sure? She might be picky."

Janet wavered. "True. But a ton of guys are going to hit on her. She's a looker and she's got money and she knows how to dress."

Recalling the plain, dusty dress Aja had been wearing in the park, that surprised me. "Really?"

Janet caught the note in my voice. "You have seen her, you bastard. Why do you lie to me when you're such a shitty liar? Tell me the truth, have you talked to her?"

I sighed. "I saw a new girl last Friday while walking home from school. She was sitting in the park, plucking flowers. I'm not sure she's the same person you're talking about."

"Right. Like this town has a surplus of beautiful girls."

"Hold on a sec. You're the one who says us guys are always judging a book by its cover. Well, what are you doing? So she's pretty. So she's got expensive clothes. She could still be a jerk."

"She's not, she's cool." Janet leaned closer, lowered her voice. "I met her, I spoke to her."

"When?"

"Ten minutes ago. We only exchanged a few words but I sensed something unique about her." Janet paused. "You know the last time I said that, don't you?"

"Ages ago. When you met me."

"That's right. That's why you need to ask her out."

"I'll think about it."

Mr. Simon stumbled in right then, smelling like Colombian Gold, and told us to open our textbooks to chapter three. It was Janet who had to remind him that we hadn't covered chapter two yet.

I spent most of the class digesting what Janet had said. I'd learned long ago to take her insights seriously. Janet was not merely smart; she had an uncanny intuition when it came to people. She said 99.99 percent of the population were sheep. If she liked Aja, it meant she was more than a pretty face.

I saw Aja in third period, before lunch, in American History.

We were in the same class. Just my luck.

Maybe, I thought, maybe not. My usual seat was in the corner, all the way in the back. Aja came in two minutes after me and sat down in the first row, but the last seat, by the windows. Basically, even though we occupied the same room, she was pretty far away. I couldn't help but think she'd somehow spotted me, remembered me staring at her the previous Friday afternoon, and had gone out of her way to keep her distance.

Of course, given the fact that she hadn't even glanced in my direction when she'd entered the classroom, I was probably just being paranoid.

She looked good, better than good. There were plenty of

heads between me and her and all I could see was Aja's. Her dark hair appeared a little shorter than last Friday, like she'd gotten a trim over the weekend. But the shine was still there. And her long eyelashes, seen in profile, were amazing.

Our teacher, Mrs. Nancy Billard, came into the room. A stuffy, old bird if you got on her wrong side, but one of the most caring people you could meet if she happened to like you. She taught AP English on top of history and I'd had her for English the previous year and had won her over with a slew of wild-and-crazy short stories I'd written. She liked students who thought outside the box.

However, those who landed on her wrong side were either flunked or ignored or both. In her AP classes she enforced a strict work ethic. She said anyone who wanted to go to college had to earn it.

"I see we have a new student today," she said, glancing in Aja's direction. "I was told you'd be joining us. What's your name?"

"Aja," she replied in a soft voice.

"Is that your first or last name?"

"It's what people call me."

Billard cleared her throat, a bad sign. "Then that's what I'll call you. But please humor the rest of the class and tell us your full name."

"Aja Smith."

"Took a moment to remember your family name?"

Aja stared at her and said nothing.

Billard continued. "Well, we're all very happy you could join us two weeks late. Another week and you'd have wandered in during the Civil War. Ted, fetch a textbook for Aja from the closet and let's all open to page forty-nine, chapter three. Time we got to the thirteen colonies and their feud with King George the Third." Billard paused and glanced at Aja again. "Do you have a problem, girl?"

"No."

"You're looking at me kind of funny. I thought maybe you did." Aja didn't reply, just continued to stare at her, which didn't sit well with Billard. "You do know something about American history, don't you?"

"No," Aja replied.

Billard blinked, unsure whether Aja was sassing her or not. "Then it's your responsibility to catch up. This is an AP class—there are no shortcuts here. Read the first forty-eight pages of your textbook tonight and I'll quiz you on them tomorrow."

Aja nodded without speaking as she accepted the textbook from Ted Weldon, a football jock with a double-digit IQ and a gross habit of farting whenever he yawned. Some might have wondered what he was doing in an AP class.

But those who bothered to contemplate the matter probably didn't know that Ted's father was best buddies with Elder High's Principal Levitt and that—despite what Billard had just said—there were always shortcuts available to those students whose parents knew the right people.

Handing Aja her textbook, Ted didn't simply look at her; he gloated over her face and body before returning to his chair, eliciting a mild chuckle from the rest of the class.

"Thanks," Aja said. Her voice was not merely soft, it was smooth, cool, confident. She obviously didn't have to speak up to make a point. Plus her answers to Billard's questions had been at best evasive, which I naturally had to admire.

Yet I could tell already that Billard didn't like her and that Aja was probably going to have a hard time in her class. That bothered me, a little, even though she was a total stranger.

Total stranger. Damn. Got to change that fast.

I remembered Janet's warning that Aja would not last when it came to Elder High's horny guys, and it got my adrenaline pumping. When class was over I caught up with her outside in the hallway and walked by her side before she stopped at her locker. *Oh no,* I thought. I wasn't ready for this. Suddenly a life-changing choice was upon me. I could either keep walking and live the rest of my days in regret or I could stop and pretend to have a locker next to her.

I did the latter, spinning the dial on the lock like it was preset to my favorite radio station. Only the volume never came on and the locker never opened because I had no idea what the combination was. Fortunately, Aja seemed to be having trouble with her own locker and I was able to swoop in and rescue her.

"It's not opening?" I asked, way too casually and with a stupid grin on my face.

Aja pulled a slip of paper from her pants pocket and stuck it out for me to take. "I was told this is the combination," she said.

Aja didn't have on ordinary pants; she wore designer jeans that had clearly been purchased far from Elder's finest clothing stores. Up top she had on an ultrathin maroon sweater; and if it was responsible for her subtle curves, then it was worth its weight in gold. Her silky blouse had red in it as well—a rusty color that made me think of desert sand dunes and romantic sunset kisses and . . .

I was losing it, I suddenly realized. Aja's big brown eyes were still waiting for me to take her slip of paper. I shook my head and took a breath. Breathing was good, I reminded myself.

"This looks like it might work," I said. *Duh!* The piece of paper said: "LOCKER NUMBER" on top. A sequence of three numbers followed: 12–18–24. All the locks in school—all the combinations I'd ever seen, for that matter—worked on the right-left-right sequence. When I dialed in Aja's three digits, the locker immediately opened. Amazing. I noticed her eyes following me closely and added, "You see how it works?"

"Yes," she replied, and it was only then I realized she'd never had a locker before. She deposited her book inside and closed it. Out of habit, I reached up and spun the dial.

"You can't be too careful," I said.

"Pardon?"

"Your lock. You need to spin it to clear the combination." She didn't respond, just stared at me. Again, I felt the need to add something. "So no one will break into your locker."

"Kids do that here?" she asked.

"Some kids do, yeah." Again, she seemed to wait for me to continue so I added, "Actually, the students here don't like being called kids."

"What should I call them?"

"Girls or guys or people. Kids—it sounds kind of young, you know."

"I didn't know that but thanks for telling me."

"No problem. By the way, my name's Fred Allen. I'm in your history class. I sit in the back."

"I saw you."

"You did?" God, the way I asked the question, the sheer amount of wonder in my tone, it was like she'd just told me she'd found a heart donor that could save my life. I reminded myself again to keep breathing and try to act normal. Fortunately, Aja didn't appear to notice my clumsiness.

"Yes," she said simply, adding, "I'm Aja."

"I know. I mean, I heard what you told Mrs. Billard." Aja nodded and again acted as if she wanted me to keep talking. I added, "She can be a great teacher if she thinks you're trying. But slack off and she'll classify you as a loser. Then you'll be in trouble. She was serious when she told you that she's going to quiz you on the first two chapters of the textbook. If I was you I'd study tonight. I'd read chapter three as well. I wouldn't be surprised if she quizzed you on the whole lot."

"I will." She looked past me as the student body converged toward Elder High's courtyard. We had an indoor cafeteria but no one ventured inside before the first snow came. The school lunch staff didn't mind. They kept a half-dozen windows open where you could order a decent hamburger, hot dog, or sandwich if you had the money. Since I was on a strict budget, I usually brought a brown bag from home and just picked up a Coke from one of the vending machines. In fact, my lunch was waiting for me back at my real locker, although I felt in no hurry to get to it.

"The kids . . . the girls and guys have lunch now?" Aja asked.

"Yeah. It's always after third period. Are you hungry?"

"This bod . . ." She suddenly stopped. "Yes."

"Bring anything from home?" I knew she hadn't because I'd seen the interior of her locker and it had been empty. She shook her head and for the hundredth time waited for me to go on. I added, "Then you should probably pick up something at the windows."

"Are you going to these . . . windows?"

"Uh-huh. I can show you where they are if you want. If you don't have other plans, I mean."

She flashed a smile. "I don't have any plans, Fred."

I liked how she said my name and loved her smile; nevertheless, I groaned inside thinking how hard Janet would be laughing if she could see me now. Honestly, my nervousness made no sense. Sure, Aja was pretty, and, sure, I liked her, or at least I thought I did. But she was the new girl in town, a stranger from another country, and English was obviously a second language for her. She should have been the one stumbling all over the place.

I assumed the language barrier was the reason she had

almost referred to herself as *"This body."* I was pretty sure that's what she'd been about to say.

I escorted her to the windows and if I'd been forced to critique my stride I'd have to say I looked like an extra on *The Walking Dead*. I was definitely taking time finding my cool gear. But eventually I began to calm down and by the time we'd waited in line and it was our turn to order I was feeling pretty good about myself. Why not? I'd just met Aja and already I was taking her to lunch. Not bad for a few minutes' work. I'd decided to pay for whatever she ordered to show what a gentleman I was.

"Hey, Fred, how's the demo going?" Carlos asked from the other side of the glass. He was from Mexico and worked three jobs to keep his family of six out of the rain. He was also a genius when it came to playing the acoustic guitar and was helping me to lay down tracks on a new three-song demo I was struggling to put together.

Yeah, I know, so I wanted to be a rock star.

But tell the truth. Who didn't?

"It's getting there," I said honestly, turning to Aja, who was staring at Carlos and not bothering to look at the overhead menu. To his credit, Carlos acted like I showed up every afternoon with a pretty girl on my arm. "Know what you want?" I asked Aja.

She looked at me. "It doesn't matter."

"Want a burger? A sandwich? A salad?"

"I'll have what you're having," she said.

"I was going to have a turkey sandwich with fries. And a Coke. That sound good?"

Aja nodded. "That's good."

Carlos whipped up our sandwiches in three minutes flat and when it was time to pay Aja pulled out a wad of cash fat enough to buy a new car with. I hastily told her I had it covered and she put the money back in her pocket.

Like the rest of town, Elder High was kind of old and kind of poor, and no part of our campus reflected those qualities more than our courtyard. It had no tables, no umbrellas to block the sun, no drinking fountains. Only peeling wooden benches that, if you were lucky, managed to catch the shade of a nearby tree.

Of course we had trees, the whole state did, except for our infamous Badlands, which I, personally, happened to love. I steered Aja toward a shady bench located somewhere between where the jocks and the bad boys gathered. Like most schools, Elder High had a variety of clearly defined social groups, none of which had ever shown the slightest interest in attracting me as a member.

For a few minutes I had Aja all to myself but I wasted

them because all I did was eat and watch her eat. It was during this time I noticed that she seemed to be following my lead. When I unwrapped my turkey sandwich, she unwrapped hers. When I reached for a fry or a sip of Coke, she did the same. She didn't take nearly as big bites as I did, though. If anything she chewed her food more thoroughly than anyone I'd ever met.

But she only mimicked me for a few minutes before quitting.

"Where are you from?" I finally asked.

Aja pointed north. "I live with my aunt Clara. In a white house by a large pond."

I had meant where she was from in Brazil but her answer interested me. "You don't live in the old Carter Mansion, do you?"

"Carter? Hmm. Yes, the realtor told Aunty that was the name of the man who built the house. That's where this . . . that's where I stay."

"That's one big house. Is it just the two of you?"

"Bart lives with us."

"Who's Bart?"

"Bart is Bart. He takes care of things."

"Is he a housekeeper? A butler?"

"Yes. He's been with Aunty since before I met her."

"How old were you when you met your aunt?"

"I was small." Aja added casually, "I ran into her in the jungle."

"The jungle?"

"The town where I was born is surrounded by jungle."

"And you just sort of bumped into your aunt?"

"Yes."

"Are you saying she's not your real aunt?"

Aja sipped her drink. "She's as real as you and me."

I frowned. "This was in Brazil?"

"Yes."

I wanted to continue my line of questioning but we got interrupted right then by Dale Parish and Michael Garcia, two close friends of mine. Actually, two members of a band I'd formed—Half Life. Dale played bass and Mike was our drummer. Dale had only been playing a year but he was a natural and kept improving in leaps and bounds every month. Mike—he'd been banging on anything that made noise since he'd been a kid. No joke, he was like a force of nature onstage. We were lucky to have him. I kept expecting to lose him to a louder and more successful group.

Yet Mike swore he'd never leave us. He had faith in my singing and songwriting abilities.

Unfortunately, he also had a temper and was unpredictable. He missed plenty of practice sessions, even a few paid gigs. We never knew which Mike was going to show up. If he was loaded, on pot or beer, we knew the "Beast" was in the room and we'd better watch out. But when he was sober he was the nicest guy. The swings could be stressful.

Worse, Mike caused Dale constant grief. Because Dale was in love with him and Mike didn't have a clue. On the surface it seemed impossible, since they'd grown up together. But the truth was Mike didn't even know Dale was gay. And Dale had begged me and our keyboardist, Shelly Wilson, never to tell him.

Carlos had warned me—and Carlos never lied—that Mike often hung out with a Hispanic gang in Balen that controlled most of the area's drug traffic. If anything was going to tear our band apart, I knew it was going to be the tension between our drummer and bass player.

"Who do we have here?" Mike asked, straddling the bench beside Aja like it—or she—was a horse he was anxious to ride. Dale nodded to me and smiled uneasily in Aja's direction but remained standing.

Physically, the two couldn't have been more unlike. Mike was dark-skinned, short and stocky, and could bench-press more than Elder's heartiest jocks. If a swinging chick was looking for a bad boy who could rip holes in the sheets, Mike was it. While Dale—well, I never met a more gentle soul in my life but there was a reason his stage name was "The Corpse." He was way beyond skinny and pale. Onstage, under a harsh spotlight, he almost looked transparent. But the boy sure could play. That was all that mattered to me.

I spoke up. "Aja, these are two musician friends of mine, Mike and Dale. We're in a band together. Dale plays bass and Mike the drums. Guys, this is Aja. She's from Brazil. This is her first day at Elder High."

Aja nodded in their direction. "I enjoy music."

"But do you like musicians?" Mike asked, teasing. "That's what I want to know. Besides, what the hell are you doing with Fred? Did he tell you he's such a wuss that he won't go onstage—and I'm talking practically every single gig we play—without me swearing that I've got his back?"

"I'm afraid it's true," I admitted. In the band, during shows, once Mike got going he created such a ferocious rhythm that he drowned out any flat notes I hit on my guitar or with my voice.

"Fred has more talent in his little finger than the rest of us combined," Dale added.

Mike slapped me on the back. "Yeah, Fred's the only one in this town that's going places. Take my word for it. So how did you two meet?"

I assumed Aja would remain silent, given her habit, and that I'd have to answer. However, she stared Mike right in the eye and said, "We met last Friday in the park. He was watching me pick flowers and I smiled at him but he ignored me. But today he's a lot more friendly."

Her comment caused my heart to skip.

She'd smiled at me?

Mike was suddenly curious about her accent. *"¿Hablan español en el lugar de Brasil de donde vienes?"* he asked.

"No muchos. Pero algunos," Aja said.

"¿Pero creciste hablando portugués?" Mike asked.

"Sim," Aja said.

"What the hell are they saying?" I asked Dale. He'd taken four years of Spanish at school but his real knowledge of the language had come from hanging around Mike's family. Dale leaned over and whispered in my ear.

"Mike asked if they spoke Spanish in her part of Brazil. Aja said, 'Not many, but some.' Then Mike asked, 'But you grew up speaking Portuguese?' And Aja said, 'Yes.'"

"Why the sudden interest in Aja's background?" I said. But Mike ignored me and continued to speak to Aja, who appeared to fascinate him.

"Your accent—you remind me of my grandmother," Mike said. "She could speak half a dozen languages. She sounded like she was from everywhere, and nowhere, if you know what I mean. Sort of like you."

Aja lowered her head. *"Ninguém do nada."*

"What was that?" I asked quickly.

Apparently she'd answered in Portuguese, which neither Mike nor Dale understood. When I asked Aja what she'd said, all she did was shake her head like it didn't matter.

Dale flashed Mike a sign that it was time to split and Mike, knowing my bad luck with girls, bid us a quick farewell. When they were gone Aja and I returned to eating our sandwiches and fries. A long silence settled between us but to my surprise it wasn't uncomfortable. I suspected Aja had spent most of her life alone and wasn't bothered by quiet.

"I apologize for Mike," I said. "He can be a handful when you first meet him."

"He has a fiery spirit."

"I suppose that's where all the smoke comes from."

Aja turned her big, brown eyes on me. "They look up to you. Are you that good?"

I assumed she was asking about my musical abilities and shrugged. "As far as South Dakota is concerned, I could be the next Mozart. But if I performed at a club in Los Angeles or New York or Seattle I'd be laughed off the stage." I took a gulp of Coke. "Trying to make a living as a singer/songwriter is probably the most irrational ambition a guy can have. One in a million—no, one in ten million—ends up making money at it."

"But it's what you want to do," she said.

"Unfortunately."

"Then you'll do it."

I chuckled. "You haven't even seen us play."

The remark was far from subtle. I was hoping she'd bite and say she'd like to come to a show. Also, it wasn't by chance that I'd switched from talking about me to talking about the band. If she didn't bite, then she was rejecting Half Life, not me. So went my crazy logic. The truth was I'd brought up being a musician to impress her. It was shameless, I know, but I figured I had to play what cards I held.

"Is it fun for you?" she asked.

"Being onstage? Sometimes—when I forget what I'm doing and that people are watching me. Then I love it. But most of the time I'm way too self-conscious and can't wait until the gig is over. Seriously."

Aja continued to stare at me and because she didn't blink often, it was a bit disconcerting. "Play for me sometime," she said.

There. I'd practically begged her to ask but now that she had I wished I'd kept my mouth shut. I shook my head. "I'm not a solo artist. Better to see me in the band."

She nodded but I didn't think she believed me.

"How about you?" I asked. "What's your favorite hobby?"

She hesitated. "I don't have any hobbies. I just . . . enjoy things."

"What sort of things?"

"Bart told me to watch out for questions like that. He said they'd get me into trouble."

Her response caught me off guard. "Huh?"

"I told you about Bart."

"I know, I heard you. But he actually told you how to behave while you were at school today?"

Aja nodded. "He spent the weekend trying to teach me what to say and what not to say."

"Isn't that a little weird?"

If my question bothered her, she showed no sign. "Bart said he had to teach me so I wouldn't appear weird to the rest of you." As if to reassure me, she reached out and touched my arm. "He was trying to help."

The instant she touched me, I felt something odd, a lapse of sorts, where I had trouble focusing. The scene around us, the guys and girls walking back and forth across the court-yard, they didn't stop but they did seem to slow down. I shook my head to clear it and the sensation eased up, somewhat. I noticed Aja had taken back her hand. I had to struggle to get out my next remark.

"I should meet this guy. Maybe he can help me with my weirdness."

Aja suddenly stood, leaving what was left of her food behind on the bench. She wasn't tall but at that moment she could have been standing on a chair and looking down at me. I worried that my peculiar sensation had not passed, after all. Again, I had to remind myself that she was new to the school, the stranger in a strange land, but right then I was certain I had it all wrong, that she was more at home in Elder than I could ever hope to be.

"I'm glad we got to talk, Fred. I hope I see you again soon."

With that she turned and walked away.

CHAPTER TWO

THAT EVENING AT TEN FIFTEEN I GOT TOGETHER with the band at Shelly Wilson's garage. The reason I was so late was because the hardware store where I worked was doing inventory and the boss wanted me counting the stock on the shelves until exactly ten o'clock. I was flying high from my lunch with Aja but the joy dimmed as I slipped back into the usual grind of my life.

Since a Walmart had opened in Balen, the hardware store was losing money and my boss was always tense and taking it out on us employees. He'd given me a dollar-an-hour raise at the start of summer but had since cut me back to minimum wage. The loss of the extra bucks hurt.

Still, I looked forward to playing with the band. We usually practiced at Shelly's garage since her parents were the only ones who'd allowed us to insulate the space. We'd fastened large bags of powdered cellulose—a fancy name for ground-up wood pulp—to the ceiling and walls so that we could play as loud as we wanted and a person standing right outside the garage door couldn't hear a thing.

Shelly's parents had been supportive of her musical career from a young age. At sixty-one, her father was twenty-five years older than her mother and was retired, but in his prime he'd played piano with the Chicago Symphony Orchestra— no small feat. He'd developed serious arthritis in his hands when Shelly was only five yet had persisted in tutoring her on his favorite instrument. As a result Shelly was the most trained musician in our band. Anything she heard, she could play back on any form of keyboard; it didn't matter how complex it was.

But despite Shelly's skill and dedication, she had a major handicap. She never came up with anything new. Whenever we jammed, chasing one crazy riff or lyric after another, just throwing stuff out into the air, she'd get lost. Though it pained her, and her father, she was devoid of creativity. The flaw showed itself in the lack of emotion in her playing. Yet, because of her technical abilities, most audiences didn't notice the problem.

But we did and so did Shelly.

Janet was also at our practice. As our manager, the one who set up our gigs and handled our finances—for 15 percent commission plus expenses—she wasn't required to be at the garage but I suspected she was more interested in cornering me on Aja than in reviewing how much I still owed on my Marshall amp. And sure enough her eyes lit up the second I walked in, which told me I'd better get her outside quick.

The reason was Shelly. She'd had a crush on me since we were in middle school. I tried not talking about my love life around her. The short time I'd gone out with Nicole, Shelly hadn't even come to practice, and it had been at her house.

"I saw everything," Janet said the second we were alone. "I followed you to Aja's locker, and the windows, and was watching the two of you the whole time you ate on the bench. By the way, that was a smart opening when you faked sharing a locker beside her."

"Thanks. I assume you were able to read our lips so there's no point in telling you what we talked about."

"Don't you dare! I want to hear everything!"

"On one condition. Get me her number."

"You don't have it yet?" Janet asked.

"No."

"Done. Speak."

Since the others were waiting, I gave her a condensed

version of my conversation with Aja. Janet listened without interrupting; she was a good listener. When I was done she appeared puzzled.

"Why'd you get dizzy around her?" she asked.

I shrugged. "It was no big deal."

"It was probably nerves."

"I wasn't that nervous."

"Fred."

"I'm telling you the truth. Look, I just met her. I like her, I don't love her." I added, "We'd better get back inside."

Janet nodded. "I'm proud of you. It took guts to go after her the way you did. It sounds like she likes you." She paused. "Why the long face?"

I shook my head. "On the surface I'd agree—she seemed to like me. The last thing she said is she wanted to talk again. But the way she sat so silent—it was like a part of her was far away, in her own little world."

"That could be good. It could mean she has depth."

"Depth can be a two-edged sword. Fall for a girl with too much depth and you can end up falling forever."

"How poetic." Janet patted me on the back. "I've got a good feeling about Aja. She could be the one, you know, who makes you feel so much you finally write a love song that sells. And if that doesn't happen, you'll at least get sex out of the deal."

"I hope you got that in writing."

Janet laughed. "Wake up! She's from Brazil! Land of thong bikinis. Plus you're cute. You always forget that. Of course she'll have sex with you."

I did *not* think I was cute. All I saw when I looked into the mirror was a standard guy: brown eyes, brown hair—which was beginning to curl now that I was letting it grow longer. Was there anything that made me unique?

Well, I suppose I did have nice hands. They were large, my fingers were long; they made it easier for me to play the guitar. And Nicole—and Janet, who seldom handed out compliments—said I looked thoughtful. I took that to mean I didn't look stupid, but they acted like it was a rare quality. Still, no one ever raved about my smile, probably because I didn't smile often. Frankly, except when I was playing guitar, my parents said I looked depressed. They were always asking me if I wanted to see someone.

Yeah, I thought. I wanted to see a pretty girl who wanted to love me, tell me I was going to be a rock star, and especially who wanted to have sex with me. It seemed too much to hope that that girl might be Aja.

Back inside the garage we had a mini–business meeting. Janet held court. First she went over the gigs we had coming up. Friday, we were playing at a high school in Stoker, which was an hour away. The pay was four hundred, not bad considering all we had to do was play our usual list of covers and break down our equipment by midnight.

Saturday night's gig was at the Roadhouse; it was located a mile outside Ellsworth Air Force Base, ten miles east of Rapid City—the largest city in the state—and a two-hundred-mile drive from Elder. We all groaned when Janet made the announcement. We'd played for the boys at the base before and we still had the scars to prove it; none worse than Mike, who'd been lucky to escape with four cracked ribs. Me, I'd needed three stitches above my right eye.

"How come we never heard of this gig until now?" Mike demanded.

"Because you'd have canceled if I'd told you about it ahead of time," Janet replied.

"To hell with the Roadhouse," Mike said. "You can't pay me enough to go back to that pigsty."

"Fifteen hundred bucks," Janet said.

"Huh?" the room gasped.

"Burrito Bill, the owner, said he'd give us fifteen hundred in cash if we play from nine in the evening until two in the morning. He promised we'd have security this time—a half-dozen MPs from the base."

"Janet," Dale groaned. "Last time it was the MPs who

beat us up. When they're off duty, they're worse than the mechanics and the pilots. They never go anywhere without their guns." He shook his head. "The money's tempting but I don't think we should go."

"And we'd have to spring for a motel room," Mike said. "No way I'm driving back at three in the morning."

"I've already reserved a room," Janet said.

"For how much?" Mike snapped.

"Cheap," Janet said.

"Why are they paying us so much?" Shelly asked.

Janet continued. "Most of the soldiers are heading off to the Middle East next week and this is their last big night to party. And Burrito Bill said they loved us the last time we played there."

"So that's why they tried to kill us," I muttered.

Janet nodded. "They're trained to kill. It's what makes them happy. The bottom line is we need the cash. Fred's two months late on his guitar and amp payments and we prom- ised Shelly new equipment. Besides, we knock them dead and we'll get written up in Rapid City's newspaper. I already put in a call to them and they promised to send someone to the show. Think about it. Now that summer's over we don't have that many gigs scheduled. We need the money."

Mike shrugged. "This means we're going to have to spend

the whole week practicing Led Zeppelin and Rolling Stones covers."

"Like I can mimic Jimmy Page," I said sarcastically.

"That's not what Burrito Bill wants at all," Janet said. "Last time, he said it was Fred's original material that blew the crowd away—especially his love songs. He told me the soldiers and their dates came in weeks after talking about Fred."

"Nice try," I said. "You just made that up."

"It's true," Dale said. "During our break, when you guys ran off to the kitchen, I hung around and felt out the crowd. Except for the animals who beat the shit out of us, most of the audience loved Fred's singing. And not just when he did covers."

"Burrito Bill told me we have to play 'Rose' at least twice," Janet added, mentioning one of my better creations.

"That's great," I said. "He wants us onstage five hours and I've got twenty minutes of original material." I paused. "Mike's right, we need to spend the rest of this week rehearsing classic rock."

"And locating body armor," Mike added.

Janet left to go do homework and we started to play a few Rolling Stones classics: "Satisfaction," "Gimme Shelter," "Jumpin' Jack Flash." Because the Stones always performed with two guitars, Shelly grabbed my old Fender and played rhythm to my lead. She was a decent guitarist but never moved an inch onstage. For that reason Dale and I kept her hidden in the back beside Mike when we played live.

Dale and I could at least act like we were enjoying ourselves onstage. Indeed, despite his "Corpse" nickname, Dale was a natural performer; he could dance for hours without repeating the same moves. Plus his voice was the only one that remotely harmonized with mine.

We jammed for an hour before we took our first break. It was then Dale got on my case about playing a new song I'd written called "Human Boy." It was a typical power ballad; it started slow, got loud, returned to a whisper, then went wild again. Dale had heard me play it at my house and thought it had potential. As usual I couldn't tell if it was inspired or if it sucked. I had no internal barometer. I only knew "Rose" worked because of the reaction I got when I played it.

I shook my head when Dale brought up the song. "'Human Boy' is way too raw to use this weekend. Let's just call it a night," I said.

"At least give us a taste," Shelly said.

"Yeah. We'll tell you if it's shit," Mike promised.

I frowned at Dale. "You swore you'd keep your mouth shut."

"If I did that we'd have nothing original to play," Dale said.

I strummed a few minor chords: E, A, D, G—I used the four of them a lot. Safe chords, I thought, easy on the ears. I usually came up with the melody first, before I got the lyrics. That's why I preferred to play my guitar for a few minutes before I opened my mouth. The truth was, I hadn't really figured out the beginning. . . .

Human Boy
The world sits on your weary shoulders
Every day is darker, colder
You cry out for your savior
Praying there's something there
It's just your human nature

Human boy
Try not to weep
You and the other boys
Can have your toys
Until the day you're buried
Six foot deep

Human boy
There are no answers to life's questions
No God to hear your confessions

No grace the sky can send
No need to weep
Even when you're buried deep
That's just the way life ends

I let my voice trail off and repeated, "That's just the way life ends." I'd made up the last line on the spot.

The room was silent a long time. Mike spoke first. "Hey, that's some pretty great shit. I like it."

Shelly nodded. "It needs editing but it's hot."

Dale spoke last. "I agree with Shelly. It's great, in spots. But . . ."

"You can tell me. I can take it," I said.

"There's a lot of darkness in that song," Dale said.

"Dark is good," Mike said. "Gives it energy."

Dale was watching me. "We'll work on it."

Dale wasn't talking about the song. I knew him too well, or else he knew me even better. He was talking about me. That I needed to work on my head.

Dale's remark stayed with me as I rode my bike home. Here I was, seventeen and couldn't afford four wheels. The few times I'd gone out with Nicole, Janet had loaned me her car. What little money I'd saved, from gigs and what I earned at the store,

I'd put into equipment. It embarrassed me the band was still paying for my brand-new Gibson guitar. But the others were cool about it. They said it was an investment in our future.

That phrase, "our future," freaked me out because it was so loaded with lies—or worse, childish dreams—that the band as a whole never really talked about. The truth was, I was the only one who had enough talent to have even a remote chance of succeeding in the marketplace. That sounded arrogant, I know, but it was a fact. Janet and Dale knew it without having to be told. And Mike—he didn't dwell much on the future; it was enough he enjoyed hitting his drums.

It was Shelly who was most troubling. Clearly she wanted to succeed to please her father, as well as to impress me. Just as bad, she'd grown up watching *American Idol* and *X Factor* and *The Voice* reruns and had it ingrained in her psyche that she had to be a celebrity to be someone. I often wondered if it was her need to succeed that blocked her creative juices. The girl never relaxed when she played; she was exhausted after every show.

Still, the bottom line was that everyone in the band was working toward a goal I was pretty sure they all secretly knew was only a possibility for me.

It was no wonder I felt depressed as I rode my bike home.

It was late, after one, and my parents were asleep. But my mom, bless her, had left lemon-and-pepper chicken and saffron rice in the oven. I was starved. I hadn't eaten since that afternoon with Aja and obviously that meal hadn't counted because I'd been completely unaware of my food.

I took my dinner and a bottle of apple juice up to my room and flipped on my computer. At home I often ate while logged on, although I wasn't addicted to surfing the Internet. I felt the anonymity of the Net gave the public too much freedom to be rude to people. Whenever I spent over an hour online, I inevitably got a headache.

The first thing I did on my computer was look up what Aja had been trying to say with her cryptic Portuguese remark—*Ninguém do nada*. I spelled it wrong a dozen times before Google's translators finally told me what it meant: "No one from nowhere." I wondered why Aja had said such a thing. She had acted happy enough.

Next I checked my e-mail and was surprised to see a note from Janet. Normally she'd text me. She'd sent it an hour ago and reading it caused my heart to skip a beat.

Dear Fred,
Forgot to mention. I didn't get Aja's number but . . .
I gave her yours.

Try sleeping on that one.
Love, Jumpin' Jack Jan

"Damn you," I said. What was I supposed to do now? If I wanted to appear cool I'd have to wait for Aja to call me. The only problem was she might not call. Indeed, the chances were a hundred to one she wouldn't. Janet, who was my best friend, and who was probably thinking she'd just done me a favor, had snatched my free will right out of my hands.

I slept that night with my phone beside my pillow.

It never rang.

CHAPTER THREE

THE NEXT DAY I LOOKED FORWARD TO MRS. Billard's class and another chance to see Aja. I arrived early but Aja didn't come in until a few seconds before the bell, sitting in the same chair as the previous day, on the far side of the room. She had on a simple red dress and looked fantastic. Only she didn't look at me. Oh well . . .

Billard started fast, handing out a quiz on yesterday's discussion, the thirteen colonies' difficulties with the king of England, chapter three in our textbook. Billard was known for her pop quizzes, but from the groans that surrounded me, I could tell the majority of the class hadn't read the chapter. I was lucky, I'd awakened early and studied it thoroughly. I knew I'd ace the quiz. I never considered myself particularly smart but I had a knack for taking tests.

As Billard had promised, she gave Aja her own special quiz. "This is on the first two chapters, all forty-eight pages. You did read them, didn't you?" she asked as she handed Aja three sheets of paper.

"Yes," Aja said.

"Good," Billard said. "If you have time, you can take today's quiz as well."

"Thank you," Aja said.

"Don't thank me," Billard replied. "All my tests are closed book. Put your textbook under your seat and leave it there. If I catch you cheating I'll flunk you before you begin. Understand?"

Aja nodded but said nothing. I wondered at Billard's harshness. Aja had just arrived in town; there was no reason for Billard to snap at her. To even be in an AP class, Aja must have scored high on the placement tests that were given to all foreign students. For all Billard knew, Aja might have been Ivy League material.

Yet I wondered if Aja had Billard flustered. The teacher was used to intimidating students and it was as if Aja's calm demeanor, her penetrating gaze, made Billard feel like she was somehow no longer in control . . .

It was just a thought.

The quiz turned out to be harder than I'd anticipated.

First off it was not all multiple choice; there were essay questions. Billard not only wanted to know *who* had started the Boston Tea Party, she wanted to know *why* they had started it. I was lucky I'd read a biography on Benjamin Franklin over the summer—a tome my mother had insisted I digest—and was up on my Revolutionary history. While taking the test, I was able to expand upon what was in the textbook, which I had a feeling would please Billard.

I finished the test early but didn't immediately hand it in. The last thing I wanted to do was show up my classmates. Yet, a half hour into the period, I was surprised to see Aja stand and hand in the test sheets Billard had given her. Billard, who was engrossed in a book about the Civil War, looked up in surprise.

"What's the problem?" she demanded.

"No problem," Aja said, giving her the tests. She returned to her seat, leaving Billard with a frown on her face. Ordinarily Billard graded her quizzes after class but today she quickly scanned Aja's work. I don't know why that disturbed me but it did; and it didn't take long before her frown changed into an expression of outright anger. Clenching Aja's quizzes in her hand, Billard stood from behind her desk.

"Class, put down your tests and listen for a moment," she said. "I want to read something that I think you'll find enlightening. As a few of you might remember from two weeks ago, on the fourth question of your first quiz, I asked how the town of Raleigh and subsequent colony of Carolina was founded. Now Aja Smith answered this question by writing, and I quote, 'During the reign of Queen Elizabeth I, Walter Raleigh, a pirate well known for raiding Spanish ships crossing the Atlantic to and from the New World, came to the attention of the queen when he introduced the English court to tobacco, which he had discovered while exploring what was later to be known as Virginia. It was this discovery, along with his handsome face and flirtatious nature, which made him a favorite of the queen and inspired her to grant him a royal patent to further explore Virginia and pave the way for future English settlements. Unfortunately for Raleigh, in 1591, before he could return to the New World, he fell in love with and married Elizabeth Throckmorton, one of the Queen's ladies in waiting, without the queen's permission, for which he and his wife were imprisoned in the Tower of London. Yet he was released during the attack of the Spanish Armada and distinguished himself in the main battle off the coast of Dover, which led to him being knighted by Queen Elizabeth . . .'" Billard stopped and spoke in a sarcastic tone. "Need I go on?"

No one responded, least of all Aja, who sat as motionless

as a statue. Billard scanned the rest of us before shaking her head in disgust. "This is not an answer to the question I asked. This is *the* answer. It is word for word exactly what is written in your textbooks, for any of you bright enough to recall." She turned her blazing eyes on Aja. "Which can only mean that you copied the answer directly out of your book, or else from cheat sheets you slipped up your sleeves. Tell me, Aja Smith, which was it?"

Aja sat calmly. "Neither."

Billard ripped Aja's test papers in half and threw them in the air. "Don't act innocent with me! I want to know how you cheated!"

"I read the chapters you told me to read. I remembered what the book said about Walter Raleigh and wrote down what it said on the papers you gave me. Bart told me that was the best way to answer test questions in high school."

Billard looked as confused as she did angry. "Who the hell is Bart?"

"Bart is Bart. He works for my aunt Clara."

Aja's reply was virtually identical to the answer she had given me. At the same time I thought it was a pretty straightforward answer but if I was hoping it would calm Billard down I was mistaken.

"You still haven't explained how you cheated," Billard

said. "Did you peek at your book or do you have cheat sheets hiding up the sleeves of that pretty red dress of yours?"

Aja didn't respond but Ted Weldon, the football jock who'd given Aja her textbook yesterday, spoke. "Mrs. Billard, I think I can help here. I was watching Aja the whole time and I swear she never looked at her book or copped a cheat sheet from any part of her mighty fine body."

Billard didn't welcome the interruption but was forced to respond to him. "Like you're an expert when it comes to cheating," she said.

Ted was so dumb he smiled; he thought he was being complimented. "Yes, ma'am, I suppose I am."

"Tell me, Mr. Weldon, how was it you happened to be watching Aja this whole time when you were supposed to be working on your own quiz?"

Ted's grin swelled into a smirk as he glanced around for support. He liked attention. "Well, it's true I have a ways to go on this test. But as far as watching Aja, let's just say she's awfully easy on the eyes. If you know what I mean, ma'am."

Billard nodded with exaggerated patience. "Thank you, Ted, for your astute observations. But now . . ." Her gaze shifted back to Aja as she added in a deadly tone, "Now I want you to either admit that you cheated on your test or else I'll have you expelled from this class."

"I can do that," Aja said calmly.

Billard hesitated. "You admit you did cheat on the test?"

"Yes."

Billard pointed toward the door. "Report to Principal Levitt's office immediately. I'll be along in a few minutes. Go!"

Aja collected her books and left the class.

"Macy, pick up all the quizzes and put them on my desk," Billard ordered as she collected the pieces of Aja's tests she'd ripped in half, along with a copy of our textbook. "The rest of you, start reading chapter four. There's to be no discussion on this matter while I'm gone." She headed for the door. "I'll be back shortly."

I stood quickly. "Mrs. Billard, may I have a moment, please?"

"No, Fred, you may not. Sit down and do as you've been told."

Naturally, the moment Billard was out of sight the room exploded. Half the class jumped Ted, the other half me—and it wasn't just because I'd tried to talk to Billard before she'd split. Elder High was like any school—the gossip highway was well paved. Yesterday, everyone had watched me having lunch with Aja. Now they wanted to know how I'd planned to defend her before I'd been told to sit down and shut up.

Naturally I didn't know. But the fact that Aja knew several languages made me suspect she had an excellent memory. I tried telling the class that but they latched on to the idea that Aja had a "photographic memory" and ran with it.

"Let's not go overboard," I said. "Billard only quoted a few lines. It's not like she read all of Aja's answers. It's possible Aja just happened to remember that particular paragraph word for word and wrote it down. If you ask me, Billard's overreacting."

"I don't buy it," Macy Barnes spoke up from two rows over. Besides being a cheerleader and the student body president, Macy was a brilliant student. She was in fact Janet's main competition to be class valedictorian. She studied for hours every night, never suspecting for a moment that Janet had no desire to graduate number one. Macy was also extremely religious. She headed a Bible-reading club on campus.

Macy added, "I think Aja cheated. I mean, she quoted the book word for word. Who the heck can do that?"

"She didn't cheat," Ted said. "I wasn't kidding when I said I had an eye on her the whole time. Anyway, she was writing fast, real fast, like she didn't have to stop and think. If you ask me she's some kind of savant."

"Why didn't you tell Billard that?" I said.

"Like she gave me a chance. You saw how pissed off she was. I tried to defend Aja, I did."

"I know," I muttered. "Sorry."

Ted grinned. "Hey, it's cool. A guy's gotta stand up for his babe."

I snorted. "She's not my babe. I had lunch with her, that's it."

"One thing's for sure," Macy said. "If all of Aja's answers are right out of the textbook, Billard's going to roast her in front of Levitt. I wouldn't be surprised if she gets expelled."

"She just moved here," Ted said. "No way that's going to happen."

I stayed silent. I knew Principal Levitt better than most. Had Elder had a local KKK chapter, he would have been washing and ironing their sheets. My dad played poker with a group of guys every month at Levitt's house and when our beloved principal got a few beers in him he inevitably ended up talking about the country's southern border—he'd grown up in the South—and how a wall was the only way to keep the "Goddamn Mexicans" out of America. My dad only went to his house because he was a hard-core poker player and it was the only game in town. But he couldn't stand the bastard.

I couldn't count how many times Levitt had tried to bust Mike for bringing a joint to school. The guy was always checking his locker. Mike was too smart for him and usually stashed his dope in Dale's locker, or in mine.

Billard wasn't back by the time the bell rang and so I left

for lunch not knowing Aja's fate. It worried me I couldn't find her anywhere on the courtyard. Eventually I caught up with Janet, who had sources no one knew about.

She told me that Aja had been expelled.

"No way!" I cried.

"Calm down, it's temporary," Janet said. "She might be back in class tomorrow, nothing's been decided yet."

"Then why did you use the word 'expelled'?"

"Because that's the word Wendy Hawkins used and she's the only honest counselor we've got. She overheard Billard's whole tirade in Levitt's office. Now, don't get upset but it does sound like Aja copied everything she wrote right out of the book. And—"

I interrupted. "Ted swears she didn't even open her textbook."

"I know that, I know everything. But look, as far as I can tell, Aja admitted that she cheated. She said it right in front of your class."

I shook my head. "That's not the way it went down. Billard gave her a twisted ultimatum that gave her no choice but to admit she cheated. She told Aja she'd be expelled unless she confessed."

Janet considered. "That might explain some of what Mrs. Hawkins told me."

"What did she say?"

"That Aja kept contradicting herself. First, Aja said she didn't look at the book while taking the test. Then she admitted that she'd cheated. She just wouldn't say how."

"She couldn't explain how because she didn't do it!"

"Fred, I know you like her but . . ."

"No, listen. Billard's got something against her, I don't know why. I saw it on day one. Billard went ballistic when she thought Aja might have cheated. And Aja saw that—she saw how upset she was. That's why she told her she cheated. Aja was just trying to calm Billard down."

Janet frowned. "That wasn't smart. Not for a smart girl."

"What's the bottom line?"

"Levitt's going to talk to her family."

"She doesn't have any family," I said.

"Well, her guardians, then, that Aunt Clara and Bart you told me about. They're supposed to come in tomorrow and have a meeting with Billard and Levitt."

"Ted should be at that meeting."

"Do you really want Aja's future depending on Ted Weldon?"

"Where's Aja now?" I asked.

"Hawkins told me a black man came and picked her up."

"That was probably Bart."

"Yeah." Janet squeezed my arm. "Relax. Aja's new here, she's from another country. Levitt's a racist pig but he can't let the town know it. He's got to at least pretend to be fair and take Aja's background into account. He can't keep her from getting an education. It's against the law."

I shook my head. "I just hate to see her treated so badly."

"Cheer up. From what Hawkins told me, Aja sounded like the coolest one in the principal's office. I don't think anything upsets that girl."

I continued to mope. "The bastards."

Janet's touch went from my arm to my hand. She continued to eye me closely. "Are you sure you're not falling in . . . ?"

I quickly raised my hand, shaking off hers. "Don't even start with that," I interrupted.

Janet smiled. "Yes, sir."

CHAPTER FOUR

I'D TOLD JANET I DIDN'T LOVE AJA AND THAT was true. I hardly knew her. But I cared about her—I wasn't sure why—and for that reason the next few days were hard on me. Aja didn't reappear and Janet's sources fell mute and there was no news to be had. I couldn't even find out if Aja's guardians had met with Principal Levitt. And Billard—there was no point in talking to her. The day after her blowout with Aja she acted like nothing had happened.

She handed back our quizzes, though, and I got an A on mine. Apparently my insightful essay answers still appealed to her.

I pressured Janet to get me Aja's number but she said she couldn't find it anywhere. I considered driving out to Aja's house and speaking to her directly. I knew where she lived.

But I didn't have the nerve, and I think it had something to do with the fact that I knew she had my number and hadn't bothered to call me. It was a poor excuse but it was how I felt.

At the same time I had to rehearse long hours with the band to get ready for our trek to the Roadhouse. Our usual source of transportation to shows was an old camper van Dale's parents let us borrow. It was the only vehicle we had that was large enough to carry all our equipment, along with the five of us.

Unfortunately, the camper's radiator overheated and cracked the night before we set out for the Roadhouse, just after we'd driven back from our gig at Stoker High. The parts and repairs would have cost us over a grand but we were lucky Janet's father—Mr. Bradley "Bo" Shell—wasn't merely a mechanic but an expert welder. He kept us from having to go out and buy a new radiator. He just welded the crack shut. Given the internal pressure an overheated radiator could generate, it was an amazing feat. On Saturday morning, before we left town, I helped him finish up with the repairs in his garage while Janet packed for our trip inside their house.

"I can't thank you enough, Bo," I said. Everyone called him by his nickname, even Janet. "When we get rich and famous, none of us are going to forget it was you who kept this RV running. Seriously, without your help we wouldn't be a working band."

Bo chuckled at my remark as he scrubbed away at the thick, rusty buildup near the spot where we needed to plant the radiator. Bo was the most popular and respected mechanic in town and was never at a loss for jobs. He worked hard—seldom less than sixty hours a week—and made good money. But the Shell home had only two bedrooms and a kitchen you could hardly turn around in. Everyone knew he was saving his money for Janet's college education. He was that kind of guy.

He was a football freak, though, particularly when it came to the NFL, and had indulged in an expensive giant-screen TV. I loved watching games with him. He always had plenty of beer on hand and three decades ago had played right tackle at the University of Michigan. He knew the game from the inside out and I usually ended up turning off the babbling commentators so I could listen to his more colorful remarks.

He still had his bulk from those days, although it was now more fat than muscle. He had put on the pounds when his wife—the relatively young and far more educated Cynthia Shell, Janet's mother—had divorced him for a Wall Street lawyer. That had been seven years ago and Janet had actually left town with her mom to live in Manhattan in a ten-million-dollar penthouse that overlooked Central Park. Talk about a step up from Elder.

But a year later Janet had returned home to be with her father and I could only assume it was because she'd had a falling-out with her mom. The woman didn't exactly have a strong maternal instinct. Janet swore her mother had been born on the planet Vulcan.

Janet had never told me why she'd left such a glamorous lifestyle to return to Elder, or why, for that matter, she'd left Elder in the first place. The topic was taboo with her, which was weird because Janet and I talked about everything.

Bo continued to chuckle at my comment. "Does that mean you'll give me a share of your songwriting royalties?" he asked.

"No way," I said.

"That's what I thought." Bo stopped to give me a serious look. He could have been a handsome man but with his weight and the grime from his job—and the hard years—he wasn't going to be meeting another Cynthia soon. Still, I never looked at him without seeing a sparkle in his eyes. He had suffered terribly when his wife had left but he had his daughter back and that was all that mattered to him.

"What is it?" I asked.

"Jan tells me you're writing great stuff. She's told me about the demo you're working on. She says it's a given—you're going to be big. Huge."

"Best friends make lousy critics."

"Jan always speaks her mind. You know that."

I shrugged. "Well, I hope she's right."

A half hour later we had the radiator in place and were good to go. The RV was already loaded with my guitars, and after taking a quick shower at Janet's house, I drove over to Shelly's and collected the rest of the band's sound system. Mike had recently picked up a used bass amp—bass amps were notorious for being heavy—and we had to struggle to fit it in the back.

We hit the road. It was still early: a quarter after nine. As usual, I drove and Janet sat up front with me while the others hung in the back and played video games on Shelly's tablet and took frequent hits off a fifth of Jack Daniel's Mike had smuggled aboard. Because I was driving, the open liquor bottle made me nervous, but there was only so much control we could exercise over Mike. I knew Shelly and Dale would inevitably take larger nips of the bottle than they would prefer just to keep Mike from walking onstage totally smashed.

"I heard you guys rocked in Stoker," Janet said as we left town. I always felt a wave of relief leaving Elder and getting on the interstate. I imagined what it would be like when I said my final good-bye to the town. My favorite part of the trip was driving over the Missouri River and visualizing how far it traveled before it merged with the Mississippi and flowed all the way down to New Orleans. If LA and New York did end up rejecting me, I thought it likely I'd end up in "Nawlins," backing up a jazz band in the French Quarter. I loved jazz but, like masturbation, it wasn't something a guy talked openly about at school.

"We sucked," I said. "The place had the acoustics of an aquarium and the students kept calling out for us to play Mariah Carey's greatest hits."

"That's sick," Janet said.

"Tell me about it. We compromised and ended up playing Coldplay, Maroon 5, and the Beatles. Eventually they shut up and danced with their dates."

"Did you get paid in cash?"

"Their student body president insisted I take a check."

Janet fumed. "That asshole. He swore on the phone he'd pay cash. If that check bounces we swing by there next weekend and torch their new hockey rink. Can you believe the good people of Stoker voted to pay two million for that rink when their only high school has computers that still use floppy disks?"

Lightning struck. "So that's why the sound was so bad and why it was so cold! We played on top of that damn rink! They must have covered the ice with wrestling mats or something."

"You're kidding me?" Janet said.

"I'm not. My hands were numb by the time we played our encore."

"What did you play?"

"Foreigner's 'Cold As Ice.'"

Janet smiled. "I think tonight's show's going to be hot. I'm glad we're spending the night."

As much as I disliked Elder, I couldn't compete with Janet when it came to wanting to get out of town. The girl took every excuse to escape. I sometimes suspected she'd volunteered to manage us just so she'd have a reason to split on the weekends.

"Any news on the Aja front?" I asked.

"Oh, I meant to tell you. Heard from Macy Barnes that she'd heard from Kathy Hawkins that Aja should be back in school on Monday, just not in Billard's class."

"Who the hell is Kathy Hawkins?"

"Our counselor's nine-year-old daughter."

"You couldn't find a better source than that?"

"Kathy's solid. Remember, it takes at least a decade of living to learn how to lie properly. Besides, Macy knows Kathy well—she's her babysitter." Janet paused. "Cheer up. You should be happy with the news."

"I am, I just, I don't know." I paused to wipe the sweat off my brow. The camper had air-conditioning but I didn't want to push the repair job we'd done on the radiator. I added, "I'd just like to know why Billard took such an immediate disliking to Aja."

"Billard's explosive. Aja didn't sass her or anything like that?"

"Not even remotely. It makes no sense."

"You're thinking about what you saw. The two may have met before Monday morning."

"I doubt it. Aja just moved here."

"According to my sources she's been here two months."

"Really? Why'd she miss the first two weeks of school?"

"I don't know why she decided to sign up at all."

"We're doing it again. We keep talking about my love life. What about yours?"

Janet shook her head. "Point to one guy in our town that I could take seriously and I'll go out with him tomorrow night."

I could think of several guys that might make a good match for Janet. But I knew if I brought them up she'd just start pointing out all their flaws.

I worried Janet was walling herself off. I wasn't sure why. She was no knockout but she was cute enough. Her hair and eyes were brown, like mine. However, over the summer she'd taken the scissors to her hair and cut most of it away. Now she looked vaguely butch. It was almost as if she'd been trying to create an image, or sign, that said: *Stay Away*.

We reached the Roadhouse at six in the evening and immediately began to set up. A few non-servicemen were having a beer and a sandwich but the Ellsworth Air Force Base crowd wouldn't begin to trickle in until later. Burrito Bill was happy to see us and offered us free dinner while we were in the middle of our sound check. Naturally we accepted—we were starved.

Yet we didn't order any Mexican food, nor did anyone who came to the joint, not anymore. Burrito Bill had earned his nickname twenty years ago when he'd been married to his first wife—he was now on his third—who had supposedly made such fantastic burritos that a Pentagon general who'd come out to inspect the base prior to recommending its closure had changed his mind when he happened to stop at the Roadhouse and sampled the first wife's cooking. He'd been so blown away he'd ordered the base kept open just so he'd have an excuse to visit three or four times a year and eat her burritos.

Everyone in the band assumed it was an urban legend until we spoke to half a dozen servicemen who'd actually been in the bar when the general had eaten there. The only real mystery, the soldiers told us, was why Burrito Bill had divorced the woman. Back then, they said, the Roadhouse had been the hottest joint in the state.

Now our band was called in to headline their biggest event.

I wondered what that said about the place. And us.

The agreement Janet had struck with Burrito Bill stated that we were to go on at nine and play until closing. But when nine rolled around the Roadhouse was only a quarter full. We stalled by pretending to tune our instruments. None of us liked to play to empty seats. Yet, as it got closer to ten, Bill got on Janet's case and Janet got on ours and Dale suggested I start by playing solo.

"Are you nuts?" I snapped.

"Chill, Fred," Mike said. "Just you and your acoustic guitar—it'll work. Pretend you're Bob Dylan playing in an old coffeehouse in New York City. Later, when the herd shows, the rest of us can quietly slip onstage and turn up the volume and blow out their brains."

"The early birds are probably here because of you," Janet said.

"I don't like it," I grumbled, although it was a fact I often played solo at some point during a show. It was just that I liked to warm up with Mike's thundering drums and Shelly's classic keyboard at my back. Simply having Dale standing by my side with his bass gave me confidence.

I continued to protest but the band, and Bill, gave me no choice. In the end I sat on a stool at the far end of the Roadhouse, the long bar on my left, the bulk of the seats and tables in front of me. I strummed a few chords on an acoustic guitar I'd bought for a hundred bucks when I was twelve. I'd practically worn a hole in the wood beneath the bottom string. The guitar was like an old friend; I'd learned all I knew about music on it.

I wasn't sure what to play but finally settled on an old Neil Young song, "Heart of Gold." I'd always looked up to Neil. His songs were mostly simple, chord-wise, but his lyrics carried powerful emotions: pain, loss, desperate hope. It didn't bother me that I hadn't even been born when he'd written his most famous hits. Great songs were like fine wines— they aged gracefully.

My voice . . . God, I honestly didn't know if I could sing or not. Most people said I was gifted, that I hit every note and had a lot of feeling. But I only truly felt my potential when I sang alone—all alone, in my bedroom when the house was empty. When I was in front of a crowd, big or small, I had to hear the cheers before I could relax.

Yet I was fortunate that night because the older servicemen

had come into the Roadhouse early and Neil Young had been a part of their youth and they clapped loudly when I finished my first song. That made me feel good. My heart stopped pounding and I ceased dripping sweat over the guitar's frets. I decided to play another song from the same era, Cat Stevens's "Wild World." The first two lines made me think of Aja.

"Now that I've lost everything to you, you say you want to start something new. And it's breaking my heart you're leaving . . ."

I sang alone for half an hour, until ten thirty, when suddenly the dam burst and two hundred men and women in uniform poured in. Bill signaled that he wanted me to take a break while he and his help filled drink orders. By then the others had joined me onstage and were tuning their instruments—for real this time.

The crowd was loud and boisterous. Janet had been right. From the gossip we could tell that most of them were shipping out to the Middle East tomorrow. They were a mob with a lot on their minds and we knew we had to meet their energy with our own.

There're two questions rock bands often ask each other when they meet backstage at a gig. The first is, "Are you a Rolling Stones or a Beatles fan?"

If you answer "Rolling Stones" you don't have to say another word. But if you say "the Beatles" you're invariably asked question number two: "Are you a Paul or John fan?" Right then, if you don't say John, you're labeled a wuss.

Why? Everyone knows that Paul was a genius but if you're going to play finger-bleeding rock and roll then you've got to have an edge and every musician knows John was the one Beatle who took the real creative risks.

Tonight I just wished I could channel John Lennon's spirit. Hell, I'd even take Paul.

We started with a classic, Nirvana's "Smells Like Teen Spirit." Except for backup vocals, Shelly didn't play on the song. I was a big fan of Kurt Cobain and our voices were similar. He was a songwriting genius, in my opinion. I loved how on the chorus of "Teen Spirit" he repeated "Hello, hello, hello," again and again, until it changed into "How low?" A simple transformation but powerful. That was the direction I wanted my own lyrics to take.

The audience went nuts, yelling and dancing. I could see Burrito Bill in the back, with Janet, his big gut swaying with the music. He was happy. The more the crowd moved and screamed the more thirsty they got and the more they drank. I signaled to the others that we should pound hard for an hour before we eased up and let our guests attack the bar.

The first set couldn't have gone better. When we finally did take a break, Burrito Bill called us over to help deliver pitchers of beer. That wasn't part of the deal but everyone was in a good mood so we said what the hell and played the part of being waiters for a spell. The air was thick with cigarette smoke and you had to yell to be heard. As usual, Mike drank more beer than he delivered and his stride began to sway.

At 11:20 we got back onstage and started alternating between old pop and rock favorites sprinkled with grunge and the occasional hip-hop hit. At first we were in a flow, playing tight, but then I began to notice Mike kept throwing off our rhythm. A glance over my shoulder told me he was nursing another bottle of Jack Daniel's. I didn't know if he'd paid for it or swiped it. But I did know nothing made a band sound like crap faster than a drunk drummer.

The crowd began to grumble. A few soldier boys threw paper plates in our direction. That was okay but when they started heaving pints of beer I quickly backed up and signaled to Burrito Bill that we had to take a break. To my surprise he crossed his arms over his chest and shook his head, which pissed me off.

It helped that our instruments—particularly Dale's bass and my electric guitar—were grounded. I'd grounded them myself with a handful of cables that were plugged into the round sockets in the Roadhouse's wall outlets. But our equipment was old and an electrical short could literally electrocute one of us. I knew from painful experience. Dale and I were up front; it was easy to get sprayed. So I started playing with my back to the crowd, trying to protect my wires. I told Dale to follow my example.

It was then I felt a waterfall of beer pour over my head.

The pickup on my guitar sparked and a scary jolt went through my body. I knew I had to get the instrument off my chest before my heart began to skip but suddenly my arms were no longer connected to my body. I began to panic.

Dale was beside me in an instant, never mind that he was stepping into the same wet pool that was threatening to send me to an early grave. He ripped my guitar over my head and tossed it aside. The hum in my nerves ceased but then my legs stopped working and I collapsed in Dale's arms. He held me to his chest.

"You're all right, Fred," he said. "You're going to be all right."

I nodded, unable to speak, although my eyes were working well enough to see Mike and Shelly unplugging our main power cords. The weird thing was Mike still had his whiskey bottle in his hand and I could tell by the look in his eyes that he was feeling the lightning as well, and that soon we'd all be hearing the thunder.

I watched helplessly as he stalked around the stage toward three buzz-cut guys in uniform who stood near the front.

From the empty beer pitchers in their hands and the smug grins on their faces I knew they were the ones who'd drenched me. For sure, Mike knew it, too, and he was going to make an example of them.

"What the hell you assholes trying to do?" Mike demanded, going toe-to-toe with them. Three to one; the odds didn't bother Mike. Two of the soldiers were short and skinny—many pilots were—but the third guy was at least as muscled as Mike and he had a six-inch height advantage and God only knew what kind of reach. He was the one who stepped forward to meet our drummer.

"Wash away the shit that's playing tonight," the guy snorted.

Poor choice of words. Mike didn't start and win fights because of his muscles, particularly when he was drunk. He won because he changed into an animal. The guy was still smirking when Mike cracked his half-empty Jack Daniel's bottle over his skull. The brown spray that erupted was mixed with a sickly red liquid and the soldier toppled to the floor.

His buddies didn't approve, and not just the two standing by his side. Every guy in uniform in the Roadhouse leaped to his feet. The women, too; they could be just as deadly. Dale and I looked at each other and neither of us said a word. We didn't have to.

We knew we were screwed.

The two skinny dudes took a swing at Mike but he took one down with a kick to the crotch and the other with a hard punch to the solar plexus. Mike laughed like a maniac and dared any and all customers to step up to the line. At least four dozen said okay and seconds later Mike was on the floor and getting the shit kicked out of him. Shelly tugged on my arm.

"They'll kill him!" she cried.

"I'll kill them!" Dale swore and dove into the fray. It was probably the bravest thing I'd ever seen a sober human being do in my life, and I felt obligated to follow. But first I tried signaling Burrito Bill. I knew he kept a sawed-off shotgun behind the bar. I figured a double-barrel blast into the ceiling would restore order in a hurry.

Unfortunately, Bill was on the wrong side of the room and the mob wasn't giving him a clear line to his weapon. And now Dale was getting the crap kicked out of him. What could I do? I was a guy, a man's man, I told myself. And they were my friends; I had to do something. Picking up my unplugged electric guitar, I raised it over my head and prepared to follow Dale and Mike's extremely brave and extremely foolhardy example. The noise was deafening, louder than when we'd been playing. I swear I thought I was leaping to my death.

Then the room fell silent.

It was eerie. It was as if every screeching voice had suddenly been sucked out of the room by a huge invisible vacuum. I didn't understand; everyone froze, myself included. The kicking stopped and slowly Mike and Dale, and the three soldiers—even the guy who'd gotten busted over the skull—all sat up and looked around in wonder.

No, they looked up at the girl standing atop a nearby table.

It was Aja but—I don't know why—it took me several seconds to recognize her. Perhaps it was because she was the last person I expected to see at the Roadhouse. She had on a short silky black dress, her long hair loose down her back. She stood with her arms raised above her shoulders, her palms faced outward as if she were trying to hold the crowd at bay, but gently. Everything about her manner was gentle. It was possible she'd been trying to calm the crowd before the sudden cessation of hostilities but it was only now that I heard her talking.

"It's okay," Aja said without raising her voice. "Everything's going to be okay. Where you're going tomorrow—none of you is going to die." She paused and repeated herself but somehow, with the repetition, an odd power entered her voice. "No one dies," she said.

That was it; that was all she said. Then she stepped down from the table and offered her hand to the guy Mike had attacked, the one who'd taken a bottle to the head. He was bleeding freely from a nasty scalp wound but didn't hesitate to take Aja's hand. The second he stood she carefully touched his cut and the whole Roadhouse seemed to sigh. It sounds crazy but that's what I heard. One huge blissful sigh . . .

"Feel better?" Aja asked the guy.

He nodded. "Thanks." He spoke louder, to the crowd. "I'm okay!"

Aja nodded toward Mike and Dale and without another word the guy helped them to their feet. All around, people began to mutter and pretty soon everyone was talking at full volume again, but more civil, less wild. A few called out for songs they wanted us to play.

Shelly and I exchanged a look and shook our heads, not sure what had just happened. I mean, wow, Aja says a few words and now suddenly everyone's acting like they're on ecstasy? No, actually it was weirder than that. Because I recalled how the crowd had fallen silent even before she'd spoken.

Mike and Dale climbed back onto the stage. Both were bruised and bloody but they assured us it was nothing serious. We all agreed we should keep playing. Before we did, though, I searched for Aja in the crowd. But she had disappeared.

It was four in the morning when I heard the soft knock on our motel door. I appeared to be the only one who heard it.

Nearby, Janet and Shelly slept soundly on one bed, while on the other Dale lay like a dead man as Mike snored loudly. At the knock, I sat up on my foldout bed. I didn't mind rollaways. If I was tired enough, I could sleep on the floor. Pulling on my pants over the gym shorts I'd been sleeping in, I slipped from beneath the sheets and answered the door.

"Hi," Aja said and smiled. She had on the same dress she'd worn to the Roadhouse. Her hair was wet, though, as if she'd just showered, and her feet were bare. I saw no car. I assumed she'd walked over from her own nearby motel or hotel.

"This is a surprise," I said. It was so good to see her I feared I might still be asleep, dreaming the whole thing up. "What are you doing here?"

"Want to go for a walk?"

"Right now?"

"Yes."

I glanced at my friends; they were still out. "Give me a second, let me find my shoes and a shirt," I said.

Minutes later we were strolling along the cracked edge of an asphalt road beside a twenty-foot fence, topped with barbed wire, that surrounded the base. The town was silent as Elder usually was at this time of morning. There wasn't a soul in sight.

The air was heavy with moisture and the ground was damp; clouds had chased away the stars. It made me wonder if it had been raining and if that was the real reason Aja's hair was wet. Had she been wandering around in the dark since we'd last seen her? I asked and she nodded.

"Are you nuts?" I said. "You should have hooked up with us hours ago."

She shrugged. "You were playing and the place was noisy. Besides, I like to take walks late at night." She glanced over. "You look surprised."

"I'm surprised you're here. What made you come?"

"You invited me to hear you play. You remember?"

"Sure. How did you get here? Did Bart bring you?"

"I took a bus."

"Why didn't you come with us?"

"I wanted to surprise you."

"Let me get this straight. You rode here all alone, across half the state, with only the clothes on your back. And since we last saw you at the Roadhouse, you've been wandering around in the dark—barefoot—in a strange town all by yourself."

"No."

"What part are you saying no to?"

"My shoes."

"What about your shoes?"

"I brought shoes. But I got tired of wearing them." She added, "They're sitting on the hood of your RV."

"Well, that's a relief. You've got your shoes to protect you. Honestly, Aja, you can't behave like this, not in this country. You're too pretty a girl. Anything could happen to you."

"Anything can happen," she appeared to agree, before adding, "Don't worry about me."

I shook my head. "I do worry about you."

"Why?"

"Because . . . maybe where you come from it's safe to wander around at night. But this can be a violent town. You saw those guys at the club. They were ready to kill Mike and Dale." When Aja didn't respond I looked over at her. "But they didn't because you showed up. How did you get them to stop?"

"I didn't do anything. They were afraid, that's all. They didn't want to hurt anybody. And when they understood that, everything was okay."

I shook my head. "If Shelly had stood on that table instead of you and begged that drunken herd to calm down, they would have beaten the shit out of her. What you did was amazing."

"Fred."

"What?"

"I can't be in danger one minute and amazing the next. You have to make up your mind."

She had a point, sort of. I was contradicting myself. Not

that she still wasn't acting naive. "What I mean is . . . ," I began.

She interrupted by reaching over and taking my hand. "I liked when you sang by yourself at the beginning," she said.

Her hand felt good in mine. "You were there at the start? I didn't see you."

"Yes. At first you were nervous, then you relaxed." She added as if to herself, "You enjoy singing in front of people."

For such a naive girl, I thought, she was perceptive.

"I do," I said. When she didn't reply, I asked, "How have you been this last week?"

"Good."

"It must have made you mad getting expelled on your second day of school."

"It doesn't matter. I'll be there Monday."

I shook my head. "I can't understand why Billard hates you."

"She doesn't hate me."

"What do you mean?"

"She's afraid of me."

"Huh?"

"We met over the summer."

"Where?"

"At the town cemetery. I often walk there."

"What happened at the cemetery?"

Aja hesitated. "Better you ask her."

"Why?"

"She'll explain."

I pushed Aja to elaborate but she just shook her head and kept walking. I finally decided to shut my mouth and enjoy the touch of her hand, which was remarkably soothing. I don't know how far we'd walked when I noticed that I was feeling awfully energized for a guy who hadn't really slept in two days. More, I felt light, light as a balloon, as if I wasn't walking but floating alongside the fence. And the clouds in the sky, they felt somehow closer, like I could touch them.

Aja suddenly stopped and faced me, her big, brown eyes bright in the dark night. She reached up and stroked my cheek, my hair, and even though I did my best to stay cool I trembled. She inched up on her toes and kissed me on the lips, just for a second or two.

"Let's go back to your RV," she said.

"You mean the motel? You can sleep on my foldout. I can sleep on the floor."

Aja shook her head and tightened her grip on my hand. She began to lead me back the way we'd come. "I want to sleep with you in the RV."

I don't recall much about the walk back. But I do remember lying beside her on the cushions in the rear of the RV, our two bodies barely fitting between the crush of our equipment. We didn't have sex—we didn't even make out, nor did she kiss me again.

But she held me and let me hold her and for the first time in my life I felt as if all my hidden fears had been deftly exposed and quietly put to bed, once and for all. I had fought with her that it wasn't safe to wander alone in the dark, but when I slept with her cheek resting on mine, and felt the brush of her eyelashes as they fluttered during her dreams, I was the one who felt protected.

The band slept until noon the next day, which was not unusual. Aja and I woke up an hour earlier and had breakfast in a nearby coffee shop. Once again, she ate what I ate: scrambled eggs, bacon, toast, coffee. I tried quizzing her about her life in Brazil but she easily turned the topic to our performance the previous night and I ended up doing most of the talking without even realizing it.

Aja was turning out to be a tough egg to crack, I thought.

I still knew almost nothing about her.

Returning from the coffee shop, we found the band loading the RV. I assumed we'd be giving Aja a ride home until the infamous Bart showed up in an ivory Jaguar. Specifically, I met Bart in the motel parking lot while Mike and Dale were collecting clothes from our room and Aja was talking to Janet while Janet settled our bill at the front desk. It seemed Mike had raided the minibar—which, technically, was supposed to be locked and off-limits to us "kids"—earlier and we owed more money than our original deposit.

"You must be Fred. Aja's told me a lot about you," Bart said as he climbed from the Jaguar and shook my hand.

The man was coal black with a handsome face and a thick Jamaican accent. He wore a flowered shirt, white slacks, and wooden sandals that looked as if they might have been carved on a Caribbean island. He was short but robust. With his strong features and smooth skin it was hard to place his age. I would have said he was in his midthirties but a tinge of white in his black hair made me wonder if he was a lot older.

"She's told me about you," I replied.

Bart glanced around. "Is she here?"

"She's with my friend Janet. She should be here in a few minutes. Don't tell me—Aja snuck out on you and her aunt."

Bart nodded. "It's a habit of hers. But I had a good idea where she'd gone. She told me where your band was playing this weekend."

"She—or you—should have called. We could have given her a ride home."

"I didn't have your number," Bart said before changing the topic. "How was the show?"

"It was going great until we had a riot. Then it got pretty ugly. I'm not sure any of us would still be alive if Aja hadn't intervened." I added, "I'm not joking."

Bart appeared to take it all in stride. "It's a good thing she came." He turned toward the motel office. "Let me check and see what's keeping her."

I stepped in front of him. "She'll be here in a minute. Anyway, if you don't mind, I'd like to ask a few questions."

He hesitated before flashing a smile. "Shoot."

"Aja told me Mrs. Smith isn't her real aunt. That the two of you ran into her in a small town in Brazil when she was a kid."

"That's true. We were staying in Selva—that's a tiny town in South Brazil—when we met her. She was eight at the time."

"How did that work? I mean, was she living on the streets or in the jungle and you saw her and took pity on her and adopted her?"

"Pretty much. She was homeless."

"What about her parents? Where were they?"

"Her mother and father were killed when she was much younger. The locals—there's conflicting stories about what really happened. All I know for sure is there's no point in asking Aja about them. She won't discuss it."

"But you assume it was something traumatic?"

"I have no idea," Bart replied, giving me a penetrating look. "You like her, Fred, I can tell. I'm glad. Growing up, Aja hasn't spent much time with people her own age."

"Why's that? Why wasn't she in school?"

Bart shrugged. "She didn't want to go to school. Not until recently."

"When the three of you moved here?"

"Yes."

"Why did you move here, if I may ask?" When he didn't answer right away I added, "Was it because she wanted to?"

Bart chuckled, keeping his eyes on me. "Good, that's good. You're beginning to understand her. Most people never do."

Janet and Aja returned right then, followed shortly by Mike and Dale. Mike had a black eye and Dale a swollen lip but no one was complaining. Burrito Bill had tipped us an extra two hundred, all of it in cash.

Yet I was disappointed Aja wouldn't be riding back with us. I'd been looking forward to having a long talk with her. However, I could see Aja was reluctant to have Bart drive home all alone after he had come so far to find her. I couldn't blame the girl for being polite. She squeezed my hand as she was leaving, which felt nice.

"I'll see you tomorrow at school," she said.

I smiled, although I hated to let go of her hand. Again, I wondered why I cared so much. And again, I told myself that I hardly knew her.

"Have a safe drive back," I said.

Aja gave Bart a quick glance—as if to check with him, I thought—before she went up on her toes and gave me a quick kiss on the lips. To my surprise no one said a word, not even Mike. Moments later Bart and Aja pulled out of the parking lot and headed for the interstate.

Janet was watching me closely. "Are things good?"

I watched as the Jaguar turned onto the interstate and vanished. "I'm not sure," I said honestly.

CHAPTER FIVE

MONDAY AT SCHOOL FELT LIKE A ROLLER coaster.

Since I didn't share a class with Aja anymore, I figured I'd talk to her at lunch. But on the way to her locker I was stopped by Nicole Greer. She wanted to talk, which I found odd because she hadn't said two words to me in the last six months.

Nicole had been my first real crush, the first girl I'd asked out on a real date. My infatuation had been intense, feverish. When she'd broken up with her boyfriend—a guy named Rick Hilton—and I'd finally managed to build up enough courage to call and ask her to a movie, and she said yeah, sure, she'd love to—I swear that had been one of the happiest days of my life.

Unlike Aja, I'd had my eye on Nicole for several years and knew her pretty well, or at least I thought I did. She was very cute: dark blond hair, hazel eyes, round face, upturned nose, brain-blowing smile. Mike went so far as to say she was the prettiest girl in the school, and it wasn't like I was in a mood to argue.

She was sweet, too; she seemed kindhearted. Our first few dates, I felt on top of the world, especially when we made out, which we did often, usually at my house, in my bedroom. We even came close to going all the way. Nicole made it clear she wanted to but it was I who held back. But it wasn't because I was a prude or lacked in horniness. Hell, I was a walking hard-on when we were dating. No, the problem was Nicole. She still talked about Rick. She talked about him a lot, at least from where I was standing.

I knew Rick, I even admired him. We had a lot in common. Like me, he was a loner, more into his oil painting than school. He was smart, too, and there was no phoniness about him. Although Nicole never came out and said it, I knew it had been Rick who had ended their relationship. I suppose a girl who looked like Nicole wasn't used to that sort of thing.

They had only been broken up three months when we began to date; that should have been warning enough. Yet I didn't see the ax coming because I was happy and I didn't want to see it. I wanted to pretend Nicole was happy, too. But I was naive and inexperienced. I didn't understand that all Rick had to do was crook his little finger and say, "I miss you," and she'd come running.

I still remember the day Nicole dumped me. We were supposed to go out that night, and when I called to ask what time she wanted me to pick her up she told me she couldn't make it that evening. That she had to stay home and wash her hair.

Had to wash her hair? What a shitty breakup line. I told her as much before I slammed down the phone. At least I had some pride, I told myself. Later, I took that line and wrote what Dale said was the worst song he'd ever heard in his life. It was called, naturally, "I Have To Wash My Hair."

Anyway, now Nicole wanted to talk and I can't say I was over the moon about the prospect. At the same time I have to admit she still had some kind of hold over me.

"What's up?" I asked. We were standing right beside Aja's locker. It was beginning to look like she had come and gone.

"I just wanted to see how you're doing," Nicole said.

"I'm great. What's new with you? How's Rick?"

Nicole hesitated. "He's fine, I suppose. You know he moved away."

"I didn't know. Where did he go?"

"San Francisco."

"San Francisco? God, lucky him. I mean, did he want to go?"

She nodded. "His father lives there. And Rick's always been kind of impulsive. A few days before school started, he just packed a bag, sent me a good-bye text, and left on a bus. Amazing, huh?"

I could see she was hurting and even though she'd broken my heart I felt no desire to increase her pain. I put my arm around her.

"How you holding up?" I asked.

She sighed and rested her head on my shoulder. "Oh, I'm a mess. I keep thinking what a fool I was. I knew Rick could dump me. He'd done it once, he could do it again. It was just that I . . . I think I got what I deserved. 'Cause of the way I treated you."

"Don't say that. You loved him. You had every right to go back to him. You and I—we were just like a couple of fireworks. We were bound to burn out fast."

She smiled. "You haven't changed. You always know how to make me smile." But then she lost her smile. "You were good to me. I'm sorry I hurt you. The way I did it, I was such an asshole. Can you forgive me?"

"Nicole, come on. I'm going to be a rich and famous rock

star. I'm going to be known all over the world. I'm going to have tons of hot girls chasing me. You wouldn't like that. You did us both a favor." I added, "Although you shouldn't have used your dirty hair as an excuse to cancel our last date."

Nicole didn't smile this time. If anything she looked more worried. "I'm not here just to moan and groan and ask for your forgiveness."

"What's up?"

"Aja, that new girl. I heard you're seeing her."

"That's not true. We haven't even gone out on a date. She came to see our show the other night. That's all."

"Don't lie to me, Fred. You forget how well I know you. In the last two minutes you've glanced at her locker six times. You've got a thing for her."

I stiffened. "If I do it's none of your business."

Nicole pulled away. "I'm sorry, I didn't mean it that way. I'm doing this all wrong. I shouldn't have talked about Rick. He's not why I'm here. She is." Nicole paused. "I need to warn you, Fred."

"About what?"

"Aja. She's playing you."

"What are you talking about?"

"Bobby Dieder and James Caruso. They've both been talking to her. Bobby's in her psych class and Jimmy's in her English class. They've both asked her out."

A cold wave swept over me, the kind of cold that can only be felt on a really hot day when your brain's so cooked a single stroke of bad news can freeze a billion neurons.

I cleared my throat. "What's the big deal? She's a pretty girl. Half the guys in the school probably want to go out with her."

"You don't get it. They've both been to her house. They've both already gone out with her."

I shook my head and backed up a step. "When?"

"Bobby went to the movies with her last Friday. Jimmy—I don't know when they went out. I just know he took her to dinner." Nicole came close, put a hand on my chest. "I hate having to tell you this. It's just that I know you. I know how sensitive you are. I don't want you to fall for—"

I interrupted. "You don't want me to fall for Aja the way I fell for you? Is that what you're saying?"

Nicole nodded. "I still care about you. I care about you more than you know. I don't want to see you get hurt again."

I stood very still. "Thank you."

"If there's anything I can do. . . ."

"Right."

Nicole was no fool. She knew when it was time to walk away. "Take care of yourself, Fred," she said and turned and left.

·   ·   ·

I decided not to talk to Aja that afternoon at lunch. Instead I ditched class, walked home, and took a nap. I needed the extra rest, I told myself. I had to put in a six-hour shift at the hardware store that evening and, besides, I wanted to work on my demo. I decided to take the next day off school as well, which I did.

I couldn't simply drop out, though, and when I did return to school, on Wednesday, I watched from across the courtyard at lunch as first Bobby Dieder and then James Caruso walked up to Aja. Plenty of smiles all around. I couldn't tell which one she liked more and I suppose it didn't really matter. Janet stood beside me and tried to be reassuring.

"So she has guys hitting on her," she said. "That's no surprise."

"Yeah."

"Talk to her. She's probably waiting for you to talk to her."

"She has eyes. She can see where I am. If she wanted to talk, she'd walk over."

"You could be wrong. Maybe I should bring her over."

"No."

"I'm just talking about checking out whether she—"

"No," I repeated.

"All right. But I still have a good feeling about Aja."

"Screw your feelings."

Janet sighed. "They're not always accurate."

Somehow, I managed to avoid Aja the rest of the week, or else she managed to avoid me. It was shocking how miserable I was. I mean, I hardly—no, I won't say it again.

One thing that helped distract me, though, was a last-minute gig Janet set up in Aberdeen, the third-largest city in our beloved state. A major sci-fi convention was taking place over the weekend in the town's swankiest hotel and Janet told our band that it seemed even nerds needed loud music to help break the ice with nerds of the opposite sex.

What she didn't tell us—at least not until we were driving toward Aberdeen—was that their first choice in entertainment, a famous hypnotist, had been stabbed to death a few days ago by his stage assistant. It appeared she'd discovered she'd only been having sex with her boss because he kept putting her in a continuous trance. Janet warned us we were the convention's second choice.

We arrived late and were hastily setting up in the hotel's ballroom when Aja suddenly appeared. She stepped from behind the hall's stage curtains, wearing a tight pair of blue jeans and a white sweatshirt with our band's name, "HALF LIFE," printed in bold letters across her chest.

I had no idea where the sweatshirt had come from.

It looked like she had made it herself.

"Hi," she said.

I was too stunned to think up a great comeback.

"Hi yourself," I said.

She came closer, took the power cord running from my guitar, and plugged it into our stack of Marshall amps. "I remember that's where it goes," she explained.

"What are you doing here?"

"I came to hear you play. You invited me, remember?"

"I didn't think you'd come twice. How did you get here? Did Bart drive you?"

"I took a bus."

"Does Bart know where you are?"

"I don't know, he might."

"You didn't say anything to him?"

Aja considered. "He said something to me."

"What?"

"Bart told me that boys usually ask girls out on dates— when they like them. He said that's normally how it's done. Then he contradicted himself and said you might be an exception to that rule and that I should give you another chance." She paused. "That's why I'm here."

"Hold on a second. What about Bobby Dieder and James Caruso?"

"What about them?"

"Aren't you dating them?" I asked.

"I don't think so. But they keep asking me to go to places with them. And they talk to me every day at lunch and try to see me after school."

"Try? I heard they do more than try."

"Not today. They both wanted to see me this evening but I told them I wanted to watch you sing with your band."

"Why?"

"I told you, because you invited me. And because I like listening to you play your guitar and sing." She paused. "Are you trying to tell me your invitation was good for only one date?"

For some reason, right then, I couldn't take it anymore. Here I'd been feeling miserable over Aja's rejection and now she was telling me she wasn't even aware what the word "rejection" meant. Or else she was trying to tell me she liked me. Either way what she was saying was so bizarre I couldn't help but burst out laughing. Pulling her close, I leaned over and whispered in her ear.

"You may not know this but you're one very strange girl."

I assume she thought she had to follow my example. She whispered back. "Does that mean you want me to stay?"

I let her go and handed her a bundle of amp cords. "What

I want is for you to get your ass in gear and help me set up our equipment."

She took the cords and smiled.

And just like that I was happy again.

It was then I knew I was in serious trouble.

To the band's relief, the crowd appeared open to almost everything we played. The nerds liked our oldies section and recent hits by U2 and Coldplay, and they even got up and danced—like normal Homo sapiens—when we played hard rock. They especially gave me plenty of applause when I played my own songs solo with my acoustic guitar. The only thing they hated was when we tried our hand at rap, which we couldn't blame them for. We were way too white-bread to pull off Jay Z or 50 Cent.

This time Aja hung around for the show, standing on the far edge of the stage on my left. Janet even put her to work: having Aja bring us drinks between songs; helping us switch out our instruments when we went from acoustic to electric; swiping cans of beer from Mike before he could finish them. All in all it was a pleasant evening.

It was only when we were breaking down our equipment that I saw a group of people from the convention crowding around Aja. I was too far away to hear what they were saying but they had a collection of tablets on hand and appeared to be grilling her about something online. I asked Janet to check it out and when she returned she looked worried.

"What's wrong?" I asked.

"Remember when I told you the *Rapid City Journal* would be sending a reporter to our concert at the Roadhouse last week?" Janet said.

"Yeah."

"Well, the reporter didn't just write an article about the show. She taped it. She taped all of it. Even the riot part."

I was busy putting my guitars in their cases. "Not sure I'm following you," I said.

"Stop what you're doing and listen." She sounded serious. I did as I was told while Janet continued. "The reporter in question is named Casey Morall. She posted the riot on YouTube. Specifically, she posted the scene where Aja raised her arms and parted the Red Sea and miraculously got the mob to calm down."

"So? What Aja said was probably true. They were probably fighting because they were scared. I know I'd be scared if I was being shipped off to the Middle East the next day."

Janet shook her head. "You haven't seen the video. Aja's sway over the audience looks a lot more impressive on film. In fact, she comes across as some kind of faith healer."

"Huh?" I said.

"There's a part two. The next morning the reporter inter-viewed the soldier Mike hit over the head with the Jack Daniel's bottle. The guy says when Mike struck him he was sure he'd cracked his skull. He says he was bleeding like a stuck pig and the footage appears to back him up. Then, and this is the weird part, Casey suddenly zooms in with her camera and shows that his scalp wound is completely healed. There's only a faint trace of a scar."

"That's ridiculous. All that means is Mike never cut the guy to begin with. The blood probably came from one of his buddies. There was so much confusion right then. Who knows what happened?"

Janet sighed and glanced toward Aja, who continued to be surrounded by the growing gang. They weren't actually hassling her; they just appeared curious. Frankly, from what I knew of sci-fi nerds, they were the last sort to believe in miracles.

"You're preaching to the choir," Janet said. "But Casey Morall is more interested in making a name for herself than in the truth. You'll die when I tell you how many hits this video has." Janet quickly checked her iPhone. "Two million, six hundred and ninety-two thousand."

"God. How long has it been up?"

"Two days. The hits are growing exponentially. Come

Monday it'll be the craze at school. Like Aja needs any more publicity." Janet paused. "I'm surprised we're only finding out about it now."

I nodded toward Aja. "How's she handling their questions?"

"Okay, I guess. She keeps saying that she didn't do anything."

I shook my head. "I wonder why that soldier would put himself out on a limb like that."

"It's possible he thought he was telling the truth. We know Mike hit him with the whiskey bottle. Even a minor head wound can bleed a lot and then be gone the next day. You remember when that drunk threw a bottle at you when we played Kelsa High? You bled like you'd been stabbed. We were going to take you to the hospital. I was sure you needed stitches. But driving home the next morning, we could hardly find the cut."

"I remember. What if you contact Casey Morall directly? Tell her the band feels uncomfortable about how she's portraying us."

Janet shook her head. "She's already saying her video has nothing to do with Half Life. That it's all about Aja and the soldier she healed."

"What's popular on YouTube one week is forgotten the next. It'll blow over."

Janet hesitated. "You're probably right."

Aja drove home with us this time—after I insisted she call Bart and explain where she was. She rode in the back with Mike, Shelly, and Dale. Naturally, the whole gang had heard about the YouTube post by the time we got on the road. Shelly had her tablet in her bag and we all got a look at the thing. Mike was excited at his fifteen minutes of fame, and that the video showed him diving into a crowd of bloodthirsty soldiers.

"It proves I've got more balls than the lot of them," he said.

Shelly and Dale were less enthusiastic. They feared Mike's behavior might make conventions, schools, and clubs reluctant to hire us. Yet Dale did remind us that any publicity is usually better than no publicity.

"At least it gets our name out there," Dale said.

"Damn straight," Mike said.

Although the clip was focused on Aja, she had little to say about it, even when the rest of us prodded her to speak. Yet, to my surprise, she did give indirect support to the soldier's story.

"The man's wound went away. Isn't that good?" Aja said.

"That's not the point," I said from my place behind the wheel. "The guy's acting like Mike split his head open when he didn't."

"Oh," Aja said.

"I'm pretty sure I saw bone when I clobbered him," Mike said.

"Me too," Aja said.

Janet turned and looked at Aja and spoke in a serious tone. "But you agree you didn't perform a miracle on the soldier, right?" she asked.

Aja hesitated. "Yes."

Janet groaned and spoke to me in a soft voice that only I could hear. "If Casey Morall shows up in town, we've got to keep Aja away from her."

"Agreed," I whispered.

Since our route back to Elder took us near Aja's home, we dropped her off first. Most people in Elder were familiar with the Carter Mansion. Before his death two years ago, Carter had been the town's only truly rich person. He'd made his fortune in oil and promoting concerts. If only he'd lived a few extra years he could have kick-started Half Life's trajectory to the stars.

He'd lavished a good chunk of his wealth on his home, which sat in the center of a plot of land two miles in diameter. The terrain looked both rich and natural; it sloped up and down and was covered with plenty of trees and acres of carefully mowed grass. The house itself, despite its size, had been designed to resemble a log cabin; the rustic style allowed for numerous chimneys. I'd once read it'd taken over a thousand truckloads of lumber to build the place. Less than a quarter of a mile behind the home was a large lake. Basically, the Carter Mansion had it all.

As we crept up the long driveway, Mike asked Aja if she ever went swimming in the lake. "Every night," Aja replied.

Mike was interested. "I bet you go skinny-dipping."

"Skinny what?" Aja asked.

I grumbled. "Mike wants to know if you swim naked."

"Sure. I don't want to get my clothes wet," Aja said.

Mike went to speak again but I slammed the RV to a halt. That shut him up. I escorted Aja to the front door. Despite the silly hysteria with the YouTube post, it had been fun performing in front of her. I'd never seen her smile so much; she really seemed to enjoy the show. She thanked me for the music and the ride as we stepped onto the porch.

"You can thank me by never going out with Bobby Dieder or James Caruso again," I said, joking. But Aja must have heard something else in my voice. She touched my arm.

"This week at school, I felt you were unhappy," she said.

I shook my head. "You just moved here, and we barely know each other. You don't owe me anything. If you want to date other guys then do it."

She looked perplexed, an unusual expression for her. "I don't want what you think I want," she said.

"So what do you want?"

"Nothing."

"Nothing at all?"

"That's right." She raised my hand to her lips and kissed my clenched fingers just before she kissed me on the mouth. Her lips felt as warm as the sun, although the night couldn't have been darker. We kissed for a while, and I prayed the others couldn't see us.

She whispered as we parted, "Talk to me this week at school."

"Sure." I let go of her and began to walk down the porch steps. I spoke over my shoulder, "Good night, Aja. I'm glad you came."

"Me too." Then she called, "Fred?"

I glanced back at her. "Yeah?"

"There's no reason to be unhappy."

"Then why do I keep finding reasons?"

"I'll tell you later," she said before turning and entering the house.

Great, I thought, another secret. From a girl who was full of them.

CHAPTER SIX

THE NEXT DAY I HAD TO GET UP EARLY TO WORK the nine-to-six shift at the hardware store. Business was slow, though, and my boss ended up letting me go at five. I had my bike and was on my way home when on the spur of the moment I decided to swing by the town cemetery. From talk I knew that Mrs. Nancy Billard always visited her child's grave Sunday evenings. I had no desire to intrude but Aja's remark about their encounter over the summer at the cemetery gnawed at me.

Billard was sitting on a bench not far from her boy's tombstone, a bundle of fresh flowers in her hands. Elder was too small a town to have many secrets. I knew what most people knew about the child's death. It was a brutal tale, and far too common.

A decade ago, two-year-old Barney Billard had been playing in the family living room under the less-than-watchful eye of his father, Stan Billard. The story went that Stan had gone outside to collect firewood, but had left the front door ajar when he came back inside. It was a freezing February morning and all of Elder was buried under four feet of snow. Back in the house, Stan stoked the fireplace with fresh lumber and stretched out on the couch and dozed off. Barney, seeing that the door was unlocked and slightly open, did what most boys his age would've done—especially when they've been locked up in the house for most of the winter.

Barney went outside. A neighbor said she saw him making snowballs and throwing them at a bunch of birds, laughing delightfully. The neighbor hurried to scoop him up and take him back inside but before she could reach him the boy wandered into the street. As fate would have it a car came by at that exact instant. The driver—a salesman from out of town—slammed on his brakes but that was probably the worst thing he could have done. The road was icy; the car went into an uncontrollable spin. Barney was crushed, dead before the ambulance could arrive.

The driver was arrested but soon released. It had been an accident, the police said, nothing more. Mr. and Mrs. Billard separated soon after, with Stan moving to Florida. Perhaps he couldn't bear the stares he'd get when he walked down the street. Everyone blamed the poor guy for his carelessness, although, over the years, I came to understand that his wife wasn't one of them. The fact they broke up so soon after Barney's death made me assume I had a less-than-complete picture of what had gone on in their house after the death of their only child.

Billard looked up as I approached. The sun hung low in the west, coloring the white carnations she held a haunting red. Despite the warm evening air, she wore a gray sweater. I was relieved she took my sudden appearance in stride.

"I hope I'm not intruding," I said.

"Not at all." She gestured to a spot on the bench beside her. "Have a seat. It's not often I have company when I visit my son."

Leaning my bike against a nearby tree, I sat beside her and stared uneasily at Barney's tombstone, particularly at the stone cross set atop the heavy block of granite. Unlike Aja, I never visited the cemetery, probably because when it came to the "Big Questions" about life and death, I had no answers. Or perhaps I should say I had no faith in the answers I'd been fed.

Both my parents were Catholic and I'd been raised in the faith. From as far back as I could recall, I'd gone to church every Sunday; made my first communion when I was in third grade, and my confirmation when I was in seventh. Up until then I assumed the local priest and nuns had the inside track on getting into heaven and I didn't give much thought to my immortal soul.

Come my freshman year in high school, however, the foundation of my beliefs began to trouble me and I spent serious time reading the Bible—a practice that wasn't, ironically, encouraged by most Catholics. For me, it was a real eye-opener.

Because the Old Testament came first, I started there and by the time I got to Noah and his ark and two of every living creature on earth, I knew either my faith was as shallow as my trust in Santa Claus or else the book I was holding in my hand conflicted with every scientific concept I knew. Frankly, because I'd devoured at least a couple of sci-fi novels a week since the time I was ten, I knew more chemistry, biology, and physics than probably any kid in town.

It was probably unfair to Jesus Christ and his Gospels, but by the time I reached the New Testament I was 99 percent certain the whole Bible was nothing but fiction. Granted, parts of it were inspiring—I really enjoyed reading the Psalms—but as a so-called manual given by God to mankind to help him understand his place in the universe . . . well, I felt a lot safer in the hands of Robert Heinlein, Isaac Asimov, and Arthur C. Clarke—famous science-fiction authors that I worshipped.

What I mean is, I lost all faith in the supernatural. Reading the holy books of other religions did nothing to change that loss. When it came to the topic of religion, I now felt as Janet did. That "faith" was a code word for a circular form of logic. To put it more bluntly, "faith," to me, now meant "Believing in something you had no logical reason to believe in."

That's why staring at the cross atop Barney's tombstone made me uneasy. I feared in the next few minutes I'd be comforting Mrs. Billard, and that I'd have to say something like, "He's at peace now," or, "You'll see him soon in heaven," when I knew damn well I'd be lying. It had been a terrible tragedy but Barney was gone.

Yet Billard surprised me with her first words.

"You don't go to church anymore, do you, Fred?" she said.

"No, ma'am."

"Is it because you no longer believe or because you can't stand the fact that Father Mackey is a senile old drunk and Sister Josephine took a vow of celibacy because the poor woman couldn't bear to tell her parents that she's a lesbian?"

I smiled. "Father Mackey and Sister Josephine have nothing to do with my crisis of faith. I can only blame myself." I added, "But it's not something I lose any sleep over."

Billard nodded, a faraway look in her eyes. "I used to feel

the same way, when I was young. I figured I'd grow old and die and that would be the end of it. But I did use to hope I'd go before Stan. I didn't want to face losing him." She stopped and stared at Barney's tombstone. "Then I lost more than I dreamed possible."

I was afraid to ask but the question seemed to hang in the air.

"Did losing your son rekindle your faith?"

Billard shrugged. "I thought so at first. The day after we buried Barney, I began reading tons of spiritual books. They didn't have to be Christian. I read about near-death experiences; books on miracles. I watched videos of séances, and all those characters on TV who say they get messages from the dead. I drowned myself in New Age literature. I even went to see several channelers. Let me tell you those people weren't cheap. Still, I got to the point where I was pretty sure there was enough evidence to believe in life after death." She stopped and brushed away a tear that had crept over her cheek. "But then I realized something was missing."

"What?" I asked.

"Proof. Hard-core proof.'"

"It's a pain in the ass that it all has to come back to that."

She looked at me. "But then I was given proof. The one thing I had prayed for since Barney wandered out our front door to play in the snow. I was given it this summer, sitting exactly where you are right now. All the proof I could ever have asked for. And it . . . it tore me apart."

"I don't understand?"

Billard reached out and took my hand. "It was Aja."

"Huh?"

"She came here one day in July when I was . . . visiting my son. Or else, I don't know, maybe she was here before me. It's strange but I can't remember which one of us got here first. All I know is when I saw her I felt annoyed. Like she was intruding on my space—on Barney's little area. I wanted her to leave. I snapped at her, I think, told her she had no business disturbing the dead." She paused. "But Aja didn't leave, at least not right away."

"What happened?"

Billard's hand slipped from mine like it had lost all strength to hold on. Her face was suddenly stricken. "She said something, something she couldn't have known."

I waited. I waited without speaking; it felt wrong to press her.

Billard lowered her head. "It was just one sentence. I don't know why it shook me so deeply. No, I'm sorry, that's not true. I do know why. Part of it was the way she said it. Like she knew what she was telling me was absolutely true."

"Tell me."

Billard quoted, "'Your son doesn't blame you any more than your husband does.'"

"Wait. From what I heard, your husband, Stan, it was his fault. He left the door open and your boy wandered . . ." I didn't finish.

"I never told anybody this except Stan and Mrs. Green, the florist. But I trust you, Fred. It was my fault the door was left open. I came downstairs after Stan had fetched the firewood. He was dozing on the couch and Barney was playing with his Legos. It was a Sunday morning. As usual, Stan had forgotten to bring in the paper. I went outside to get it. It was snowing lightly and there were five sparrows walking over a nearby snowdrift. They looked like a family—there were two big ones and three baby ones. I remember how I wished Barney could see them. Maybe he did. Our neighbor, Margaret, said she saw him playing with some birds before he stepped into the road."

Billard stopped talking and once again I waited. The woman rubbed her hands together as if they were cold, like she was back on that frosty morning. She continued:

"I came back inside and took the paper upstairs to our room, where I spread it on our bed so I could clip the coupons I wanted to save. I have no recollection of not shutting the door all the way but it had to have been my fault. The door automatically locked when it was closed. Plus the handle was old and rusty. There was no way Barney could have opened it without help if I'd shut it properly." She paused. "I was upstairs when I heard the squeal of the car's brakes."

"I'm so sorry," I said.

"You're too kind. What you really want to say is why didn't you tell your husband that it was your fault and not his? Why did you let the entire town think that Stan had been responsible for his son's death?" She paused. "The truth is—I don't know. Maybe I needed someone to blame. Somehow it was easier to keep silent and let Stan take the heat. Of course it tore him apart. Until one day—it must have been two months after the funeral—he found the pile of coupons I'd cut out of the paper that Sunday morning. A few were dated and right then he put two and two together and he knew."

"Did he blame you?" I asked.

"No. He was too good a man. Too good for me, that's for sure. That's one of the reasons I begged him to leave."

"So it wasn't guilt?"

"It wasn't *his* guilt, it was *mine*. He didn't want to leave but the way people kept staring at him—I don't know if he had a choice. Not unless I owned up to what I had done."

"Why didn't you?"

Billard shook her head. "Stan said what was done was done. He was a long-distance truck driver. He was gone a lot. I taught in our only high school. Everyone in town knew me. Not many people talked to Stan. He said if my lie came out I might lose my teaching job. We talked about it a lot—his leaving. He was positive it was the right thing to do." Another tear rolled over her cheek and she wiped it away. "But I've always wondered if deep down inside he wanted to get away from me. That he did in fact blame me for Barney's death." She stopped and looked me in the eye. "That doubt went away when Aja said what she said."

I was confused. "Did she say anything else?"

"Just those eleven words. I swear to you, Fred, everything that mattered was contained in those eleven simple words."

I gestured. "She must have heard the story about what happened to you. She was probably trying to comfort you. It doesn't mean—"

"I checked," Billard interrupted. "Aja had gotten off her plane from Brazil that same morning. She didn't know a soul in town. I doubt she had talked to anyone in Elder before we met. And yet she came straight here, at the exact time I'd be here, and said one line that freed me from a burden I'd carried for a decade."

"Then why weren't you . . ." I didn't want to say it.

"Grateful? I was grateful. My gratitude knew no limits. My heart swelled with such relief it burst in my chest. I went home that night and wept myself to sleep. With tears of joy. Tears of gratitude."

"Then?" I said.

Billard shook her head. "Then the monster in me awakened. The same monster that had so casually put the blame of my son's death on my husband when it was my fault. That creature came back to life and said no, it's too good to be true. It's a miracle and there are no miracles, and besides, Aja's just a pretty girl from Brazil. She's no angel. I convinced myself that somehow she had heard about my past, and had gone to the cemetery that day to play a cruel trick on me."

"But no one knew, except Stan, that you left the door open?"

Billard nodded. "That's right."

"I don't understand."

"Yes you do, Fred. Aja showed up here from halfway around the world and immediately—with eleven ordinary words—healed a wound that could not be healed. Not only did she absolve me of my guilt over what I'd done to Stan, she reassured me that, yes, a part of Barney was still alive and that that part forgave me for leaving the front door open and depriving him of his mortal life."

"Hold on. Aja never said she spoke to Barney's soul."

Billard grabbed my hand tightly. "You weren't here! You didn't hear the certainty in her voice when she spoke. I did and I believed her."

"Then why do you hate her?"

"You know why!" Billard cried.

I sat silent for a whole minute before I realized the truth. "Because it's easier to hate her than to keep on believing her," I said.

Billard nodded weakly. "Easier and less terrifying."

I remembered what Aja had told me in Rapid City.

"I can't understand why Billard hates you."

"She doesn't hate me."

"What do you mean?"

"She's afraid of me."

"It scared you having her in your class," I said.

"Yes."

"You made up that story about her cheating."

"Yes."

"Did she really give the exact answer that was in the book?"

"Yes." Mrs. Billard smiled. "She's quite amazing, that one."

"Did you see her again—between when you met her here and when she walked into your class?"

"No."

"You hadn't talked to her on the phone?"

"No."

"Didn't you want her to explain her remark?"

"No."

I felt like I'd hit a wall. "Are you still afraid of her?"

Billard hesitated. "Sure. But I'm . . . I'm mostly grateful to her."

I shook my head. "This is weird."

"I hear the two of you are dating."

"Who told you that?"

"You know Elder. Word gets around."

"What you told me just now, I won't repeat it to another soul."

"I know that."

"But I'm worried about your reaction to her remark."

"The weight I give it?" Billard sighed. "I suppose it's possible she had heard about my history, although I don't see how. Or else she could have seen me sitting here mourning over Barney's tombstone and made a wild guess about what had happened and just ran with it. Believe me, I've gone over every angle in my mind—again and again. But I keep coming back to how I felt when she spoke. The way her voice touched me like some kind of magical key that unlocked not only my deepest secret, my deepest pain, but my deepest doubt."

"I'm not following you."

"You don't give yourself enough credit, Fred. You never do. You understand everything I'm saying."

I stood up; I felt I had to move. Yet I couldn't very well walk away.

"There's no reason for you to say Aja restored your faith."

Billard nodded. "I agree, it's not logical. It's certainly not scientific. It just happens to be true."

"But she didn't do anything!" I protested.

Billard also stood and stepped to her son's tombstone. There she knelt and lovingly placed her flowers so the petals touched the name of her boy. She had more tears now but for some reason they didn't seem so sad.

"I saw the video about Aja on YouTube," she said as she stood back up and wiped her face. "What it showed didn't surprise me. In fact, it reminded me of when Aja was here with me and Barney."

"You honestly believe she was aware of your son's feelings?"

"Yes."

"How?"

"I have no idea. But I do know this. Aja is no ordinary girl. I don't know if I'm telling you that because I want to warn you or because I want to congratulate you. I just know it's true."

I shook my head. "You're acting like she's some kind of saint."

Billard studied me. "You wouldn't be reacting the way you are unless she had touched you as well. Touched you in some way you can't explain."

"That's not true. I hardly know her."

"You sound almost as scared of her as I am." She offered me her arm. "Do me a favor and walk me back to my car. This whole 'confession' has left me feeling exhausted."

I escorted Mrs. Billard to the parking lot, before returning to collect my bike. But I didn't leave the cemetery right away. For a while I stared at Barney's tombstone and thought of all the scriptures I had laughed at a few years ago.

CHAPTER SEVEN

AT LUNCH THE FOLLOWING DAY, AT SCHOOL, I spoke to Aja only briefly. There were too many people around her asking questions about the video. According to YouTube, Aja's encounter with the Roadhouse mob had now collected over eight million hits. Its popularity continued to soar. What struck me as odd was that half the people chumming up to her seemed to think she had in fact healed the soldier. Never mind that they were talking about a miracle and miracles were impossible.

But—and this was a big *but*—Mrs. Billard's talk had gotten to me. I couldn't stop thinking about what she had said, or what Aja had said to her. That didn't mean I was ready to canonize Aja. Still, a part of me, a tiny part deep down inside, began to wonder . . .

For her part, Aja continued to insist she'd done nothing; and I found her denials strangely comforting. Also, although we only spoke for a few minutes, I'd managed to ask her if she wanted to go out with me to a movie that night. All talk of miracles aside, hearing her say "Yes" did more for me than the video and Mrs. Billard's mysterious tale combined.

Technically, our band had practice that evening but everyone was cool about my canceling, with the exception of Shelly. As usual, she didn't say anything but I could tell she was jealous. Janet agreed with me. She even worried that Shelly might quit the band.

"Then we'd have no place for the band to practice," Janet said as we walked home from school together.

"Shelly won't quit. Her father wouldn't allow it."

"She's a rejected woman. Trust me, she might. You should talk to her."

"And say what? 'I like you as a friend but I don't find you sexually attractive'?"

Janet frowned. "Don't cancel any more practices because of Aja. And she doesn't have to come to every show, you know."

"I feel more confident when she's around."

"I told you this would happen. You're falling in love." Janet suddenly paused and sucked in a breath. "Do you think tonight will be the night?"

"That I propose? Yeah, let's go pick out a ring."

"No, silly, that you have sex."

"We're not having sex tonight. For your information, tonight's going to be our first official date. All the other times she showed up at our shows, remember? Which reminds me, I need to borrow your car."

"What's wrong with your parents' car?"

My father and mother shared the same car, which they drove to Balen every morning. They usually didn't return until after seven in the evening. Because I planned to take Aja to dinner before the movie, I needed to get an early start. I explained all this to Janet and she said it was okay with her as long as Bo wasn't using it. She doubted that he was. They had another car—a Mustang that Bo had turbocharged. That sucker could do over a hundred and twenty miles an hour.

"You know, technically, he still owns the Camry," Janet said.

"I thought he gave it to you on your last birthday?"

"He did, sort of. But he never signed it over to me. I wouldn't worry—Bo never says no to you."

"Nor to you."

"I wouldn't go that far."

"What are you going to do right now?"

"I've found this new yoga teacher I like on YouTube. I'm going to check out a few of his videos."

Janet's latest craze was learning to meditate, which was curious because I always associated meditation with New Age movements, and Janet was an even bigger atheist than I was. To my way of thinking, most people who meditated were trying to contact their soul, and to do so I would have assumed a person would have had to believe he or she had one.

Yet Janet saw no conflict in her spiritual beliefs—or the lack thereof—and her desire to quiet her thoughts. She told me she was just looking for peace of mind and meditation gave her that and the end result was all she cared about. Fair enough, I thought.

Still, I couldn't imagine meditating myself. I was more interested in increasing my creativity; in seeing where my thoughts could take me. The last thing I wanted to do was get rid of them.

Later, driving Bo's Camry out to the Carter Mansion, I was feeling pretty jazzed. When I thought of all the times I'd been with Aja, I realized we'd never been alone for a sustained period where we could talk, just talk. I was looking forward to getting to know her better.

Yet, a voice inside kept nagging me that she might be *impossible* to get to know.

Bart answered the door and informed me that Aja was still dressing and would be down shortly. While I was waiting, he asked if I'd like to meet Aja's aunt—Mrs. Clara Smith. I said sure and he led me to a large bedroom on the first floor loaded with tons of medical equipment. It was only then that I learned the woman had suffered a stroke shortly after they had arrived in America.

"She's lost the use of the left side of her body and her words are too slurred to understand," Bart said. "But she communicates fine with the help of a voice box connected to a tablet she types on with her right hand. Her fingers are nimble—she has no trouble keeping up a natural conversation."

"Does she know who I am?" I whispered as we neared the bed and I got my first look at the woman. She was old, probably in her mideighties. But her hair was dyed an agreeable blond; and add to that the fact she wore makeup that had been applied by an expert, and had on a lovely white silk dress—she somehow reminded me of an old-fashioned movie star. Her stroke notwithstanding, the lady had a style about her.

"Most definitely," Bart said before he turned to his boss and formally introduced us. "Clara, this is Fred Allen, the singer/songwriter Aja told you about. Fred, Mrs. Clara Smith, Aja's legal guardian."

"Pleased to meet you, ma'am," I said as I shook the frail hand she offered. She let go quickly though, to type on the pad lying on a pillow near her waist.

"I've heard a lot about you, Fred," a mechanical voice sounded from a speaker above her bed. The words were more natural in tone than Siri's.

"I hope some of it was encouraging," I said.

"Oh yes." Clara must have hit a special button because a string of laughter followed. She gestured to a nearby chair. "Please, have a seat."

Sitting, I wondered if her gesture had contained a hidden message because I noticed Bart had suddenly split. I didn't mind. I was curious to talk to the woman alone, and hopefully find out what kind of person it took to adopt an eight-year-old girl who'd been roaming the streets of an obscure shantytown since God knew what age. I did the best I could to explain my interest in Aja's background—and in Clara for that matter—and the woman immediately put me at ease.

"Please, ask any question you want," she typed.

"How did you first meet Aja?"

Clara's fingers flew over the pad.

"Bart and I had heard stories about the *Pequena Maga*—that means 'Little Magician' in Portuguese—before we actually met Aja. That's what the people in Selva called her. The majority were fond of her and for most the nickname was an affectionate title. But even before we met Aja face-to-face we spoke to a few who feared her, probably because she was something of a mystery. They didn't understand how she lived, what she ate. You see, since she was a child, Aja lived almost like an animal. She had no home, no family. She wandered in and out of the jungle, and when she was in town, no one ever saw her begging for food or asking for help. And no one ever touched her or tried to harm her. They just let her be."

I frowned. "Are you saying no one spoke to her?"

"Oh no. She spoke to anyone who spoke to her, although she usually had little to say. But you have to understand the people of Selva. They're a kind people but simple. In their own way, they too live close to nature. For the most part they're very religious and they seemed to sense a saintliness to Aja."

My frown deepened. "Are you saying they worshipped her?"

"They respected her deeply. They spoke of odd events that happened around her: hearing the voices of dead loved ones; seeing lights in the sky or in the trees. There were reports that Aja could predict the future and heal the sick. It was these stories that piqued my interest in her. But when I asked where I should go to meet her, the townspeople said I'd never find Aja that way. That she had to come to me." Clara paused in her typing before adding, "And that's how we met."

"She appeared on your doorstep one day?" I asked, not bothering to hide the skepticism in my voice. If Clara was offended she didn't show it. She continued.

"One day I was taking a long walk in the jungle outside of town. But I had wandered too far off the path and was lost. It was a hot day and I had foolishly forgotten to bring water with me. I don't want to exaggerate and say my life was in danger but I was becoming concerned. It's very humid in that part of the world. Feeling dizzy, I stopped under the shade of a tree to rest. It was then I saw Aja. She just walked up to me and pointed with her arm, saying, 'There's a stream of fresh water up ahead. Come, I'll show you.' She took me completely by surprise. All she had on was a short, white dress. It was dirty and so was she. Her hair was long—it looked like it had never been cut, never been combed. Yet she looked— how should I say it?—beautiful."

"She's a beautiful girl," I said.

"Yes. But that's not what I mean. She had an inner beauty—I felt it right away. I followed her to the stream, and, without a moment's hesitation, she pulled her dress over her head and dove stark naked into the water. It was like the most natural thing in the world to her. I can't say I followed her example but it was a relief to splash my face and head and take a deep drink. My dizziness passed and

I sat and rested on a rock while Aja swam lazily in the stream, mostly on her back, staring up at the blue sky. I didn't know if it was because of the coolness of the water, or the prettiness of the spot, or the presence of Aja herself, but I began to feel a deep peace settle over me. And I knew that my meeting with Aja had been no accident."

"What do you mean?" I asked.

Clara eyed me closely. "I think you know what I mean."

"I don't, honestly. Tell me."

The woman shrugged as best she could with her half-paralyzed body. "I just knew that Aja and I were supposed to be together from then on. But when she got out of the water, after dressing, she took my hand and showed me a way back to the path. Yet she didn't go with me back to town, not that day, and a part of me felt confused and hurt."

"Mrs. Smith, may I ask a question?"

"Clara, please. Yes, ask anything you wish."

"Do you have any children of your own?"

"No. I know what you're thinking. That I'd always longed for my own child and that meeting Aja was the fulfillment of an old and painful wish. No, you don't have to apologize. I'd be thinking the same thing if I was in your position. But the truth is, and it might sound cold, but I'd never really wanted children." Clara paused. "Not until I met Aja."

"Tell me more."

"I didn't see her again for a month. Then, one day, she just showed up while Bart and I were having lunch on the porch. We invited her to stay and eat. She was obviously half-starved—you only had to look at her. It took a while for her to open up but eventually she began to answer our questions."

"What did you ask her?"

"Normal things. Where do you live? How do you feed yourself? What do you do when it rains? Does anyone ever try to hurt you? This last question made her laugh. She acted as if the idea of her being harmed was totally foreign to her."

"Excuse me, I meant to ask this earlier. Were you speaking Portuguese the whole time?"

Clara hesitated. "No. Initially, we were only passing through Selva when we heard about Aja. For that matter, we were just visiting Brazil. It wasn't as if we lived there. Neither Bart nor I spoke Portuguese. When we talked to Aja, it was always in English."

"Did many of the people in Selva speak English?"

"Very few. It's a small town and doesn't get many tourists. If people speak a second language, it's usually Spanish."

"Then who taught Aja English?"

"I don't know. She never said."

"What led you to Selva in the first place? From what you've said, it sounds like a pretty remote place."

Clara raised her head. "I had a dream about the town."

"A dream?"

"Yes. A few days before we set out on our trip. The dream was the reason I scheduled a visit to Brazil."

"Where are you from originally?"

"Los Angeles."

"I see. So I take it Aja started to stop by regularly?"

"She'd show up once every week or so. Then, after a couple of months, she began to come by more often. Bart and I set up a room for her and she began to stay overnight. After a year or so she almost never left."

"This started when she was roughly eight years old?"

"We don't know her actual birth date. And we don't know anything concrete about her parents, except that they both died when she was around four or five. But the villagers never told us how they died, and Aja would never talk about them."

"But you believe a few of the villagers did know how they died?"

"Yes. But I think they were afraid to say how."

"Why?"

"I don't know."

"How many years has Aja been with you now?"

"Ten years, almost to the day."

"Bart gave me the impression it was her idea to move here."

"That's true."

"Do you know why she wanted to come to this particular town?"

Clara looked at me a long time. "You know Aja, she seldom says much. But from hints she's dropped, I've gotten the impression she came here because she was looking for someone."

"Who?"

Clara smiled. "You."

I felt my skin burn with fresh blood, although I can't say her answer surprised me. All along, talking to the woman, I had felt she was leading up to some sort of revelation.

Clara was clearly intelligent; the stroke that had impaired her left side had not damaged her mind. Yet I found her story of meeting Aja disturbingly vague. It had an almost fairy-tale-like quality to it. Indeed, it reminded me of Billard's encounter with Aja in the cemetery.

At the same time I was certain Clara was not lying.

"I know what you're thinking," Clara said when I didn't respond. She reached out and took my hand, squeezed it for a moment before her fingers returned to her pad.

"I'm glad one of us does," I said.

"You're thinking I'm no different from the primitive

villagers who lived beside Aja all her life. That I've romanti-
cized the story of her life. But the truth is I haven't told you a
fraction of the wild tales surrounding her."

"You mean I haven't heard anything yet?"

"Exactly."

"Then tell me."

"No."

"Why not?"

"Because you're not ready to hear it all, not yet. But I
promise you, before I sleep tonight, I'll write down a few
things that will help you better understand her."

"Fred," I heard a voice speak at my back.

I turned. It was Aja, standing in the dim doorway, wearing a tight red dress, tall black boots, looking anything but
saintly, more like sex incarnate. She flashed a bright smile.

"Do you want to go?" Aja asked.

I stood clumsily, somehow feeling that it was rude to
leave Clara so abruptly but at the same time anxious to be
alone with my date. With my head turned away, I felt Clara
pat my hand.

"It was nice to finally meet you, Fred."

"Likewise," I replied. The way she said "finally"—I got
the impression the woman had been waiting a long time.

CHAPTER EIGHT

IN THE CAR I SAW THAT MY MOTHER HAD LEFT A message on my cell. I picked it up and was surprised to hear my parents were spending the night in Balen. It seemed my mom's company was celebrating a huge quarterly success and was throwing a party at a nearby hotel. Because they were going to be out late, and drinking, they thought it best not to try to drive home late. It sounded like my mom's company was springing for the hotel room.

Aja noticed my uncertain expression. "A change of plans?" she said.

I started the car. "Well, I wanted to take you to Balen so we'd have some privacy. But I just found out my parents are going to be gone for the night. In fact, they're spending the night in Balen."

"So there's no reason to go there."

I felt like such a dick for blushing. "We could go to my house and hang out but it's not very exciting there. Besides, I promised you dinner in a fancy restaurant. You're probably hungry."

"Do you have food at your house?"

"Leftover turkey. It's only a day old."

Aja shrugged. "I like turkey leftovers."

"You really want to go to my house?"

"Yes."

I was fortunate I didn't have to worry if the house was clean. My mother loved to tidy up as much as my father loved to work in the garden. Our house was always immaculate, with the exception of my bedroom. It was not that I was a slob but my space was limited, what with my guitars, amps, and keyboards, never mind my computer and books.

My parents had bought me a tablet the previous Christmas but, for me, there was a special pleasure in holding and reading a *real* book. I doubted that I'd ever throw out my collection of novels. Besides science fiction, I'd collected tons of mysteries. I had every book Agatha Christie had ever written.

If my friends could have seen me the first half hour I was alone with Aja I'm sure they would have died laughing. For some reason, hanging out with her in the place where

I'd grown up made me feel especially nervous and clumsy. For example, in the kitchen, suddenly I couldn't find a damn thing. I even had trouble finding a pot to boil rice. Then I had trouble remembering how long I was supposed to let it cook. Finally, though, I began to calm down and by the time I had the food on the table I was back to my usual witty self.

"Does Bart do the cooking at your house?" I asked as I sat across from Aja, the width of the table separating us. I'd offered her a beer or a Coke but she seemed to prefer water. She also kept me from piling too much rice, turkey, and steamed broccoli on her plate. Given that she weighed no more than a hundred pounds, I could see why.

"I do most of it," she said.

"Really? Where did you learn to cook?"

"Aunty taught me. She and her husband owned a restaurant when they were young."

"She didn't mention her husband to me."

"He died not long after they married."

"She never remarried?"

"She told me there was no point—that she'd never be able to love someone else as much." Aja added, "I disagreed with her."

"Isn't it possible she was right? I mean, isn't it possible there's only one special person out there for all of us?"

"No," Aja said and there was a peculiar authority in her

voice, as if she was absolutely certain what she was saying was true.

"You'd never make it in the music business," I teased. "Almost every song recorded nowadays is about finding your soul mate."

She spoke in a serious tone. "That's not what you write about when you compose your songs. I've heard them. You write what comes to you from the Big Person."

"The Big Person?"

She gestured. "I don't know what you call it. When you write a song, don't you listen inside, first, before you come up with the lyrics?"

I nodded. "Yeah, usually. I know I write better when I'm alone and the house is quiet. Silence seems to help me connect with my muse."

"Your muse." Aja appeared to savor the word. She added, "The Big Person must be the same as the muse."

"Is 'Big Person' a phrase they use where you come from?"

"No."

"Then why do you use it?"

Aja continued to struggle to find the right words. "To separate it from the Little Person."

I chuckled as I took a bite of turkey. It didn't taste bad for leftovers. The rice was pretty good, too. My mom preferred basmati and, like her, I put plenty of ginger in it.

"You're losing me," I said. "Who's the Little Person?"

Aja went to answer but then stopped and smiled. She shook her head. "It doesn't matter," she said.

After we finished our meal and cleaned up—it was my idea to wash the dishes—we watched a movie. Aja had never seen *The Lord of the Rings*—she had only seen a handful of films—so I played her a tape of the first installment: *The Fellowship of the Ring*. She watched the whole thing without uttering a word. But it was obvious she loved it.

It was after midnight when we went up to my bedroom. Aja sat on the edge of my bed and I picked up my acoustic guitar and took a seat beside her and began to strum a few chords. The instrument was out of tune but I remedied that fast enough. Since I was a kid and had first picked up a guitar I'd been able to tune it automatically. It wasn't bragging to say I could hear notes, precise notes, much clearer than your average person.

"What do you want to hear?" I asked.

"A new song," she said.

"All my new material is rough."

"No. Play something brand-new."

"I don't know . . ."

"You can do it. Just . . . let it find you."

"Let it find me?"

She nodded. "Let your muse find it for you."

Aja sounded so confident that I could do what she was suggesting I didn't have the heart to tell her I didn't think my muse was actually alive and on call. Like I often did when I was alone, I strummed a few minor chords—E, A, D, G— switching them around randomly before I began to play individual notes in the same chord structures.

For a while I just let the hypnotic flavor of the chords ease over me. I love the sound of the guitar; I love to just randomly pick at the strings. This time, however, after ten minutes or so, I began to feel a soothing heat inside. It seemed to radiate from my gut and rise up and flow through my fingers. I noticed I'd begun to play faster, my fingers flying between the frets. It was odd but I felt as if I'd touched something special and if I just reached a little farther, a little harder, I'd know what it was and I'd be able to play it.

Then I had it, a brand-new melody. I began to hum along with it, occasionally throwing in a line now and then. I was far from having a complete song but I knew I'd stumbled onto something.

I began to sing aloud. . . .

"Strange girl
Where did you come from?

Where have you been?
Strange one
You're so full of secrets
I can't see within

Strange girl
You move so softly
Across the stage
My eyes can't leave you
I'm hiding backstage
You're a closed book
I can't read a page

I suddenly stopped, feeling embarrassed. "God, I'm not sure if that worked. The words I mean. But the melody—there's something there. What do you think?"

"I liked the words. I liked them a lot."

I chuckled. "That's because you're not a songwriter. I was just throwing out lines. That's how I compose songs. I'll throw out a dozen lines and if I'm lucky I keep one."

Aja was curious. "What lines would you keep tonight?"

"Well, maybe the first handful. They might work as a chorus. Maybe a few others."

"Maybe all of them?"

"No way."

"Why not?" she asked.

I hesitated. I wanted to tell her that the words made me think of her too much. That she, and not my muse, had inspired them. But there was no way I was going to tell any girl something like that on a first date.

Aja appeared to sense my shyness and put her hand on my knee. "You're worried you won't succeed. But you will."

The certainty in her voice, it was odd, it seemed to vibrate a chord deep inside.

"How can you be so sure?" I said.

Squeezing my knee, Aja stared at me with her big, brown eyes. "It will be okay, Fred," she said.

"You didn't answer my question. How can you be so sure?"

"The Big Person."

I smiled. "He told you?"

"Yes."

She kissed me then, or else I kissed her. I honestly don't know who made the first move. It wasn't a brief kiss, nor was it long; somehow it was timeless. The next thing I knew we were lying on my bed. I was stroking her hair and running my hand over her shoulder and down the side of her hip and leg. And Aja was touching my face and the feel of her fingers—there was something extraordinary about them.

Her touch was not merely loving. I felt as if her hands were actually *made* out of love. I knew that was crazy, yet it felt so real. I'd like to say that I felt as if I was falling in love with her right then but the love I felt coming from her—it seemed so much bigger than anything a normal human heart could conjure up. It was like a tidal wave of caring, of intimacy—of something so big that perhaps only a Big Person could really understand it. All I knew for sure was that I'd never met anyone even remotely like Aja.

Then my phone rang. It rang and rang and I was forced to answer it. The screen on my cell said it was Dale. He wouldn't call this late unless it was important. I propped myself up on the bed with my elbow.

"Hello?" I mumbled.

"Fred, it's Dale. We have a problem."

"We do?" I said. He sounded bad.

"It's Mike. When you canceled practice he got restless. He drove over to Balen. I tried to stop him but he said he had some business to take care of. I knew it could be nothing good. Turns out he went to pick up five pounds of pot at the home of some big dealer. Someone must have tipped off the cops. He was followed by the police, and when he was inside the dealer's house, completing the deal, the cops hit the place.

There was a shooting. Mike didn't get hit with a bullet but he got hit over the head hard. I don't know the full story, only what the cops told me. The dealer might have struck Mike, thinking he'd set him up, or else Mike might have gotten into a fight with the cops. You know how he gets when he's cornered. They might have cracked him over the head with a baton. But his injury—it's serious. I spoke to the emergency doctor just before Mike was wheeled into surgery. He told me there could be brain damage." Dale started crying. "Fred, I don't know what to do. The doctor said I have to prepare myself for the worst."

"Are you at Balen Memorial?" I asked. Balen had a decent hospital, good doctors. I assumed they'd called in their main neurosurgeon. The guy was famous in our part of the country.

"Yeah. I'm on the third floor. Please, can you come? You've got to come, I don't know if I can take this."

"Of course I'll come. I'll leave now. Hang tight. Everything's going to be okay."

Dale was crying. "I don't think so."

I hung up the phone. Aja was staring at me; she didn't ask anything. I assumed she'd heard enough to know Mike was badly hurt. I felt a pain in the center of my own chest. It felt odd after all the joy I'd felt only seconds ago. I sighed heavily.

"I should take you home," I said.

Aja shook her head. "I'll go with you to the hospital."

"Are you sure? I'll probably be there all night."

"I'm sure."

We drove to the hospital in silence. It was ironic that my parents were in Balen that very night. I considered calling them but what was the point? My mother would just get upset and pace miserably in the waiting room. She had known Mike since we were in kindergarten. And I couldn't call Mike's mother, not yet. I had my reasons.

But I considered calling Janet. I knew she could comfort Dale better than I could. I also knew she'd want me to call her. But something held me back. I told myself it was best to wait and see how serious Mike's condition was before dragging everyone out of bed. The truth was I didn't know what I was doing.

Balen Memorial was a five-story cube. Whoever had designed it had been lacking in imagination. Yet the building was relatively new and the hospital had a good reputation. Considering where we lived in South Dakota, Mike had ended up in probably the best facility within three hundred miles.

We found Dale on the third floor in the surgical waiting room. He was alone; he looked so frail. He burst into tears when Aja and I arrived. He hugged us both and I could feel him trembling in my arms. He kept thanking us for coming; I finally had to tell him to stop it.

"Have you heard any updates from the nurses?" I asked.

He nodded weakly. "A nurse came out. She said Mike's skull was swelling inside and that the doctor—Dr. Rosen—had to drill a hole to relieve the pressure. But she warned me that that was just the beginning. The blow—it sent tiny fragments of bone into Mike's brain. The nurse said that Dr. Rosen is trying to take them all out before he closes him back up."

Doctor Albert Rosen was the famous neurosurgeon I'd heard about. That was the good news. But the rest of what Dale told us made me feel sick to my stomach. Holes in Mike's head. Bits of his skull in his brain. It felt so unreal; like a nightmare.

Yet, ironically, none of what I heard surprised me. It was as if a part of me had waited for years to get this exact call in the middle of the night. Mike's crazy drinking, the wild crowd he ran with when he was out of our sight, his explosive temper . . .

It had made this night all but inevitable.

Still holding on to Dale's hand, I collapsed into a chair, with Aja on the opposite side, her head resting on my shoulder. It was a quarter till two in the morning. There was nothing to do but wait. The nurse had warned Dale the surgery could take all night, maybe longer.

Around three in the morning Aja seemed to drop off to sleep. Her breathing became soft and regular; she wasn't snoring but she was close. Dale, too, to my surprise, blacked out, his head lying back against the wall. I was glad; he needed a few hours of peace. His pale face looked so weary. I worried if Mike died that Dale wouldn't make it. Dale loved his friend that much; Mike was the center of his life. And Mike didn't even know.

What a messed-up world, I thought.

At six in the morning a nurse came out and spoke to us. The news was all bad. Mike had *major* swelling of the brain; the fact his head was open due to the ongoing surgery was the only thing that was keeping his gray matter from pressing against his skull. Plus the doctor kept finding more fragments of bone; he'd already removed a dozen. I still didn't know what Mike had been hit with or who had hit him. The nurse certainly didn't know. She told us to try to be patient. When she left, Dale collapsed in his chair, sobbing.

"It's no good! It's no good!" he cried. "Even if he lives he'll never be the same."

Sitting beside him, I pulled Dale close. "You don't know that. He's got a brilliant surgeon working on him. And the brain is an amazing organ. Why, some people get in car wrecks and fall into comas for a year and are ten times worse off than Mike. Then, out of the blue they wake up and a few months later they're out playing baseball. You have to keep a positive attitude."

Dale nodded miserably. "I'm sorry, I know you're right. I just feel . . . I just feel like it's going to turn out bad. I don't know why."

There was a question I had put off asking Dale.

"Don't you think it's time we called his mother?" I asked.

Dale cringed. "No. Don't, Fred, let's wait. Please."

On the surface Dale's reaction might have appeared weird. But since Mike's father had died when Mike was only five, Mrs. Garcia had never been right in the head. It was not as if she went around doing crazy stuff but she was usually disengaged from the world and seldom answered questions beyond saying yes or no. Most people in town assumed she'd had a nervous breakdown when her husband died—one she'd never recovered from. Dale believed, as I did, that the only thing that kept her alive was her son.

I'd discovered that the hospital had called Dale because they'd checked Mike's cell and had seen Dale listed first in Mike's saved numbers.

I patted Dale's hand. "We'll wait."

But I felt I'd waited long enough when it came to Janet. I called her and told her the bad news. She swore at me for having left her in the dark so long but I could tell it was a defense mechanism. She was badly shaken. She said she'd come right away.

"Have Bo drive you," I said.

"I'll be fine."

"No. Listen to me. Call Shelly. You two should drive together."

She hesitated. "All right, we'll see you soon."

Time crept by. The large round clock on the wall above us reached seven o'clock. Dale stood and went off to find some coffee. Aja continued to rest with her head on my shoulder. She appeared to have gone back to sleep. It was only then that I realized she hadn't called her aunt or Bart to let them know where she was. Knowing her unreliable history when it came to checking in, I took it upon myself to call her house.

Bart answered. "Hello?"

"Hi, Bart, this is Fred. Aja's with me and she's fine. We're in Balen. A friend of mine was in a serious accident. He's in surgery now. I tried to take Aja home but she insisted on coming to the hospital with me. I hope that's okay."

Bart didn't immediately say it was fine like I thought he would. Instead, he was quiet a long time. "Is your friend in danger of dying?" he asked.

"It's serious. He's suffered major brain trauma. He's been on the operating table all night."

"Then you must listen to me. Do not let Aja anywhere near your friend. Even if it's just to see him for a few minutes in the recovery room. Don't take her with you if you go see him. In fact, it would be better if you took Aja home right now. She shouldn't be at a hospital."

Aja continued to breathe deeply on my shoulder. I spoke softly. "I don't understand. You're acting like my friend can hurt her."

"He *can* hurt her. You must trust me on this. Take her home now."

"I don't think she'd go. She insisted on coming with me. You know how stubborn she is."

Bart paused. "She told you she had to be there?"

"In so many words, yeah."

He sighed. "Then let her stay. But swear to me, even if she insists, that you won't let her get near your friend."

"Why not?"

"I told you why not. He'll hurt her. He might even kill her."

"How?" I asked.

"I can't tell you how. You have to take my word for it. You know I've been with Aja a long time. Just trust that I know what I'm talking about. Now swear to me you'll do what I said."

I swallowed. "I swear."

Bart wished my friend all the best and hung up, leaving me utterly confused. His request, his demand—it had been so odd. He was acting like Mike would suddenly rise from his death-bed and transfer all his pain and injury directly into Aja's head. Frankly, Bart had sounded more crazy than Mike's mother.

Yet I had sworn to him.

I saw no reason why I couldn't keep my word.

Dale returned shortly and brought me a coffee. Janet and Shelly arrived close to eight o'clock and woke up Aja. The waiting room was starting to feel claustrophobic to me and we moved to the hospital cafeteria, which was open and serving breakfast. None of us was really hungry but I picked up some scrambled eggs, toast, and a few slices of bacon, as well as a pot of coffee. Janet and Aja poked at the food, eating little. Dale and Shelly stuck to the coffee.

"You should have called us hours ago," Janet said.

I shrugged. "Would it have helped? You and Shelly got to sleep. That's a good thing. Mike's going to need us today."

"I know you told us everything the nurse had to say," Shelly said. "But what was her attitude like? Was she opti-mistic?"

"She was professional," I said. "She didn't give anything away."

"She sounded like a cold fish," Dale muttered.

"We're lucky Dr. Rosen is doing the operation," Janet said. "People fly from all over the country to see him. Mike couldn't be in better hands."

I chewed on a piece of buttered toast; it felt tasteless in my mouth. "I don't understand why we haven't seen any cops all night," I said.

"You know the answer to that question," Janet said. "They're the ones who cracked Mike over the head. Trust me, their lawyers have already warned them to keep a distance and to not say a word to anyone."

"How could Mike be so stupid as to get caught in the middle of a drug bust?" Shelly said.

"Because he's an idiot," Dale said, and there was so much pain in his voice.

After eating less than half our food, we returned to the waiting room. It was eleven before Dr. Rosen finally appeared through the swinging doors. He'd obviously come straight from the operating room. There were splashes of blood on his blue scrubs. Although his dark eyes were weary, bloodshot actually, and he was on the short side and balding, the man had a strength to him. We jumped to our feet the moment he entered the room.

"Are any of you family?" he asked.

"We're the only family he has," Janet said. "Talk to us."

Dr. Rosen told us the news. My fatigue might have dulled my mind but it seemed to me the man used a lot of long-winded medical terms I could have done without. The bottom line was that he'd been able to remove all the bone fragments but he feared the overall trauma to Mike's brain would cause it to continue to swell. The next twenty-four hours would be critical.

"Could he die?" Dale had the guts to ask.

Dr. Rosen could tell, of all of us, that Dale was the most shaken. He patted him on the shoulder. "We'll do everything we can to see that doesn't happen," he said.

"Is he conscious? Can we talk to him?" I asked.

Dr. Rosen sighed wearily. "We can only wait and hope he regains consciousness. Two of you can see him—no more—and only for a few minutes."

Dale was the obvious choice to go, of course, and he wanted me to come with him. But Aja stepped forward. "I should go," she said.

"Why?" Janet asked. "You hardly know him."

Aja didn't respond. Pulling her aside, I spoke so only she could hear. "I called Bart to tell him where you were. When I explained to him what had happened, he freaked out. He made me swear that I wouldn't let you anywhere near Mike."

Aja stared at me with her big eyes. "Bart knows not to interfere."

"With what? You?"

"Yes."

"I'm confused. Bart acted like Mike could hurt you somehow."

Aja shook her head. "I need to see him."

Dr. Rosen cleared his throat. "The two who are coming with me had best come now," he said with a note of impatience as he turned toward the door that led to the recovery rooms.

"Come on, Fred," Dale said, grabbing my arm. He literally pulled me away, leaving Aja following me with her eyes.

The recovery room was open; there were not even curtains separating the patients who had been operated on, perhaps because they were all males. I saw two elderly fellows who'd had their sternums sawed open; obvious heart patients. And a guy in his forties who had metal bolts holding his lower right leg together.

Yet Mike looked the sickest of them all.

It was his color—he didn't have any. Being Hispanic, always out in the sun, it seemed impossible but Mike was white as a bedsheet. The top of his head was encased in bandages; the gauze came down to near eye level. On the left side it was stained with blood. "Soaked" would have been a more accurate word. A narrow tube ran from his nose to an air pump. The latter hissed as it rose and fell. He was being mechanically ventilated.

"Can he breathe on his own?" I asked.

"I'm afraid not," Dr. Rosen said. "But that can change. All we can do is wait and see." He turned to leave. "My prayers are with your friend."

"Thank you, Doctor," Dale whispered, wiping away a tear. He turned to me as if looking for a miracle. "Fred?"

I pulled Dale close. "There's hope, you heard what Dr. Rosen said."

Dale's head sagged heavily. "I wish I hadn't heard what he said."

We stayed with Mike ten minutes, both of us taking turns squeezing his right hand, the only limb that didn't have an IV stuck in it. Dale spent most of the time talking to Mike, telling him that he was going to be all right, that he had a lot of living left to do, a lot of concerts left to play with us. He told him how much he loved him and it was all I could do to keep from crying. I hated crying in public. Even more, I hated what the oozing blood in Mike's bandage told us about his odds. He looked so lifeless; like no one was home.

Finally a nurse came and kicked us out. It was just as well. Seeing Mike, who'd never been sick a day in his life, in such bad shape had been too much for Dale. He was beyond overwhelmed. I practically carried him back to the waiting room. Janet and Shelly were anxiously waiting for our report. But Aja was missing.

"Where is she?" I demanded.

"She went to the bathroom," Janet said.

"You're sure?" I asked.

Janet was in a rotten mood. She snapped at me. "Who cares? She's human, Fred, you know. She uses a toilet just like the rest of us. Now tell us how Mike looks."

Dale had already collapsed in a chair and covered his face with his arms. I did my best to put a positive spin on what we'd seen. My lies were not very convincing. I probably should have lied more. When I mentioned that Mike couldn't breathe on his own, Shelly broke down and Janet turned away so no one could see her crying. She was worse than me when it came to public displays of grief.

Aja didn't reappear in the next fifteen minutes. I finally went looking for her and found her sitting near the hospital entrance. She was bent over and clutching her abdomen as if she had a bellyache. I sat beside her.

"You okay?" I asked.

She slowly raised her head and looked at me. She hadn't seen me approaching. Her gaze looked somehow off. She kept blinking and a muscle in her cheek was twitching. "I'm fine," she said.

"Do you want me to take you home?"

"Yes."

I didn't bother returning to the waiting room and the others. I just texted Janet a brief message saying I would catch up with them later and that one of them should pick up Mike's mother and explain to the poor woman what had happened. I knew Janet would take care of it herself.

Aja and I were no sooner in the car than she passed out, her loose hair hanging over her face. I wasn't really worried about her. At best she had only slept four hours. She must be exhausted, I told myself. It had been a little selfish of me to bring her in the first place. Then again, I had not been lying to Bart when I had told him she had insisted on accompanying me. On the surface Aja acted easygoing but I was beginning to see she was not used to being told no.

I didn't disturb her until we were driving up the long driveway to the old Carter Mansion. It was then she gave me a bit of a scare. I had to shake her hard to wake her up. "Aja?" I said loudly.

She finally stirred, raised her head. "It's okay," she whispered.

"What's okay? Are you all right?"

She nodded, her eyes half-closed. "Fine."

Bart came out the front door, onto the porch, and down the steps as I stopped at the mansion entrance. I'd hardly put the car in park when he flung open the door and undid Aja's seat belt. He practically lifted her from the front seat, all the while glaring in my direction.

"I told you that you should have taken her straight home!" he screamed at me. His venom threw me off guard.

"She was just taking a nap," I said.

Yet Bart had a right to be concerned. Suddenly I could see Aja was far from all right. She was having trouble staying awake; she kept sagging into Bart as they went up the stairs. Finally, and this really scared me, he lifted her off the ground and carried her into the house. Jumping out of the car, I tried to follow but he shouted for me to leave.

"You've done enough for one day!" he cried, slamming the door in my face. I stood there for several minutes feeling like a complete fool. I wanted to knock, talk to him, explain that I had kept my word. What made it worse, of course, was that I had no idea what was wrong with her.

In the end, though, I accepted that I was not wanted and trudged back to the car. Driving back to town seemed to take an eternity. The weird thing was, I suddenly felt more worried about Aja than I did Mike.

CHAPTER NINE

GOOD NEWS CAME LATER THAT DAY. WHEN I returned home, I passed out on the living room couch and was only awakened at six o'clock, about an hour before I expected my parents home. Janet was calling.

"He's awake!" she cried into my cell. "He's talking and everything. Dr. Rosen can hardly believe it. He says it's a miracle."

I sat up, wiping the sleep from my eyes, relief swelling in my chest. I'd passed out thinking I'd never see Mike again. "Thank God," I said.

"And Allah and Krishna and the rest of them!" Janet exclaimed. "Seriously, Dr. Rosen said in thirty years of practicing medicine he's never seen anyone recover so fast from such a severe head wound. The swelling in Mike's brain has totally stopped. Except for being tired, he's not showing any side effects of the surgery. Think about that! He was on the table ten hours with his skull sliced open!"

"I don't know what to say. It does sound like a miracle."

Janet lowered her voice like she didn't want anyone else to hear. "Fred, you've got to get back here. Since he woke up Mike's been saying he has to talk to you. That it's real important."

"Do you know what it's about?"

"No. I only know he's desperate to talk to you."

"I'll leave now. I've still got your car, you know."

"Glad you brought that up. I've got Bo's car. Could you swing by and pick him up? He wants to see Mike and, besides, he needs the Camry back. I can drive you home later in the Mustang. Bo has somewhere he has to go tonight. I've already told him to expect you."

"No problem. I'll pick him up," I said.

Bo was waiting on the porch when I drove up; he hopped in the passenger seat. Janet had given him the full scoop on Mike, and Bo kept shaking his head in wonder.

"If something like this doesn't force Mike to clean up his act I don't know what will," Bo said. "He's been given a second chance in life. Tell him those don't come around too often."

"I will. Hey, do we know yet who attacked him?"

"From what Janet told me, it sounds like an entire SWAT team surrounded the house seconds after Mike went inside to collect his dope. The SWAT leader called out on his bullhorn for them to surrender. The dealer and his gang figured Mike was working for them. They tried using him as a hostage to help them escape. You can imagine how that worked. The SWAT team swept in and opened fire. One guy was killed, two others besides Mike were wounded. The SWAT leader says the dealer hit Mike over the head with a baseball bat. The dealer says it was the cops who did it."

"What does Mike say?" I asked.

"I don't know if he knows."

"Were any police hurt?"

"No."

"There were no cops at the hospital after the raid. That's pretty odd, don't you think?"

Bo shrugged. "They were probably avoiding the press. Your main problem now is Mike was the catalyst for the shoot-out. Chances are he's going to do time. Your band's going to need a new drummer."

"I'm not worried about the band right now," I said.

The others were still at the hospital: Janet, Dale, Shelly. Dale was so relieved Mike was going to make a full recovery he wept as he hugged me. "That bastard," he said. "That god-damn bastard. I'll never forgive him for the hell he put us through."

"Yes, you will," I said. "You always forgive him."

Dale came close and whispered in my ear. "Mike's going to tell you something bizarre. Trust me, you should believe him. Everything he has to say checks out."

It took permission from Mike's mother—who looked to be holding up better than we had expected—for me to be let in to see Mike. I was led by a nurse to the critical area, where he'd been given his own room. Before leaving, the nurse warned me not to tire him.

I couldn't believe this was the same person I'd seen that morning. The ventilator had been removed and he had regained his normal color. Actually, he looked like he was glowing. It made no sense; he was sitting up in bed, drinking a bottle of apple juice, and grinning away. His bloody bandage from that morning had been replaced with fresh gauze and there was no sign of further bleeding.

"Hi, Fred," Mike said and shook my hand like he hadn't seen me in years. His grip was firm.

"Welcome back," I said. "You gave us quite a scare."

He spoke in a tone I'd never heard before. It was like another miracle; he sounded mature. "I know exactly how you and the others felt. That's why I told Janet to get your ass back here. I need to tell you what happened during the surgery." He gestured to a nearby chair. "Pull up a seat."

I sat down. "Don't tell me you went into the light."

"I saw something. I saw a lot of things."

"Mike, I was joking." I saw he wasn't. "Tell me what happened."

He considered before speaking, something I'd never seen him do before. Whatever he'd experienced had moved him.

"At the dealer's house, I remember the SWAT leader calling to us on his megaphone. There were six of us inside; three were carrying. But we could all hear the sound of the cops loading their clips. They wanted us to hear. They wanted us to know we were surrounded. I remember thinking how screwed I was—that I'd probably end up spending years behind bars. I thought how that would break my mom's heart. I thought of you and Dale, too, and how much I'd miss playing in the band. Then I felt a huge bang on the back of my head and everything went black."

Mike sipped his juice before setting the bottle aside. He cleared his throat. It sounded hoarse, probably from the ventilator.

"The next thing I knew I was here in the hospital," he said. "But I wasn't in the operating room. I was floating along the hallways, looking into different rooms. I knew I was looking for someone but I wasn't sure who it was. I wasn't worried or upset. If anything, I felt real peaceful. It felt so cool to move without walking. It was like I could fly. I didn't stop to worry about what had happened to me. I just went with the flow. But I wanted to find the person I was searching for.

"Then I saw you guys: Janet, Shelly, Aja, you, and Dale. I could tell you were worried about me and that bothered me. That was the first time I felt anything negative. I was mainly concerned about Dale. I could feel his pain like it was my own pain. Like I was inside him." Mike paused. "Does that make sense?"

"Yeah, sure. Go on."

Mike was thoughtful. "I wanted to do something to make you guys feel better but when I tried talking to you I saw that you couldn't hear me. It was then that I thought I might be dead. That this was what death was like and I wouldn't have a chance to say good-bye to any of you. It shook me up pretty hard.

"Then Dr. Rosen came out and spoke to you. I heard every word he said. I already compared what I heard with what Dale said the man told you guys. It was identical— you can ask Dale when you go out. But right then, at that moment, what the doctor was saying sounded pretty bad. So

I wasn't dead yet, I realized, but I was going to be pretty soon.

"I followed you and Dale when you went into the recovery room. It was then I saw myself from the outside. Saw how messed-up I was. I could feel how little life was left in my body. I touched my hand and it was like holding a dead battery or an old lightbulb. You just know it's not going to work. I knew my brain was so messed-up that even if I tried to slip back inside my body, I wouldn't be able to talk or move around. It sounds crazy, I know, it was just something I sensed. Something I was certain of. You following me so far?"

"Yes," I said. "Keep talking."

"I was still tied into Dale's emotions. I could feel your grief but it was his pain that overwhelmed me. For the first time I saw how connected we were. That we'd always been connected all our lives, ever since we were kids. More than anything else I wanted to tell him that I was right there beside him. It was so frustrating—that I couldn't talk to him or to you. By then I was pretty sure I was going to die and I wanted you both to know that God, or the universe, or whatever, hadn't erased me and that a part of me was going to go on. But I didn't stop to think where I was going.

"You guys didn't stay very long and when you left I wanted to go with you. But now I felt stuck to my body. You know how some people, when they get in accidents, they talk about how there's a silver cord that connects them to their body? Well, I didn't see anything like that but it was like it was there. It was like some force was keeping me near my body and forcing me to feel how mushy the left side of my brain was. It was scary. I didn't like it, I wanted to get away. I prayed to God to let me go."

Mike paused for a moment before continuing. "This next part's hard to talk about. If you don't believe me I understand. I mean, if you told me what I'm about to say, I would have said, 'Yeah, right, Fred. You got hit over the head with a bat and you saw your guardian angel. What else is new?'" He paused. "You know what I mean?"

"Not really. Did you see your guardian angel?" I said.

"Maybe." Mike coughed again to clear his throat. He grabbed his bottle of apple juice and sipped it. Finally he was ready to go on.

"Something entered the recovery room. I didn't know what it was but I sensed right away it was what I had been looking for when I first woke up outside my body. It hadn't been you guys, it was this being, this creature. I don't know what to call it. If I had to describe it I'd say it looked like a pinpoint of blue light. It was indescribably loving and kind. It was so—you know I never use this word—charming. It was like the most precious thing in the universe. A jewel of some kind. When I looked at it I didn't want to look at anything else. I was mesmerized.

"But as it drew closer I realized it wasn't small. No, it was actually huge. It was so big it frightened me. I must sound like I'm contradicting myself but this is just what I experienced. It was terrifying. I'm sure you remember that old Nietzsche quote where he says, 'When you gaze into the abyss, the abyss gazes into you.' You should remember because you're the one who gave me his book. This *thing*—this wonderful terrible thing—was the abyss. And it had come for me."

"What do you mean?"

"It had come to ask me to make a decision."

"To die or to go on living?"

"Yes. I mean, that was the question. But suddenly I wasn't sure if I wanted to go on living. The thought of leaving this thing was unbearable. It scared me but it was like a billion times greater than any angel or god you could imagine. Now that I'd found it there was no question I could leave it. Except for . . . Dale. His pain haunted me. I knew it would kill him if I died. I didn't want to do that to him. And the more I thought about it, I didn't want to leave you, either, or my mother, or Janet or Shelly. So I told the being I wasn't ready to go. At the same time, I told it I didn't want to come back a drooling, brain-damaged vegetable."

"It's good you remembered to mention that . . . Carrot Head."

Mike nodded seriously. "I felt like I got my message across. But then another weird thing happened. Another being came into the room. It was similar to the first one. I'm not a hundred percent sure there were two of them they were so much alike. Except this one seemed to touch my body."

"Touch you? How?"

"With its hand."

"I thought it was a point of light. I didn't know it had hands."

"That's what's confusing. It didn't have hands. It didn't have a body, it wasn't a human being. But, for a moment, I saw it reach out and touch me—with a human hand."

"That's weird."

"It gets weirder. Somehow, I knew when it touched me that I was going to be okay, physically. That I wasn't going to come back with my brain scrambled. I felt so grateful I could have wept. The glowing blue point of light, the second one, seemed to pick up how I felt. It seemed to smile at me."

"Now it had a mouth?"

"A mouth, hands—what the hell do I know? If it really was the abyss, couldn't it take any shape it wanted?"

"I suppose. Why not?"

Mike looked at me. "You think I'm crazy. Say it. Don't worry, I can take it. I know what I saw."

I considered before answering. I wanted to be honest.

"I don't think you're crazy. I saw Dale outside and he told me that I should believe what you told me. Which means you did hear everything Dr. Rosen told us. Which is physically impossible. So you're a lucky guy. You not only got healed by an angel, you returned with proof that you saw him."

"Or her," Mike said.

"Or her," I agreed.

Mike continued to study me. "But you still don't believe it."

I shrugged as I stood. "Give me some time to absorb it all. You have to admit, it's a lot to take in."

The nurse came and told me it was time to scram. Outside in the waiting room, I cornered Dale and had him repeat what Mike had said Dr. Rosen had told us. Unless Dale was lying—and he had no reason to lie—Mike had heard every word the neurosurgeon had said even while his comatose body lay a hundred feet away in the recovery room.

"It makes you wonder, doesn't it," Dale said.

"That's the understatement of the year," I said.

Bo had already taken the keys to the Camry and left the hospital. The nurses had told Bo that Mike couldn't have any more visitors. Janet was preparing to drive me back to Elder when we spotted Casey Morall, the reporter who worked for the *Rapid City Journal,* entering the building. We knew what she looked like from her YouTube video. We lowered our heads and tried to look the other way as we crossed the lobby but she saw us and hurried over. She had a professional-quality digital video camera hanging around her neck.

"Hello, Fred Allen, Janet Shell. I'm glad I ran into you guys. I've been wanting to talk to you about a story I'm working on."

"We're not interested in your stories," Janet said, while keeping us moving toward the exit. But Casey had no intention of letting us go; she quickly matched our pace.

"You're the one who invited me to the Roadhouse," Casey shot back. "I just wrote what I saw."

"And posted a bogus video on YouTube while you were at it," Janet snapped.

"The video spoke for itself. The same with the soldier. He spoke from his heart."

Janet groaned. "Gimme a break."

"It can't be a coincidence that wherever Aja shows up, people get healed," Casey said.

The reporter's remark stopped me cold, much to Janet's displeasure. She wanted me to keep moving. But suddenly my legs weren't cooperating. I realized I was missing something.

"Why are you here?" I said.

Casey spoke a mile a minute. "Ms. Shell hasn't told you? I was here earlier this afternoon. I spoke to several nurses in critical care. All of them confirmed that Michael Garcia underwent a miraculous healing after being touched by Aja Smith. His vitals immediately stabilized and he began to cough, indicating he no longer needed to be ventilated. In fact, Aja was still in the room when they took him off his ventilator."

"Huh?" I said.

Casey continued. "They also believe that other patients in their ward were healed by Aja. Mr. Alex Spender had a tibia break so severe his doctor feared he might eventually lose his leg. At the very least the nurses and his doctors knew he'd have to undergo several more surgeries. But now the bone in his leg is almost completely healed. The nurses can't explain it." Casey gestured to her camera. "I have all this recorded."

I looked to Janet. "You knew about this?"

"This is bullshit!" Janet said. "This woman is turning gossip into miracles. The only reason Mike's awake and talking is because of the skill of one of the best neurosurgeons in the country—Doctor Albert Rosen. He worked on Mike for over ten hours. He's the one who picked the pieces of bone out of Mike's brain. He's the one who stopped Mike's brain from swelling. To ignore all the work he did and to say Mike's better because a girl who's only attended high school for a few days happened to touch his head is utterly ridiculous."

"Aja touched Mike's head?" I mumbled, totally confused.

"When she went to the bathroom," Janet said.

"Ah!" Casey Morall said. "But Aja didn't actually go to the bathroom, did she? She went to the recovery room instead. Where she was seen by RN Kimberly Leroash and RN Barbara Spinoli. They're the nurses I have on tape who verified that it was only after Aja touched Mike's head that he began to show sudden and remarkable signs of improvement. How do you explain that?"

"Very easily," Janet said. "You swoop in here and give everyone the impression that you're some big-shot reporter that was sent here by the *New York Times*. You act like some miracle has already occurred and that you're just here to verify it. And because most people love being in the spotlight, and you know all the right questions to ask, you manage to get these two nurses to lend credence to your bullshit story." Janet paused to catch her breath. "Forgetting all along that Aja has said over and over again that she's never healed anyone in her life."

"I'd like to hear that from Aja herself," Casey said. "Is she here?"

"No," Janet said.

"But she was here earlier? When your friend Mike was on his deathbed?"

I held up a hand. "Aja was here when Dr. Rosen was operating on Mike. She was in the waiting room like the rest of us. As far as I know she never got near Mike."

"Why do the nurses in this hospital say otherwise?"

"Beats me," I said.

"They have sworn on record that Aja—"

"Enough!" Janet interrupted, grabbing my arm. "We're leaving."

Janet swept me outside to her car. But before we climbed inside, I asked her if it was true Aja had snuck into the recovery room to see Mike.

"That part of Casey's story is true," Janet said. "After she told us she had to go to the bathroom, she must have circled around and snuck into the room right after you and Dale left."

I remembered how long Aja had been gone.

"Why didn't you tell me earlier?" I asked.

"You just got here. And what does it matter if she saw him or not?"

I worried when I thought of how weak and listless Aja had been on the ride back to Elder. I had tried calling her on her home phone before I'd left for the hospital but there had been no answer. Aja had never given me a cell number; I don't think she had one.

"I wonder," I muttered. That tiny doubt I'd felt after listening to Mrs. Billard's story returned; I felt it as a crack in the ground beneath my feet. I believed in science, in facts, and I wasn't about to toss the laws of physics and chemistry and biology out the window just because of a few puzzling events, never mind Mike's fantastic story.

But—and the "but" just kept growing in size—I felt as if I'd mentally stumbled right then on a mythological rabbit hole. Why had Aja gotten so weak after seeing Mike? And how had Bart known that seeing Mike could harm her? It made no sense.

Of course, there was no point in trying to explain my confusion to Janet. She'd smack me on the side of the head if she saw even the slightest sign that I was buying into this wave of "miracle madness."

"What?" Janet said.

I shook my head. "It's nothing. I wouldn't get worked up over Casey Morall's story. It will die down when Mike refuses to verify that Aja healed him."

Janet nodded. "You're probably right. Mike's as much the key to her story as Aja is. I wonder if we should have both of them post a video on YouTube saying that the woman's a big fat liar, a beginning reporter who's desperate to publish something sensational."

"No. Respond to her stories and you'll add fuel to the fire. Best to just ignore her."

"That's true, I suppose." Janet continued to study me. As usual, she was sensitive to my mood. "What's bothering you?" she asked.

I shrugged. "This investigation and reporting by Casey Morall—it feels so over-the-top. Why'd she make such a big deal about what happened at the Roadhouse? And how did she know to come here to interview Mike's nurses? We're missing something."

"What?" Janet asked.

The most obvious answer was the most disturbing.

"She knows something about Aja that we don't."

CHAPTER TEN

THE NEXT DAY—IT WAS A WEDNESDAY—AJA wasn't at school. I called her home number. Bart answered and was extremely curt. He told me Aja was sick and would be out a few days. When I tried to ask what was wrong with her he hung up. Seemed I was no longer welcome by everyone at the Smith residence.

I felt concerned but there was nothing I could do. When I got home that same day, though, there was an e-mail from Aja. I'd given her my e-mail when she'd been at my house. The note was short and to the point.

Fred,
Don't worry, I'm fine.
Love, Aja

I kind of liked the last line. Read it a few hundred times.

Knowing Aja was okay and that Mike's brain was on the mend, our gang was able to turn our attention to Mike's legal situation. His near-death experience notwithstanding, Mike still had his street smarts and knew not to talk to the police. We agreed the first thing we had to do was find him a good lawyer. Our problem was money, or the lack of it.

But to our surprise—and in no small part due to Janet's prodding—Bo stepped up to the plate and loaned Mike ten grand to hire an attorney in Balen named Randall Clifford. The man had an excellent reputation. After meeting with Clifford, Mike told us the lawyer was optimistic. It seemed the police had broken a few rules when their SWAT team had gone in shooting. The man was confident he'd get Mike off with a misdemeanor and a year of probation. The wonders of high-priced legal advice, I thought. Now *there* was a miracle Casey Morall should have been talking about.

Three days went by and we began to relax about the reporter. No new videos appeared on YouTube and no amazing miracle articles ran in her newspaper.

Unfortunately, on the weekend, Casey made up for lost time. She'd probably taken the extra time to write her article and then purposely ran it in the Sunday edition of the *Rapid City Journal*, when the paper's circulation was at its largest.

The article started on the front page; it was long and detailed. It first reviewed what had occurred at the Roadhouse, before moving on to Mike's miraculous healing and the two nurses' long quotes. The only positive was that Casey was unable to get a doctor at Balen Memorial to substantiate her claims.

The new video she posted on YouTube was far more chilling. It contained a long interview with the man, Alex Spender, whose tibia had been broken into two distinct pieces. The video showed X-rays of the gap between his bone, or bones—before and after Aja's visit to the recovery room. God knows how Casey had obtained them. Of course Alex had just had surgery to repair the problem but he swore on tape that his doctors had been completely befuddled by his sudden recovery.

Worse, Alex was an eyewitness to Aja's visit to the recovery room. He spoke with feeling about how he watched as Aja snuck into the room and touched Mike's head and how instantly the beating of Mike's monitors changed and he began to cough as his body rejected the ventilator. This was minutes after Dale and I had exited the recovery room. Alex said Mike suddenly sat up and gestured frantically for the nurses to remove the tube from his throat.

All in all it was a moving piece. Casey spoke briefly at

the beginning and at the end, letting "The facts speak for themselves." Within two days the twenty-minute tape had nine million hits. We felt lucky that reporters from the major networks and papers hadn't shown up in Elder to chase Aja down. But their absence didn't surprise me as much as it did my friends.

Crazes on the Internet didn't usually translate into reality. What Casey was claiming sounded too phenomenal. I suspected she had gone too far with her article and video and had scared off the legitimate media. But I knew she was clever; I worried she was holding something in check.

It was for that reason I agreed to meet with Casey. Alone.

The only one I told about the meeting was Janet.

No surprise. She exploded.

"You were the one who said it would be a mistake to engage her!" Janet yelled when I told her about my intention to have dinner with Casey midway between Elder and Rapid City.

We were on Janet's porch. It was three in the afternoon on a Tuesday and we had just walked home from school together. Janet paced as I told her my plan while I sat on the swing chair. Janet's father, Bo, was working on the engine of a big rig in the garage.

Aja had returned to school today. Except for looking a

little tired, she seemed okay. Still, I worried about her. Why was she tired? What had she done?

"I know but the situation's changed," I said.

"How?"

I shrugged. "Nine million hits."

"It's the Internet. You said yourself that it will blow over."

"Casey Morall shouldn't have taken up this crusade in the first place. I'm telling you she knows something."

"What?"

"Something from Aja's past."

Janet paused in midstride. "Did Aja say that?"

"No. She doesn't talk about her past. But it's a good guess."

"Have you asked her straight out if she did anything to Mike?"

"Yes. She says she didn't do anything."

"Then why did she sneak into that room?"

"She says she had to see him."

"That's it?" Janet asked.

"You know Aja. If our class gave out an award for 'Most likely not to say much,' Aja would win it." I paused. "I'm worried about her."

"All the publicity?"

"Not just that. Since she's come back to school, she hasn't seemed herself. She looks weary."

"She's probably getting over a bug."

"You don't believe that any more than I do."

"What are you suggesting?" Janet asked.

"I don't know."

"Fred!"

"All I know is that after she sat with Mike in the recovery room for a few minutes, she couldn't keep her eyes open. By the time I got her home, she was so sick she couldn't walk."

"I spoke to her today. She seemed fine to me."

"You don't know her as well as I do. Look, I'm not saying she healed Mike. I don't believe in healings. I believe in Dr. Rosen and his incredible skill. But we do know that Aja's different than anyone we've met before."

Janet made a dismissive gesture. "That's because of her background. If I grew up spending most of the time in a jungle I'd be as strange as her."

I smiled when I thought of our date at my house.

"I'm writing a song about her called 'Strange Girl.'"

"I told you. Nothing inspires great songwriting like falling in love."

"It's got an awesome melody."

"You're changing the subject. If you're going to meet

Casey Morall to talk about Aja, bring Aja with you. Let her set the reporter straight. By erecting this wall around the girl you just make her into more of a mystery."

"No. It's too far a drive. I want her to stay home and rest."

"Then take me."

"No way."

"Why not?"

"You'll attack Casey the moment you see her, like you did at the hospital. No, I need her to open up to me. To confide in me."

"Good luck with that."

"Everyone thinks I'm Aja's boyfriend. I'll bait Casey with the prospect of sharing secret knowledge with her."

"She's an experienced reporter. She's not going to fall for that. She'll get more out of you than you get out of her."

I stood. I was meeting Casey in three hours. I wanted to get on the road. "Impossible. I don't know any of Aja's secrets."

Janet gave me a good-bye hug. I was taking her car again.

"Just make sure she's not recording your conversation."

"I'll frisk her from head to toe," I promised.

Alone on the road, with only the radio for company, the drive felt long. I spent a large part of the time trying to come up with a strategy that would make Casey leave Aja alone. But I realized that probably wasn't going to happen. The woman sure had a bug up her ass when it came to Aja. If I could at least find out the source of her obsession, I'd call the evening a success.

We met at a diner just off the interstate in the middle of nowhere. Casey had a bag and camera with her but I insisted she leave them in the car. I also told her I wasn't going to talk unless she let me frisk her. She threw a song and dance about what a pervert I was but a minute later I was holding a tiny digital recorder she'd fitted into the top of her boot.

That shut her up.

Casey was an attractive woman; I put her age at twenty-five. She'd cut her dark blond hair short and sassy-like; and she'd highlighted her blue eyes with black mascara. She was stout without being overweight. I was sure she could handle herself in a fight. Hell, she could probably take me. She'd struggled when I'd frisked her. The fact that she'd tried to tape me without my knowledge showed she had no scruples.

Then again she was a reporter. What did I expect?

We sat in a corner booth and ordered dinner. I had a hamburger and fries. Casey asked for halibut and rice. We both drank tall glasses of iced tea. Casey asked where Aja was and I told her she had no interest in being a fake celebrity. Casey didn't bat an eye at my opening dig.

"If she's not interested then why are you?" she asked.

"We're close. I hate seeing her harassed."

"I'd hardly call it harassment. I'm making her into a star. You must know the number of hits my videos are getting on YouTube."

"YouTube's like Disneyland. It's the happiest place on earth if you're bored or stoned. No one takes it seriously. I doubt CNN and Fox are knocking on your door."

"You take me seriously. You just drove three hours to talk to me."

"Because I'm bored and stoned. You're the busy reporter. Why'd you drive so far to see me?"

"You're Aja's boyfriend. You're in the same band as Michael Garcia. It's simple. You're connected to the people I need to connect with. I'm here to work out a deal."

"What kind of deal?" I asked.

"You talk Aja and Mike into granting me interviews and I'll tell you everything I know about Aja's past." She paused. "You'd be amazed what you might learn."

"I'm already close to the family and Aja's told me plenty. I doubt there's anything new you could tell me."

"You're saying you know all there is to know about your *Pequena Maga*?" Casey said, trying to shock me.

"The Little Magician—yeah, I know what they call her in Selva. But I'm curious how you know."

The fact that I knew what the name meant in English surprised Casey. I could see I'd scored a point. She frowned as she stopped to light a cigarette in a no-smoking area and blew smoke over my head.

"Give me something and I'll give you something," she said.

"Give me something significant and I'll talk to them about granting you interviews." I glanced at my watch. "Start now or I'll be gone before our food arrives."

"You'd stick me with the bill?"

"That's a given."

Casey studied me. "You're smart, Fred. I like that about you."

"You mean you've been told that. By your mole."

Casey blinked. "What are you talking about?"

"You have someone in Elder feeding you information about Aja. Someone told you she and I were a couple. The same person told you about Mike's head injury."

"You're guessing."

"I don't think so. You heard about Mike too fast. You were at the hospital too quick. Someone called and told you what was going on."

"My, you are a clever boy. So who is this secret agent of mine?"

"It's a student at Elder High. Someone who doesn't wish Aja well. Or at least someone who wants me to stay away from her." I paused. "Are you paying Nicole Greer or does she do your bidding for free?"

Casey smiled wickedly. "You're in the wrong profession, Fred. You should be a mystery writer, not a rock singer."

"In your article you praised our band."

"I did that to get on your good side. Although I have to admit you have talent. But the rest of your group—you'll dump them the day you leave Elder. I'd do the same thing." Casey took a drag on her cigarette. "What other secrets of mine have you uncovered?"

"You're new to Rapid City. You only arrived three months ago. Around the same time Aja arrived in Elder."

"Who told you that?"

I shrugged. "As Hannibal Lecter would say, 'Quid pro quo, Clarice.' I mean, Casey. It's your turn. Tell me something interesting."

The woman suddenly ground out her cigarette in a nearby potted plant. "All right, I admit I've been chasing the Aja story for some time. She intrigues me."

"How did you come across her?"

"By accident. Five years ago I graduated from UCLA with a major in journalism. Two years later I picked up a master's in creative writing at USC. I love a good story and know how to tell a good story. But I'm not so great at making them up. Writing a nonfiction bestseller or being a TV journalist is probably my most promising career route. But 'promising' is a relative term. There's ten thousand young women like me out there. I need a major scoop to get my foot in the door. I think Aja's that scoop."

"Why?" I asked.

"A year ago I was visiting an uncle in São Paulo. He was throwing a party at his penthouse and I heard this woman from Selva talking about Aja. She'd known her from when she was a child. She was full of stories about her, mostly crazy shit. Aja was a wild girl from the jungle who could turn stone into gold. She could heal the sick and talk to spirits. Wild animals never attacked her. She'd sleep under trees and snakes would gather and form a protective circle around her." Casey reached for another cigarette. "The woman was a staunch Catholic but swore Aja was an angel who'd been sent to earth by Jesus."

"You believed her?" I asked.

"I believe that where there's smoke there's fire. Obviously ninety percent of what the woman was saying was nonsense but she was traveling with her ten-year-old daughter and the little girl told me a story I knew had to be true. The girl was too scared to be acting. She'd been playing on the edge of town when she'd been bitten by a bushmaster. In Brazil, in the deep jungle, they're the most feared snakes. Their venom is way worse than a rattlesnake's. Her father was nearby and picked her up and tried rushing her to the hospital. But he was on foot and already her throat was swelling shut. She was turning blue, she couldn't breathe. Her father wept; he knew she was as good as dead." Casey paused. "Then they ran into Aja."

"Go on," I said.

"He'd heard the stories about her and he believed in her. He stopped and begged her to help. Aja didn't say anything—she didn't even touch the girl. She just told the man his daughter would be okay but he should still take her to the hospital." Casey stopped and shook her head. "The girl made a miraculous recovery."

I couldn't help but smile. "Aja didn't touch her? Aja told the man to take his daughter to the hospital? I'm sure the doctors at the hospital gave her an antidote to the venom. That's why the girl recovered. Really, Casey, how could you be moved by such a cliché story?"

"You weren't there!" Casey snapped. "If you had been, if you'd seen the fear in the girl's eyes as she recalled what she'd gone through, then you would know something significant had happened. Still, like I said, the girl's story was only one in a hundred. The mother had followed Aja all her life."

"I take it you went to Selva?"

"Yes. I spent a month there, my first visit. The whole town knew about Aja and believed she was special. I taught myself Portuguese so I could interview as many people as possible who had seen Aja perform some magical act. For some reason they preferred to call her powers 'magical' rather than 'miraculous.' It might have been their Catholic upbringing. Because she never spoke about Jesus or Mother Mary, not everyone saw her healings as miracles." Casey paused. "Actually, Aja hardly spoke to anyone."

"I take it she refused to speak to you?" I asked.

Casey hesitated. "Yup."

"How many times did you go to Selva?"

"Three times total. I spent a month each time."

"And kept collecting secondhand accounts of Aja's amazing powers from what had to be a very superstitious village. What made you think you could take all this talk and turn it into a bestselling book? And how did you afford to keep going there? Didn't you have college loans to pay off?" I paused. "Or was Daddy paying the bills?"

I'd hit a nerve. Casey slammed her fist on the table. "My father's as interested in my research as I am. So what if he agreed to foot the bill? It doesn't make my investigation any less valid."

I sipped my iced tea. "I'm glad it doesn't bother you."

"I'm not chasing after Aja to avoid getting a real job, if that's what you're saying."

I shrugged. "Let's cut to the chase. You still haven't said anything that gives me a reason to talk Aja and Mike into giving you an interview." Again, I checked my watch. "I'm sorry but I'm feeling unimpressed."

"Aja's come here for a reason," Casey blurted out.

"What do you mean?"

"Before she left Selva, she spoke to a bunch of children who used to chase after her in the jungle. They gathered around her before she left. She said she had to go to America because the Big Person had told her to go. That she had something important to do here." Casey paused. "I'm not sure who this 'Big Person' is. It's possible she's in contact with someone rich or famous or powerful here."

"I sort of doubt that's who he is," I muttered.

"Pardon?"

"Never mind. Look, Casey, you admit you haven't even spoken to Aja. It's safe to say I know her better than you do. And I can assure you that you're trying to make something out of nothing. Yes, she's charismatic for someone who hardly speaks. Yes, she's very pretty. Otherwise, she's a normal teen-age girl. She's not a superhero. She has no special powers. I'm sorry if that ruins the big story you've been chasing all this time but it's the simple truth."

Casey considered. "I suppose we'll have to agree to dis-agree."

I decided it was time to up the ante.

"It's more complicated than that. I came here to warn you. Aja's not what the courts would call a 'public person.' That's an important legal distinction because with the articles you're printing and the videos you're posting online, you've opened up yourself and your paper to a harassment suit. Her guardian, Clara Smith, is a very wealthy woman and she's told me bluntly that if you don't back off she's going to take legal action against you and the *Rapid City Journal*."

I sounded awfully convincing; I impressed myself. Of course, Clara had not told me anything but I assumed she'd back my play. For the first time all evening Casey looked con-cerned.

"She never took legal action against me in Brazil," she said.

"I doubt they had a court building in Selva. But it's dif-ferent here in America. For your own sake back off. Think about it. Keep printing this garbage and the real press will never take you seriously. You'll ruin any chance you have at becoming a respected journalist."

"I can't be sued for slander for reporting the facts."

"But you can be sued if you distort the facts." I stood to leave. "I promise to ask Aja and Mike if they'll meet with you. But I can tell you already their answer will be no."

Casey was angry that I was leaving. "What about 'quid pro quo'? You haven't given me a single insight into Aja."

"Yes, I did. I gave you the most important insight of all." I leaned over and spoke in her ear. "Aja's just a girl, like any other girl."

On that note I left. I knew that later, when I told Janet about the details of the meeting, she'd tell me I'd wasted my time and gasoline. But I was glad I'd come. It had been useful to confirm that Nicole was reporting to Casey. It had also been good to hear another take on Aja's life in Selva. It reminded me of the John of God phenomenon in Brazil. It seemed there was something in the mind-set down there—or else there was something in the water—that made the people crave saints and angels.

The meeting had also given me an insight into Casey herself. It was clear she'd been pampered all her life and was now desperate to prove her worth—or self-worth—to her father. Her admission that Daddy was interested in Aja was revealing.

People believed what they wanted to believe, I thought. All you had to do was be pretty and walk around and not say much and the public would assume you were extraordinary.

It was a pity I didn't meet either criteria.

It probably would have helped my music career.

But—and this time the "BUT" inside my brain had swollen to a much greater size—Casey's comments on Aja's early life had done nothing to erase the doubts that continued to gnaw at me. Just when my mental picture of who Aja was would begin to steady inside another ripple would come along and blur what I knew to be a fact.

Or else what I *hoped* was a fact.

It struck me as I raced along the dark interstate that the more I learned about Aja the more she freaked me out.

Yet none of it made me care for her any less.

I told myself that was all that mattered.

"Maybe I am falling in love," I said aloud.

When I got home I heard from Janet that Aja's aunt had died.

CHAPTER ELEVEN

THE SERVICE WAS SCHEDULED FOR FRIDAY.
Bart drove Aja to school on Thursday and she didn't seem the
least bit upset. Her reaction may have been justified. She told
me Clara had hated living in a crippled body after her stroke
and was anxious to move on. She also said her aunt had had a
wonderful life. There was no reason to grieve, in her opinion.

The service—I suppose it could have been called a
funeral—was held in the afternoon at the edge of the lake
behind the Carter Mansion. Except for Aja, Bart, and myself,
no one in town really knew Clara Smith. She had not attended
any local church and seemed to have no set religious beliefs.
In her will she'd asked that her body be cremated and that her
ashes be spread by Aja in the waters of the lake.

Mike, Dale, and Janet came to the service. They drove

over in the same car with me. Aja and Bart were waiting for us on the porch when we arrived. Aja had on a black dress but no shoes. She looked as serene as ever, even with the silver chalice of Aunt Clara's ashes in her hands.

Bart gave me a warm hug and thanked me for coming. It was clear he was taking Clara's death badly. His face was puffy with tears. Bart had been with Clara for twenty years, Aja had told me.

"He'll miss seeing her around," Aja said about Bart as we walked toward the lake through the thick grass. Bart strode in front of us, out of earshot, seemingly lost in his own thoughts.

"What about you?" Janet asked, and it almost appeared as if she was testing Aja. If she was, I'm not sure Aja passed the test. Aja shrugged.

"The body's not important," she said.

"That makes sense to me now," Mike said, obviously referring to his near-death experience. Janet gave him a puzzled look. Mike had not told Janet or Shelly what had happened to him at the hospital. I had a feeling he was never going to tell them.

This was Mike's first day out of bed and Dale had not wanted him to come, fearing the walk to the lake would be too strenuous. But although Mike was clearly frailer than usual, he looked in no danger of collapsing.

"You sound like one of my meditation teachers," Janet said to Aja.

Aja nodded but didn't reply.

There was no formal service. We gathered at the edge of the lake and Bart spoke of how he'd met Clara while he was a struggling actor in LA, not many years after her husband had died, and how she'd taken him as first a housekeeper and then as a friend. He told several endearing stories of the times they'd shared together and it was only then that I realized they'd been lovers. More power to them, I thought.

Bart looked to me next and I spoke of how I'd only met Clara once but how charming I'd found her. "I'm only sad I didn't get to spend more time with her," I said.

All eyes went to Aja next, Bart's especially. It's like he wanted to hear something special from this girl so many others thought unique. Aja looked at him and smiled.

And she did say something special.

"When a baby's born people celebrate. They're happy a new person has come into the world. But when a man or a woman dies everyone weeps. They're sad the person is gone. The reverse should be true. Birth is difficult, for the child and the mother. But death is like being embraced by warm loving light." Aja glanced at Mike right then, just before she stepped forward in her bare feet into the water and removed the lid from the chalice and began to sprinkle the ashes over the surface of the lake. She added, "Let us celebrate this death."

Bart broke down then; he wept loudly. But they were happy tears. It was as if Aja's words had pierced his heart and soothed the pain of his loss. From my side, I was stunned. Her words had really touched me.

Back at the house there was plenty of food and drink. It was, after all, lunchtime. Bart took me aside and explained that Clara had written me a letter before she'd died but he'd somehow misplaced it. He swore he'd find it soon.

"I never lose anything," he said. "I don't know what happened to it."

"I'm sure it will turn up." I added, "Sorry about what happened at the hospital."

"It wasn't your fault. I heard Aja snuck away on you. She'll do that when you least expect it. But let it be a warning to you."

I wasn't sure what kind of warning it was meant to be.

We didn't stay long. Dale was anxious to get Mike back home and back in bed. Janet, too, said she had to get home. Apparently she had to reschedule Half Life's gigs for the next month.

"Hey, I can play before then," Mike said.

"Like hell you will," Dale said, taking him by the arm

and leading him toward the car. I cornered Aja before I lost my chance.

"When will I see you again?" I asked.

Her eyes shone; she appeared to be her old self. "When do you want to see me?" she asked.

"Tomorrow night."

"Great," she said.

The next evening I borrowed Janet's Camry again and picked up Aja at six. I planned to take her on the date I had originally promised her. The one that included dinner in a nice restaurant in Balen followed by a movie. On the drive to our neighboring town, Aja volunteered that she could pay for the date.

"There's going to be a reading of Aunt Clara's will later in the week but I know I'm in it," she said. "Bart already told me I'm a rich girl."

"How does that make you feel?"

"It doesn't make me feel anything."

"Probably because your aunt's money has always been there."

"I have no interest in money. You can have it if you want."

I had to laugh. "I wouldn't make that offer if I were you. I might just take you up on it."

Aja glanced at me. "Maybe you will."

I wasn't sure what Aja liked to eat. She acted like she didn't care what was put in front of her. But I figured she had to enjoy certain dishes more than others so I had made a reservation at Benny's, which was not only the most expensive restaurant in Balen but the only one that served a little of everything.

Wearing a short, white silk dress and a string of her aunt's pearls, Aja made a stunning entrance. Heads turned as we were escorted to our seats. At first I assumed it was because of her beauty but then I worried Casey's videos might be at work. I heard a wave of whispers as we sat down. I tried to ignore them.

"Why has it taken me so long to take you out on a real date?" I said.

"You were just waiting until I could pay."

"Was that a joke? I didn't think the Big Person cracked jokes."

"I might be developing some Little Person."

"You think?" I teased her.

Aja hesitated, although her eyes were bright as she looked at me. "Yes. And I think you're the cause," she said.

"Well, at least I'm good for something." The menus came and we opened them. "What are you in the mood for?"

"At home I ate a lot of fish," she said. It was the first time I'd heard her refer to Selva as home.

"What kind of fish?"

"Whatever I caught in the river."

"Are you serious?"

"Yes."

"Okay. Here, tonight, we're in a fancy restaurant. Here they cook the fish and serve it on a clean plate. You won't have to get your hands wet, or bloody. Hey, look, they have swordfish. I love swordfish. Would you like that?"

"That would be good."

Dinner was lazy, fun, delicious, and wonderful. If other people in the restaurant were gossiping about us I didn't care. Aja got me talking about my music and, again, I suppose, I monopolized the conversation, which was easy to do around her. I didn't bring up all the chatter about her "healings" and frankly I was glad that she appeared to have no interest in discussing the matter. The time flew by and at some point I realized we'd missed our movie. I didn't care. All I wanted to do was stare into Aja's eyes and hear her voice. I can't remember ever having so much fun.

During dessert, we were interrupted. A thin, Japanese woman in an exotic red dress and a Japanese man in an Armani tux came up to our table. The woman led the charge;

the man appeared reluctant to approach us. At the same time, the woman seemed nervous.

"I'm sorry but I need to speak to you," the woman said to Aja. "I know who you are. I've read about you. It's about my daughter. She's very ill, she has leukemia. She's had three courses of chemo but it keeps coming back. The doctors say there's nothing else they can do. Her name is Keko." She fumbled to open a tiny, red purse. "I was wondering if I could show you her picture."

I stood. "I don't know what you've heard or read but my friend can't help you. Please, if you could just leave us alone. I don't mean to be rude. Truly, I am sorry about your daughter."

The woman persisted. "You don't understand, Keko is dying! The doctors have given her only two months to live. She needs help." The woman shook as she stared at Aja. "She needs you."

Aja went to speak but seemed to think better of it and remained silent. I appealed to the husband. "There's nothing my friend can do for Keko. I'm telling you the truth."

The man reached for his wife's arm. "This was a mistake. My apologies."

His wife shook him off and pulled a photograph from her purse. "For God's sake, look at her!" she cried, slamming the picture down on the table. Aja picked it up and stared at it for several seconds.

"Her body is very tired," she said, before handing the picture back to the woman. "It will be okay."

The woman trembled with excitement. "Keko's going to live?"

"No," Aja said.

The woman's face fell. Grabbing her daughter's photo, she slapped Aja hard in the jaw. I saw it coming but was too slow to block the blow. Blood flew from Aja's mouth onto the tablecloth. The husband wrapped both his arms around his wife and tried pulling her away. She fought him.

"You're a witch!" the woman screamed at Aja. "Satan's witch!"

The restaurant erupted in noise; people jumped to their feet. Blood continued to drip from Aja's mouth onto the table. She grabbed a napkin and tried to stanch the flow. I hurried to the other side of the table and put my arm around her.

"How are you? Did she break anything?"

Aja stretched her jaw and shook her head. "I'm fine."

The manager of the restaurant scurried over, looking worried. He was probably envisioning a lawsuit. "Are you okay?" he asked Aja. "Should I call 911?"

"I'm fine," Aja repeated.

"Your lip's swelling." The manager turned to a waiter. "Fetch ice from the kitchen. Ice is the best thing."

"Don't bother, we're leaving," I said, helping Aja to her feet. She was not totally fine. The blow had hit the sweet spot on the jaw. The woman had poured all her anger into it. Aja's legs wobbled as I helped her up.

"I'm so sorry about this," the manager gushed. "The Takasus—they often dine here. They're usually so polite. I know their daughter is ill but this type of behavior is inexcusable. They'll be hearing from me this very night, and from the owner."

Aja touched the man's arm. "That's not necessary. Let the woman grieve in peace."

The manager seemed struck. "You're sure?"

"Yes, she's sure," I said. "Now we're leaving. Good-bye."

"I understand, of course. There'll be no charge for the meal."

"That's very thoughtful of you," I muttered.

Aja needed help getting to the car but once there she seemed to rally. She still had the napkin from the restaurant and continued to hold it to her lips. The bleeding had stopped.

"Are you sure you're okay?" I asked.

"Yeah. I love their swordfish."

Just like Aja. She cared more about the fish than the fact a complete stranger had slapped her in the mouth. I burst out laughing. "The fish was fantastic. We should come here again."

"Maybe we could eat in the kitchen with the staff," Aja said.

"Before we do we'd better make sure none of the cooks have any sick relatives. They might demand you do a healing at knifepoint."

Aja smiled, although her lip was already swelling. "It doesn't matter. Let them carve away. This body is just a body."

"The hell it is. I love your body."

"You do? Why? It's no different from Aunt Clara's body. Soon it will be nothing but ashes."

"I hope not too soon." I finally began to calm down. "That was my fault in there. I saw her draw back her hand but didn't move fast enough to block it."

"You like to blame yourself, Fred. It's not necessary."

I saw she was serious. She was staring at me again.

"Why do you say that? I'm not a martyr," I said.

"Maybe a little one? Maybe? Yes?"

She had me. "All right. I admit it, I'm always trying to fix things. But people expect me to do it, I don't know why. Like in the band, if there's an argument, everyone looks to me to settle it."

"You've been playing that role since you were young."

I wasn't sure if she was asking a question or making a statement.

"That's true," I said. "It probably started when I was six. My parents were going through a rough time and it looked like they might get a divorce. My dad moved out of the house, although he didn't go far. He got an apartment around the block. Anyway, I remember going to see him every evening after he came home from work. He would tell me things to say to my mother and then she would tell me stuff to say to him. There I was, in first grade, playing the role of a marriage counselor. But the weird thing is my parents *expected* me to fix their problems. And that was all right with me—I wanted to help them."

"And you were happy when they got back together."

"Sure," I said. "What kid isn't terrified of the thought of their parents divorcing?"

Aja nodded but I wasn't a hundred percent sure she was agreeing with me. I didn't take it personally. The last thing I wanted to do was to get into a major psychological discussion. I changed the subject.

"What do you want to do next?" I asked. "We've already missed the movie. I could take you home, if you want, or we could, I don't know, do something else."

"Let's get a hotel room," Aja said.

It was the last thing I expected her to say.

I came oh so close to having a heart attack.

"Huh?" I gasped.

Aja spoke casually. "This body's never had sex. I've often wondered what it would feel like, especially since meeting you. I think tonight would be a good night to experience it." She paused. "If that's okay with you?"

I nodded. I nodded again. And again.

"Sure," I said.

We stopped at an all-night drugstore on the way to the hotel. I ran in, bought a packet of condoms, and ran out. Aja wanted to see what I had bought. I obliged her, and she opened one.

"Oh," she said, and she smiled.

The room had a huge Jacuzzi bathtub. I'd never been in one before but Aja was interested. Maybe it reminded her of skinny-dipping in the lake behind her house, or in the streams of Selva. I remember turning on the hot water and slowly watching it fill. Aja silently came up from behind me and hugged me. She rested her head on my back, listening to my breathing instead of my heart. Both were pounding fast.

There were bath salts for good health and bubble mixes for fun. We threw the whole lot in and took off our clothes and jumped in the steaming water. Well, I slowly climbed in. Aja, she was the one who jumped. And here she was supposed to be the quiet one, the shy one, and I was supposed to be the rock star. But the truth was I was just as much a virgin as she was and far more nervous.

She had me hypnotized. Her big, brown eyes never left my face. Sliding toward me through the gushing hot water, the swirling steam, and the swelling bubbles, she sat naked on my lap and wrapped her thin but surprisingly strong legs around my waist. God, I felt I was about to have my own near-death experience. Then again, it would have been just fine if I had died right then. Why? Because I'd never been so happy in my life. I'd reached my ceiling, I thought. No, the top of my skull had burst through it. Everything that came after in my life would be anticlimactic.

But I felt that would be okay as well. I'd have this memory, I'd have this night. When we began to kiss—I kissed her very lightly—to touch each other, the feel of her skin gave me so much pleasure I felt as if my body was no longer bound to the earth. Holding her naked in my arms transported me to another world.

Honestly, I felt she was an angel.

My angel. Aja . . .

Later, lying together on a Hilton king-sized mattress, a

single sheet covering our bare bodies, I stared at the ceiling and thought I saw stars. I saw them through the roof of the hotel room. Was it so impossible? We were on the top floor of an eight-story building, and with Aja resting in my arms, the stars did not seem so far away.

Her breathing became soft and regular, like it had in the hospital when she had dozed off while Mike was in surgery. I assumed she'd fallen asleep and began to drift off myself. But then I felt her palm reach up and rest over my heart, which was now beating slow and lightly, almost sighing with a newfound rhythm it had found. I almost pitied it. My heart wasn't used to such joy.

"Hi," she said.

"Hello," I replied, drowsy.

"I told you it would be okay."

"When?"

"Many times."

I smiled. I felt many miles away, still floating, and yet, at the same time, I'd never felt so close to anyone in my life. It was pleasant to drift along beside Aja, through the moments, the seconds, the instants . . .

"I guess you were right," I heard myself say.

"Are you happy?"

"Yes."

"Do you feel the Big Person?"

"I feel you. Are you the Big Person?"

"Yes."

"Am I?"

Her next words sounded like a child's lullaby in my ears, so sweet, so innocent, and yet, ironically, so wise. My drifting sensation slowly picked up speed. Now I felt like I was going somewhere, somewhere nice.

"There's only one Big Person. He's the same in everyone. But you don't often feel him. Your Little Person gets in the way."

"Who's the Little Person?" I asked.

Her palm slipped from my heart to my forehead. "He's up here. His name is Fred. He thinks a lot, he worries a lot. He thinks he's a body. He thinks he's his mind. But he's neither."

"Who is he then?"

"He's everywhere and in all things. He never grows old, he can never die. And he's never sad. He's always happy and at peace."

"Like I am right now?"

"Yes. Right now you're getting a glimpse of the Big Person."

I could hardly think, nor did I want to. I felt it disturbed the joy I was feeling and it seemed much easier just to let my thoughts run down. To turn them off with a switch that suddenly seemed close at hand. Intuitively, part of me knew she was helping me find this switch by using the touch of her fingers to steer me from my head down to my heart where my mind belonged. To what felt like an endless space suffused with peace and happiness.

"Do you always feel this way?" I whispered.

"Yes."

"So this is the real you?"

A million light-years away I felt her kiss my cheek.

"Yes. Now go to sleep and remember."

CHAPTER TWELVE

THE NEXT DAY I ONLY REMEMBERED HAVING
sex with Aja. In my defense the sex had been absolutely
incredible and what had followed had been very abstract.
Even though I'd felt the memory of being with her would
sustain me for the rest of my life, I wanted to be with her
again as soon as possible. It was the lover's eternal paradox.
One night was enough but a thousand nights would never
satisfy me.

I felt I was in love.

Honestly, I only vaguely recalled what she'd said as we
fell asleep. But I'd had such amazing dreams. I felt I'd spent
the whole night flying.

We slept in and ordered room service: breakfast. We
ordered half the menu. Aja begged me to let her use Aunt

Clara's credit card and I gave in. She continued to show no grief over the woman's passing. With anyone else I would have been concerned but with Aja it all seemed so natural.

We didn't start back to Elder until one o'clock. There were clouds in the sky. The first sign of summer coming to an end. Knowing South Dakota, I thought, the weather would skip autumn and head straight into winter. It occurred to me that Aja had probably never seen snow before. I asked and she said that was true.

"You're in for a treat. Sort of," I said.

"This body has never been cold before."

I smiled. "You like to say 'this body' rather than 'I.' I know you'd say it all the time if Bart hadn't lectured you about it. Why do you do that?"

She glanced at me. Her lower lip was still swollen from the previous night. "Because I'm not the body," she said.

A feeling of déjà vu swept over me and I felt a mild dizziness. It reminded me of the first day I had met Aja, when she had touched me while we were eating lunch on the bench. I struggled a bit with the wheel of the car.

"You told me that last night," I said.

"Yes."

I frowned. "Why am I having trouble remembering?"

"It's hard for most people to understand. Don't worry, it'll come back to you with time."

"What will?"

"What you need to know."

"About you?"

"About you." Aja touched my shoulder. "It will be okay, Fred."

The dizziness caused by my déjà vu fled and I was able to steady the car on the road. I smiled at her reply. "You like to say that as well. But I don't think it's true. The world's a brutal place. Life is seldom okay for very long. Just look at what happened to Mike."

Aja squeezed my shoulder and nodded.

But she didn't say anything.

I dropped her at home before I returned the Camry to Janet's house. Bo met me in the garage. He joked about providing transportation for my love life. "You should just buy the damn car from me," he said.

"Didn't you already give it to Janet?"

Bo shrugged. "It's impossible to give that girl anything. She keeps insisting it's my car when I keep telling her it belongs to her."

"Whose name is it listed under at the DMV?"

"Mine. She won't let me put in under her name."

"That's weird."

"That's her mother in her. Hey, she told me to tell you she's over at Shelly's with the rest of the band. They want you to go over. Mike can't play yet but they still want to practice."

"Thanks. And thanks again for the car."

Bo grinned mischievously. "Just tell me if you got lucky last night?"

"A gentleman never says."

"Since when are you a gentleman?"

I laughed. "Since last night!"

Bo patted me on the back. "That's my man!"

I walked straight to Shelly's house. My two main guitars were at home but I could always use my old Fender if we decided to jam. Walking up to our heavily insulated garage, I was surprised when a middle-aged couple jumped out of their car and hurried over to me.

"Excuse me, are you Fred Allen? The lead singer of Half Life?" the man asked. They were both overweight with pleasant faces. Yet they were tense as well and I was reminded of the incident at the restaurant. Suddenly, I knew what was coming. Their car plates said they were from Ohio.

"Who wants to know?" I asked.

"Please forgive us. My name is Dustin Alastair and this is

my wife, Eileen. We know who you are. We saw you in that first video Casey Morall posted on YouTube."

"That video didn't exactly focus on my singing."

"I'm sorry. But to be honest we're not here because of you," Mr. Alastair said. "Our ten-year-old daughter, Lisa, is in the car, lying in the backseat, resting. She has an inoperable brain tumor." He paused. "The doctors say she doesn't have long to live."

"We need Aja to heal her," Mrs. Alastair blurted out.

"I'm sorry, I can't help you." I tried slipping past them but they blocked my way.

Mr. Alastair continued. "Look, Fred, may I call you Fred? We've checked around town. Everyone says you're Aja's boyfriend. We've been out to her house. But no one answers when we ring the doorbell. And we understand that. Tons of people must be showing up and begging her to heal them. I realize we're nobody to you." He began to choke up. "But Lisa's all we have. And if it wouldn't be too much trouble, if you could just ask Aja to look at her."

"We'd be so grateful," Mrs. Alastair said, her eyes watering.

This couple wasn't like the one Aja and I had run into the previous night. They were in terrible pain but they were still striving to be kind and polite. Yes, maybe they were a little pushy, I thought, but if I was in their position would I be any different? I mean, if I honestly believed Aja could heal my child. The answer, of course, was no. So it made it harder for me to brush them off.

Yet I had a problem. Well, actually I had a few problems. First off, I didn't know if Aja could help Lisa. On the other hand, I wasn't certain Aja *couldn't* help their daughter. Somehow, sleeping with Aja, having sex with her, and listening to what she had told me—whatever it had been—had altered my mind in some mysterious way. All the doubts I'd had about her healing ability, they had not vanished. Not completely, at least. I mean, it wasn't as if I'd suddenly been transformed into a true believer. But the idea that she could work miracles no longer seemed ridiculous. And that in itself was something of a miracle, I thought.

Yet I was terrified what would happen to Aja if she did try to heal Lisa Alastair. Touching Mike's head had wiped her out for a week. She was my girlfriend now—at least in my mind she was—and there was no way I was going to risk hurting her, no matter how dire the Alastairs' situation was.

It was all very confusing and difficult.

"Are you staying in town?" I asked.

Mr. Alastair spoke. "We just got a room at the Great Western. Room sixteen."

"Okay, room sixteen. I'll remember that. Look, I'll be

talking to Aja later today and I'll ask her about Lisa. But I must warn you, the chances of her doing anything to help your daughter are small. Really small, I mean, extremely remote. So please don't get your hopes up."

"Can I give you our cell number?" Mr. Alastair asked, handing me a card.

"Sure," I said. I put it in my back pocket.

"But she can heal people, right?" Mrs. Alastair said. "You've seen her cure people?"

I shook my head. "Honestly, I've never seen her heal anyone. Not with my own eyes."

That seemed to shock the Alastairs. They didn't know how to respond. I took the opportunity to slip away. I headed for the garage and went inside. Mike, Dale, Shelly, Janet—everyone was waiting for me. Only no one looked ready to play music. The mood was somber. I didn't have to ask if they'd spoken to the Alastairs. It was written on their faces.

"We have a problem," Janet said.

"I told you guys about my meeting with Casey Morall," I said, taking a seat beside Mike and Dale on the dumpy yellow couch we kept pressed against our amps to smooth out our sound. We also used it to crash on.

Shelly sat behind her keyboards, Janet behind the drums. In a pinch Janet could play the drums. She had the few times

Mike had been too drunk to go onstage. But she wasn't very good.

"You didn't tell me," Shelly said.

"Sorry," I said. "The bottom line is Casey's got too much time and emotion invested in 'Aja's story' to back off."

"Aja should sue her," Shelly said.

Janet spoke. "Yesterday, I would have said no way. But today I wonder if it's not a bad idea."

"Casey's not our problem," Mike said abruptly.

A long silence followed his remark.

"What do you mean?" Janet asked.

Dale spoke. "Aja's the problem." He turned in my direction. "Fred knows what Mike and I are talking about."

I hesitated. "Not really. What do you mean?"

Mike spoke. "You must have noticed we left the garage door open. We heard you talking to the Alastairs."

"So? They drove a long way. They seemed like nice people. I didn't want to just brush them off."

"You gave them hope," Janet said. "You shouldn't have done that. It doesn't matter that you told them the chances Aja could help their daughter were remote. All they heard is that it's possible and that hope will torture them. You should call them right now and tell them to take their daughter home."

"I agree," Shelly said.

"I don't," Mike said.

"Neither do I," Dale said.

Janet jumped up, knocking over the snare drum with her leg. "Hold on a second! What in God's name are we talking about here? You guys are acting like Aja really can heal people. Do you know how nuts that is?"

Again, another long silence. It was weird that Mike and Dale had stirred the pot with their remarks but everyone was looking to me to tell them what we should do with what was already in the pot. I lowered my head and kept my mouth shut.

"Well?" Janet said finally. "Somebody say something."

Dale stood. "Fred knows Aja better than any of us. I don't think we should be so quick to judge what he said to the Alastairs."

Janet groaned loudly. "Didn't you guys hear what he just said? He didn't brush off the Alastairs because he was too much of a coward to hurt their feelings. Not because he thinks Aja can save their daughter." She paused. "Right, Fred?"

I shrugged. "I didn't know what to tell them."

Dale spoke carefully. "There's an elephant is this room that none of us wants to talk about. But I think it's something we need to face. Now."

Shelly frowned. "Huh?"

Janet fumed. "Dale's talking about Mike's amazing recovery. He's implying that Aja had something to do with it. And Mike, to my surprise, is saying the same thing, without really saying it. Why is everyone afraid to just say what they mean? Could it be because Fred's here? And he's sleeping with Aja?" Janet paused to catch her breath. "Am I right or am I right?"

Shelly looked stunned. She looked at me. "You had sex with Aja?"

I stood. "I'm sorry, guys, but I'm awfully tired. I'm going to go home and sleep." I headed for the door. "Good-bye."

I left in a hurry.

At home I spoke to my parents for a few minutes before disappearing into my room. The previous night, to keep my mom and dad from worrying, I'd called them when Aja and I had checked into the Hilton. But I'd lied and told them I was with Mike and would be at his house the whole night.

I don't think either of them believed me because they repeatedly asked when they were going to get to meet Aja. Apparently they'd heard people around town talking about her. But they seemed to know nothing about Casey Morall's videos. My parents had no interest in the Internet. They could send and read e-mail but that was about it.

Upstairs, lying on my bed, I blacked out. Although I'd slept well with Aja, the last few days had been stressful and I really was exhausted. I slept soundly for two hours and may have gone longer if my cell hadn't rung.

"Hello?" I mumbled.

"Did I wake you?"

It was Janet, the last person I wanted to talk to. I couldn't believe she had told the others I was sleeping with Aja. I wasn't even sure how she knew, although I had kept her car the entire night. "What do you want?" I growled.

"I want to apologize," Janet said.

"Great. Apologize after you let the cat out of the bag."

"I know, what I said was totally rude, especially with Shelly in the room. I was just feeling pissed off about how everyone keeps acting like Aja is the second coming of Christ. Stuff like that really pushes my buttons. But it's no excuse for what I did. I swear, Fred, I just blurted out the thing about you and Aja. I didn't know I was going to say it until I did."

The remark had annoyed me, especially since it had been so out of character for Janet. Growing up together, I'd always been impressed how she respected people's privacy. Indeed, she was something of a fanatic on the issue.

But we were too close. I never could stay mad at Janet for more than a few minutes.

"It's all right. She was bound to find out," I said.

"Thanks. Thanks for letting it go. I'll let you get back to sleep."

I sat up in bed. "No, wait. In a way, I'm glad you called. I've been wanting to talk to you about these yogis you've been studying."

"You want to discuss yoga the day after you lost your virginity?"

"How do you know I was a virgin? How do you know I never had sex with Nicole?"

"By the way you walk. A girl can tell. Why the sudden interest in yoga?"

"Aja told me some pretty weird stuff about herself last night. We need to talk about it. I'm beginning to realize that girl is stranger than we thought."

"I can come over right now if you like."

"I'll come to your house. I'm the one asking the favor."

"I'd rather talk about it at your house. Is now a good time?"

"Sure," I said.

Janet arrived twenty minutes later with several books in hand. By then I was strumming my acoustic guitar, trying to work out more verses for "Strange Girl." I was making progress. I played Janet my latest version of the song and she liked it. She said she loved it, actually, which meant a lot to me. Janet was hard to please.

"You should put it on your demo," Janet said, sitting on the edge of my bed. I was in the chair beside my computer.

"I've already laid down the tracks for three songs."

"This might be your strongest piece. I'd include it."

"I'll think about it." I gestured to her books. "Once, when we were talking about yoga and meditation, you mentioned a specific system where you realize everything is one. I forget what you called it."

"Advaita. It literally means 'non-dual' or 'not two.' It's the form of meditation I'm into."

"And you believe in this system?" I asked.

"I don't believe in anything, you know that. Advaita isn't based on beliefs. It teaches you how to quiet your mind. It works for me. It calms me down." Janet paused. "What does this have to do with Aja?"

I tried my best to relate what Aja had told me about the Big Person and the Little Person; not being the mind or the body. I followed that by saying how Aja had given me a glimpse of the experience. Janet laughed when I explained it had happened right after we'd had sex. Yet I could tell she was listening closely. When I finished Janet sat silent for a long time, thinking.

"So?" I said finally.

"I'm not sure. Aja sounds like she's describing the goal of Advaita. Not only that, she seems to be saying she's realized the goal."

"Is that possible?"

"Yeah. It's also possible she's just nuts."

"Aja's not nuts," I snapped.

"I hear ya. I'm just saying that it's more likely that she's crazy than that she's in cosmic consciousness. Listen, there's an old saying from the Bhagavad Gita where Krishna says that out of a thousand people who are born, only one seeks the supreme state. And out of the thousand who seek the supreme state, only one finds it." Janet paused. "That gives Aja only a one-in-a-million shot."

"Those are pretty lousy odds."

Janet shrugged. "Tell me about it. But for most people even a little peace of mind is better than jumping off a ten-story building."

"I hope that's not why you took up the practice."

"Nah. There are no ten-story buildings in Elder."

"This goal of Advaita, seeking the supreme state—what does it mean?"

"It's the oldest goal in mankind's history. 'Know thyself.'"

"Are you talking about some sort of enlightenment?"

Janet frowned. "I hate that word. It sounds so New Age. Advaita is an ancient system of meditation where you don't meditate on anything. No god, no mantra, no philosophy."

"So you don't chant 'Hare Krishna'?"

"No."

"What do you do?" I asked.

"You've asked me that before. You don't do anything."

"You just sit there?"

"You sit there with your eyes closed and stay with the awareness that you exist. Nothing else. You don't pretend you exist. You don't make a mood of it. You don't have to because everyone already exists. You just turn your mind in that direction and let go."

"Why bother? I mean, what do you get out of it?"

"I just told you. Peace of mind."

"Okay, I get that. But let's stick with Aja. She seems pretty damn peaceful. You yourself have said nothing seems to bother her."

Janet hesitated. "That's true. She is unique. I mean, for someone who hardly talks, she's highly charismatic. She just had to say a few words at the Roadhouse to shut up that crazy mob. And she definitely has a strong presence about her. And you're right, I've never seen her upset."

"So . . ."

Janet interrupted. "Let me finish. I can think of a few more points in Aja's favor. In fact, you just gave me a few extra with what you told me she said to you. It's obvious she's never studied classical Advaita. She doesn't use any of the common Sanskrit words that teachers use to describe it. Still, it's clear that's what she's talking about. Take the way Aja described the 'Little Person' to you. She told you it's what most people think they are. Advaita would agree with that. Most people are ignorant. I've been studying Advaita for months and I'm still ignorant."

"Ignorant of what?" I asked.

"Who I am. I still see myself as 'Janet Shell.' I see myself as having a certain kind of body. When I look in the mirror I see brown eyes, dark hair, an average face. I know I'm attractive but I know I'm nowhere close to being beautiful. That's the body my parents gave me. Then there's my mind, my personality. I know I grew up in Elder, and that I'm a senior in high school. I know I'm the smartest one in my school but I try not to brag about it. All these facts, all these characteristics—they're how I define myself. And that's what Aja calls the Little Person. Right?"

"She uses different words but it sounds like you're talking about the same thing," I said.

Janet continued. "Most Indian Advaita teachers call the Little Person 'maya,' which means illusion. Basically they say that who we think we are is not who we really are. Who we really are is the Brahman. The Brahman's like a universal being, some kind of supersoul. Going by what you just told me, Aja's Big Person sounds a lot like the Brahman."

"This Brahman—a person who's experienced it, how do they behave? How do they feel?"

"Well, if you can believe the Advaita teachers, a person who knows the Brahman lives in infinite bliss. They're not bound by the mind or the body. They're beyond all suffering."

"Can they work miracles?" I asked.

"It says in the books I've read that the person who reaches that state can do anything he or she wishes. But I doubt they would go around interfering with nature. Chances are they would accept whatever was happening to someone else as their karma or their fate or their destiny. Whatever you want to call it."

"What if a child's dying of cancer? Wouldn't they try to help them?"

Janet shook her head. "I've read lots of books on the few people who have supposedly realized the Brahman. None went around curing people of cancer or heart disease or even impotence." She paused. "At least, none of them did it as a regular practice."

"What's that mean?" I asked.

"Nothing."

"Janet."

She sighed. "I'm not saying I believe this—I don't—but witnesses say that sometimes miracles do happen around such people."

"You're saying they happen spontaneously?"

"That's what the books say." Janet was troubled. "I'm telling you the pros for Aja's high state because that's what you're looking for. But like I said at the start, there are a lot more cons against her being that one-in-a-million soul. Hell, the very idea of the Brahman might be bullshit for all I know. I told you, I meditate because it works for me. It gets rid of my stress. That's all I know for sure." Janet paused. "And you already know I don't see Aja as some kind of miracle worker. That's not even on the table."

"Why not?" I asked.

Janet groaned. "Because I've never seen her work a single miracle. Not in front of me. Neither have you. Admit it, all we've heard is a bunch of talk."

I studied Janet. "You know, just now, when you spoke about the Brahman and the goal of Advaita, there was an enthusiasm in your voice. Like you really want to believe it's true. And as much as you pretend to doubt Aja, I hear the same tone when you talk about what's special about her."

Janet chuckled, although it sounded a bit forced to me. "If you're trying to label me as a true believer, you've got the wrong girl."

"I'm not saying that. I'm saying you're more open-minded than you're willing to admit. And I can tell all this talk about Aja healing people fascinates you. Sure, you dismiss it—hardheaded Janet Shell can't admit to having faith in anything too weird. But I've seen how protective you are of Aja. How you study her when you think no one else is watching."

"What can I say? She's different. That makes her interesting to me. Her talking to you about Advaita, in her own way, also interests me." Janet paused. "If Aja's here to help teach people about their Little Person and the Big Person, then I say more power to her. I mean it. It's a relief to meet a girl with more on her mind than 'is my mascara smeared?' or 'does my hair need to be blow-dried?' You have no idea how much shit like that drives me crazy."

That made me smile. "You know as well as I do Aja isn't here to teach anything. Hell, I can hardly get the girl to talk."

"Hmm. You've got a point there." Janet considered for a minute. "Does Aja ever talk about how she underwent this awakening? When it happened?"

"No. I get the impression she's always been this way."

Janet plucked a book from her pile. "There was a woman saint in India called Anandamayi Ma, which means 'Joy Permeated Mother.' She was born in 1896 and was supposed to have been enlightened from the time of her birth. She was supposed to be unique in that respect. This book is all about her life. She was extremely beautiful. And she had Aja's same habit of calling herself 'this body.'"

My ears perked up. "She really called herself that?"

"Yeah. We're talking about a famous person here. Many in India consider her their country's greatest saint."

"What did she teach?"

"She didn't teach Advaita, not per se. She embraced all paths."

"Was she married? Did she have children?"

Janet snickered. "There are funny stories about that. You know how marriages in India are arranged? She was married off to this guy when she was pretty young and on their wedding night, just when they were about to have sex, he was supposed to have realized who she was and prostrated before her. But another story says that later, when he did get horny for her, when he touched her, he received an electric shock that almost killed him." Janet paused. "I take it that didn't happen with Aja?"

I shrugged. "It was her idea to have sex."

"Why doesn't that surprise me?"

My cell phone rang. I picked it up. "Hello?" I said.

"Fred, this is Dustin Alastair. I can't thank you enough for speaking to Aja on our behalf. She told us Lisa's going to make a complete recovery and that we have nothing to worry about. I'd say it's too good to be true but already Lisa's up and running around like there's nothing wrong with her. And neither her mother nor I told her anything about the healing Aja did on her."

I felt dumbfounded. I wasn't alone. It was silent in my room and I had the volume on my cell up high. Janet's eyes had suddenly swelled wide. She'd obviously heard most of what Mr. Alastair had said. I moved onto my bed beside her.

"Mr. Alastair, would you mind if I put you on speakerphone for a moment?" I asked.

"No problem."

I pushed the speaker button. "I'm here with my best friend, Janet, who is a close friend of Aja. We're both a little puzzled by what you just said. When did Lisa and Aja meet? What happened exactly?"

"Oh, they never met. Aja said it wasn't necessary. She just called us here at the Great Western."

Janet and I exchanged a look. Boy, was it a long look.

"When?" I asked.

"An hour ago. That's when Lisa suddenly felt better. I tell you, Fred, you probably think I'm a gullible man but I've been around. If I hadn't seen such drastic improvement in Lisa, I wouldn't have believed a word Aja said. But you can't argue when your daughter rises from her deathbed and wants to go for a swim in the hotel pool."

I looked to Janet for support. She shrugged helplessly.

"Well, I'm happy for the three of you," I said. "You have a safe drive back to Ohio. But please do me one favor. Don't tell anyone what Aja did for Lisa. I think you understand why."

"I understand perfectly. God bless you, Fred. You, too, Janet."

The man hung up. "What the hell's going on here?" I said.

"I don't know."

"I'm serious."

"So am I." Janet looked stunned. "I don't know."

I bowed my head as I crouched on the edge of my bed. "And here I thought everything was about to calm back down. When the craziness has just begun."

Janet put her arm around my shoulder. "You want my advice?"

"Sure," I said.

"If all you want is an ordinary girlfriend to have sex with, then get out of town quick. And don't come back."

I sat up with a jerk. "Aja could be sick!"

"Huh?"

"Remember, she got sick after she healed Mike." I frantically dialed Aja's home number. She answered on the third ring.

"Hello, Fred."

"How did you know it was me?" I gasped.

"It says so on the caller ID."

God, I was losing it. I was seeing miracles everywhere.

"I heard you worked your magic on Lisa Alastair. I just wanted to know if you were feeling okay."

"I'm fine. Are we still going to a movie tonight?"

"Sure. But—how did you know Lisa was sick?"

"Her father called and told me."

"I got the impression you called him?"

"I did. He called me and left his number and I called him back," Aja said.

"So you're not sick from working on her?"

"I didn't work on her. The Big Person did. What movie are we going to?"

"If we go to Balen we'll have our choice of eight different films."

"What time are you picking me up?"

"In an hour. I'll see you in an hour."

Aja said good-bye and I set down the phone. Janet read my mind.

"Mike was right," she said. "Aja is the problem."

Again, I borrowed Janet's Camry and drove out to pick up Aja. On the way to the Carter Mansion, Dale called and asked if he and Mike could hook up with us after the film. They were going to a movie in Balen as well—a horror flick. I'd already decided to take Aja to a romantic comedy. The films ended at the same time so I said okay. We agreed to meet at ten at the restaurant in the Hilton.

The film turned out to be pretty funny and I laughed a lot, along with Aja. She seemed to have a thing for the theater's popcorn. She ate a king-sized container all by herself. She told me she hadn't had any dinner.

"Bart's still grieving over Aunt Clara," she said. "He left home to be alone so I didn't bother cooking anything."

"It normally takes people a while to get over a death in the family."

Aja nodded. She understood.

Meeting up with the guys was fun. Mike looked much better than he had at Clara's funeral, although he continued to wear a one-inch-wide head bandage. There was no arguing the obvious. His recovery was nothing short of a miracle. But my relief was short-lived. Not long after we each ordered dessert, Dale told me he'd heard Lisa Alastair had been healed.

"Damnit! Her father told me he wouldn't talk about it," I said.

"I think Lisa herself started the rumor," Dale said. "She'd made friends with some kids who were staying at the Great Western. And she'd told them she was too sick to play. But after—well, after Aja got involved and Lisa was suddenly better, she went out to play and told her new friends that an angel had healed her. And the kids told their parents."

I groaned. "Casey Morall's going to hear about this."

"Hopefully it won't turn into a big deal," Dale said. "If the man swore to you he wouldn't talk about Aja, then Casey won't have anyone close to Lisa to interview and it'll just be another rumor if she posts it on YouTube."

"Everything she's posted has been secondhand," Mike said. "That hasn't stopped the millions of hits."

"Is she still hounding you for an interview?" I asked.

Mike snorted. "Three times a day, every day. The chick doesn't know when to quit."

Dale stared at Aja across our table. "Can you tell us one way or the other—so we can quit arguing among ourselves— did you heal Mike and Lisa?"

Aja was slow to answer. "This body you see, that you call Aja, she can't heal anyone."

"But you're more than the body," Mike said. His remark surprised me. As far as I knew, he'd never heard Aja talk about the Big Person and the Little Person. Yet, it was possible, given his near-death experience, that he understood Aja better than any of us.

Who had been the second being of light?

Whose hand had he seen while outside his body?

"Yes," Aja said.

"Can you explain that to us?" Dale asked carefully.

Aja repeated her explanation of the Big Person and the Little Person that she'd given me the previous night. Most of it sounded new to me, not just because I had only a foggy memory of what she'd told me, but because hearing it again, straight from her mouth, made it somehow real again. As she spoke I felt my mind quieting, my worries fading away. Watching the faces of my friends, I suspected they were feeling the same way.

Yet I still had plenty of questions. "If the Big Person worked on Mike, as well as Lisa, how come you only got sick when you healed Mike? How come you're not sick now?" I asked.

Aja hesitated. "It's hard to explain."

"Could you try to explain?" Dale said gently.

Aja considered. "When I lived in Selva, I used to lie in the river and stare up at the sky. I loved it. The current would pull me downstream and occasionally I'd feel a fish swim beneath me. Sometimes it was a big fish and it wouldn't even have to brush my skin for me to know it was there. It's the same whenever I feel the Big Person heal someone. I feel a motion in the vastness. Before, I seldom caused the motion. The Big Person would just do what it would do."

"But with me?" Mike said and let the question hang.

Aja glanced at me and Dale. "Your friends were worried about you. Dale was crying and Fred was struggling to figure out a way to make things better. While the doctor operated on you, I slept in the waiting room with my head on Fred's shoulder. But I didn't feel any motion in the Big Person. No big fish swam by. Then morning came and the doctor spoke to us and he acted like you were going to die. It was then this body—no, it was then Aja thought to do something to fix you."

"That's when you said you had to go to the bathroom but you really circled around and snuck into the recovery room right after Dale and I left," I said.

Aja lowered her head. "I did have to go to the bathroom."

"But you did sneak into the recovery room," Dale said, and there was a tear in his eye. A tear of gratitude.

"Yes," she said.

"Are you saying you overruled what the Big Person wanted to do for Mike?" I asked.

"The Big Person cannot be overruled."

"Then why did you get sick after healing Mike?" I persisted.

"I let the Little Person get involved," she said.

"Which means you must have a Little Person," I said, more to myself. I began to feel like we were interrogating the girl and that we should stop. At that instant she reached under the table and squeezed my hand. She didn't say anything.

"There is one point I hate to bring up," Dale said. "It's not an opinion I share, but I worry others might think it's the case. If you start talking to them about having a Big Person and a Little Person inside of you, they'll think you're suffering from dissociative identity disorder."

"What's that?" I asked.

"It's the new name for people who have multiple personalities," Dale said. "It usually stems from a trauma experienced in childhood. The person creates another personality as a coping mechanism. The 'alter'—that's what psychologists call it—holds on to the trauma and shelters it from the main personality."

I couldn't help but remember what Bart had told me.

How Aja's parents had been killed when she was a child.

"So the person is able to totally block out what happened to them?" I asked.

"Yes," Dale said, and smiled. "But it's not like I'm worried Aja's suffering from DID. People with that condition are almost always miserable. They can't function in the world. And they certainly can't work miracles," Dale added as he gazed at Aja. "Besides, you seem like the least traumatized person I've ever met."

She smiled. "I feel fine."

Our dessert came and the guys talked about the movie they'd seen and I told them about ours. Aja and I shared a huge banana split while Dale had a vanilla shake and Mike had chocolate cake with ice cream. We all drank coffee. What was interesting was how easily we switched from discussing the secrets of the universe to stuffing ourselves.

It wasn't until near midnight when the restaurant was closing that we stood and prepared to drive back to Elder in our separate cars. We paid the bill and headed for the door. But Dale pulled me aside while Mike and Aja walked on ahead. He spoke in a hushed tone.

"You know Aja's becoming a celebrity. Tomorrow's Monday—the start of a new school week. Already people have been asking her questions, but come tomorrow they'll be swarming all around her. How's she going to take that?"

I sighed. "I was thinking the same thing. For all her hidden power, it's not like she's very good at defending herself."

"What should we do?" Dale asked.

"I was hoping you'd have some idea."

Dale stared after Aja and Mike. "Maybe we should pray to the Big Person to protect her," he said.

Any other night, I would have laughed at the idea.

"Something bothering you?" Dale asked when I didn't respond.

I shook my head. "It's nothing. Everything's fine."

And it was, I told myself.

Aja had said she was fine.

Still, I kept wondering how her parents had died.

CHAPTER THIRTEEN

I PICKED UP A HINT OF AJA'S FAME WHEN I arrived at school the next day. People talking in the locker halls about her YouTube videos, or the fact that Mike was still alive and walking around with a hole in his head. I took it in stride until I entered Mrs. Billard's class a few minutes before the bell rang. Our teacher had yet to appear; the class was gossiping.

"Nobody returns to school a week after brain surgery," Macy Barnes, our head cheerleader and student body president was saying. "There's no question that she healed Mike. I don't know why you guys are still arguing about that."

"She says she didn't do anything to Mike," Ted Weldon, everyone's favorite football jock, countered. "You calling her a liar?"

"I'm just saying there's something spooky about that girl," Macy said. "You've seen the way she stares at people. And the way she talks—you're lucky if you can get more than a yes-or-no answer out of her. Then there's her photographic memory."

"I thought you didn't believe in that," Ted interrupted.

"I believe in it now," Macy said. "That girl's got some kind of power. But you've got to ask where that power comes from. We know she healed Mike and that soldier at the concert. But how come she never gives God credit for the healings? That's what I want to know."

I couldn't take it anymore. "You mean she doesn't give Jesus credit," I said. Macy shrugged like I was stating the obvious.

"Same difference," she said. "It's like she wants all the glory."

I snorted. "On one hand you say how quiet she is. On the other hand you accuse her of seeking glory. Face it, you're threatened by Aja because she doesn't fit into your black-and-white world. To you a person's either righteous or evil—a Christian or a nonbeliever."

"I believe in good and evil," Macy said. "I'm not ashamed of that. And before you start ridiculing my religious beliefs, has it ever occurred to you that America is a Christian nation?

Sure, I know Aja didn't grow up here. She's from Brazil. But that's a Christian nation as well. How come she refuses to acknowledge Christ when she does a healing?"

"Maybe she's Jewish," Ted said. "Her last name is Smith."

Christ, I thought. Smith wasn't a Jewish name.

"She adopted that name when Clara Smith adopted her," Macy said. "It's not her real name. She's kept that secret. If you ask me she keeps a lot of things secret. I bet even Fred doesn't know her real name." Macy added, "And he's sleeping with her."

I glared at her. "I like how cleverly you slipped that in. How you implied that she can't possibly be a good person because she's a slut on top of everything else."

"I didn't say that," Macy said.

"Liar," I snapped.

"Everyone stop talking," Mrs. Billard said as she strode into the room just as the bell rang. She was all business. "Open your textbooks to page one-twelve. We've got a lot of ground to cover today."

For the next fifty minutes Mrs. Billard talked nothing but American history. I didn't even try listening. I was too heated up. Yet when the bell rang Mrs. Billard asked that I stay behind. She wanted to talk. She told me to close the door.

"I was listening before class started," she said.

I wasn't surprised. "Why didn't you speak up?"

"You're asking why I didn't defend Aja? After our talk the other day you probably think I owe the girl. And you're right. But I didn't intervene for one very simple reason. I think Aja can take care of herself."

"Because you feel you've been touched by her power?"

"I wouldn't put it that way but yes."

"She may not be as powerful as you think." I told Mrs. Billard about how sick Aja got after working on Mike. The woman listened closely. She appeared touched.

"Thanks for sharing that with me," she said when I finished. "I'm almost glad to hear she has a chink in her armor. It makes her seem more human."

"She is human."

"I know that, Fred. And I know that you love her and want to protect her. But you're just going to create more enemies for her by attacking those who have every right to question what she's doing."

"Macy's an idiot. I had a right to call her on her bullshit."

"Macy's on track to be class valedictorian. She's far from stupid. She also happens to be Christian. Do you want to shut her up because of her beliefs? Because she has faith?"

"If Macy stuck to what Jesus said I wouldn't have a problem. 'Love thy neighbor' and all that good stuff. But Macy's attacking Aja for one reason—she doesn't give Jesus credit for her healing abilities. And that's wrong. I don't care what you say, it's just wrong."

Mrs. Billard shook her head. "You think you're going to get the whole world to see Aja the way you do? I'd be surprised if you changed a single person's mind. Listen, Aja's something new and exciting. Now you know how people react to what's new. Half are intrigued while the other half are fearful. That's natural. But the half that are scared of her—you're not going to help Aja by going around telling them how stupid they are."

"So what do you want me to do?" I asked.

"Let Aja take care of herself."

"She won't! That's the problem. She won't lift a finger to defend herself."

"Maybe that's the best defense of all." Billard paused. "Trust Aja. I do."

"You don't fear her anymore?"

"No. The opposite. I find her inspiring."

I expected Mrs. Billard to elaborate but she told me to go enjoy my lunch. On the way to the courtyard I ran into Nicole Greer. She wanted to explain why she'd been spying on Aja for Casey Morall.

"Don't bother," I said. "I know why you did it."

"Why?" Nicole asked.

"You were trying to break us up."

"That's not true." Nicole paused. "So you're together, then?"

"Yup."

Her face fell. "Why?"

"What do you mean why? I'm with her because I like her." I tried to step past her but Nicole blocked my way.

"I don't believe you. You've been in love with me for the last two years. Something like that doesn't vanish overnight. The only reason you're with Aja now is because she's popular."

"Oh, brother," I muttered.

"All right, fine, poor choice of words. She's not popular, she's a freak. There's no way you can have a normal relationship with her. But we can have that. I swear to you, I'm over Rick. I shouldn't have been with him in the first place. I should be with you."

I stopped and stared at Nicole. "No," I said.

"No what?"

"No, I'm not with Aja because she's popular or because she's a freak. No, you're not over Rick. And no, we should not be together."

It was a universal truth: Girls as pretty as Nicole did not comprehend what the word "no" meant. It was genetic, I think. She stomped the ground, unsure whether to weep or scream. In the end she did a little of both.

"I know you still love me. Don't deny it," she said.

"I don't love you."

"You can't love Aja! You just met her!"

People were beginning to stare. I raised a hand, cautioning her to get a grip. I leaned closer. "I want you to stop."

"Stop what?"

"This whole song and dance about you and I living happily ever after. And stop spying on Aja. It's beneath you." I pulled away. "I've got to go."

Nicole called after me. "Casey Morall knows about Lisa Alastair."

I halted in midstride, turned. "You told her?"

"No. She found out on her own. And right now, she's in Ohio. She's just beginning to ramp up her investigation." She sniffed. "I just thought I should warn you."

"Thanks," I said.

I found Aja on the same bench where we'd shared our first lunch. Dale, Mike, and Janet stood around her the same way the Secret Service stood while guarding the president. When anyone got too close to Aja, Mike would glare at them. His head bandage added to his intimidating look.

"How are we all doing today?" I said.

"I'm fine," Aja said.

Janet grumbled. "This isn't working. Wherever Aja goes

there's always someone asking for her help. They've got a sick aunt. A sick uncle. A dying pet. Someone—it was Carl Burger in chemistry—came up to her and asked if Aja could help fix his sister."

"What's wrong with Carl's sister?" I asked.

"He says she's ugly," Janet said. "She's got too many pimples and her nose is too big. Can you imagine that?"

"I can when I think of Carl's face," I said.

"He's uglier than his sister," Mike agreed.

"All I'm saying is the honeymoon's over," Janet said. "Aja's never going to have a moment's peace. This town—hell, this country—is full of sick people. They're all going to want Aja's help."

"Did this happen to you in Selva?" Dale asked Aja.

She considered. "The people there were simple and polite. Only if there was an emergency, someone might come running and try to find me. But I explained that talking to my body didn't tell the Big Person anything new. That if there was going to be a healing, it would happen all by itself."

"Like with Lisa Alastair?" Dale asked.

"Yes."

"You mean it didn't matter that her father called you?" I asked. The possibility had never occurred to me.

242 / CHRISTOPHER PIKE

"No," Aja said. "The people of Selva understood that. For the most part they left me alone."

"Does it help that you're physically close to a person?" Dale asked.

"Yes," Aja said.

"So the Big Person does use your body as a tool?" Dale said.

Aja hesitated. "In a way."

"Fascinating," Dale muttered.

"Maybe you should hire a private tutor and stay home," Mike said.

"No. This body is meant to be here at this time." Aja turned to me. "Can you come to my house tonight? Aunt Clara's lawyer is going to read her will and he wants you there."

"What for?" I asked.

"He didn't say," Aja replied.

That evening, I waited until my parents arrived home so I could borrow their car to drive to the Carter Mansion. Bo had been more than patient with me borrowing the Camry. I didn't want to overdo it.

John Grisham was the name of Clara's lawyer. I thought it was a joke at first; he didn't look anything like the thriller writer. The man promised us that was his real name—"us" being Bart, Aja, and myself.

Mr. Grisham was around sixty, heavyset; his gray suit looked as if it had been bought several belt sizes ago. He had a nicely tailored beard and mustache and a twinkle in his eye. For a lawyer he seemed like an okay guy.

It was clear Grisham knew the layout of the house, especially when he led us into one of the mansion's four living rooms and had us take a seat. The room was heavily insulated, soundproofed—perfect for meetings about money. Opening his briefcase, he took out a thick sheaf of papers. I'd never seen such a fat will. Well, actually, I'd never seen any kind of will before.

According to Aja, Bart had only returned that morning. She had no idea where he'd been and in typical Aja fashion had no interest in finding out. She was dressed in red sweats; her feet were bare. If she was worried about the will she gave no sign. She sat on a love seat beside me and held on to my hand.

"I'm glad you could come," she said, giving me a quick kiss on the cheek. I smiled.

"No problem. But I should tell you the truth. The only reason I've been dating you is because I knew you came from money."

"I thought it was because you loved me," she said.

"I tell all the girls that."

The remark just came out of my mouth.

The fact was I'd never told Aja I loved her.

John Grisham spoke. "The dispersal of Clara Smith's wealth is fairly simple. I hope there will be no surprises. But the will itself—and the living trust it's connected to—is a complex legal document that was prepared in my law offices last summer. It's designed to have you, Bart Lewis, and you, Aja Smith, pay the least amount of taxes possible. Later I can explain in detail what this means but for now I'll just go over how the inheritance is to be divided."

Mr. Grisham cleared his throat before continuing. "As you may or may not know, Clara had much of her wealth in major stocks and various real estate holdings spread all over the world. This last summer she converted these investments into cash—with the exception of this property. At present, the sum total of her estate is worth two hundred and sixty-two million dollars."

Bart gasped. "I had no idea."

Mr. Grisham turned to Aja. "Are you surprised?"

"No," she said.

Mr. Grisham raised an eyebrow at her lack of reaction and continued. "It was Clara's wish that this sum be shared equally between the two of you. You will, therefore, each receive one hundred and thirty-one million dollars and change—minus whatever taxes you're required to pay." He paused. "I hope this meets with both your expectations and that there will be no contesting of the will?"

"It's fine with me," Bart said. "Aja?"

"It's good," she said.

"Great," Mr. Grisham said. "Now, let me explain why Fred Allen was invited to the reading of Clara's will. First off, Clara asked that he be here. Second, she prepared a document for him to read." The lawyer removed a standard legal-sized envelope from his briefcase and handed it to me. "She wrote this in her final days."

"I knew she'd written something for Fred," Bart said. "I was looking all over for it."

"She mailed it to me the day before she died," Mr. Grisham said. "I didn't know you were aware of it. I apologize if there was any confusion."

Bart shrugged. "All that matters is Fred's got it now."

Mr. Grisham spoke. "There's one other item Clara prepared for you, Fred. Her late husband, Eric Smith, was a childhood friend of Richard Gratter, the founder of Paradise Records. I assume you're familiar with that company?"

"Sure," I said. "They're one of the biggest in the music business."

"They are indeed. Before passing, Clara arranged an

audition for you with Mr. Gratter. Specifically, Paradise Records will fly you out to Los Angeles anytime in the next month, where you will be given an opportunity to audition your music to the firm's top executives, including Mr. Gratter himself." Grisham paused. "I hope this meets with your approval."

I could barely speak. "Gratter wants to hear my songs?"

"Yes," Mr. Grisham said.

"How does he know I'm any good?"

"Clara told him you were extremely talented."

"How did Clara know how talented I am?"

"I played her the demo you gave me," Aja said.

"I told you not to show that to anyone."

"I didn't show it to her. I let her listen to it."

"Aja! Did she send it to Gratter?" I asked.

"I don't know," Aja said. "Probably."

I shook my head. "Oh God."

"The offer is good for a month from today," Mr. Grisham warned. "After that, Mr. Gratter might presume you have no interest in his firm."

"But I'm in a band," I said. "Can't they come to the audition?"

"No," the lawyer said. "Paradise made it clear they are only interested in you."

"What am I supposed to tell my friends?"

Mr. Grisham stood. "I'm sure you'll think of something. Now I must be off. But I need to tell you, Bart and Aja, it's best I prepare your own wills as soon as possible. You're both extremely wealthy now. You need to be prepared for any eventuality."

"We'll get back to you on that," Bart said, showing the lawyer to the door. Aja and I had stood as the man left but suddenly I felt my legs turn to rubber and collapsed back onto the love seat. Aja sat beside me.

"Don't be scared," she said. "I'll go with you. It'll be fun. They'll love you."

"Is that the Big Person talking?"

Aja smiled. "I'm not telling."

Bart returned to the living room. He continued to marvel over how much money Clara had made in her life, and how she'd kept most of it secret from him. "I knew she was well-off but two hundred and sixty-two million—it makes me dizzy thinking about it," he said. "It's an almost obscene amount of money."

"You can always give it away to the poor," Aja said, a serious note in her voice. Her tone did not escape Bart. He nodded.

"There's a town in Jamaica near where I was born that's desperate for help," he said. "It might be fun to go back there and play Santa Claus for a few hundred families." Bart stood back up. "It's something to think about. Now, if you'll excuse me, I'm still tired from my travels. I'm going to bed."

"Good night," Aja said.

"Night, you two. Try not to be too loud."

When Bart left the room I asked her what he meant with that last remark. Again Aja smiled. "I've never met such a naive Little Person."

She was talking about sex, of course; the two of us making love in a bedroom only two rooms away from where Bart ordinarily slept. It was odd but in all the time I'd known Aja I'd never seen her bedroom. I assumed it would be rather austere—given the fact she wasn't attached to anything.

I couldn't have been more wrong.

From Selva, Aja had brought with her a large assortment of throw rugs and exotic handcrafts. Plus there were paintings and sculptures, the latter made from a deeply tanned wood. Almost all were of a woman's face; a female that bore a striking resemblance to Aja. I pointed out the similarity and Aja nodded.

"My father painted them, carved them," she said.

"That's your mother, right?"

"Yes."

I hesitated. "You never speak of your parents."

"There's no need."

"I understand. But if you ever want to . . ."

"There's no need," she repeated.

Her voice sounded as calm and cool as ever. I told myself there was no need to worry.

At some point we got into bed. Like the first time, everything seemed to happen in slow motion and very fast at the same time. I suppose my adolescent brain was unable to see Aja naked without shorting out. It was incredible to hold her in my arms again.

And it was magical to feel my thoughts and emotions slip into another dimension as our bodies entwined. Being close to Aja created an invisible bubble that somehow had the power to make me forget myself. Not that I forgot my name—Fred had never been happier—but the constant activity of my mind quieted as I sank deeper and deeper into her. She had only to put her hand on my heart and I was at peace.

Later, as Aja slept beside me, I turned on a lamp by her bed and opened Clara's envelope. It was typed; she had obviously created it on her tablet with her one good hand.

Fred,
When you get this letter I expect I will no longer
be of this world. Aja has already told me that my

breaths are to run out in the next few days. Did you know we're all born with so many breaths? That's just one of the many remarkable things Aja has taught me. I know as you spend more time with her even more miraculous pieces of knowledge will come to you—mostly from inside and in a form that will be impossible to explain to others. That's why this letter might sound like nothing more than the crazed ramblings of an old woman. Very little of what Aja has taught me can be put into words.

Why am I writing this letter, you must wonder? Already I've heard that Aja's healing ability has begun to be felt in Elder. That's inevitable. The universal soul—what she calls the "Big Person"— is lively wherever she goes. In Selva, when I first witnessed it in action, I sought to control it by controlling her, although at the time I told myself I was trying to protect Aja from people who were trying to take advantage of her. I can see already you care for her; I suspect you'll try to do the same. You'll try to isolate her. And you'll try to keep others from knowing what you know about her.

My advice is simple. Don't do it.

There's an arrogance built into us "Little

People." We think we know what is best, especially when it comes to those we love. How truer is that when we chance upon a person such as Aja—a beautiful young woman with powers that make her appear to be an angel incarnate. It's as if we can accept Aja's power but not her intelligence. Again, I tell you that's a mistake.

The same consciousness that allows her to heal also directs her to where she should be and what she should do. It was the Big Person that told us to move to Elder. It was the Big Person who brought you into her life. You'll have trouble believing that; any sane person would. You'll recall seeing Aja for the first time, and thinking how cute she was, before deciding—for yourself—that you wanted to get to know her better. You're probably certain your relationship was driven by a normal high school crush, and I'm here to tell you that you're absolutely wrong.

How can I be so sure?

Aja told me about you before you even spoke to her.

She said she saw you while she was in the town park. She saw you walking home from school. I doubt you noticed her; she wasn't even going to Elder High then. But when she saw you she knew *she'd seen her reason for moving us all to Elder.*

What is that reason? Why are you so important?

I don't know.

I just know that I like you and that I trust you.

Let me tell you something else you don't know.

Aja possesses the ability to heal wounds that are mostly hidden, that are not physical. I've seen demonstrations of this far more often than I've seen her heal a sick child. Probably because we all carry these type of wounds. You and I are no exceptions. No matter how many hints I've picked up from Aja as to how the Big Person operates through her, I've never gotten a clear idea of why it chooses to heal one person over another.

Yet I've glimpsed a definite pattern when Aja has healed me, or Bart, or healed other close friends of psychological scars. The healing inevitably results in a clearer vision of what the Big Person is. In other words, it's as if this vast consciousness is trying to make itself known in the lives of the people who come in contact with Aja. I tell you this now, Fred, although I'm pretty certain you'll eventually come to the same conclusion. A pity I won't be here to hear if that's true.

I can only pray you have as many years with Aja as I did. Frankly, despite what I said at the top to trust what Aja is doing, America scares me. Selva was much simpler. The people were unsophisticated—by our standards—but they were kind. I was loath to take Aja out of such a natural sanctuary, especially when I knew my days were short. But I knew I had to trust her. And now that I've met you, I feel that trust has been rewarded.

Take care, Fred. Take care of Aja.

All my love, Clara.

I held the letter to my chest and looked at Aja's sleeping face, only inches from my own. How innocent she looked right then; how sweet and uncomplicated. And yet behind her softly sighing breath and the flutter of her long eyelashes, I sensed something vast. A being so huge that my paltry concepts of time and space could not contain it.

What was that something?

Was that the real Aja?

Clara's letter suddenly felt heavy in my hand.

I set it aside and turned off the light.

CHAPTER FOURTEEN

IT WAS TIME TO LISTEN, TIME TO STOP TRYING TO fix everything. It went against my nature but maybe my nature had been shaped by the type of psychological scars Clara said Aja could dissolve. Looking back at my childhood, how desperate I'd been to keep my parents together, and then at my teenage years, how I'd struggled at every step to help my friends even when they hadn't asked for my help, I had to wonder if I was carrying more baggage than I knew.

No wonder Aja had called me a martyr.

I told Janet, Mike, and Dale that our new policy with Aja was "hands off." We wouldn't stand around her at break and lunch like security guards. Whoever wanted to talk to her could talk to her. And I told them Aja would go along with our new approach, even though I hadn't spoken to her about it. She wouldn't complain because she never complained, about anything.

Also, I shared Clara's letter with them.

They read it Tuesday morning as we huddled together in the school parking lot. Hopefully, the letter helped explain our new hands-off policy. Mike and Dale seemed to take Clara's advice to heart but Janet had her doubts.

"Elder isn't Selva," Janet said. "And this idea of trusting in the Big Person sounds like nothing but wishful thinking. Let's not fool ourselves. We drop our wall and Aja's going to get swarmed. Every kid in school is going to hassle her to fix some sick relative."

"She'll learn how to handle them," I said, not really believing what I was saying.

Janet snorted. "Wait until she tries to heal someone who makes her sick. You'll drop your 'Trust in the Big Person' attitude faster than any of us."

I smiled. "So you do think that she can heal people?"

"That's not what I said," Janet said.

"Aja won't get sick if she doesn't get emotionally involved," Dale said.

"Forget about her healing for a second," Janet said. "Can Aja control her emotions twenty-four/seven? Because if she can't—and she couldn't with Mike—then how is a shy girl who basically grew up in a jungle going to handle throngs of people pestering her all day? It would drive anyone nuts."

"She can handle it," Mike said, not a trace of doubt in his voice.

Janet shook Clara's letter in front of us. "And what's all this crap about her healing psychological wounds? It's bad enough people think she can heal sick people. Add this new power to the mix and half the guys and girls in this school won't be bugging her to cure their aunts and uncles. They'll be begging Aja to fix their own screwed-up lives."

"We probably shouldn't advertise the 'psyche repair' thing," Dale suggested.

"I agree," I said.

Janet studied me. "Has she ever done a psychic probe on you?"

I acted nonchalant. "She's said a few insightful things. Nothing that's rewired my brain. I mean, I'm not walking around thinking my demo is going to get me a million-dollar advance from EMI or Sony Records."

Shit, I thought. Talk about a Freudian slip.

I hadn't shared with the others Clara's offer to fly me out to LA to audition for Paradise Record's top executives. They'd never shown any sign of jealousy over the fact that most of

Half Life's fan base raved about how great I was, without mentioning them.

Still, a part of me worried that Clara's offer might push buttons, particularly when it came to Shelly. She knew she was lacking in the creative department. She knew she couldn't sing or write songs. But her father was a musician; we practiced at her house. And to top it all off, she was jealous of Aja. Considering all these points, I wouldn't have been surprised if Shelly insisted on going to LA with me.

Janet was suspicious of my answer, as she had a right to be. I was, after all, lying. "Are you saying Aja hasn't helped you resolve at least one traumatic event in your life?" she asked.

I shrugged. "You know me. I've led a pretty boring life."

"She's nailed me on a few things," Dale said.

Janet jumped on him. "Like what? Give me an example."

Dale glanced at Mike, who gave him an encouraging pat on the back. Dale cleared his throat before answering. "She knew I was gay and that I've been in love with Mike for the last four years. She gave me the strength to acknowledge that and to talk about it openly with Mike."

Janet was staggered. She wasn't the only one.

"You're kidding me!" Janet gasped.

"He's not," Mike said.

"But how—" Janet began.

"The rest of it's none of your business," Mike interrupted.

Janet backed up a step. "But Mike, you're not saying that you're . . ."

"What? Gay? What if I am? What if I'm not? Either way it doesn't matter. What's going on between Dale and myself is private."

Janet shook her head, not because she disagreed with Mike, but because she was still trying to process what they'd just said. The issue between Mike and Dale had been with us for years. To have it suddenly resolved, in the blink of an eye . . . well, let's just say I was struggling as much as Janet.

Maybe more. Maybe because Dale was saying that Aja had, with a few well-chosen words, made everything between him and his best friend okay. Adding another layer of proof to the possibility that Aja could in fact work miracles.

But whatever the source of Dale and Mike's new relationship I was happy for them. So was Janet. She hugged both of them together, making it a threesome.

"I'm happy for you guys," she said. "And I'm proud of you, Dale. It takes a lot of guts to come out of the closet."

I spoke up. "Hey, maybe Aja can inspire all the gay people on campus to come out. Think about it—Elder High could be the first school in the nation to enjoy total sexual acceptance."

"You're forgetting Principal Levitt," Mike said. "He'd flip. He'd break out the white sheets and torches and organize lynch mobs."

Dale punched him playfully. "Thanks for making me feel loved and secure at what's probably the most sensitive moment of my life."

Mike spoke. "Have no fear, bro. God works through that girl. Whatever Aja's set in motion—I know she's got the Man Upstairs looking out for both of us."

Janet backed off a step and shook her head. "I feel like I'm being dragged kicking and screaming into a cult—the Aja Cult. You know when I first met her all I was worried about were all the hearts she was going to break at Elder High. Now it's like the four of us are grooming her to be a modern-day Virgin Mary." Janet poked me in the gut. "No offense to your virility."

"None taken," I said. "So it's settled. Our new marching orders are—we let Aja be Aja. And if CNN or NBC shows up, we'll deal with it."

"Heard any more word on Casey Morall's investigation of the healing Aja did on Lisa Alastair?" Dale asked.

"All I know is Casey's still in Ohio," I said. "Nicole texted me this morning."

"She's spying for you now?" Dale asked.

"One can only hope," I said.

• • •

At lunch that afternoon, a few people approached Aja while the rest of us sat on the other side of the courtyard. No one spoke to her long but they all seemed to go away satisfied. I had no idea what they asked and no clue what she told them. I wasn't sure I wanted to know. Janet watched uneasily. Mike and Dale looked optimistic.

The next day at lunch Aja was swarmed. A line formed around the courtyard. Someone started handing out numbers. Aja continued to sit on the bench where we'd eaten our first lunch together. She spent roughly two minutes with each person. It was like she was a priest hearing confessions. At least that's what Janet said.

I quit my job at the hardware store. Business was slow and my boss couldn't afford me. I did him the favor of not having to fire me. Besides, I hadn't forgotten that Clara had given me only a month to fly out to LA. Aja had warned me Clara liked to put time limits on tasks to get people moving. I took the deadline seriously and used the extra time to work on my demo.

After going back and forth, I decided to put "Strange Girl" on as a fourth track. To my surprise, Shelly, more than Dale or Mike, helped me with the arrangement. She had a keyboard that could play any instrument that had been invented by man, and she ended up laying down not just a minute of piano that complemented my acoustic guitar, but a string section that came near the end and heightened the emotion of the song. I asked her where she'd been hiding such a far-out composition and she told me Aja had helped her with it.

"How?" I asked. "She doesn't play an instrument."

We were in my bedroom. Shelly was sitting on my bed with her keyboard on her lap. I was at my computer, juggling my tracks, and playing with the volume of each one. If the digital age had not come along I would have been toast. I was the sort who polished a song forever. I never got to the point where I felt something was perfect.

My Achilles' heel was my singing. Because I was so self-conscious about my voice, I had to fight the tendency to drown it out with music. My voice I couldn't change. But I could control the music. Left to my own devices I'd create the classic "wall of sound" over everything I composed. Probably because walls were oh so easy to hide behind.

"You going to tell me?" I asked when she didn't answer.

Shelly hesitated. "She told me to ignore my shadow."

"Huh?"

"That's what I said, 'What do you mean?' Aja said, 'The one with the stick. Ignore him and he'll go away.'"

"Weird."

"It wasn't so weird, not when I thought about it. When my father tutored me as a kid, he always stood behind me, snapping, 'Practice perfect. Practice perfect.' He never let me hit a false note. If I did he'd whack my hands with an old violin bow he carried. I was young—it hurt. But you see, he was old-school. He thought he was doing me a favor. He believed any bad habit would get ingrained in my brain and in my fingers. I swear, before I spoke to Aja, I felt a shadow hanging over me every time I sat down at the keyboard."

"How did she help you let him go?"

Shelly shrugged. "I suppose by telling me that my father was the key. After talking to her for one minute I went away and thought about what she said and felt a huge weight lift. It was then I realized I don't have to be afraid when I jam with you guys in the garage or when I play alone. I can make all the mistakes I want and no one will hurt me. I went straight home and laid down this track. I knew it would fit perfectly with 'Strange Girl.'" Shelly stopped. "But I don't want you to use it."

My reaction to Shelly's comments was mixed. I was grateful Aja had been able to help her. Was I stunned? No. It was getting to the point where nothing Aja did surprised me. It was kind of a bizarre attitude to have about your girlfriend but I suspected if Aja began building an ark I'd probably start gathering two of every animal while I kept an eye on the weather reports.

Now as far as Shelly and her strings—we had just spent two hours fitting them into my song. They made the song better; I wanted them. Yet I couldn't use them without her permission so I waved my hand like it was no big deal but inside I was annoyed.

"It's cool," I said. "I wouldn't just hand over a piece of music like that."

Shelly came over to my desk and put a hand on my shoulder. "I'd give you the strings in a second if I thought they helped. But they don't—they distract from you. Leave my piano in the background and go with your voice and guitar. Think about it. The song works because the girl you're singing about is probably going to leave you. You're alone and you need to sound alone when you sing about her."

What she said made sense but I couldn't help teasing her. "You're just being a greedy bitch," I said.

Shelly smiled. "Hey, this is the first thing I ever wrote that you wanted to steal. It must be good."

"It's brilliant."

"Not. I know the difference between clever and genius. And you're the genius." She leaned over and hugged me. "You need to get your demo out there."

I told her about Paradise Records' offer right then. Even though it scared the shit out of me to do it, I felt the urge and just went with it. To my amazement she got all excited and danced around the room. I'd never seen Shelly dance before, not even onstage. She was happy for me and promised she'd keep the audition secret.

But I knew right then I'd have to tell Mike and Dale before the day was over. I'd been a coward not to tell them the instant I'd heard about the audition. We were a band, and although I doubted I could convince Paradise Records to sign the four of us, my friends deserved to know the truth.

CHAPTER FIFTEEN

COME FRIDAY THE LINE LEADING TO AJA ON the courtyard had shrunk. By my estimate no more than twenty new people tried to speak to her. Already I was beginning to think we'd made the right decision to stop protecting her. Of course, for me, it was still hard not to worry.

Walking home from school that afternoon I spotted a beautiful, black woman picking daisies in the park. There weren't many black people in South Dakota. It was kind of sad—in all of Elder there were only three black families. But what caught my attention was she was picking the daisies in the exact spot Aja had been gathering them when I'd first seen her.

As I watched, the woman carried her flowers to a nearby bench and sat down in the broiling sun. I couldn't take my eyes off of her. She was far from young yet her age did nothing to dim her regal appearance. Dressed in a stunning blue gown, she looked like a queen from a lost kingdom. She noticed I was staring at her and flashed a smile and raised an exquisite hand and gestured to me: *Come.*

Seconds later I was standing beside her, staring down at a deck of tarot cards she'd spread over a white towel she'd covered her half of the bench with. She'd waved me over but the cards held her attention. Without raising her head, she motioned for me to sit beside her.

"Have a seat, Fred," she said. She had an accent, but I couldn't place it. It made me wonder where she was from.

I sat. "You know who I am?"

She nodded to the cards. "I know a few things about you."

"Who are you?"

She looked at me with her bright, dark eyes. She had the most amazing black hair: long and braided, tied with shiny gold thread. "A visitor."

"What brings you to Elder?"

She gestured to the students pouring out of Elder High and to the rest of the town. "We're all here for the same reason."

"And what might that be?"

"Aja."

"I take it you've seen the videos?"

"I have. I must say you're much more handsome in person."

"Thank you. I assume you have a sick relative that needs to be cured?"

"My daughter was sick but she no longer needs healing."

Her voice had changed when she mentioned her daughter.

"Is your daughter all right?" I asked.

"She's dead. She died twelve years ago. Cancer."

"I'm very sorry to hear that."

"You say that as if you mean it. I'm grateful." She studied me. "I can see why Aja chose you."

"Chose me for what?"

"To be close to."

I shook my head. "Who the hell are you?"

"Call me Angela."

"Is that really your name?"

"Does it matter? I like the name, and on my better days I like to think I'm an angel here on earth doing God's work."

I gestured to her tarot cards. "Are you a psychic? Is that what you do? Readings for people?"

"Yes. But I'm different from most psychics."

"Your rates are low?"

"Actually, they're quite high. But that's not what makes me unique." She leaned closer. "My readings are accurate."

"Don't all psychics say that?"

"Most do. But most are liars." She paused. "Would you like me to do a reading for you? It would be on the house."

"Oh, I get it. The reading's free but in return I have to introduce you to Aja."

Angela, whoever she was, stared at me. "I'm not here to hustle you. I've already met Aja." She paused. "But it was a long time ago."

"Did you know her when she lived in Selva?"

"Yes and no. She was a child then. I knew her father."

"What was your relationship?"

"Far from pleasant. I'd rather not talk about it."

"If you say so. But you're in town to see Aja. You already said as much."

Angela considered. "I confess it would be nice to see the young woman she's grown up to be. But I understand a lot of people are asking for her time. I'm not here to bother her." She paused and searched the park. "I haven't been here in years but it doesn't look like much has changed."

"Do you have friends in town?" I asked.

"One close friend." She pointed to the tarot cards. "Do you want to know what the cards have to say about your life?"

"You'd be wasting your time. I don't believe in the tarot."

"But you're curious, admit it. You keep looking at the cards."

"They're beautiful. The paper—it doesn't look like normal paper. What are they made of?"

"Skin."

"Skin?"

"Human skin."

Was she serious? "The colors—they're dark but they look—"

She interrupted. "Full of life?"

"Yes. Where did you get them?" There were sixteen; she'd arranged them in four rows of four.

"That's a long story. Let's just say they came to me after Aja's parents died. It was only then I was able to give readings." Moving fast, she picked up the cards and shuffled them as smoothly as a dealer in Las Vegas. She added, "If it makes the reading any more palatable to you, I only use the cards as a tool to channel. My gift comes from elsewhere." She handed me the deck. "Now hold them, touch them, feel the cards. Let whatever's on your mind, whatever you're feeling, enter into them."

I did as I was told, at least the physical part, although I doubt I gave much of my inner soul to the cards. But when I handed her the deck back she put the cards on the towel and suddenly took my hands in hers. Slowly, she began to trace the lines on my palms with her nails. Besides being long, her nails were sharp; they dug into my flesh as she moved over my hands. The sensation wasn't unpleasant; rather, it was like she was scratching an itch I'd never been aware of before.

"You've led a normal life, up until recently," she said.

I assumed she was talking about Aja having entered my life.

"Kudos to you," I said.

She continued to study my palm. But her nails—it was like she was using them to dig lines she couldn't find. She pressed deeper into my skin; I wouldn't have been surprised if I'd started to bleed. Still, the pain was more than balanced by a strange pleasure. Her touch was almost erotic.

"You have a great soul," she said. "You're destined for great things."

"I bet you tell all your customers that."

"I've never told anyone that." She pointed to a line just below my pinkie. "Your heart line. Note how it breaks at the end of the first quarter. That signifies a great change will occur in your life when you're seventeen or eighteen."

"Just looking at me you've got to know I'm that age."

Angela ignored my sarcastic remarks. She continued. "You pretend to believe in nothing when you secretly believe in everything. Yet you want proof. You feel you need it."

"Proof of what?"

"Your destiny." She let go of my hands and turned over the top card on the deck of cards. "Perhaps this will help you find it."

I felt a chill in the center of my chest.

I recognized the card. It was the only tarot card I knew.

"Is that the devil's card?" I asked.

She seemed surprised at the card I'd drawn. "Some call it that. Others call it the card of death."

I snorted. "So I'm going to die soon? Is that it?"

She hesitated before answering. "I'd rather not say."

I stood. "Thanks for the reading. I think it's a bunch of bullshit."

Angela nodded sadly. "I thought the same thing."

I walked home in a foul mood, annoyed with the woman. Yet by the time I reached my house I realized I was more upset with myself. I'd let her get to me. It had been her remarks about Aja's past that had drawn me in. Still, I suspected they were nothing but lies; that she'd just been scheming to get to Aja.

When I got home, I finally read up on DID—dissociative identity disorder. Except for possibly suffering a major trauma as a child, there was nothing in the literature that linked Aja to the condition.

"Except for the Big Person and the Little Person," I said to myself.

I was not seriously worried.

She was too sane.

And she sure as hell was too happy.

Later, Aja called and that brightened up my mood. She asked me out for Saturday night: dinner and a movie. I liked her chasing me. She said she wanted to return to the same restaurant in Balen—Benny's. I begged her to reconsider—to no avail. She insisted she liked their food, then taunted me by asking what the chances were of her getting belted in the jaw again.

The next day we drove to Balen in a brand-new car Bart had bought her—a Mercedes C-Class, with the incredible 4.0L AMG biturbo V-8 engine. Aja let me take the wheel; she said she didn't have a driver's license. For that matter, she said she didn't know how to drive. I offered to teach her.

The night ended up mimicking our original date. We talked so long over dinner we missed the movie and ended up checking into the Hilton for another dip in the Jacuzzi and another round of fantastic sex. The only difference this time was Aja didn't mention the Big Person. I was hoping it was because she was enjoying what pleasures us little people had to offer.

The storm hit on Sunday, figuratively and literally. We'd just checked out of the hotel at noon and were driving back to Balen when thunder ripped the sky and it began to rain so hard I had to struggle to keep the car on the road. A stream formed on our right, in the overflowing gutter. On top of that Janet texted me. Her note said it was an emergency; that I had to call her immediately. I pulled off at the next exit.

"What's wrong?" I asked Janet when she answered. I had her on speakerphone so Aja could hear. I figured it was probably about her.

"We need to talk. But first—watch," Janet said, before linking us with a video on YouTube. It showed a nurse being interviewed by Casey Morall. I assumed we were in for a rerun of what had happened with Mike. Except this nurse sat hidden in the dark and her voice had been distorted so she couldn't be easily identified.

Worse, much worse, this time Casey had X-rays of Lisa Alastair's head. MRIs of Lisa's brain. CAT scans. The unidentified nurse provided most of the vocal commentary while the images flashed on the screen. The theme of the video was simple—a running stream of images of Lisa's tumor before and after Aja's healing.

When Lisa's father had told me his daughter had a brain tumor, I had never imagined it was the size of a golf ball.

How could such a thing fit inside the head of such a small girl? But there it was in black and white.

It was still there two days after Lisa's father spoke to Aja and was told his daughter would be fine. Except by then the tumor had shrunk to the size of a walnut. A week later it was the size of a pea. Finally, two days ago, the nurse reported it had vanished altogether.

At the end of the visual display and the nurse's commentary, Casey wisely kept her remarks brief. Why talk when her pictures were worth a million words? Indeed, studying the number on the bottom of my cell screen, I could see they were worth over twelve million hits on YouTube.

And it was still early.

Yet Casey did take time to remind viewers of the mystery surrounding Mike Garcia's healing, and the healing of the soldier at the Roadhouse. For the first time, Casey stated that Aja was from Selva, Brazil, where she was well-known as the *Pequena Maga*, the "Little Magician." Casey closed her presentation by showing Lisa playing in the front yard of her house with other kids her age.

Janet's voice came back on my cell. "It was posted at four in the morning our time. I just found out about it now. We're lucky Casey wasn't able to interview any doctors, and the nurse refused to give her name. But it's weird the nurse was able to get hold of so many X-rays and pass them on to Casey. Medical records are supposed to be confidential." Janet paused. "Unless Mr. Alastair broke his word and just gave Casey the pictures."

I had a different take on the situation. "It's no surprise Lisa's parents would take Lisa to be examined after Aja worked on her. Especially since she seemed so much better. I'd do it if I was her dad. But I don't think Mr. Alastair broke his word. He seemed like an honest man and you remember how grateful he was to Aja—to all of us."

"Then where did the MRIs and CAT scans come from?" Janet asked.

"Money," I said. "Casey's father's been supporting his daughter's investigation of Aja from the start. I bet the nurse we heard on the video stole the images and was paid a pretty penny for them."

Janet was interested. "That could be a good thing. The whole video could be illegal, an invasion of privacy. YouTube might be forced to take it down."

"That won't help," I said. "You can bet a million people have already made copies of it by now. It will keep circulating. But what might help are the holes in Casey's story. It's sloppy reporting at best. She doesn't identify the nurse. She doesn't identify the hospital where the X-rays were taken. She doesn't even say what Aja did when she worked on Lisa."

"Because Aja never met her!" Janet cried.

"That's right. We need to get that fact out there."

"No," Aja interrupted. I'd almost forgotten she was listening.

I looked at her. "This could be the beginning of the end. If this video doesn't get discredited, immediately, you might never have a minute's peace for the rest of your life."

Aja didn't respond right away. Janet took it as a sign she was hiding something. "Do you want the publicity?" Janet asked, speaking to Aja.

Aja shrugged. "All this is inevitable. If Casey Morall didn't post these videos, someone else would have weeks from now."

"This video will alert the national media," Janet warned. "Are you ready for that?"

Aja acted indifferent. "I'd prefer to be left alone. I'm used to solitude. But moving to America—I knew crowds would come. There's no point fighting it."

I spoke to Janet. "I take it you still don't believe in miracles? That Aja can heal people?"

Janet took a long time to answer. "I don't know. I don't know anything anymore."

I could tell by her tone she was shaken up.

"Let me get back to you later," I told Janet.

We exchanged good-byes and I sat with Aja for a few minutes while the rain pelted the roof of the Mercedes. The muddy water on the road was up to our hubcaps. If the downpour continued we'd flood the interior of an eighty-thousand-dollar car. But I was no more worried about that than I was worried about Aja's mental health. A girl who could erase a brain tumor was not suffering from a multiple personality disorder.

"So you knew this would happen?" I said.

"Yes," Aja said.

"When I first spoke to you—you knew then?"

"Yes."

"You should have warned me."

Aja smiled. "You still would have chased after me."

"Is that the little you or the big you talking?"

She leaned over and kissed me and reassured me in her usual way. "It will be okay, Fred," she said.

At six that evening, three hours after I'd dropped Aja at her house, I broke my vow to let Aja be Aja and leave her unprotected. At dinnertime what most people call the "real media" arrived in Elder. A reporter and film crew out of Rapid City appeared first. The reporter wasn't Casey Morall. Her name was Dana Sharone and everyone knew her. She was our capital's biggest and brightest face when it came to TV news.

It didn't take long before Dana was knocking on Aja's door. Bart answered and lied and said Aja wasn't at home and he didn't know where she was. I got the news from Bart, who called while the reporter was still standing on the porch. It was the first time he had ever called me.

"I think we got a problem," Bart said.

"I know you do. Is Aja there with you?"

"Yes. She's with your friend Janet."

"What's Janet doing there?"

"They're talking in Aja's room."

"Can I speak to Aja please?" I said.

"She asked that I leave them alone."

"But this is important. We should all be on the phone together."

"Her talk with Janet must be important. Aja seldom asks not to be disturbed. But when she does, it's best to leave her alone."

This was sounding weirder every minute.

"All right, let's talk about these reporters," I said. "Everyone in South Dakota knows Dana Sharone. She's the most aggressive reporter in the state. She's not going to leave you alone. She'll keep knocking on your door until you answer or else someone forces her off your property. You've got to hire private security."

"Do you think that is absolutely necessary?" Bart asked.

"Yes. I thought this might happen. I've been on the Internet for the last two hours researching South Dakota security firms. There's one that comes highly recommended. They're expensive but they have tons of positive reviews. The people who recommend them say they can be mean but that's what you need right now. Dana Sharone is standing on your porch but I promise you she's just the tip of the iceberg."

"Is this firm local?" Bart asked.

"Sort of. Their name is Max and Mercer and their main office is located in Aberdeen. That's three hours away. Call them as soon as we hang up. They have a twenty-four-hour line. Stress how much you and Aja are worth and explain how large a property you have. That will tell them how many of their people they need to send out."

Bart was in the mood to listen. I could hear someone knocking on his door in the background. "Do you have their number?" he asked.

"Yes. Let me give it to you," I said.

After a quick shower, I drove out to Aja's house in her Mercedes. She had loaned it to me. Well, actually she'd told me to keep it. Going from a ten-speed bike to a car that was worth more than half the homes in Elder took some getting used to. To be blunt, it felt kind of weird to drive. I kept expecting a cop to pull me over.

I know I should have been more excited about her inheritance but I wasn't. And it was not because I feared she'd moved into a higher social sphere and that I'd lose her because of the money. Aja cared about her millions as much as Mike cared about the AA meetings he'd been ordered by the court to attend.

By the time I arrived a van from a TV station out of Boise, Idaho, had joined the fray. It was raining hard but they didn't mind. The reporters and their crews were setting up their cameras as if they owned the place. They tried to interview me on the way to the door but I had brought a large, empty pizza box with me and acted like I was making a delivery. Bart answered when I rang and I slipped inside.

Bart told me the security firm already had people on the way. But I was surprised to discover Janet had already left.

"Where'd she go?" I asked.

"Home, I think," Bart said.

"New York," Aja said, entering the room. She had just taken a bath. She took two or three a day. She said she loved to lie on her back and float on the warm water. She was wearing a blue bathrobe and nothing else. Her hair was soaked. From experience I knew she was never in a hurry to dry it.

"Very funny." I assumed she was joking. "What were you and Janet talking about?"

"I can't say," Aja said.

Odd, I thought. Janet wouldn't have gone to Aja for counseling. It wasn't like her.

"How many people are Max and Mercer sending?" I asked.

"Three teams of four," Bart said. "They said twelve people would be the minimum they'd need to secure a property this size." He added, "I told them they could sleep here if they want."

"You're assuming Elder's local hotels and motels are going to be booked?" I asked.

Bart shook his head. "I've seen the same videos you have."

"How do you feel about them?" I asked.

Bart glanced at Aja, who was sitting cross-legged on the couch. "I can't say I'm happy about it," he said.

"Hopefully this will blow over soon," I said. "Usually only top-level celebrities stay in the news more than a week."

Bart sagged wearily into a chair. I noticed the streak of gray in his curly black hair had grown. "We should be so lucky," he said.

The security personnel arrived two hours later. By then there were five TV stations jammed together in the mansion's driveway, all wanting to interview Aja.

Max himself had driven out from Aberdeen. He was more imposing than the photo his firm had posted on their website. Six five, three hundred and fifty pounds; he wore a bulging black leather sports coat that did a poor job of hiding the two guns he carried, never mind his knives. His black eyes matched his intimidating stare. But ironically, when he smiled, he suddenly looked as harmless as a teddy bear.

Then again, I only saw him smile once.

He knew his business. Bart asked Max to clear the property and fifteen grumbling minutes later the reporters and their crews were all encamped at the junction of the driveway and the road that led back to Elder. It was clear they weren't leaving anytime soon. I wondered how that worked in real life in a nasty storm. I mean, what if Aja didn't come out for a week?

But Aja said that wasn't a consideration. She was going to school tomorrow. I tried to talk her out of it.

"I think it would be a good idea to remain out of sight for a few days," I said.

"I agree," Bart said.

"No," Aja said. "If necessary the guards can follow me to school. But I'm going."

"The guards won't be allowed on campus," I said.

"They can keep the reporters off the campus," Aja replied.

"Principal Levitt isn't going to like all this commotion," I warned.

Aja didn't care; the topic simply didn't interest her. She asked if I wanted to watch a movie on TV. I knew I should be at home, working on my demo. But it was hard to leave her surrounded by a growing horde.

"Why not?" I said.

I spent the night. Several times before going to bed I tried calling Janet. I still didn't believe Aja had been serious. Janet wasn't answering, though, which was unusual for her. I tried her cell and her home number. The latter should have at least got me Bo but he wasn't picking up either. I asked Aja if Janet had said anything before leaving and she told me to ask Janet.

What the hell, I thought.

Monday morning I entered the twilight zone. It started when I drove Aja past a dozen reporters and their cameramen. They shouted out a whole list of questions as we cruised by. "Can you heal people, Aja?" "Are you a virgin?" "What's the source of your power?" "Are you a Christian?" "Is your boyfriend a Satanist?" I have to admit I wanted to stop and answer the last question. I'm sure I would have come up with something that would have gotten me on the evening news.

The media—they didn't care that we ignored them at the end of the driveway. The bigger half was waiting for us in the school parking lot. It was here Max and his team briefly lost control of the situation. I shouldn't have blamed Max, he didn't have enough men, but I yelled at him anyway. It scared the shit out of me when I saw the crush surround Aja and pin her against a fence.

I'd dropped her off beside a small flight of concrete stairs that led onto the campus, thinking that would give her a head start. But Aja, as usual, never in a hurry, never worried, let the reporters catch her at the fence. At that point there was nothing for her to do but lower her head and hide beneath her umbrella and wait for Max and his people to rescue her.

The reporters surrounded her on all sides. The onslaught of their questions matched the stormy sky; it was like thunder. But then something unexpected happened. Perhaps the Big Person flexed its power. I saw the sea suddenly part—the crowd of reporters abruptly backed off—and Aja was allowed to continue on her way. After parking the car, I yelled at Max to block all entrances to the campus.

My demand was silly and I knew it. Elder High was old. It had been built in the decades before city councils even dreamed of putting tall fences around schools. The truth was anyone could get on campus from almost any direction. To his credit,

Max didn't use that as an excuse. He shouted at the reporters to stay back and caught up with Aja and escorted her to her locker. Then he called for reinforcements—that meant more security guards—but before they could arrive the police showed up.

It seemed that somewhere during the night Max had read a copy of Elder's city bylaws and discovered that no adults— outside of faculty and hired staff—were allowed on campus when school was in session. That included Max himself but he ignored that point until the cops arrived. By then Aja was sitting safely in her first-period class—chemistry.

What a morning, I thought.

I headed for my own first period. Along the way I tried calling Janet. I didn't get her but Bo finally picked up and told me that Aja had not been joking. Janet was in New York City visiting her mother and stepfather. Just like that she'd flown to the East Coast without telling me. I asked Bo why she'd left so unexpectedly and he said he didn't know. But going by the tension in his voice I wondered if he was lying.

By second period Max had a dozen more guards surrounding the school and Aja was free to wander Elder High unmolested. But since the bad weather had flooded the courtyard, effectively soaking "Dr. Aja's" office space, she didn't have to attend to a long line of teenagers and their problems. The two of us spent lunch together in the school library—basically alone. Reading had never been a particularly popular pastime among my classmates.

"I'm surprised these reporters are so intent on talking to you," I said. "They must have a source beyond Casey's YouTube videos."

"Yes," Aja agreed in that special tone of voice that told me she knew for a fact what I was saying was true while I was just speculating.

"Have you healed someone I don't know about?" I asked.

"Healings happen around this body, you know that."

"For some reason your answer isn't very comforting."

"Have you finished your song about me?" she asked.

"Almost. I should work on it tonight."

"Do you want me to come over?"

"Ordinarily I'd say yes. But then I'd have to explain to the reporters and to my parents why I became a Satanist."

Aja smiled. "If I tell the reporters that I'm the Harlot spoken about in Revelation, do you think they'll get scared and leave me alone?"

"There's an idea." I paused. "I didn't know you'd read Revelation."

"I started reading the Bible a few days ago."

I gestured to the outside world. "To better understand the questions you'd be asked?"

Aja laughed. "Don't be silly."

Only Aja would think it silly to prepare for anything life might happen to throw at her. "Read the Gospels yet?" I asked.

"Yes."

"What's your take on Jesus? Was he connected to the Big Person?"

"Yes."

"You sound certain?"

"I am."

"The reporters and their audiences will like that. Wait, no, I might be wrong. You can't say anything that compares you to Jesus. People will say that's blasphemy."

Aja laughed some more. "Fred, don't worry, it will be fine."

"I'll try," I said, reaching for my cell, trying Janet again, failing to get her to pick up. "At least tell me if Janet was upset when you last saw her."

"She was upset."

"About what?"

"I can't say. It's private."

"Since when does the Big Person keep secrets?"

"I've always kept your secrets. Since the day we met."

"I would hope so. I'm your boyfriend." I paused. "I think."

She took my hand. "You are definitely my boyfriend."

After fourth period, after lunch, I began to hope we'd

escaped the day unscathed. That I'd be able to return Aja to her house and that she'd be able to barricade herself inside and life would go on pretty much as normal. But come fifth period the principal's office sent a message to every class in the school. It seemed Principal Levitt was annoyed with all the security guards and police and wasn't going to allow it to continue. Tonight, at eight sharp, he was calling for an emergency PTA meeting and asking all students who were "interested" to attend. The topic would be—in his words—"the Aja Smith issue."

Aja was required to attend, I was told.

But no reporters would be allowed inside.

"It sounds like a trial," a friend of mine, Stephen Makey, said as the rest of the class looked in my direction to see if I was freaked-out. I thought Stephen was right, although it made me wonder if there would be jurors and how they would be chosen.

I wished Aja hadn't brought up the Gospels. Her casual remark had somehow steered my imagination toward a bleak gray zone where I felt like I was flashing back on an acid trip. I was being silly, totally paranoid, yet I couldn't help but see Principal Levitt as another Caiaphas, the Jewish high priest, and my Aja as Jesus, about to be dragged before the Sanhedrin. Sure, I admit, my fear was running ragged with my reason, yet I couldn't stop from wondering what kind of punishment would be doled out if Aja was found guilty.

CHAPTER SIXTEEN

I WANTED AJA TO LIE. I SPENT THE GAP BETWEEN the end of the school day and the PTA meeting trying to get her to lie. Begging her to say nothing about the Big Person. To not admit to healing anyone. Pleading with her to say she was just an ordinary teenage girl who studied hard, who wanted to get accepted at a good college, and who enjoyed going to concerts with her boyfriend.

I needed her to tell everyone she was normal.

How did Aja respond? She just yawned and told me that everything would be okay and that she was sleepy and wanted to take a nap. Really, she didn't appear to give a damn that the whole town was being assembled to judge her. To her the PTA meeting was just another get-together of little people where her body would show up and enjoy whatever was happening.

The line from my song had been prophetic. To Aja the world was nothing but a stage.

I didn't think that was a good thing. Not this evening.

Later, when she awoke from her nap, she made the two of us dinner—grilled Cajun chicken, brown rice, and steamed broccoli. Bart was away for the day. I had no idea where. It didn't matter—legally. With the death of Aunt Clara—and because she was eighteen years of age—Aja no longer had or needed a guardian.

"Every kid who shows up will have a cell," I warned Aja as she handed me a plate of chicken and rice. I preferred the white meat, Aja the dark. Boy, what a perfect couple. I continued. "It won't matter if Principal Levitt orders them turned off. No one will listen. They'll record everything that's said at the meeting. Which means the reporters waiting outside in the rain are going to get a copy of what you say and it's going to be plastered on TV and across the Internet. Do you understand what that means? Don't lie and the world's going to find out who you are."

It was a matter of debate if Aja had dressed up for the big meeting. She had on a silky red blouse, tight white pants, and tall black boots. She held a pitcher of iced tea in her hands.

"Want some?" she asked.

"Yes." As she began to pour, I added, "You're not listening."

"I am," she said, pouring herself a glass before sitting across from me. She began to dig into her rice; she seemed hungry. She added, "I'm just not worried about it."

"That's easy for you to say," I said. "You've got 'Mr. Happy' in your head. You can disappear into . . . wherever it is you go. You're not thinking about me. About us. How are we going to have a normal relationship if the world finds out you can work miracles?"

"There are no such things as miracles."

"Oh yeah? You've worked plenty since you got here."

"The healings are only seen as miracles because people don't know they have the Big Person inside. Once a person knows who they really are, performing a miracle is no different from going for a walk in the park or having sex on a bed."

"Please don't use that analogy this evening."

"Why not?"

"I'm serious, Aja. This meeting scares me. If you say whatever pops into your head, the crowd and the media are going to crucify you."

She reached over and squeezed my hand. "Have faith."

"In what? You?"

"Yes."

I felt her fingers in mine and there was something reassuring about her touch. "Faith isn't my strong suit," I said.

"I know. But tonight you'll be strong."

"You sure?"

"I'm positive."

I didn't drive Aja to the meeting. I let Max and his people take her. They were better equipped to protect her and, besides, I wanted to make a quick stop at Janet's house. I needed to talk to Bo; he'd stopped answering his phone since he'd told me his daughter was in New York.

The visit turned out to be a waste. I could tell Bo was home. Both their cars were in the driveway. But it didn't matter how hard I knocked or how loud I called out, Bo didn't answer. For the life of me I couldn't imagine what was wrong.

I drove to a diner downtown, the Hot Plate. Janet had a close friend, Mindy Paulson, who worked there as a waitress. Mindy was two years older than the rest of us; she had already graduated. Over time I'd noticed that Janet would tell Mindy stuff she wouldn't even tell me. I didn't take it personally. After all, Mindy was a woman.

The Hot Plate was jammed when I arrived. Listening to the buzz coming from the crowd, it sounded like most of them were headed to the PTA meeting. Dozens of pairs of eyes locked on me the moment I stepped inside. I ignored them. All I cared about was Janet and finding out from

Mindy what she was doing. I saw her talking to a cook in the back and hurried to a nearby corner, standing not far from the open grill. Mindy saw me and walked over.

"She's in New York at her mom's place," she said.

"I know that. Why is she there?"

"She didn't tell you?"

"No."

Mindy hesitated. "I'm sure she'll call you when she's ready." She went to leave. "I gotta get back to work."

I grabbed her arm. "I need to know what's going on."

Mindy was cool. "You're her best friend. You've known her since kindergarten. How can you not know?"

"What are you saying?"

She shook free. "Open your eyes, Fred. Janet never told me the truth either. I just knew. So should you."

Mindy walked away, leaving me alone beside the blazing heat of the grill. I staggered toward the door, struggling to see what was supposed to be so obvious.

I drove to the school. Ordinarily a PTA meeting would be held in the library and maybe a dozen parents would show up, along with half a dozen teachers and Principal Levitt. The only students who'd attend would be someone like Macy Barnes, who was student body president. Otherwise, I don't think a local teen would be caught dead at a PTA meeting.

I knew it would be different tonight and I was right. The meeting had been moved to the gym and it was jammed.

The building had been constructed in the fifties; it was old as well as run-down. The wooden benches sagged and there was an offensive mildew odor that each humid summer magnified. Worse, if you happened to be playing basketball, there were so many dead spots on the court that the gym had earned the nickname "The Graveyard."

Welcome to the Sanhedrin, I thought.

Standing behind a raised podium, Principal Levitt called for order. Even though my father played poker with the man once a week, I didn't know his first name. We students either called him "Levitt" or the "Imperial Wizard," in reference to his time in the Ku Klux Klan.

The guy definitely would have looked better with a sheet over his head. His body was strong. He worked to keep in shape. But his features somehow *burned*. Even in the winter his skin was red from the sun; and his thin yellow hair, self-cut and combed rudely back, reminded me of a fuse. But it was his pale green eyes that were the source of his fire. Mike had once said they were the same color as grass that had died under the summer sun.

I agreed. Levitt was not a pleasant person to lock eyes

with. I'd never seen him smile. Although, I suppose being universally hated didn't give him much to smile about. God only knew what had attracted him to education.

I didn't know how true the rumors about him being a member of the Ku Klux Klan were. But he'd never denied the fact, at least not publicly. The story went that he'd been born and raised in South Carolina. That he'd grown up on an honest-to-goodness cotton plantation and that his family had been so poor he'd had to work in the fields from the time he was eight years old.

Upon reaching high school, though, he'd found a way out. He'd taken up boxing and discovered he was good at it, better than good. At the age of nineteen he qualified to fight at the Olympic trials. The U.S. team only sent one fighter per weight class and Levitt made it all the way to the final fight. Only to be stopped by a seventeen-year-old black kid who ended up medaling at the Olympics.

Like all good stories, there was a twist. Levitt had lost, so he said, because his opponent had oiled his gloves with a special concoction that had temporarily blinded Levitt in the second and third rounds. In effect destroying Levitt's dreams in one cruel stroke.

That part of the story might have been true because my father said that whenever Levitt talked about the fight the bitterness in his voice was so great it couldn't have been faked. Levitt had grown up in a house where blacks were not welcome—not an unusual thing in that part of the world—but after the Olympic trials Levitt had supposedly gone off the deep end. Not only had he joined the KKK, people said, he'd put his heart and soul into it and eventually worked his way up to a leadership position.

Yet now, at sixty years of age, he was our beloved principal.

Levitt called for order and the jammed gym quickly quieted down. We students were stuffed in the stands, six hundred strong. The teachers were arranged in a half circle around the podium, while the parents—there had to be at least a hundred couples—sat on cheap foldout chairs that reached to the back wall. My parents weren't present. I doubted they even knew of the meeting. I certainly hadn't told them about it.

Outside it poured but somehow the interior of the gym was stuffy. When Levitt told everyone to turn off their cells I heard a few clicking sounds but noticed that most of the students had taken the order to mean they should rearrange their phones atop their knees. As I feared, everyone was recording the meeting.

"As most of you probably know, this is no ordinary PTA meeting," Principal Levitt began in his usual raspy voice. "It wasn't scheduled until today at lunch. I called it because

Elder High is under siege. We have police, security guards, and reporters and their film crews from over two dozen TV stations—all camped out on the borders of our campus. This isn't right. This has to stop.

"How we're to solve this problem—well, usually that would be up to me to decide. But I don't want to handle it that way. What's going on here is too important to our community for one man to simply sweep it under the rug. This is America, you know, this is supposed to be a democracy. I've called you all here so we can decide together, as a town, what we should do."

Levitt paused and took a sip of water before continuing.

"By now you've all heard of Aja Smith. She's new here at Elder High. She moved here from Brazil this summer. When it comes to our students, most of you have probably met her, spoken to her. I never did see a transcript of her educational background but I was told by Mrs. Hawkins, one of our counselors, that she scored extremely high on our placement tests. So high, Mrs. Hawkins automatically put her in several AP classes. Talking about Aja with Mrs. Hawkins before the school year began, the two of us were confident she'd make a fine addition to our student body.

"Unfortunately we got off to a rocky start. Her second day in class Mrs. Billard sent her to my office to be disciplined for cheating on a test. When I asked Aja if it was true she'd cheated she said yes. When I asked her why, she didn't say a word. Nope, she just sat there staring at me. I'll admit her behavior didn't impress me. I saw her as just another lying . . ."

Levitt caught himself and changed his tone. "But maybe I'm wrong about her. I hope I'm wrong. I've got an open mind. Despite the gossip I've heard floating around, this meeting is not about putting Aja on trial. Quite the opposite. I called you all here tonight because I want to know who this young woman is and why so many of you are fascinated by her. I want to let her speak—that's only fair—and then I want to let the rest of you speak. Only when we're all done talking together . . . then we'll decide what to do. Are you with me?"

To my utter disgust many of my classmates and virtually every parent clapped. It was the parents that scared me. I knew most of them and I wasn't surprised that the more conservative ones had chosen to come out on this stormy night. In fact, I wouldn't have been surprised if Levitt had personally called and invited them.

They'd ask the questions Levitt was too smart to ask. That would spare him from having to dirty his hands.

Levitt called for Aja to stand beside a microphone he'd set directly in front of his podium. The positioning was silly. Not only was she forced to stand three feet below him—to address him directly, she'd have to twist her body around, which in turn would cause her to place her back to the stands.

I was pleased that Aja saw the problem and, without asking Levitt's permission, moved the microphone off to our right. I almost applauded.

Levitt began by offering his condolences to Aja on the loss of her "Aunt Clara." He waited for her to thank him for his kind words but she said nothing. He shrugged and went on, barely hiding his annoyance.

"Aja, I have a few questions I want to ask," he said. "I want you to swear to answer them honestly. Agreed?"

"Yes," Aja said.

Levitt continued. "A month ago in Rapid City you attended a concert where your boyfriend, Fred Allen, was performing with his band. It was at the Roadhouse beside the air force base. During the show, a riot broke out and you stopped it by supposedly healing a soldier named Dennis Krane. It's been said that you healed him of a head wound given to him by Mike Garcia, who struck the soldier on the head with a whiskey bottle. What I want to know is—is this true?"

"I don't know," Aja said.

"What don't you know?"

"I don't know if Mike really hurt him. And I don't know if a healing occurred."

"You're saying you don't know anything?"

"I know some things."

Levitt flashed a fake smile. He acted like he was dealing with a child. "Tell us what you do know," he said.

"You have a deep wound you wish you could heal."

Levitt looked startled. He took a moment to collect himself. "That's nonsense. I'm healthy as a horse. Besides, we're not talking about me. Don't change the subject."

Aja didn't respond.

"Answer my original question," Levitt said. "Did you heal Dennis Krane? Yes or no?"

"I don't know."

"How can you not know?"

"This body is like all bodies. It's limited. It's born, it grows old, it dies. It's incapable of healing anyone. But inside this body is something great—the Big Person. It's the Big Person who heals."

Many in the audience drew in a deep breath. They were listening; they were interested. A few might have heard about the Big Person before, when Aja spoke to them in private in the school courtyard. I couldn't be sure. But hearing her speak of it now—it was as if the majority of the audience sensed the power in her words. The truth.

A woman behind Levitt stood. I recognized her. It was Ted Weldon's mother. Our principal let her ask the next question.

"Are you speaking of God?" Mrs. Weldon said.

As a student I hated everything about our gym, but as a musician I had to admit the acoustics were superb. The wooden walls, softened with over a half century of wear, absorbed any and all sounds and somehow smoothed them out before reflecting them back amplified. Even without the benefit of a microphone, we could hear Mrs. Weldon's voice.

"I don't use that word," Aja said.

"Why not?" the woman asked.

"It means too many things to too many people."

Mr. Weldon stood. "Who is your God?" he asked.

Aja shrugged and said nothing.

"Is Jesus Christ your Lord and God?" Mrs. Weldon asked.

"I never met him."

"Please answer yes or no," Levitt insisted.

"No."

"So you're not a Christian?" Mr. Weldon said.

"Yes."

She'd answered a negative question with a yes, I thought. Which meant she was saying no. I doubted many noticed.

"What religion are you?" Mrs. Weldon asked.

"I don't have one," Aja said.

"Who do you worship?" Mr. Weldon asked. "Where does your power to heal come from?"

Nothing from Aja. Mrs. Weldon shook her head, unhappy. Levitt tried hard not to look smug. An old boxer, he knew he'd won the first round without even having to lay a hand on Aja.

"How do we know if she even has power?" Levitt posed the question to the audience before turning back to Aja. "Roughly two weeks after the concert in Rapid City, you went with Fred to Balen Memorial. During the night his friend, the same Mike Garcia I already mentioned, had suffered a serious head wound during a drug bust. Mike was operated on by a nationally known surgeon named Dr. Albert Rosen. Mike was on the table for ten hours and according to the nurses on staff wasn't expected to live. But he did survive—he made what some are calling a miraculous recovery." Levitt paused. "Care to comment?"

Aja remained silent.

"Did you heal him?" Levitt asked.

"The Big Person heals. But this body—with Mike—this body was involved."

"What are you saying?" Levitt said.

"It's difficult to explain with words."

"Words are all we have, child," Levitt said. "We only want to know the truth. Who helped Mike Garcia more? You or Dr. Rosen?"

"I don't know."

"They both helped save my life," Mike called out, standing up beside me. "But Aja helped me more."

"Sit down. I didn't call on you," Levitt said.

"You're talking about my head. I have a right to speak."

Levitt paused, no doubt sensing the crowd was on Mike's side. He said, "It's my understanding you were unconscious when Aja supposedly worked her magic on you. How do you know what she did?"

Mike glanced at me; I shook my head. There was no way I wanted him to bring up his near-death experience. It would take too long to explain and it would sound too fantastic.

But our gang *had* decided that since Aja refused to lie and act like an ordinary girl, then there was no point in us trying to hide her healing abilities.

"When I woke up the nurses told me what happened when Aja put her hands on my head," Mike said. "My vitals stabilized. The pressure inside my skull vanished. The nurses were the ones who said it was a miracle."

"I'm impressed," Levitt said. "But to be frank I'd be more

impressed if you hadn't been in a drug dealer's house when you got hurt."

Mike was ready for him. He addressed the crowd. "I screwed up, I admit that. But thanks to Aja, I was given another chance. I'm not going to screw up again, I promise you."

Many in the audience applauded, including the parents.

"Let's move along," Levitt said. "It's time we discussed the young girl who brought so much attention to our school. Most of you know who I'm talking about—Lisa Alastair. If we are to believe the stories that are being told, up until one week ago Lisa had a giant tumor in her head. I'm sure you've all seen the X-rays of her skull on the Internet—the 'before Aja' and 'after Aja' pictures. At first the media didn't give the story much weight, especially when Lisa's parents denied Aja had healed Lisa. But with pressure from the press the parents finally broke down and admitted their daughter had been healed by Aja. Personally, I find their flip-flopping disturbing. If Aja did in fact heal Lisa, why did they lie about it at the start?"

Dale stood on my other side. "They were trying to protect Aja."

"Dale," Levitt said. "Raise your hand if you wish to speak."

"I apologize, Mr. Levitt," Dale said. "Do I have your permission to respond?"

The principal glanced around the stands. He personally liked Dale. Everyone liked Dale. "Go ahead," he said.

Dale turned and gestured as he spoke, trying to address everyone at the same time. "Most of you know that Mike, Fred, Janet, Shelly, and I are close to Aja. From the start we knew she was special but it took us time to realize just how special. By the time we knew she could heal, we saw something else—that sometimes the miracles she worked wore her out, made her sick. For that reason we tried to protect her. We were the ones who asked Mr. and Mrs. Alastair to lie about their daughter's healing. And we were the ones who—"

"How exactly did Aja heal Lisa?" Levitt interrupted.

"Excuse me?" Dale said.

"It's my understanding Aja didn't meet with Lisa. That she only spoke with her father on the phone. So my question is—how did Aja heal someone she didn't touch? Someone she couldn't even be bothered to drive over and see?"

"Aja should probably answer that question," Dale said. "But before she does I'd like to say something I've observed about her healing. All the stuff we've seen in the movies and on TV—the laying on of hands and the staring in the eyes—none of that seems to apply to her. She just has to be told that someone's sick and that's enough for the Big Person to heal that person through her. Whether Aja meets with them or not is irrelevant."

Levitt snorted. "I find that hard to believe."

A freshman named Stacey Kataekiss jumped to her feet. "Believe it," she said. "It happened to my mother yesterday."

Levitt was taken aback. "What happened to your mother?"

Stacey went to speak but emotion got the best of her. She broke down sobbing. "I don't know," she wept. "I just know she's better."

"I know Barbara," a woman named Mrs. Evelyn Green said, standing. Beside her stood her husband, Mr. Samuel Green, holding on to the handles of a banged-up wheelchair he had maneuvered into the gym. In the chair sat a dark-haired girl around ten years old. She was spastic; she kept jerking in her seat. I didn't recognize her but I knew Mr. Green. He taught chemistry and physics at a small four-year college in Balen. The guy was a genius; he had two PhDs.

Mrs. Green was well known in Elder because of the successful florist shop she ran downtown, two doors away from city hall. I'd once bought a dozen roses from her for Nicole and she had shocked me by saying that I was wasting my time and money. That Nicole was still in love with Rick, which turned out to be true. Mrs. Green was a great one for tough love. She was also extremely religious. She headed up the choir for a large Baptist church in Balen.

Mr. and Mrs. Green's son, David, was in my physics class and was an unfortunate example of how intelligence often skipped a generation. But the girl—I had no idea who she was. Or why the Greens had brought her.

"Most of you know Barbara," Mrs. Green said. "She has multiple sclerosis. She's spent the last two years in a wheelchair. Her legs, arms, and hands—they're useless. Or I should say they *were* useless. I saw her today—after you, Stacey, appealed to Aja for help. Barbara still can't walk. Her muscles and tendons and ligaments have atrophied after being sick so long. But she's regained feeling in her arms and legs. It came back to her overnight, like a miracle." Mrs. Green paused and stared at my girlfriend. "Did you do that, Aja?"

Aja had been standing with her head bowed but now she looked up. Mrs. Green had spoken to her in a gentle tone and perhaps Aja sensed her sincerity for she looked at the woman a long time before answering.

"This body is flesh. It cannot heal other bodies."

"But this Big Person you speak of . . . can it heal?" Mrs. Green said.

"Yes."

"I'm a Christian. I've been raised to believe that Christ is the only begotten son of God. That's what the Bible says— that Jesus is the ultimate source of all true miracles. Even if a saint or prophet appears to do the healing. Are you saying the Bible's wrong?"

Aja spoke clearly, without hesitation. "People all over the world believe in their own holy books. They read them in search of wholeness. But wholeness cannot be found when you see yourself as your body. It cannot be found when you see only through your mind. True wholeness—what I call the Big Person—is beyond the mind and body."

Mrs. Green was intrigued. "So you're saying this Big Person is inside me as well as you?"

"Yes. The only difference is you call it Jesus Christ."

A sigh went through the crowd. They liked that answer. They liked when Aja said things that made them feel comfortable about their existing beliefs. But I knew my girlfriend and I knew comfort was not a priority with her. I waited for the ax to fall.

I didn't have long to wait.

"Lies!" a tall, burly gentleman in a navy blue suit shouted from the back row of the adults. It was the Reverend Todd Basken. He lived in Elder and his son went to school with the rest of us but his Pentecostal church was in Balen, where there were a hundred times more people to draw upon. He called himself "God's Todd," and he sure knew how to pack them in. He was an intense fire-and-brimstone kind of guy who loved to call on the Holy Spirit and "JESUS!!!" to get the juices flowing up and down the spines of his worshippers.

"This Big Person is not Christ!" Reverend Basken shouted. "That's blasphemy and I'm disappointed you're even listening to her, Evelyn. Now let's quit messing around and get down to it. Aja, obviously you have some kind of power. I didn't come here to label you a charlatan. But it distresses me that you don't heal in the name of God. It disturbs me even more that you refuse to call upon the name of Jesus when you heal. Why don't you? Why do the names of God and Jesus Christ frighten you so?" He stopped to shake his fist. "Tell us the truth! What is the real source of your power?"

Aja smiled. She looked as happy as a child on Christmas morning. She glanced in my direction, and I knew, I just knew, she was going to say something that would bring the house down.

"You're thinking I'm the Harlot in Revelation," Aja said.

God's Todd slapped his hands together. "Yes, by God! Are you her?"

"No. But I wish I was."

The gymnasium exploded. There was laughter, booing, hooting—close to a thousand people basically losing it. Dale and Mike just looked at me. There was nothing to say. Again, it didn't matter how serious the situation. Aja was onstage and she was playing a part. She didn't care about the consequences. The noise shook the building. It took forever before things settled down.

Reverend Basken, God's Todd, looked like the cat who had just swallowed the canary; reveling in the fact that he had exposed Aja for the demon succubus that she was. His arms were lifted high. He was thanking Jesus for helping him deliver the truth to our poor, misguided high school.

"So the truth is finally told!" he shouted from the top of his mountain as he lowered his right arm and pointed a damning finger at Aja. "Now I command you in the name of Jesus to tell us who your master is!"

The gym fell dead silent. Except for Aja.

She giggled like a little girl.

Mrs. Green walked over to Aja's microphone stand and gently gestured to Aja to stand aside. She spoke to Basken. "For heaven's sake, Todd. Don't be a goat's ass. This girl hasn't said a word against Christ or our beliefs. And she's certainly not working for the Devil."

Reverend Basken suddenly looked like he might be having a little trouble with that canary he just swallowed. Nevertheless, he managed to respond in a booming voice. "How do you know?" he demanded.

Mrs. Green quoted, "'Beware of false prophets who come to you in sheep's clothing, but inwardly are ravenous wolves. You will know them by their fruits. Grapes are not gathered from thornbushes nor figs from thistles, are they? So every good tree bears good fruit, but the bad tree bears bad fruit.'" Mrs. Green paused. "You know Barbara. You know how she's suffered. Only someone anointed by God would have the power to heal like Aja does."

God's Todd didn't have an answer for that one. But perhaps Levitt did. He spoke from atop the podium. "I disagree. We have absolutely no proof this girl has healed anyone," he said.

"Oh, shut up, William," Mrs. Green said. "We have all the proof we need. The question is how does her ability fit in with our own view of the world? That's what I'm wrestling with." Mrs. Green turned back to Aja. "Can you tell us more about this Big Person? How it came to you?"

Aja didn't respond, but she did continue to study the woman, who stood only three feet away. They were basically sharing the microphone.

"Please," Mrs. Green said. "It would help us to understand."

Aja finally nodded. "You are sincere in your search. I was very young when the change happened to me but I believe

I shared that quality with you. Keep going the way you're going. The Big Person will seek you out."

"She's saying something important," Dale whispered.

"Thank God for Mrs. Green," Mike said.

"This change—what triggered it in you?" Mrs. Green asked.

Aja shook her head. "It was years ago. It's not important. Now is what matters. Your sincerity is what's important. Keep seeking the truth and it will find you."

"But is there a way? A path?" Mrs. Green asked.

Aja considered. "I'm no teacher. I only know this—the Big Person is here now. In each and every person in this room, in an equal amount. As much as you long for it, it longs for you more. Take one step toward the Big Person and it will take a hundred steps toward you."

Did the auditorium sigh again? I was sure of it. I had never heard Aja speak with such passion. It was like the Big Person itself was speaking through her. I sensed a timelessness all around. I knew Mrs. Green felt it as well.

"May I ask a favor of you, Aja?" Mrs. Green said.

Aja waited, saying nothing.

Mrs. Green pointed to the girl in the wheelchair. "I've brought my niece here tonight, Katie. Recently her mother—my sister—died in a car accident. My husband and I have been taking care of Katie since then. As you can see, Katie is badly handicapped. She suffers from cerebral palsy. It's a different condition than Barbara has but . . . well, I was just wondering if you could help her." Her voice broke and she wiped away a tear. "God help me, I hate putting you on the spot."

Again, the auditorium fell silent.

I could have heard a pin drop. . . .

If not for the pounding of my heart.

"Your friends were worried about you. Dale was crying and Fred was struggling to figure out a way to make things better. . . . But I didn't feel any motion in the Big Person. No big fish swam by. . . . It was then this body—no, it was then Aja thought to do something to fix you."

Aja walked toward the pale, young girl who seemed to be clawing at the right side of her wheelchair. Yet Katie took note of Aja. She looked up as she approached. Maybe she saw something in her the rest of us couldn't. Aja knelt at her shriveled feet, hidden in a pair of red slippers, and a wave of relaxation went through the girl. Her clawing motion stopped. Her fingers lengthened and straightened as Aja took her hands. But then I saw Aja wince, a momentary flash of pain.

I stood. "Aja! Stop!" I cried.

Aja turned her head in my direction.

"It will be okay," I thought I heard her say. I was not reassured. I dashed onto the basketball court, wove around

Principle Levitt's stand. When I reached Aja, I literally ripped her hands off Katie. I heard a groan from the audience; I don't think many approved. But I didn't give a damn what they thought. I spoke to Mrs. Green, who stood nearby.

"Please, don't ask this," I said, my palms resting on Aja's shoulders. "Whenever Aja heals, it has to happen automatically. If she does it because you begged her to do it—it'll hurt her."

Mrs. Green looked back and forth between Aja—who continued to kneel on the auditorium floor—and Katie. The woman sighed. "Fred's right, Aja, you have to stop. Katie's hurting you."

Aja finally rose to her feet, her gaze still fixed on the girl in the wheelchair. "I can help her," she whispered.

Mrs. Green approached and took Aja's hands in hers. "I know you want to heal her, child. That's enough—that you tried. Some things are meant to be." Mrs. Green let go of Aja and touched her niece's head. "This is God's will."

I took Aja by the arm, began to pull her away. Aja stumbled right then; I feared it was because she was drained. Katie appeared to understand that Aja had improved her condition. She managed a twisted smile and Aja smiled back. Mrs. Green wiped away a tear.

As far as I was concerned the evening was over. The meeting should have ended then. Mrs. Green had turned the tide of the inquisition. Aja was an angel, a kind soul at least, she wasn't a demon. I felt Aja had proven that much. But then, I'd never understood how deeply true believers felt about their beliefs.

Macy Barnes, our student body president, raised her hand and Levitt quickly called on her. Wearing blue jeans and a thick, wool, white sweater, she stepped to the microphone on the floor, standing only a few feet off to our left. If Macy was nervous she didn't show it.

"I'm grateful Mrs. Green quoted that portion of the Bible," Macy began. "'Beware of false prophets who come to you in sheep's clothing, but inwardly are ravenous wolves. You will know them by their fruits.' Those lines have guided me throughout my life. Because I've discovered that people can say anything—it doesn't matter whether they're young or old. They can promise you anything. Listening to Aja's deeds, it sounds like she can promise a lot. A friend of hers hits a soldier over the head with a whiskey bottle. No problem, Aja is there to fix the man. The same friend gets caught in a drug bust—a bust where he was buying drugs to sell at our school. Again, no problem, Aja heals his head and he walks out of the hospital—and out of the courtroom—a few days later. Like he's done nothing wrong." Macy paused. "I'm sorry, I have a problem with that."

"Why?" someone shouted from the top bleachers.

Macy nodded. "That's a fair question. Most of what Aja has done has seemed—on the surface—to be wonderful. She's healed the sick and she's handed out sound life advice. But when I study how she conducts her own life I have to wonder if any of us should be listening to her. Let's take the example of what happened at Benny's a week ago. Benny's is an expensive restaurant in Balen. Friends of my parents were dining there that night and told me what happened. I have a word-for-word transcript of what was said." Macy held up a piece of paper. "A couple walked up to Aja and Fred—you all know Fred—while they were eating dessert. The woman was distraught. She tried to tell Aja about her sick daughter, Keko, who had leukemia. Fred got annoyed and told her to leave them alone. The woman persisted—she told them her daughter was dying. That she had only two or three months to live. Again, Fred told them to go away. Aja didn't say anything. The woman pulled out a picture of her daughter and placed it on the table. She begged Aja to look at Keko. Finally, Aja picked up the picture and said, and I quote, 'Her body is very tired. It will be okay.' Instantly, the woman was overcome with relief. She thought Aja was giving her hope. She was so excited she cried, 'Keko's going to live?' Then Aja said flatly, 'No.' Just no."

Macy stopped to glare at Aja. "I don't know if any of us can imagine the agony that woman felt at that instant. It's true she struck Aja right then. But let's be honest—can any of us blame her?"

"The woman shouldn't have hit her!" a student called out.

Macy nodded. "I agree. Aja was under no obligation to heal Keko. But couldn't she have treated the woman with a modicum of compassion? And make no mistake—the woman didn't really hurt Aja. I know because the friends of my parents who were at Benny's were spending the night at the Hilton in Balen. Guess who happened to be in the room beside them? Aja and Fred. I'd rather not go into detail but from the noise the two of them made we can safely assume Aja was feeling no pain."

The audience laughed. I forced a smile to show I got the joke. But I could feel my face burning. Did no one in the crowd stop and ask themselves what a coincidence it was that the couple who was watching at the restaurant just happened to be in the room next to us at the hotel? I wanted to step to the microphone and shout out that we'd been followed but the way Macy was watching me I could tell that was exactly what she was hoping I'd do.

"Like Principal Levitt, I'm a Christian," Macy continued. "I know many of you here are. As I said at the start, I look to the Bible to guide me in life. I try to treat others the way I want to be treated. I do my best to live as I believe Christ would want me to live. That's not to say I try to model my daily life after Christ. I know that would be impossible. I just do the best I can. But studying Aja from a distance I have to ask myself if she does the same. Why does she give so much help to a guy who deals in drugs? Why couldn't she comfort Keko's mother even a little bit? Did Keko mean nothing to her because she was Japanese? Or was Aja distracted because she was anxious to check into the hotel with Fred? I asked myself these questions when I was waiting in line in our courtyard for a chance to speak to Aja. After hearing so much about her power, I thought it only fair that I talk to her face-to-face."

Macy turned and again glared at Aja. "But you know what Aja told me? Nothing. It didn't matter what I asked. It didn't matter how sincere my questions were. She wouldn't give me the time of day. It was like I meant nothing to her." Macy paused. "Admit it, Aja, you blew me off."

Aja just stared at her, silent, unblinking.

The fact that she'd been unable to goad Aja appeared to annoy Macy. She pointed an angry finger at Aja, raised her voice. "I think the jury's still out on you! Like Reverend Basken, I still have grave doubts about where your power comes from!"

Macy was a performer. That's how she'd gotten elected

student body president. She knew when to make her exit. She did it right then, stepping away from the microphone and striding triumphantly back to her seat. I was stunned, and depressed, to hear more than a few people applaud.

Principal Levitt spoke from the podium. "Thank you, Macy, for your insightful words. For my part I think you made more sense than anyone else who spoke tonight. Now I think it's time we—"

"Excuse me, Mr. Levitt, I have something important to add," Mrs. Billard called out. Levitt turned suspiciously in her direction.

"What is it?" he asked.

"My Aja story. I want to tell it."

Levitt appeared uncertain. "Really, Nancy, it's getting late and I think we should decide—"

"We're not deciding anything until I speak," Mrs. Billard interrupted, stepping past us, toward the podium. "And you're not going to stop me."

I wanted to stop her. And I would have if I didn't fear it would make Aja and me look like we had something to hide. Yet I knew Mrs. Billard's intentions were noble.

Bless her brave heart, she was going to tell the same story she had told me in the cemetery. The tale of how her two-year-old son, Barney, had died in a car accident and the lie she had spread that had eventually forced her husband, Stan, to leave Elder. I knew her story would serve as a powerful antidote to Macy's big speech, especially when she came to the part where Aja gave her the eleven-worded line beside the grave of her son.

Yet I feared what the telling might do to Mrs. Billard.

I wasn't alone.

Mrs. Green stepped forward and stopped her.

She stopped Mrs. Billard in front of the microphone. They spoke fast and furiously but they kept their voices low and I wasn't able to hear a word. I don't know if anyone did. But it was apparent to me that Mrs. Green knew of Mrs. Billard's deep dark secret and wanted it kept secret. I felt a wave of relief when Billard finally stopped arguing with her old friend and allowed Mrs. Green to escort her back to her seat. Levitt himself looked relieved.

"All right," Levitt said. "It's time we decide what to do with Aja. The choice is a simple one. Do we allow her to remain a student here at Elder High, and put up with police and reporters and guards at our door for the remainder of the year? Or do we expel her and go back to the way things were before she moved here? The members of the PTA will now vote on this matter. And I promise you the way they vote will guide me as I make my final decision."

So much for democracy in America, I thought.

Principal Levitt had already decided to expel her.

"No," Aja said firmly, standing beside me.

"What did you say, young lady?" Levitt said.

Aja strode to the microphone stand beneath the podium. "There'll be no vote until I've had a chance to defend myself," she said.

"What do you think you've been doing all night?"

"Answering other people's questions," Aja said.

"Let her speak!" someone shouted from the top of the bleachers. He was soon joined by others, tons of students, all shouting for Aja to be given a chance to speak. Levitt shrugged and said, "All right, I'll give you a few minutes. Talk away."

"Come down from the podium and join me," Aja said.

"Why?" Levitt asked.

"The Big Person wishes to heal you. Come."

Levitt grinned. "It'd be a waste of time. Like I told you at the start, I'm healthy as a horse."

"Then you have nothing to fear. Come."

"Fine," Levitt said, acting as though he was indulging a difficult child. He stepped down from the podium and stood beside Aja and the microphone stand. "Are you going to put a spell on me?" he joked.

"Let me see your palms," Aja said, offering her own hands.

The suggestion shook him, more than it should have.

"Why?" he asked.

"Give them to me," she said.

Levitt resisted, for a moment, then gave in. I wasn't sure if he had a choice. "What are you doing?" he asked as she began to trace the lines on his palms with her nails. I was perhaps a dozen feet away.

"Helping you remember," she said.

"Remember what? I don't need your help."

"Shh. You've done this before. It works for you. It worked for her."

"Who?"

"You remember." Aja caught his eye. "Now close your eyes."

"No. I don't want—"

"Close them."

Levitt closed his eyes, breathing heavily.

Aja continued to stroke his palms and stare at his face. "Tell me about May," she said.

Levitt shook; the tremor went through his whole body. But he didn't take back his hands or open his eyes. "Last May? Why? Nothing special happened then."

"I'm not talking about the month. I'm talking about May."

He shook his head. "No."

"It's hard, I know. It hurts to talk about her. But you'll

feel better if you do." Aja added, "It's your choice."

He kept trembling. "No! You're not giving me a choice."

"But I am. You can let go of my hands right now."

"How do you know about May? Why do you bring her up?"

"Because thinking about her is hurting you."

"I don't care. I can live with it."

"Yes, you can. That's one choice. Or you can make another choice. One that will stop the pain."

"I can't talk about her in front of all these people!"

Aja let go of his hands; they continued to hang in midair.

"Okay," she said. "We don't have to talk about her."

Aja turned her back on him. For his part, Levitt looked as if he'd been hit with a train. His eyes were still closed and he was shaking badly.

Aja stood silent for several seconds, her head bowed. Then she turned toward Levitt again. She took a step closer, went up on her toes, and whispered something in his ear. Whatever it was, Levitt nodded, and Aja reached out and turned off the microphone. The sound system went dead. The audience stirred restlessly. They didn't like being excluded. Neither did I, actually; I stepped closer.

Aja turned and faced our principal. "Let us begin," she said softly. Except for me and Levitt, I doubted another person in the auditorium could have heard her.

Levitt suddenly looked weary, confused. In the space of two minutes she had disarmed him. "I don't understand how this can help me."

What was *this*? I wondered.

Was it Aja's healing? Or was it May?

Aja took back his hands and returned to tracing the lines on his palms. No surprise, I knew exactly how her nails felt as they dug into his skin. Aja spoke in a gentle tone.

"In this world your conscience is like a whisper in the mind. Soft and wise, it's always there, always guiding you. But should you fail to listen—in the next world it sounds like thunder." Aja paused. "What does that whisper tell you about May?"

Levitt groaned, spoke faintly. "I should never have denied she was mine."

"Go on."

"I was afraid people would talk. I was afraid what they'd say if they saw me with her mother."

"Angie," Aja said.

Levitt drew in a deep shuddering breath. "Yes. I loved her and her daughter."

"Your daughter."

"Yes. But I never got to . . ." He didn't finish.

"You never got to tell her that."

"Yes."

"Why don't you tell her now?"

"You don't understand. I can't. It's too late."

"May died?" Aja said.

"Yes. I can never tell her anything, ever again."

"That's not true. Tonight, you'll have a chance to tell Angie how you feel. And in the future, you'll see your daughter again." Aja paused. "Now open your eyes."

Levitt opened his eyes, wiping at the unexpected tears on his face. He looked dazed. His raspy voice sounded like the gasp of a dying man.

"How did you know?" he said.

"Talk to Angie." Aja turned and gestured to someone I couldn't see at first, not until she stepped free of the crowd at the rear of the gym. It was the black woman in the blue gown I'd met on the bench in the park. Tonight she wore a white dress. Seeing her, Levitt almost fainted. Aja had to grab his arm to keep him upright. But then the woman, Angela, was hugging our principal and Aja was able to let go. The audience watched rapt, silent, overwhelmed. They had not heard what had transpired at the end but it didn't matter. The sight of the two embracing was what counted.

Aja turned toward the door and walked out of the gym.

It was her moment; I just watched her go.

The PTA meeting was over.

CHAPTER SEVENTEEN

MY MIND REELED AS I DROVE OUT OF THE school parking lot. Naturally I was happy Aja had ended on such a positive note. Yet I wasn't sure exactly what had happened. Had Aja spoken to Angela before the meeting? Had the healing of Levitt's emotional wound been partially staged? For the life of me I couldn't imagine Aja planning such an act ahead of time to impress the crowd. The girl was so spontaneous it was a wonder she remembered to wake up in the morning. Nor did she give a hoot what other people thought about her. Also, when she had turned off the microphone, she had gone out of her way to protect Levitt's privacy, despite the fact the two of them had been standing in front of a large crowd.

No, I told myself, Aja would never have set out to con anyone at the PTA meeting.

Yet she had known things about Levitt she shouldn't have known. It had seemed . . . well, like another miracle. I suppose it was odd that I found her insights more difficult to accept than her healings. It was easier for me to grant the Big Person infinite power but harder to accept that it was all-knowing.

Before I drove out to Aja's place, I decided to swing by Janet's house one last time. Mindy Paulson had shaken me up. She had acted like Janet's situation was obvious and I was a fool not to see it. I didn't like playing the part of the fool. I'd made up my mind I wasn't leaving Janet's front door until her father opened it. I'd kick it in if I had to.

As it turned out I only knocked once before Bo answered. Maybe he was weary of playing hide-and-seek. From the miserable look on his face he was clearly exhausted. He let me in without a word and I followed him into the living room, where we had watched so many football and baseball games together. A corner lamp was the only source of illumination; otherwise, the room was filled with shadows. He had a bottle of Jim Beam in hand and wordlessly offered me a drink but I shook my head. He took a deep slug and sighed, plopping down on a chair. I sat on the sofa across from him.

"How did the meeting go?" he asked.

"Aja blew them away. I doubt she'll be expelled."

"Huh."

He fell silent, staring at a nearby framed picture of Janet, her mother, and Bo. I'd seen it a hundred times but had never given it much thought. The photograph was probably ten years old. Janet looked about eight years old and Mrs. Cynthia Shell was smiling radiantly, along with her husband.

Was Bo drinking because he was dreaming of the good old days? I'd never understood fully why their marriage had crumbled. All I knew was that Cynthia hadn't met her present husband until after she'd left Bo and moved to New York. Back then Janet had split town with her mother, only to return a year later. At the time Janet had said she had come back because she missed her friends—me in particular. But I'd always wondered if there was more to the story than that.

"Is Janet still in New York?" I asked.

"As far as I know."

"She's not answering her cell. I've left a dozen messages."

"I know the feeling."

"I'm sure you do. Just like I'm sure you know why she left."

Bo stared at me with bloodshot eyes. "It's none of your business."

"Don't give me that shit. Your daughter's my best friend. I have a right to know what's going on."

Bo snorted and took another hit of the bottle. "Ask that bitch you're sleeping with. I'm sure she'll tell you whatever you want to know."

His choice of words shocked me.

"Why are you calling Aja a bitch?" I snapped.

"What do you want me to call her? She's the one who stirred up this whole mess."

I pondered his choice of words. *Stirred.* He was implying that Aja had brought up something from Janet's past, or from his past. I shouldn't have been surprised. I'd just witnessed Aja's miraculous ability to pluck buried sins and old scars out of the ether.

Bo returned to staring at the photograph of his once joyful family. There was something wrong with the image that my gut sensed but my eyes couldn't see. What was it? The trio looked so textbook happy the picture could have been used as a poster to advertise a new sitcom.

"Whatever Aja tells someone in private, she keeps private," I said. "She won't tell me anything about Janet."

"Well, bless her heart. She should write the Pope in Rome and ask if he can make an exception and ordain her as Elder's next priest. Then she can hear all our confessions."

I stood. "You know, if you weren't drunk right now I'd beat the shit out of you."

Bo tried smiling but it ended up closer to a grimace. He drank again. "Don't let the old bottle hold you back, Fred. I can drain it to the last drop and still kick your ass any day of the week."

"Like you kicked Janet's ass?"

He winced at my remark and I knew I'd hit a nerve. But I'd just been fishing. Except that it was something painful, I had no idea what the nerve was connected to. His reply didn't help.

"I suppose," he said.

"You didn't beat your daughter. You wouldn't have done that."

He nodded, more to himself, and began to lean forward in his frumpy chair, coming close to falling out of it. I noticed he had tears on his face. He couldn't stop looking at the framed picture. I took a step closer.

"Bo, come on, talk to me. I can help."

"You can't help. It's not something that can be fixed." He coughed before adding, "Or forgotten."

Stirred. Forgotten. He was definitely talking about something that had happened in the past, something that Aja had awakened in her contact with Janet. And the photograph appeared to remind him of that something. Yet, except for their exaggerated gaiety, I couldn't see what Mindy had told me was so obvious. . . .

Frustrated, I took three long steps across the room and snatched the photograph off the table beside Bo's chair. The move took him by surprise; it angered him. Dropping his bottle, he tried to snatch it back. But I held it out of his reach. I looked at it, I studied it. Boy, did I scan it inch by inch.

Finally, I saw something odd.

Cynthia had always been somewhat of a distant person. She was smart and extremely organized. She'd worked full-time as an accountant in Balen—she actually made more money than Bo—and still managed to keep a tidy home. She wasn't greedy; she splurged on her daughter. Whatever Janet wanted her mom bought her. No one would have said the woman was cold. At the same time, no one would have said she was overly affectionate.

Cynthia was definitely not the type to smother her daughter in kisses, not like Janet's dad. That's why it hadn't surprised me when I'd first looked at the picture that it was Bo who had his arm wrapped around Janet's waist, while her mother had an arm on Bo's shoulder but wasn't touching Janet. Nothing about the positioning was unusual, at least given my memories of Cynthia.

But what was strange was the hint of uneasiness in Janet's expression. She was smiling for the camera; her bright teeth sparkled in the old-fashioned flash. Yet there was a darkness in her eyes, a tension buried in her body, that told me she disliked her father holding her. Going more by my gut than my eyesight, it almost looked as if she was trying to pull away from him even as he struggled to pull her closer.

In that instant a thousand pieces of a puzzle I hadn't known existed fit together in my mind and I understood everything.

Why Janet had left Bo when her mother had left.

Why, to this day, Janet jumped at every excuse to leave home.

Why Janet was uncomfortable accepting a car from Bo.

Why Bo was no longer affectionate with Janet.

Why Janet never went out on dates.

Why Janet had spoken to Aja and then fled to New York.

And why Janet was so desperate to find peace of mind.

I dropped the photograph, hearing the glass frame shatter on the wooden floor, and cocked my fist back. All I could think about was breaking every bone in his face.

"You bastard!" I swore. "You molested her!"

"No! I never touched her!"

"Liar!"

"It was nothing!"

I reached out and grabbed him by the throat, yanked him to his feet. "You filthy sonofabitch!" I yelled. "Admit it!"

"No!" he moaned, choking under the pressure of my clenched fingers.

"Admit it or I'll break your goddamn neck!"

His face began to turn blue. "I can't . . . Fred, I can't breathe."

I released him but didn't back away. "The truth! Tell me the truth!"

He gasped for breath as tears streamed down his face.

"It was a long time ago! I made a mistake! I didn't mean to hurt her! I love her!" His head dropped as sobs shook his body. "I'm sorry!"

I left the house. I made myself leave.

I was afraid if I stayed I would have killed him.

When I reached Aja's house she told me she had good news. She said Mr. Richard Gratter from Paradise Records had called and wanted to fly me out to LA to meet with him Wednesday morning. I was horrified.

"That's two days from now," I said, my heart still pounding from my encounter with Bo. "I'm not done fixing my demo. I can't go."

"The demo doesn't matter. They're flying you out to LA to hear you sing. That's what Aunt Clara set up for you. A live audition." She paused. "What's the matter?"

"Nothing."

"You're breathing rapidly."

"I'm fine." Like I was going to spoil her happy mood by telling her I'd almost just killed a man I'd looked up to my whole life. I spoke quickly to hide what I was really feeling. "A personal audition doesn't make sense. These guys are professionals. They see a hundred guys like me a week. I'm a nobody."

"You must be somebody. They've seen Casey Morall's recording of you and Half Life playing at the Roadhouse. They told me you have what it takes to front a band."

"You really talked to them?"

"Yes."

"Well, that's nonsense. Casey only posted the part where you stopped the riot and healed the soldier Mike hit on the head."

"You forget. Casey showed you singing for at least a minute before the riot started."

"Oh, wow. One whole minute," I said.

"A star is born in a second." She smiled as she put her palm on my chest. "You're excited, admit it."

"A part of me's excited. A bigger part of me is scared shitless." I stopped and shook my head. "This isn't the time to try to score a record deal. Too much is going on. There's a lot we have to talk about. Tonight's meeting. The reason Janet flew to New York. I'm worried—"

"Shh," Aja interrupted, kissing me briefly with her incredible lips. "Forget all that. Tomorrow we're flying to LA. We'll stay overnight in a big hotel with a big hot tub and order room service. The next day you'll meet with the record company and knock their socks off." She kissed me again. "You've dreamed about this all your life. Now it's time to live your dream."

The very idea of chasing after a fantasy when I knew Janet was struggling and needed my help should have stopped me cold. Somehow, though, holding Aja in my arms, I no longer felt a compulsion to fix the situation. A peace settled over me as she hugged me. We had our clothes on. We were not making love. Yet I felt so close to her right then I could have been inside her. A gentle voice seemed to speak inside my head.

The world will turn just fine without your help.

CHAPTER EIGHTEEN

THE TRIP TO LA WAS DIFFICULT. AFTER CHECK-
ing plane reservations, we realized the best route was to
take Sioux Falls to Denver to LAX. A pity Sioux Falls was a
four-hour drive from Elder. And with the security measures
in place, which demanded we get to the airport two hours
before our flight, we ended up leaving Elder at three in the
morning. Aja didn't mind. While I drove, she slept the whole
way across half the state.

Our layover in Denver was three hours. I was exhausted
by the time we got to LA. But Sleeping Beauty was full of
energy. After we checked into the Century Plaza, the hotel
Paradise Records had booked for us, Aja wanted to go to
Disneyland.

"The sun sets in two hours," I said after calling my parents to tell them that we had arrived safely. They already knew about the audition and were beyond excited. I continued. "We can go tomorrow, after the meeting with Richard Gratter. If you want."

Aja was walking around our two-room suite, checking out all the nice touches. She'd already eaten the heart-shaped chocolates the maids had left on our pillows and raided the minibar for a ginger ale.

"I want what you want," she said.

"Gimme a break. You may have the Big Person in your head but I think I know you pretty well by now. You have your likes and dislikes like everyone else."

Aja stopped to stare at me. "I like what you like. That's it."

"Are you saying you honestly don't have any personal desires?"

"Yes."

"That's not true. Those chocolates you just ate—you liked them."

"I did. They were wonderful."

"Then what are you saying?"

"That I enjoy everything."

"Every minute of every day?" I asked.

"Yes."

"But you're with me. You chose to be with me. Surely you

must get at least a little extra pleasure being with me than, say, Mike or Dale."

"I love being with you. I love you."

She had never told me that before. It was silly how much the three little words meant to me. Or maybe it wasn't so silly. Every poet, every songwriter in history, was forever trying to convey how magical those words could be. I shouldn't have been surprised when my heart beat faster.

But I was surprised I'd never said the words to her.

"I love you," I said.

She smiled. "That makes me happy."

I should have quit while I was ahead.

"But my question remains—do I make you happier than you usually are?"

Aja shook her head. "I can't answer that question. It has no meaning to me. I . . ." She struggled for words. "There is no Aja. How can there be when I don't have an 'I'?"

"You have no individuality at all?"

"Not as you understand it."

"But you've said that at certain times, like when you healed Mike, you acted as an individual. That's why you got sick."

"For moments, especially when I'm with you, I'm not just the Big Person. But even if a glimpse of what it means to be

'Fred's girlfriend' comes, the Big Person still dominates." She stopped. "I'm sorry. I've upset you."

"No," I lied. She loved me, great, but she didn't exist, not as a human being. How was I supposed to take that? "It's just hard to imagine what it's like being you. Can you describe your moment-to-moment state? In a way a Little Person like me can understand?"

She considered before switching to a wicked smile. She pointed to the suite's bathtub. It wasn't technically a Jacuzzi but it was big enough to fit several couples and it had water jets.

"Later," she said. "I'm having one of those 'Fred's girl-friend' moments. Let's take advantage of it."

Hours later, after we'd made love, ordered room service, eaten more than our fill, we lay in bed watching a movie neither of us cared about. It was then my cell rang. It was Janet; I wasn't surprised. I'd called earlier and left a message on her voice mail: *"I know what Bo did."*

"So Aja couldn't keep her mouth shut," Janet said. "I should have known she'd talk."

"Aja never said a word. I figured it out on my own."

"Right. After all these years you suddenly had a flash of inspiration."

"Talk to Bo if you don't believe me."

Janet snickered. "That ain't going to happen."

I sat up in bed, Aja watching me.

"Are you saying you're not coming back?" I asked.

Janet was a long time answering. "I can't."

"That's crazy. You've got to finish out the school year. You can stay at my house. My parents would love to have you."

Again, she took forever to respond. "No. Then everyone would know. And that's the last thing . . ." She struggled to speak. "I hate that you know. I hate how you must see me now."

"Janet, you did nothing wrong."

"Didn't I?"

"Janet . . ."

"I have to go. I'll call you."

"Wait!"

She hung up. Feeling sad, I tossed my cell aside. "I know you have a strict privacy policy when it comes to those who come to you for help. But since I already know what's hurting Janet I was wondering if we could talk about it."

Aja took my hand. "You feel for her."

"What I feel like is a fool. That Bo sexually molested her and I didn't know. Especially when all the signs were right in front of me."

"It happened when she was young."

I felt awkward. "Do you know exactly what happened?"

"Yes."

"Did she tell you or do you . . . just know?"

"I just know."

I shook my head. "Damn that Bo. Walking around like he's the greatest dad in the world. Like nothing in the world means more to him than his daughter. I can't believe I fell for his act."

"It wasn't an act. He loves her."

"How can you say that? Do you know what that kind of abuse can do? It can wreck a person for life." I stopped. "I feel like killing him. I'm not joking—I've been thinking about it. Sneaking into his house at night, knocking him out, driving him out to the country, burying him alive. Pretty sick, huh?"

"You're not a violent person."

"I wouldn't bet on that."

"Hurting Bo won't help Janet."

I looked at her. "Can you help her?"

"Not now."

"Why not?"

"She doesn't want my help."

"I thought that's why she spoke to you about her father."

"It was."

"Oh, I get it. Janet was too proud to ask for your help. That's no surprise."

"No. She asked."

"What did you tell her?"

"Nothing."

"Nothing?"

Aja squeezed my hand. "Words cannot heal Janet."

"Can the Big Person?"

Naturally, I waited for Aja to say yes. Hadn't she told us again and again the Big Person could do anything? But she remained silent.

Paradise Records sent a limo to pick us up. Their headquarters were in Beverly Hills, fifteen minutes from the hotel. A pretty blonde met us at the entrance and escorted us to Richard Gratter's office—a corner suite with floor-to-ceiling windows. It was a clear day and we could see the ocean.

The boss kept us waiting. But he sent along two VPs to keep us from bolting: Marc Kroff, who was in charge of marketing; and Jimmy Hurt, who focused on finding new talent. Jimmy told me at the start he'd loved my demo and the footage of Half Life playing at the Roadhouse.

"The sound quality wasn't very good on the video," I said.

"Who gives a damn about that?" Jimmy said. "You had

the audience eating out of the palm of your hand."

"Thanks. Our band is pretty tight."

"Your band is okay and they'll always be only okay," Marc said. "It's important you understand that up front. You have the voice, you have the looks. And it's our understanding you write all the original material you play?"

So much for Paradise signing the whole band.

"That's true." I fiddled nervously with the jump drive in my hands. "I brought a new demo. I improved the first three songs and added a fourth."

"Save it for when Richard gets here," Jimmy said.

"Did he hear the original demo?" I asked lamely.

Marc smiled. "I can say yes if that will help you relax."

Richard—Mr. Gratter—walked in half an hour later. Because he'd been close to Clara and her husband, I'd assumed he'd be old. But he appeared to be an incredibly fit fifty. His brown hair was long and stringy with streaks of gray. He wore his shirt open to show off his Hollywood tan; it looked like he'd gotten it during a partial eclipse. He had a friendly smile but his gray eyes were as cold as coins. He said all the right things but I could tell he was a bottom-line kind of guy. If I signed a deal with his company and didn't make money on my first record there wouldn't be a second one.

"I hear you have a demo," Richard said finally, settling

into a seat behind a huge desk. "How long is it?"

I stood and handed it over. "Sixteen minutes, four songs. The last one might be the strongest."

"Why didn't you put it first?" Jimmy asked.

"Because I'm from South Dakota," I said.

The three of them thought that was funny and laughed. Richard slipped the jump drive into his computer and turned up the volume. The demo started with "Rose," which had always been a favorite with our audiences. It was a basic love song about a guy who's getting rejected. As it played, none of the executives looked too impressed.

The next two numbers were rock ballads. They started with me on acoustic guitar before the drums and electric guitars upped the amps. By the time song number three was done I knew I was finished. Richard was staring out the window and Jimmy and Marc were looking anywhere but at me. It didn't matter if the two VPs liked the demo. If their boss didn't, I was out the door. The only ammunition I had left was "Strange Girl." I closed my eyes as it started to play. I felt sick to my stomach.

Strange girl
Where did you come from?
Where have you been?

Strange one
You're so full of secrets
I can't see within

Strange girl
You move so softly
Across the stage
My eyes can't leave you
I'm hiding backstage
You're a closed book
I can't read a page

Strange girl
Where did you come from?
Where have you been?
Strange one
You're so full of secrets
I can't see within

Girl, it's okay
If I can't solve your riddle
As long as you stay
My heart feels troubled
You're slipping away

Strange girl
I'm just your lover
Who'll never discover
What you keep covered
Hidden inside . . .

The song ended and the room was silent. Aja nudged me and I opened my eyes. Jimmy and Marc were smiling. Richard was still staring at the sea but slowly he turned his chair in my direction and I saw he was laughing.

"Shit! That was brilliant," Richard said.

I shrugged. "I like to think so."

Richard leaped from his chair. He began to pace. "I want to get that song out before Christmas season. I can put you with a young producer Jimmy found. The guy's a genius— he'll get what you're doing. Name's—what's his name?"

"Ralph Varanda," Jimmy said.

"Yeah, Ralph," Richard said. "He'll rework your song a million different ways but don't let that scare you. The guy's obsessed with having tons of shit to mix. It's just a process he goes through." He paused. "You got an agent? A lawyer?"

"No." I patted Aja's arm. "But I've got a cool girlfriend."

Richard liked that. For the first time he checked Aja out. "I bet you're the one who inspired that song."

Aja smiled but didn't reply.

Richard frowned on top of his smile. "Hey, you look familiar. Wait, you're not that chick they're talking about on YouTube? The sexy healer?"

"This is her," I said. "She's a strange girl."

Richard stabbed a finger toward us. "Perfect! We'll put her in the video with you. We'll have her heal someone on camera. The public will love it."

I frowned. "I don't know if that's a good idea."

"Why not?" Richard said.

"Aja, she's kind of shy," I said.

Richard studied Aja. "Think about it," he said.

"I don't—" I began.

Marc stepped forward, interrupting. "Fred, for us to do a deal fast you need to get representation. I can recommend a dozen agents you can speak to. Just be sure to choose the one you trust the most. And we'll need you back here within ten days. Ralph has a break then. It'll be a perfect time to put you two together in the studio. How does that sound?"

I stood, pulling Aja to her feet.

"It sounds wonderful," I said.

That night, an hour after turning out the lights in our hotel room, I found myself sitting in a chair by the window looking out at the city lights. Except for a trip to Honolulu with my parents when I was a kid, I'd never been to a major city before. The size of LA staggered me, and the fact that it was after midnight and the streets were still busy with cars and pedestrians. Back home, even on the weekends, it was hard to buy a cup of coffee after eleven.

Of course I gazed at LA with rose-colored glasses. I'd just arrived and already it was offering to make me a star. It seemed too good to be true, which made me worry that it wasn't true. I knew enough about the business to know that even if Paradise Records recorded "Strange Girl" and brought it out right away there was no guarantee it would hit the charts and change my life. Ninety percent of songs died the week they were released. A contract for one song meant nothing, I told myself.

Aja stirred in bed. "Can't sleep?" she asked, her voice drowsy.

"I'm fine. Go back to sleep."

She pulled herself up on her pillow. "You're worried your dream is still a dream?"

"You reading my mind?"

"I read it once when I met you. That was enough."

I had to smile. "Then you know I'm afraid to be happy."

Aja yawned. "All human beings are afraid to be happy."

"We are. How come you're not? What makes you so special?"

Aja sat up all the way. "I'm not human."

"Are you an alien?"

"I told you yesterday, I'm no one."

"And that lets you be everyone?"

"Yes."

"You know, I don't think it will matter how long we're together. I'll never really know you."

"Is that a bad thing? You love mystery novels. You told me it's your favorite genre, along with science fiction."

I stood, wearing only a bathrobe, and walked toward the bed, sitting on the side. I took her hand. "I love a mystery story I can solve. But you and your Big Person—you keep saying you're beyond words. What kind of story could anyone write about you when all he or she has to work with are words?"

Aja stroked my hand. "You write about love in your songs. And love is every bit as mysterious as the Big Person."

"Is that true?" I asked.

"Yes. If you were forced to label the Big Person, you could call it absolute love."

I leaned over and kissed her forehead. "So you're love incarnate?"

"Yes."

"You love everyone equally?"

"Yes."

"And yet you love me more?"

"Yes."

"Now you're contradicting yourself."

"Who cares?" She lifted my hand and kissed my fingers. "Talking about the Big Person always leads to paradoxes. That's why I took so long to tell you about it."

I stroked her hair and gazed into her eyes, which reflected the colored lights of the city outside our window. I felt so much love for her right then I feared I would explode.

"Tell me what you are experiencing right now," I said.

"I wish I could."

"You say the Big Person is infinite. Are you infinite this second?"

"Yes."

"Are you bigger than this world?"

"Yes."

"The solar system?"

"Yes."

"What's it like, Aja? Tell me?"

She gestured to the window, to the few faint stars visible above the glow of the city. "The stars are all there, inside me. And the whirlpool of a million galaxies—they float inside the ocean of love that gave birth to them and to me. When I became no one, when I dropped the silly idea that I was limited to a body and a mind, I became that ocean. I see the stars backward and forward in time. I see them being born. I see the worlds circling them. The people living on them. And I see them dying at the end of time, only to be reborn again."

I was beyond astounded. What she was saying was impossible. That was clear. No human being could experience what she was describing. But what was even more clear was that she was not exaggerating. I felt it as she spoke. Her words had the naked power of truth.

"Tell me about the creatures on other worlds," I said.

Aja grew thoughtful; her gaze turned inward.

"Some look like us, most look very different. No two worlds are exactly alike. But every world, no matter how alien or strange, is part of a vast mosaic that floats on an ocean of love. Here I'm only talking about the physical worlds. There are dimensions beyond those you can see with your eyes. There are the realms of the gods, the lands of the demons, the vast kingdoms of the angels. All these places are spoken about in ancient scriptures but somehow people have forgotten that they're true."

"What are angels like? Have you ever spoken to one?"

Aja grinned. "I'm talking to one now."

"What do you mean?"

"You were an angel before you were born as a human."

"Really? Were all people?"

She shook her head. "The people on this world come from so many different places. It's the reason it's so hard for them to get along with each other. But when it comes to angels—there are only a few on earth." She took my hand and pressed it to her heart. "You're one of them."

"If I'm an angel why am I so horny all the time?"

Aja laughed. "There's nothing the angels love more than love. That's what makes you such a hopeless romantic. That's why you were so quick to chase after me."

"Because as an angel I recognized you were a goddess?"

I meant it as a joke. But she nodded.

I went to speak, to ask another question, to take advantage of what was clearly a rare opportunity to get her to talk about herself. But I could think of nothing to say. Not only could I not find the words, I couldn't find the thoughts. It was as if my mind was a candle she had blown out with the staggering admission of what she was.

Aja pulled off my robe and pulled me into bed. We didn't make love, not again, but she held me inside a living image of what she had described. I saw other worlds. I saw angels and demons. But most of all I sensed all around me the ocean of love she had told me was beyond the worlds. It was inside as well as outside. It just was, forever and ever.

And I knew I was nothing but a child standing on the

shore of that ocean, carefully dipping my toes into the water before dashing away each time a foaming wave washed ashore. All the time, though, I realized Aja was the sea; and no matter how much I loved her, and no matter how much I wanted to believe she was mine, she would forever remain the sea. While I would have to wait until the child in me was old enough and wise enough to dive into the ocean and to swim out to where she lived. Beyond the stars, beyond the worlds, beyond time.

It was so wonderful and yet so tragic. Where I stood was limited. Where she existed was unlimited. There were tides in her ocean that ebbed and flowed. An unexpected prompting had brought her to Elder and into my life. The pull of another current could take her away, to places I could only imagine.

Aja may have been able to hold on to me, but I would never be able to hold on to her. As I drifted off to sleep in her arms, I felt sorrow amid my joy. A faint and yet distinct foreboding that our time together would soon come to an end.

CHAPTER NINETEEN

BUT ALL THAT WAS FORGOTTEN WHEN WE FLEW home the following day.

There were two reasons.

Early in the morning, the producer Richard Gratter had mentioned, Ralph Varanda, called at the hotel and told me to meet him at his studio in Malibu. Apparently he had an unexpected opening in his schedule.

Again, Paradise Records sent a limo for us. Upon arriving at the studio Ralph handed me a guitar and asked me to play "Strange Girl" alone, without backup. So with a massive microphone in front of my mouth and an unfamiliar guitar in hand, I sang with only acoustic chords to back up my voice.

If my demo was good this was better.

It may have been the superb acoustics of the studio. I'd

never sung in a room where my voice sounded so rich. Or perhaps my swelling confidence lent a fresh potency to my voice. Just knowing that the song was going to be recorded and marketed to the public had done wonders for my ego.

Then again, it didn't hurt that the guitar Ralph had lent me was light-years beyond any brand sold in South Dakota. Plus having both Aja and Ralph cheering me on from the other side of a two-inch-thick sheet of Plexiglas definitely gave me a boost.

Whatever, it all came together and it was magic.

"I'm not sure but that might be the take we use," Ralph said, before asking me again, and again, to play the song. I sang "Strange Girl" a dozen different times and all of them sounded great. When I was finished Ralph doubted I'd have to fly back out again. "Probably not until we're ready to cut the album," he added.

"Richard didn't say anything about doing an album," I said.

Ralph smiled. "He will after he hears this."

Reason two for my excitement while flying home was Janet. She had called from Kennedy Airport and said she'd meet us in Sioux Falls at two in the morning. We only spoke briefly but she asked if I'd been serious if she could stay at my house. I said sure. I knew my parents wouldn't mind.

"You look happy," Aja said as I stirred from a nap as our plane began to descend through our ever lovely South Dakota sky. I'd fallen asleep with my arm wrapped around her.

"It's been a hell of a week." I yawned and stretched. "Someone should probably shoot me now."

"You're still afraid," Aja said.

"Who wouldn't be? I just went from dreaming about being a rock star to having a chance to cut an album with the hottest record company in the nation. And my best friend, who I thought I'd lost forever to the Big Apple, is coming home with us. Honestly, Aja, us mere mortals don't get many days like this."

"So enjoy it while it lasts."

"I can't. Not totally."

"Because it won't last?" she said.

"You know me too well. I keep waiting for disaster to strike."

Aja nodded. "The world you live in is always changing."

"And your world is always the same?"

"Always the same and forever new."

"You know what? You may be one with the universe but I swear you're crazy."

Aja smiled. "Finally, you're beginning to understand me."

Our plane landed an hour before Janet's and we killed

time by picking up sandwiches in the airport cafeteria. We'd slept through our meals on the planes. For being so enlightened, Aja seemed to like meat as much as sex. She picked up a roast beef sandwich while I chose turkey. She drank half my Coke and ate most of my fries.

"And you say you don't have any cravings," I taunted. "What about eating? You obviously love it."

"Maybe I'm eating extra for a different reason."

"Huh?"

Aja took a bite of her sandwich. "I read a girl gets really hungry when she's eating for two."

I almost choked. "Aja, you're not saying you're—"

She interrupted. "I might be. Don't girls get pregnant after they have sex with boys?"

"But . . ."

"Disaster is striking."

"Aja!"

She laughed. "Relax. I'm teasing."

I sat back in my chair. "You're dangerous. I'm dumping you as soon as my record comes out and I'm rich and famous."

"If that's your plan you'll never be rich and famous."

"Why? Because all my good luck is because of you?"

"You said it not me."

Our playful banter was suddenly interrupted. Bo, walking

none too straight, swept by outside the cafeteria. Although I knew Janet hadn't called him, I wasn't surprised to see him. Bo must have spoken to Janet's mother and gotten her flight plans.

"Damn," I said.

Aja followed my gaze. "He's drunk."

"Tell me something I don't know."

"He's very drunk. What are you going to do?"

I stood. "Wait here. Let me handle this."

I caught up with Bo in the terminal where the flight from Chicago would arrive. I knew Janet would be on that plane. Bo prowled the black window that looked out on the icy landing strip. It had snowed a couple of inches since we'd been in California.

"She doesn't want to see you," I said, sneaking up behind him. He whirled, scowling.

"I've come to take my daughter home," he said.

I took a step closer. "No way. She's gone through too much shit the last few days, and all because of you. I promise you, Bo, make a scene right now and I'll bust your face."

"To hell with you. Stay out of our business."

"*Your* business? What kind of business is that? The kind where you creep into your daughter's bedroom in the middle of the night?"

Bo took a swing at me but Aja was right. He was very drunk. I took a step back and allowed his momentum to spin him around and dump him on the carpeted floor. He bounced back up, though, raising his fists, acting like I'd hit him with a sucker punch.

"Come on, Fred. Show me what you've got."

I should have let it go but I was angry. More angry than I'd ever been in my life. He'd hardly finished his last remark when I stepped forward and rammed my fist deep into his solar plexus. I didn't go for his head because I knew how hard the human skull was and didn't want to mess up the bones in my right hand, not weeks before I was supposed to cut my breakthrough album.

The one punch was enough. The blow popped the air out of his lungs and he crumpled in a heap, gasping for air. I would have kicked him in the ribs if others hadn't been watching. I crouched down beside him and spoke softly.

"Talk to her when she gets off the plane and I'll break your neck," I said. "No joke."

He groaned and coughed up a dark fluid that stank of bourbon. I strolled back to the cafeteria and sat down across from Aja. She hadn't moved from her place. She couldn't have seen our fight. But she looked none too happy.

"Feel better?" she asked.

"He swung first."

"Fred . . . ," she began.

I pounded the table. "How can you defend him?"

I'd never yelled at Aja before. Yet she didn't blink.

"I'm not defending him." She added, "They're both hurting."

I sat back in my chair. "He's a monster."

"Who are you trying to help here?" Aja said.

When Janet's plane landed a few minutes later, Bo was nowhere to be seen. I assumed he'd taken my advice to heart and left the airport. Janet appeared happy to see us. Still, there was an awkwardness. She was not totally at ease. She hugged me, but barely looked in Aja's direction.

Nevertheless, while we headed for the baggage area, she pumped me for details of how it had gone in LA. I gave her a brief summary. When I got to the part where Ralph put me in his studio with only an acoustic guitar and told me to sing "Strange Girl," Janet shook her head in amazement.

"You must have been sweating bullets," she said.

"It was weird but I felt confident. The guitar he had loaned me had an incredible tone. I could have sung 'Mary Had a Little Lamb' in that studio and it would have sounded great."

"And you had Aja rooting for you," Janet said, loosening up a bit.

"Nah. She flirted with Ralph the whole time. It was distracting."

Aja laughed at my jab. In reality, Ralph *had* flirted with Aja but I couldn't say I blamed the guy.

As we neared the baggage area, Aja volunteered to get our luggage. Janet and I headed for the Mercedes I'd left in the parking lot three days ago. Aja must have known Janet and I needed to speak alone. For all the talk about Bo abusing Janet, I still had no clear idea what he'd done.

However, I thought it might take her time to open up.

Days if not weeks.

But she filled me in as we stepped out into the icy air.

It had started when Janet was seven or eight; at least as far as she could remember. Again and again, as she spoke about the abuse, she said she couldn't recall exact details, which was odd because she usually had an extraordinary memory.

In either case, she said when she was in second or third grade, she remembered Bo coming into her room late at night, when her mom was asleep. He'd just sit on the edge of her bed and stroke her hair and talk to her and it was nice. At least she thought it was nice. He did this off and on for a year. But later, when she was in the fourth grade, he started to climb into the bed with her, wearing only his underwear, and she remembered him touching her and asking her to touch him.

"Touching me," and *"Touch him."*

That was as detailed as she got.

"Did you tell your mom?" I asked as we climbed into Aja's car. I felt in no hurry to start the engine. Aja would wait.

"Not until I was in fifth grade." Janet added hastily, "I was young. I didn't know what was going on."

"What did your mom say?"

"She told me she'd talk to my dad about it. And she told me not to talk about it to anybody else."

"But she believed you?"

Janet hesitated. "I'm not sure."

It might have been a coincidence, but Janet was in fifth grade when her mother suddenly filed for divorce and moved to New York. She took Janet with her but only because Janet asked to go. Not because Mom was anxious to have sole custody or was desperate to protect her daughter.

"That's a pretty lame reaction," I said. "I hate to say it but I don't think she believed you."

"That, or else she didn't give a damn," Janet said. "Don't forget, I just spent a week with the woman. Mom never changes. She's nice and friendly and attentive and yet—all the time you're in the room with her—you feel like a robot's been assigned to be your chaperone. She was like that when I was growing up."

"Is that why—when you were a kid—you came back home after a year?"

Janet hesitated. "Yeah."

"You said before you missed your friends."

"I missed you."

I didn't believe her, I thought. She was telling me only part of the story and not the most important part. Something else had dragged her from New York City back to Elder.

I spoke carefully. "Did you miss Bo?"

Janet ignored me and looked toward the terminal. "Aja's waiting with our bags. We should get her."

"What did Aja do to drag this skeleton out of the closet?"

Janet stared straight ahead, her gaze thoughtful. "Nothing. I mean, nothing I can put my finger on. But just hanging out with her I started to remember what had gone on, you know."

"Wait a second. Are you saying you'd blocked it all out?"

"No. I knew it'd happened. It's just . . . whenever I did remember it, I pretended like it hadn't really happened. Does that make sense?"

"Sort of. Has anything happened in the last seven years?"

"No. Not since I was ten years old. Bo's been great."

Great, I thought.

Aja was waiting outside with our three sets of bags when we drove up to the loading-and-unloading zone, shivering in a thin leather jacket she'd bought in a shop in the hotel in LA. I yelled at her for not waiting inside the baggage area.

"That's a great way to catch pneumonia," I said as I loaded the bags into the trunk.

"I'm fine," Aja said, starting to climb in the backseat.

"Sit in the front seat with Fred," Janet said.

"I don't care where I sit," Aja said.

"You should be with your boyfriend," Janet insisted. She may have been trying to put distance between us to stop all the Bo questions. That was my thought anyway. I hadn't told her about Bo being at the airport or the fact I'd punched him in the gut. For the first time since I'd known her, Janet appeared delicate. I didn't want to add to her burdens.

It was after three in the morning before we left the airport. We had a long drive ahead of us. But I felt awake enough to drive. I'd slept on our flight home, and it was good to be with my two favorite people in the whole world. Plus I was still riding the buzz from my impending record deal.

While Aja and I had been in the air, Marc Kroff and Jimmy Hurt had both called and left messages reminding me that I had to get an agent right away. Their hurry to finalize the deal added to my excitement.

It was important I stay alert. The recent snowfall had been light but it had left the road icy. I held our speed below fifty and kept my distance from other cars. The last thing I wanted to do was hit the brake; we'd spin out of control for sure.

We'd been driving for roughly an hour when I saw Janet stir in the rearview mirror and yawn, waking up from a nap. Aja sat silently on my right. I was surprised she hadn't dozed off.

"I don't want Mike, Dale, or Shelly to know what's going on," Janet said.

I nodded. "Understood."

Janet sighed. "Of all the families in the world I could have been born into. I get a mother who's so closed down inside she can't show affection and a father who's so desperate for love it's turned him into a pervert."

"All human beings are desperate for love," Aja said.

Janet chuckled. "You know, Aja, I appreciate you give good advice and all that, but do you ever stop and look at your own problems? I mean, I doubt everything in your life has been bright and rosy since the instant you popped out of your mother's womb."

"You're right," Aja said. "My family life was far from perfect."

I glanced over at her. She was staring out the side window. "How so?" I asked.

Aja shrugged. "My father was a criminal and my mother was a saint. It made for a difficult combination."

"What did your father do?" I asked.

"He worked for a drug cartel."

"Shit," Janet muttered.

"Was your mother like you?" I asked. "Was she aware of the Big Person? Is that why you call her a saint?"

"A saint is someone who does no harm. That was my mother."

I spoke carefully. "How did they die?"

Aja hesitated. "My father was greedy. He could never have enough money. He stole from his bosses. They didn't like that. When I was five years old, they sent three men and a woman from another country to kill him."

"God. I'm so sorry," Janet said. "What happened?"

A car close behind us suddenly honked. I'd seen the car approaching in my rearview mirror, or at least its lights. Now it was practically on top of us. It kept honking, edging closer. Janet peered out the back window.

"That's Bo's car!" she cried.

"Damnit!" I swore. "I didn't tell you, I ran into him at the airport. He came to pick you up. He was drunk. We ended up trading blows."

"He hit you?" Janet gasped.

"It was more like I hit him." Our car lurched as he struck our rear bumper. "Christ! He's trying to run us off the road!"

I wasn't exaggerating. Bo struck us twice more before he accelerated into the left lane and came up on our side. I could just glimpse him through the glare of our headlights and the fury of the flying snow. Hunched over his steering wheel, craning his head in our direction, he looked insane. I suspected he'd drowned the pain and humiliation of my blow with another bottle of booze. He had to be totally smashed to be risking his daughter's life.

Aja's Mercedes was powered by one of the finest engines the company had ever built—the 4.0L AMG biturbo V-8. The car could do over a hundred and fifty miles an hour without straining. Outrunning Bo wasn't a problem. It was the damn ice on the road. The frozen sheets could spin us into the steep grassy slopes on either side of the interstate just as easily as his ramming routine.

Bo swung partway into our lane and gave us a light tap.

A light tap that almost sent us careening out of control.

I felt I had no choice but to accelerate. I pushed our speed up to ninety. But doing ninety on icy asphalt in the dead of night felt like jumping out of an airplane without a parachute. Still, Bo stayed with us, the lunatic. I increased our speed to a hundred. No good. The bastard was an expert mechanic and he'd supercharged his Mustang. He caught us easily.

"Roll down your windows!" Janet cried.

"Why?" I yelled.

"He's rolled his down! Do it!"

I hit the buttons that rolled down my window alone, while locking the others in place. Freezing wind flooded our car. Janet pounded the back of my seat in frustration. I ignored her. I couldn't handle another distraction. Bo's Mustang was a foot away and the road up ahead looked like a frozen lake. We had at most ten seconds before the combination of gravity, speed, and an extreme lack of friction would become every bit as dangerous as a cliff.

Bo screamed at me across the gulf. "I'm taking my girl home!"

"She's not your girl, you prick!" I yelled back.

"I'll go with him! I'll go!" Janet cried.

"Fred," Aja said.

The ten seconds were cut in half and all I could see was a thick, white sheet in front of us that appeared to glisten—I had the high beams on—with a million hidden diamonds. On the upcoming stretch it was clear the wind had funneled the two inches of snowfall into a two-foot blanket of powder. If we hit it doing a hundred there was a chance we'd flip over and become airborne.

I had no choice, I hit the brakes. On our left, Bo's Mustang vanished. For all I could tell he'd smashed into a tree.

Our wheels gripped the asphalt for perhaps three seconds. We were lucky to get that; it cut our speed to sixty. Then we hit a sheet of invisible ice that lay camouflaged beneath the blanket of snow and we went into a spin. My life didn't flash before my eyes but the dark landscape did. We were a clock running backward, subtracting potential years instead of hours from what was left of our lives. We were totally out of control.

We hit the two feet of powder; it could have been a ten-foot wall of granite. I heard a loud, grinding noise. It sounded as if the Mercedes's driveshaft was cracking. But maybe it was my back that was breaking. I felt my body jerked in every direction at once.

The air bags exploded in our faces but rather than softening the blow I felt as if I'd been slugged by a prizefighter. I heard a loud snap followed by a warm wet gush. I felt pain inside my nose, terrible pain, and knew it was broken. Agony swelled through my head as a black wave washed over my brain. I passed out; it could have been for five seconds or five minutes.

The next thing I heard was silence, nothingness. I was freezing cold. The window on my left was still open and I had the makings of Frosty and his pals sitting on my lap. In other words, I was buried in snow. I couldn't help noticing the white powder was soaked red. A sticky red as in blood.

Our wild momentum had caused a six-foot-tall mountain of powder to build up on the driver's side. It had us half-buried. There was no way I'd be able to open my door. I'd have to crawl over to the passenger door. As long as Aja was . . .

I thought of her then. Looked at her.

She smiled. "Your nose looks like a snow cone."

"Which flavor?" I said in a nasally voice.

"Strawberry."

"How are you feeling?"

"I'm fine." Aja twisted around. "You okay, Janet?"

I could still see Janet in the rearview mirror. She'd smashed into her own air bag and seemed to be holding up her left arm to keep it from hurting. The arm didn't look a hundred percent straight. I assumed it was broken.

"I've been better," Janet groaned. "Where's Bo?"

Aja gestured to our cracked windshield. Her side was relatively clear, at least she could see past the powder. "His car's a quarter mile up the road. It's lying on its side. His lights are still on."

"We have to help him," Janet said. "Fred!"

I raised a hand. "I'll check on him. But we need to light a few flares and spread them over the road. We need to do that immediately. The next car or truck that comes along could crush us. Aja, can you open your door?"

"It's stuck," Aja said, struggling with it, before suddenly spinning on her butt and raising both her legs and kicking it open. I hit the button that should have popped the trunk but didn't hear anything. Snapping free of my seat belt, I held out the keys to Aja. She leaned back in the car and grabbed them.

"Get the flares," I said. "Light them far away from the car, up the road, back the way we came. Hurry."

"Gotcha," she said before she turned and vanished.

Crawling over the armrest and across Aja's seat let me know just how banged up I was. Everything ached; my progress was pitifully slow. I felt as if I'd been kicked by a gang of thugs. I imagined how nice it would be to soak in a hot tub. I was so cold!

I spoke to Janet. "Can you get out? Can you stand?"

"My door's jammed. And my left arm . . . it's numb."

"I'll work on your door once I'm out. I'm worried about a gasoline leak. There's a chance the tank cracked. I don't want us staying in here any longer than we have to."

"You have to check on Bo," she said.

"I promise, I'll check on him as soon as we're clear."

I stumbled and fell the instant I got outside. There was something wrong with my left knee; it wasn't working. Aja returned to my side and helped me to my feet. She had four flares in hand and already had two burning behind our car—at distances of forty yards and fifty yards. I took two and stuffed them in my back pocket. Aja had also retrieved a flashlight from the trunk.

"Good work," I said. "Let's get Janet out and get jackets on. I've got my cell. I'll call 911 and tell them our situation. Then I'll check on Bo."

"Can you walk?" Aja asked.

"I'll walk."

It was actually Aja who popped Janet's door loose. My knee was in worse shape than I thought. It didn't hurt, not like my dripping nose, but it made a disturbing clicking noise when I put weight on it and it felt *mushy*. Great, I thought. My first advance from Paradise Records would go to an orthopedic surgeon.

I called 911 and explained where we were and what had happened. The dispatcher was blunt. She explained we were in the middle of nowhere and it would take forty minutes for an ambulance to reach us. I told them to please hurry.

Minutes later the three of us huddled together outside the slightly crumpled Mercedes. The car was heavily reinforced with steel bars; it scored high on crash tests. In that respect we were lucky. The vehicle had kept us alive and free from serious injury.

Yet, except for Aja, we were still pretty banged up. We

managed to light another two flares and spread them across the road but the way I was limping, the four hundred yards to Bo's Mustang looked like a marathon. Frankly, judging by how far it had skidded on its side before coming to a halt, I wasn't optimistic what we'd find inside it.

I explained what the 911 gal had told me. Janet swore under her breath. "Where's a cop when you need one?" she said.

I spoke. "They promised to hurry. I'll check on Bo. You two stay here and try to flag down any cars that drive by."

"You can't even walk," Janet said. "I'll go."

"Your arm's broken. You're not going anywhere," I said.

"I should go," Aja said.

"Yeah. Have Aja go," Janet said quickly, too quickly for my taste. It was clear she was thinking about Aja's healing abilities, while conveniently forgetting how sick she'd gotten after healing Mike.

"No way," I said. "Aja's not getting anywhere near Bo."

"How can you say that?" Janet asked.

"I just said it," I snapped. "Now stay here and take care of each other. I'm going."

The strength of my order might have prevailed had I been able to follow it up with a brisk pace in the direction of the overturned Mustang. But as I started up the road, my left knee went from bad to useless. I was basically forced to hop on one leg—not a very efficient way to traverse a blanket of snow. The girls, not impressed with my progress, caught up with me within minutes. Aja took my left arm and told me to lean on her.

"We're all going," she said.

I gave her a hard look. "As long as you keep your distance from Bo."

To an outsider we must have looked like a pitiful trio. Even though it was Janet's arm that was broken and not her leg, she moved no faster than me. Her arm needed a cast and a sling. The way she kept grimacing—and Janet wasn't one to complain—I suspected the ends of her cracked bones were grinding against each other every time she took a step.

I could do nothing to help her. I could hardly help myself. Without Aja propping me up I would have been crawling on my knees. And Aja was not a big girl. Whatever supernatural powers she possessed didn't translate into physical strength. Every time I leaned on her, every step I took, I came close to knocking her over.

It took us fifteen minutes to reach Bo's car. When we got there I let go of Aja and used the body of the Mustang to keep me upright. The air was freezing but stank of gasoline. I warned the girls to stay back.

"The car could blow any second. Aja, give me your

flashlight and help Janet to the divider rail. I'll get Bo out."

"His neck might be broken," Janet said. "His back. It might be a mistake to move him."

"I'll take that into consideration. Now get back!"

Finally, the girls listened to me. They headed for the rail. I suppose the thought of being engulfed in a ball of fire was enough to get anyone's ass in gear. But to be blunt, I wasn't in love with the idea of rescuing Bo. He was the one who had caused the accident. He had caused a lot of grief lately and had I been alone with Aja I probably would have waited until the paramedics arrived and let them deal with it.

Yet Janet was pushing me to hurry. In the space of minutes she had gone from hating the guy to pleading for me to save him. As the girls trudged through the snow to the divider, I slowly made my way along the upturned bottom of the car. I could see the fuel tank in the beam of my flashlight. It had cracked open; and gasoline was continuing to leak out onto the snow. I would have felt safer if the toxic puddle showed signs of freezing but no such luck. I saw a nauseating mist rise from it at the same time I saw sparks crackling in the direction of the engine.

"Great," I said, pondering the irony of my situation. The very day I'm promised a record contract I get incinerated in a car accident caused by a drunken pervert.

Given the fact that the car was lying on the driver's side, there should have been no way in hell for me to pull Bo out of the wreckage. But I'd thought of a way to get to him the instant I'd seen the overturned Mustang. Bo loved to drive fast with the sun and wind in his face; and for that reason he'd installed an extra-large sunroof. As I made my way around the top, I was relieved to see the sunroof had totally shattered. That meant all that stood between me and Bo was a wall of snow.

I fell to my knees and began to dig. The stink of the gasoline and the red rattle of the sparks inspired me to hurry. As far as I could tell, Bo could have a broken neck and a crushed spine and I'd still have to drag him out of the car. Otherwise he was going to be toast.

"Bo," I called when I'd cleared away enough snow to see him flopped around an air bag in the crumpled front seat. Trails of blood poured from his forehead and his breathing was ragged and wet but he was alive. "Bo, it's Fred. Can you hear me?"

He moaned in pain. "Fred? How are you doing?"

"All right. How are you feeling?"

"Like shit." He coughed and a mouthful of blood splashed over his tan leather coat. He added, "I think I'm dying."

I chipped away at the jagged edges of the sunroof with

my flashlight. "Nah. You can't die yet. Janet's pleading for me to rescue you and if I fail she'll never speak to me again. You've got to help me help you get out of here. You've got your seat belt on. You've got to unlatch the belt. Can you move your arms?"

Bo groaned mightily as he dragged his right arm over the swollen air bag. The damn thing was supposed to deflate after impact. "Where is it?" he gasped.

I focused the beam on his bloody fingers. "Keep going. Two more inches. That's it—your hand's right on the latch. Can you feel it?"

He sounded weak. "I don't know. Sort of."

"Good. That means you're not paralyzed, that you'll make a full recovery. If you move your ass. Your tank's gushing gas and someone threw a handful of sparklers in the engine. We've got maybe a minute or two to get you out of here before we're both barbecued. Are you hearing me?"

Bo fumbled without luck with the seat belt. The effort exhausted him and he coughed up another wad of blood. "It's no good. Get away, Fred. Save yourself. I'm not worth it."

"Not an option. Janet's waiting and she says I've got to save your ass. So here's what we're going to do. You're going to undo that latch and I'm going to pull you out. Do it!"

Bo made one last desperate grasp at the seat belt latch

and I heard it pop loose. Quickly, chipping away a few last jagged spikes of glass from the sunroof, I kicked with my right leg and propelled myself, headfirst, into the front seat of the Mustang. I could just reach the collar of Bo's jacket. I got a grip on it.

Unfortunately, I had another problem. My position was way beyond awkward. I was practically falling into the car. I had no leverage, nothing substantial to brace against to pull him out.

"Are we there yet?" Bo babbled. He sounded delirious; he probably had a concussion.

"Bo, I need some more help. I need you to push with your feet. Push with one of them if that's all that's working. But push now and push hard. Okay?"

"Okay."

"Great. On the count of three: one, two, three!"

Bo pushed and screamed simultaneously. He probably had a broken leg; he might have had two of them. Whatever, the stab of pain seemed to reawaken him. His eyes popped open and he looked around at the mess he was in. Luckily, his shove had pushed him high enough to where I could wiggle back a couple of feet and still wrap my right arm around him.

I used my left arm to press against the edge of what was left of the sunroof. It was lousy leverage but it would have to do. Bo began to move. Shards of glass dug into my palm but I chose to ignore them as I continued to pull him up and out. I had never felt such an urge to hurry in all my life. I smelled smoke. Something was burning and I knew we had only seconds before we would join it. The car was about to explode.

I yanked Bo free of the Mustang. Using one hand for support on the side of the car and the other to drag him over the ground, I pulled him clear of the heavy powder and onto what I hoped was a sheet of ice. A pity I had forgotten about my lame knee. As soon as we moved away from the car, I collapsed beside Bo. He looked at me and tried to smile.

"Thanks for saving me," he said.

"Don't thank me yet," I replied as I struggled to get back on my feet. It was lucky for Bo and myself that the girls chose that instant to disobey me. Suddenly they were by our sides. Janet fighting with me to pull her dad clear of the car; Aja struggling to keep me upright. Except for Aja we were all a mess, all in agony, but we didn't stop working until we were a hundred feet from the Mustang.

It was then the bomb went off; a mushroom of fire; and a shock wave so powerful it knocked us back on our butts.

"Daddy!" Janet cried as she tentatively embraced Bo. "Are you all right?"

I had not heard her call him "Daddy" in ages.

Not even "Dad." Not since she was a little girl.

"Don't worry about me." He coughed, more blood spilling from his swollen lips. His breath was scary; a wet wheeze. It sounded like a death rattle. I suspected the impact had cracked a dozen ribs. He didn't seem able to catch his breath. I tried rolling him on his side but he cried out. I rolled him back. His jacket was soaked red. He was bleeding from so many places. There was no question he had major internal injuries.

Janet fretted over him but was afraid to touch him. "What do you need? How can we help you?" she said.

Bo opened his eyes and looked up at his daughter, managed a feeble smile. More blood dripped from his mouth. "You're here. That's enough," he gasped.

Janet looked at me with pleading eyes. "How long before the ambulance gets here?" she asked.

I checked my watch; it was broken. "Soon."

"That's not good enough. He's dying." Her eyes went to Aja. "We have to do something."

Aja stood silent, her face calm in the orange rays of the burning car, staring down at Bo. She did not look at Janet, which pissed her off. Janet stood and grabbed Aja with her good arm and shook her.

"Do something!" she cried.

Aja stared at her but said nothing.

I stood and pushed Janet back, wrapping a protective arm around Aja. "We're not doing this," I said.

Janet gestured to her father lying on the road. His condition was deteriorating rapidly. I feared yanking him out of the car had not helped; that my tug had caused the sharp edges of his shattered ribs to puncture his lungs. He tried to say something to his daughter but couldn't. His struggle to take in oxygen had become all-consuming. He kept sucking at air that couldn't help him. The sad truth was he was drowning in his own blood. It didn't matter that I was supposed to be furious with him; it was agonizing to watch.

"So it's okay for her to heal total strangers," Janet said bitterly. "But because it's my dad you're not going to let her help him. Why is that, Fred? Huh? Is it because he doesn't measure up to your moral code?"

I pulled Aja closer. "You know that has nothing to do with it. Bo's near death. Healing him could kill Aja. We can't risk it."

"Liar! You want him to die because of what he did to me!"

I went to speak and stopped.

Was it true? Did I hate him that much?

Janet turned to Aja, pleaded. "Can you do it? Can you save him?"

Aja stared at her before shaking her head.

Janet wept. "Why not? You did it for Mike. So you get sick for a few days. You'll live. And he'll live. . . ." She lowered her head as tears fell from her face. "You can't let it end like this. You can't."

Was she speaking to Aja? The Big Person? God? I wasn't sure but I could have sworn, the way Aja was studying her, that Aja believed Janet was talking to herself. And that Janet was the key to what would happen next.

Perhaps Janet sensed that. She raised her head and defiantly threw out a challenge. "You're waiting for me to forgive him, is that it? If I do that, will you heal him?"

I worried Janet might be right. I pulled Aja back.

"Forgive him all you want," I said. "She's not risking her life to save his."

Janet pointed an ugly finger my way. "You're not in charge here. She is."

I let go of Aja and took a wobbly step toward Janet. "You're wrong. I'll drag him back to the Mustang and throw him in the fire before I'll allow her to heal him. I'm not bluffing."

Bo began to choke; he shook on the ground. He could cough blood out but he could no longer draw air in. His whole body began to convulse. The back of his head banged the ice. Janet hastened to his side, gripped his hands, trying to steady him. She looked up at me with scorn.

"You let him die and I'll hate you until the day I die," she said.

"Aja doesn't owe you a miracle," I said.

Janet stood. "Maybe not but you do. How many times have you told me that you're my best friend? That you would do anything for me?"

Her words pierced me like a sword. Suddenly I felt unsure of what I was doing. But it wasn't as if my resolve to protect Aja wavered. I knew in my heart how much I loved her; knew I'd die before I'd let her risk her own life. Especially to save Bo.

Yet my doubt remained and it was odd because I suddenly questioned whether Janet had anything to do with it. I sensed a power gathering around us, an ancient force that was uninterested in my desire to save Aja or Janet's efforts to guilt me. Something switched, inside and outside, and I suddenly felt as if we stood on a wide-open plain where no horizon existed. I sensed a huge presence approach, which should have been a comfort. Yet I felt lost and very much afraid.

Janet moved close to Aja, reached out with her good arm, tried to take her hand. "Tell me what to do. I'll do anything you ask if you'll heal him."

Aja stared at her a long time.

What she said next stunned us both.

"Let him die," she said.

Janet winced. "What?"

"He's dying. Let him die."

"But you can heal him. You have the power. How can you say that?"

Aja shrugged. "He sexually abused you. You were just a kid. Why do you want to save a man like that?"

"Because he's my father!"

"So what? It's not like he was a good father."

Bo choked hard and long; he coughed up so much blood.

Janet grabbed Aja by the arm, went to slap her. But then her eyes met Aja's eyes and she stopped. I understood that, why Janet halted, even if I had no idea what else was going on. I'd felt the heat and intensity of Aja's gaze many times. Janet shook her head in disbelief.

"What's gotten into you? What's wrong with you?"

Aja spoke in a firm tone. "What's wrong with me? What's wrong with you? Why are you begging me to help a man you hate?"

"That's not true. I don't hate him."

"Of course you hate him. You have every reason in the world to hate him."

Aja's words hit Janet like physical blows. Janet groaned as if she were trying to ward them off. But I knew not to interfere even though it was hard not to. Aja was up to something—something I didn't fully understand. Yet I could see Aja had transported Janet to another world, to *her* world, and that she was determined to do with Janet what she willed.

Janet yelled. "Damnit, Aja, can't you see? I'm trying to save his life!"

Aja just stared at her. "Why?"

Janet was as confused as she was hurt. "Why what? Stop saying that. This isn't like you. You always help people. Please, you've got to help my father. He's dying."

"And I told you, let him die. He's not worth saving."

"How can you say that?"

"It's true, isn't it?" Aja said.

"No. You don't know him. He's a good man. He made a mistake but it wasn't his fault."

"It's always the pervert's fault."

"He's not a pervert!" Janet screamed.

Aja turned back toward me. "Let's go, Fred. I'm getting tired of this."

Janet dashed forward and grabbed Aja by the arm. "Wait! He's not who you think he is. It wasn't his fault." She cried in desperation. "It was my fault!"

The sphere of invisible power around us seemed to tremble.

In a mad rush I recalled the conversation I'd had on the phone with Janet when I was in LA.

"Are you saying you're not coming back?"

"I can't."

"That's crazy. You've got to finish out the school year. You can stay at my house. My parents would love to have you."

"No. Then everyone would know. And that's the last thing . . . I hate that you know. I hate how you must see me now."

"Janet, you did nothing wrong."

"Didn't I?"

Aja's demeanor suddenly shifted. She stopped and stared at Janet. "How was it your fault?" she asked gently.

Janet lowered her head as if in shame. It was as if she had been broken. I had never seen her so wounded. Tears streamed down her face.

"Because I let him . . ." Janet stopped, started again. "I let him . . . I didn't stop him. I let him do it."

"Did you?" Aja asked.

"Oh God, I don't know what you want me to say! Yes, I let him do it! I let him do it because I loved him!"

Slowly Aja shook her head. "Janet, you were a child. You were what? Six? Seven? Eight years old? Of course you loved him. He was your father."

Janet looked doubtful. "But I came back to him. Even

after what he did, I came back to Elder to live with him."

Aja spoke with authority. "Your love for your father isn't why he abused you. Your father abused you because of his own problems. You were never to blame." Aja paused. "Love—your love, all love—it's always good."

What Aja was saying—it was true. It was such an obvious truth. It pierced Janet like a living flame, burning away the deeply entrenched lies she had been telling herself for ages.

Janet trembled. "Can it be . . . ?"

"It's true," Aja said.

"It wasn't my fault?"

"It wasn't your fault," Aja said.

Janet shook her head. "I was only a child."

"Yes," Aja said.

Janet wiped the tears from her face. It did no good— more came. "All this time," she sighed.

"It's done," Aja said.

Janet hugged Aja right then, with her one good arm, and Aja hugged her back. They held each other for a long time, before Janet finally let go and turned to stare down at Bo's face. He had stopped struggling. He lay still, and for all we knew he was dead.

"Can you heal him?" she asked.

"If that's what you wish," Aja said.

The decision had been given back to Janet, or perhaps it had always resided in her hands. That frightened me. I did not know what it meant. I did not know what was to follow.

Janet stared up at the sky and shuddered. Then she looked again at Bo, staring hard at her father, before finally turning to Aja. One last time.

"I want the Big Person to decide," Janet said. "Just don't . . . I don't want you to get hurt."

Aja nodded faintly and stepped past her, before stopping beside Bo. Every fiber in my being cried at me to rush forward and swoop her up and carry her away from this dangerous situation. But I couldn't move. It wasn't my injured knee. It was the ocean that blocked my way—the endless ocean upon whose shore I could only stand and gaze out.

I could beg Aja all I wanted not to heal Bo and it would make no difference. Right then, at that instant, Aja was the Big Person. Everyone was equally dear to her. I liked to pretend otherwise but she loved Bo as much as she loved me. She would give her life to save him.

Aja looked in my direction and her eyes seemed to say that she was sorry but that this was the way it had to be. I wished I could have fought with her but all I could do was watch as she knelt beside Bo and placed her right hand over his heart and her left hand over his forehead. I heard her draw in a deep breath. I did not hear her exhale but I did see her eyes close and watched as her head fell forward and the life seemed to drain out of her.

The ambulances arrived fifteen minutes later. By then Bo was sitting up and talking with Janet, not far from the burning front of the car, while Aja and I sat at the rear of the Mustang, near the flames, trying to stay warm.

The paramedics were attending to Janet and Bo. She had a broken arm, after all, and Bo was obviously soaked in blood, although from what I could hear from the paramedics they couldn't find anything wrong with him.

I accepted their offer of a blanket and asked them to examine Aja. But she waved them away. She whispered in my ear that there was nothing they could do.

"You don't know that," I said anxiously. "These people are trained. They're practically doctors. They have drugs, all kinds of fancy equipment. They can shock your heart if it stops. Aja, please?"

She shook her head wearily. "It's too late for that."

"It's not too late. It's never too late."

"Oh Fred." She sagged into my arms as I wrapped the blanket tightly around her. "Hold me, just hold me. That's what I need the most."

I held her but inside my mind was screaming. "It can't be too late."

She looked up at me, raised her arm, wiped a tear from my cheek. "I should have told you at the start. The days of this body were numbered."

"Why?" I said.

"The Big Person doesn't tell us why. But it knew. That's why it sent me to your town. That's why it sent me to you."

I swallowed thickly. "To break my heart?"

"No. To love you. To be loved by you."

I couldn't believe this was happening. "How long do we have?"

"Not long," Aja said, snuggling close to me beneath the blanket, my arms wrapped around her, clutching her, struggling to keep her from slipping away.

"It's not fair. I thought we'd have more time," I said.

"The time we had together was good."

"Did you know it would end tonight?" I asked.

"No, not tonight. I'm like you with those mystery books you love. I try not to look ahead to the last page."

"You should have looked." I closed my eyes and fought for control. Every second was precious now. Because I knew I'd cling to every one of them for the rest of my life. I forced myself to recall what she'd told us in the car just before Bo had attacked. "Did your mother give you that name? Aja?"

"Yes. My father was away when I was born."

"What does the name mean?"

With the tip of her finger, she touched between my eyebrows. "Two inches beneath that spot, inside your head, is the 'Aja.'" Then she put her hand on my chest. "It's also here. Aja is the spiritual eye through which the Big Person can be seen."

"Did your mother know you would be born a saint?"

"I wasn't born one."

"What happened? How did you change?"

She spoke in a weary whisper. It was all she could manage. "Like I said, I was five years old when the cartel sent three men and a woman to kill my father. I was playing outside when they came. They carried machetes. My mother rushed to pick me up and carry me away but they stopped her. They herded the three of us inside. They'd come to kill my father. But they wanted him to suffer. They made him watch as they . . . they cut my mother's throat."

"Oh God." I wanted to weep for that little girl. "They made you watch?"

"Yes. It was horrible. So horrible the child in this body—her mind, her identification with this body, even her sense of 'I,' they all fled and ran away and tried to hide and were lost.

That's how I was changed. Nothing was left of that girl. In the deepest way possible she became . . . no one."

Aja stopped to struggle to catch her breath. The same way Bo had struggled. All of us had been so in awe of her healing ability but I couldn't have hated it more right then.

"That was the day I became the Big Person," Aja said.

"Why did the men let you live?"

"The woman felt the change in me. She felt something powerful enter the room. She dropped her machete and picked me up and carried me away, into the jungle."

"And your father?"

"The men chopped him to pieces. The same with my mother. They left nothing behind. Nothing but blood." Aja paused. "The woman who saved me was Angela. You saw her at the PTA meeting."

I was stunned. "Principal Levitt's lover?"

"Yes. Being there, at that moment, changed her."

"She became psychic?"

"Yes. But I think for her, the gift was something of a curse."

"She knew her daughter would die."

"Yes."

"From then on you lived mostly in the jungle?"

"Yes. It was more comfortable for me to be in nature than

to be near people." Aja nuzzled my cheek and I felt her dry lips. "Don't feel sorry for me. I was happy after the Big Person came. I was always happy."

I struggled to keep my voice from cracking.

"Are you happy now?" I asked.

She sighed. "Yes and no. I'm sad that you're sad."

"I've been sad most of my life. Why should it change?"

"That's not true. Everything changed the day we met."

I nodded, sniffed. "I'm sorry, Aja. Honestly, I'm happy you came into my life. And I'm happy just to hold you right now."

"That's better." Her head fell back on my chest; she lacked the strength to hold it up. I could hear her heartbeat, could feel it slowing down. Taking her hand I squeezed it. She tried to squeeze mine back but she was too weak. It wouldn't be long.

"What does the name 'Fred' mean?" she asked.

"'He who loves goddesses.'"

"Really?"

"It does now."

Aja smiled faintly, her eyes closing. "I knew I chose the right boy when I chose you."

I felt a stab of fear; I shook her gently. "Don't go, not yet. Please?"

Her eyes opened. "It's okay, Fred. I'm going home."

I felt a wave of panic sweep over me. It was a tidal wave but I was no ocean, not like Aja, and suddenly I felt as if I could not bear it. Tears burned my eyes. I pulled her closer.

"No! Wait!" I cried, losing all control, sobbing. "Please don't go! Use your power! For God's sake, Aja, heal yourself!"

"Shh, Fred. It's okay. You will be okay." Straining, using the last of her strength, she placed her hand over my heart. "I will be with you here. I will always be with you. I promise."

My agony did not stop.

Yet somehow her touch made it bearable.

I leaned over and kissed her. "I love you."

She closed her eyes and settled back on my chest.

"I love you," she whispered.

She died minutes later.

EPILOGUE

TWIN AMBULANCES TOOK US TO A NEARBY hospital—St. Vincent's. I rode with Aja in the back. Janet stayed with her father. The paramedics who examined Aja were dismayed. They could find nothing wrong with her. No logical reason why she had died. They kept apologizing to me, telling me how sorry they were that they hadn't attended to her from the start. I told them it wasn't their fault. They covered Aja with a white sheet, from head to toe.

I was in shock.

At the hospital Aja's body was taken to the morgue. I managed to get ahold of Bart. I told him they wanted to perform an autopsy. That it was the law. That they needed to find out exactly how she had died. Bart told me to wait and he would call me back in a few minutes. When he did he told me that his lawyer, Mr. Grisham, had made an "arrange-ment" with the hospital and they would no longer press for the autopsy. I assumed money or favors had changed hands.

While Bart drove from Elder, Janet and I were treated by a couple of competent ER doctors. They set my nose back in place, taped half my face, and did an MRI on my knee. I hadn't torn any ligaments but they said I'd need arthroscopic surgery to remove three large chunks of frayed cartilage. I was given a pair of crutches to get around and a bottle of Vicodin for the pain. I swallowed a couple of the blue pills but didn't feel any better.

Janet's broken arm was more serious. The ER doctors called in a specialist to operate. She ended up needing a metal plate and a host of screws to stabilize the bone. While she was in surgery, Bart arrived and obtained the release of Aja's body. The two of us spoke briefly about what we should do next and swiftly came to an agreement. A local mortuary was contacted to bring her body back home.

The ER doctors performed a dozen tests on Bo.

They never did find anything wrong with him.

I rode back to Elder with Bart. We followed the white hearse from the mortuary. We didn't talk much; I suppose there was nothing to say. But one thing was clear. Bart was not in the least bit surprised that Aja had died. His absence of shock, though, did nothing to alleviate his grief. He looked as if he'd aged twenty years since I'd last seen him.

"She told us before we moved here that the days of her body were numbered," Bart said.

"Is that why she wanted to come here? Was there a purpose to her coming?"

Bart nodded. "It's nice to think so. That the Big Person was kind enough to give the rest of the world a glimpse of who she was."

I shook my head. "My classmates turned out to be almost too loyal. As far as I can tell not a single student gave the press a recording of what went on at the PTA meeting. And without proof that Aja could heal people . . . well, she's already becoming just another fading headline on YouTube. Outside of Elder, I doubt anyone will be talking about her a month from now."

Bart looked at me. "You're forgetting one thing."

"What?"

"You."

"What about me?"

"You're the one who will keep Aja alive in people's memories."

"Are you serious? How? And why me?"

"'Why you' should be obvious. You were closer to her than anyone. And that includes Clara and myself. And as to 'how' you'll keep her story alive—I'm not worried about that. You're a smart guy. You'll think of something."

It was dawn by the time we reached the Carter Mansion. Bart told the two guys from the mortuary to lay her body on her bed upstairs. They did so and left. And after spending a few minutes with Aja, Bart left me alone with her. But I could hear him down in the garage; I knew what he was up to.

It was peaceful to sit beside her, to be alone with her in the bedroom where we'd spent such wonderful nights, surrounded by the paintings and sculptures her father had made of her mother. She had on the same black slacks and white blouse she'd worn in LA. I tucked her under a woolen blanket Clara had knitted for her when they lived in Brazil and brushed her hair so that it spread over her pillow and down around her shoulders.

I couldn't stop staring at her face. Honestly, I couldn't believe she was dead. All the love I'd always felt in her presence, the power, the grace—they were still there. Her body may have died but was she dead? Sitting on the edge of her bed, holding her hand, staring at her serene expression, the idea seemed ridiculous.

Still, I couldn't talk to her anymore and I knew I'd never hear her voice again. Nor would I ever hold her again. The Big Person inside her may have been alive, as unchanging as ever, but I was just a guy who loved her, a very mortal guy, and already I was beginning to miss her.

TV shows that deal with death and dying, along with cop shows and medical dramas, often speak about how quickly the human body decays. I was lucky Aja granted me one last miracle. The odor emanating from her could not have been more sweet. Her body smelled like a combination of daises and camphor, sandalwood oil and fresh air. I know it makes no sense but somehow she smelled like the dawn breaking outside her window.

Sadly, on top of the divine aroma, through a crack in her bedroom door, I caught a whiff of gasoline and knew it was time to say good-bye. One last time, I leaned over and kissed her lips.

"Thanks, Aja. Thanks for everything."

I stood and, using my crutches, walked out of her room and down the stairs to the front door. Bart had been busy—the odor of gasoline was growing. Yet he had not overdone it. The fumes would burn off quickly and by the time the firemen arrived there'd be no trace left to say the fire hadn't been caused by an electrical short. And if later Aja's remains were found, then it would be up to Bart and his lawyer to talk to the authorities. Yet I had a feeling the police and firemen would find nothing.

Standing on the front porch, Bart handed me a single wooden match. I was surprised to see him smile. "What is it?" I asked.

"In her will Aja left everything she owned to you. Besides the money, that includes a half interest in this house. If you light that match, you'll be several million dollars poorer."

"Does that bother you?" I asked.

"Not at all."

"Good," I said, striking the match on the top of a nearby wooden post, watching the tiny flame flare bright, before I tossed it through the front door and onto one of the many expensive rugs spread throughout the house. The fire ran from us in half a dozen different directions. A gust of smoke forced us back.

Within minutes flames were pouring out of both ends of the house and again we were pushed away and had to jump in Bart's car and head to the end of the driveway. There we got out and watched as geysers of flame shattered the mansion's many windows and leaped toward the gray sky. Fortunately the house was isolated. We were two hundred yards from the blaze and still we could feel our cheeks burning.

"Good-bye, Aja," I said as I stared at the inferno. At some

point Bart took my hand and I thought I heard him utter a few last words. But what they were I could not say, lost as I was in my own thoughts.

Ten years have gone by since I met and fell in love with Aja. I don't think it would be an exaggeration to say I've spent the better part of that decade trying to figure out who she was. I suppose like most people I like to think the years have granted me more insight—not just into Aja but into life itself.

Yet I'm afraid, even after all this time, that Aja remains as much a mystery as when I first saw her sitting in the park across the street from my old high school, picking flowers and staring at the students as they walked by in the hot summer sun.

Writing about the time I spent with her has been very satisfying—therapeutic in its own way. It's caused me to recall with razorlike clarity moments that the years had begun to blur. It's also caused me to *feel* her near me. That, I think, is what's most precious about her story. Because simply reviewing what she said or where she went or who she spoke to or even what miracles she performed doesn't begin to convey who she was.

Of course most people will say that's crazy, especially when it comes to her miracles. They'll say that healing Mike

Garcia and Lisa Alastair and Barbara Kataekiss—and others we don't even know about—was what made Aja unique. Just as the miracles Christ performed in the Bible are what caused Christianity to become the most popular religion on earth.

That's fine, I say. I still think I'm right. Aja was much more than the person we saw walking around and living in Elder. She said it herself many times. She wasn't the body. She wasn't the mind. She was none of those things we like to think about when we stop to remember a person.

But that said—how are we to remember her? Even more important—for those who never met her—how are we to imagine her?

Fair questions that deserve reasonable answers.

I only wish I had the answers to give.

But let me come back to that in a minute.

Two months after Aja died, after the nasal sound caused by my broken nose had vanished, I flew back to Los Angeles and rerecorded "Strange Girl." The song was released too late to take advantage of the holiday season but it managed to get decent play on the radio and rose as high as number ten on the Billboard Chart. Paradise Records asked me to cut a full album. I asked if I could wait a few months. My grief over losing Aja had yet to diminish; if anything it was getting worse. Richard Gratter said no problem, he understood, take all the time you need. I don't know why I was surprised when he refused to take my calls when I called him four months later. But hey, that's the music business. You're lucky if you get one shot.

Yet my music career was far from over. After graduating from Elder High, I left town with my acoustic guitar and bummed around the country, playing short and long gigs at whatever clubs would hire me. I didn't have a manager—Janet had gone off to Harvard—but I got by. Although "Strange Girl" never became a major hit, it quickly developed a cult following. That one song became my calling card. And since I refused to live off of Aja's money—I gave it all away to charities—the song literally fed me for years.

Still, no major labels came knocking.

Maybe it was my voice, I thought. Maybe it was my face. Whatever, I eventually decided I could make more money writing songs for existing stars rather than trying to become a star myself. And that's what I've been doing up until this day. I've written exactly one dozen top-ten hits. Naturally, out-side of the business, no one knows my name. A funny thing about the celebrities I write for. They like to take credit for everything they sing. Actually, they insist upon taking credit. I'm well paid but I never get invited to walk the red carpets.

That's okay. I get to do what I love for a living.

I can't complain.

After graduation, Mike and Dale moved to San Francisco and got involved in the health food industry. They started a company that sells herbal formulas that are supposed to do everything from increase a person's IQ to make Viagra a thing of the past. I tried their products but didn't notice much. Then again, what do I know? They're making money hand over fist and they're lucky. Because Mike married only two years out of high school and his wife quickly popped out four kids.

I played at Mike's wedding; Dale was his best man. And the male actor Dale was with that day—two years ago I heard they got married. I was in Europe at the time, playing mostly London clubs, and didn't make it back for the ceremony. But I just heard through the grapevine that Dale and his partner are close to adopting a child.

Shelly . . . it's hard to talk about Shelly. Only a year after Elder High released us into the big bad world, she entered a liquor store late at night in New York City where she was attending NYU and stumbled upon a holdup—a messy one. It appeared at the start that the owner didn't mind handing over his money, but the instant the robber turned to leave, the owner went for a shotgun he kept behind the counter.

The owner got off one shot; the robber two. The robber's

first bullet hit the owner in the shoulder, which threw off the man's aim. When the owner did pull his trigger his shotgun was pointed at Shelly's left leg. The blast came close to amputating the limb; it definitely ruptured her femoral artery. Shelly bled to death before the ambulance could arrive.

The robber's second bullet struck the owner in the hand. The man made a full recovery, while the robber escaped with fifty dollars in cash. Dale, Mike, Janet, me—we all returned home for Shelly's funeral. It was good to see everyone again, especially Janet, but it was a grim affair. I was told Shelly had finally met a guy she was wild about. Actually, I met the guy; he was at the funeral. Everyone said how much he looked like me.

I still think about Shelly every day. It makes no sense but I seem to care more about her now than when she was alive. But I don't blame myself for what happened to her and I have no regrets about how I treated her when we were in high school. Aja taught me a few things. One was that guilt had nothing to do with love.

My parents, they divorced. They split up right after I left home. My mom kept the house and remarried within a year. Another wedding I played at. My stepfather—he's all right. He doesn't talk much, which is never a bad thing.

My dad, he remarried as well, twice. The first time was

bad. The woman was coming out of a marriage too and the double dose of rebounding made them both sick of each other before the honeymoon was over. But the third time was the charm for old Dad. He's happy; at least he acts like he is. Yet it does worry me that he just happened to buy a house around the block from where my mom lives.

Janet, being Janet, finished her undergraduate degree at Harvard in three years instead of four and got accepted into their prestigious law school and naturally graduated number one in her class. The girl who said she had no interest in money took a job on Wall Street and is currently making more cash than she can possibly spend. More impressive, to me at least, is the fact that she's married to a guy who's at least as smart as her and she has a baby daughter named . . . Aja.

Janet and I keep in touch online. She says she sees her father at least once a year, although less since her daughter was born. I always tell her how happy I am for her. But when it comes to Bo I keep my mouth shut.

To my surprise Janet admits she still goes to therapy to deal with what happened to her as a child. Indeed, she started seeing a psychologist only a month after Aja died. In my mind that doesn't take anything away from the miracle Aja performed on her. Aja opened the door so that Janet could see the truth. No one could have asked for more.

Yet I still don't know why Aja healed Bo. Did the fact that she'd seen her own mother killed in front of her play a role in what happened that cold and dark night? If that's true then it means she ignored Janet's request; that she didn't let the Big Person decide whether Bo should live or not. That the Aja we knew, the one we could see with our eyes and hear with our ears, simply decided to lay down her life for him, probably for Janet's sake.

Or else it's possible Aja wasn't influenced by her personality; that the Big Person was fully in charge from start to finish. I lean toward this belief because only moments before Bo was healed it was obvious the Big Person was in control.

Now, looking back, I realize that every word that came out of Aja's mouth during those tense moments had been aimed at Janet's wound. That the phrases Aja chose meant nothing to her. They were simply finely crafted sounds spoken aloud to pluck a splinter from Janet's heart.

But if Aja didn't act on her own volition, if she was wise enough to set aside her personality and let the Big Person decide Bo's fate, then why did she die? I think the answer is simple. So simple it's near impossible to believe.

I think healing Bo killed Aja because Bo was already dead.

The guy was just lying there, not making a sound.

He wasn't moving. I couldn't see him breathing.

A life for a life. Is it so impossible to believe that Aja had the power to raise someone from the dead? She said on several occasions that she was one with the Big Person. And who's to say the Big Person does not operate by certain karmic rules—necessary rules that keep the scales of cause and effect balanced. For example, perhaps for Bo's body to stand up and walk away, Aja's body had to lie down and breathe no more. Jesus said he was the Son of God. Aja never said she was His daughter. Perhaps she could raise a person from the dead but only once.

I never got a chance to ask her the answer to that riddle.

And I know the answer shouldn't matter.

Yet it still bothers me.

I've never spoken to Bo since that night.

Hell, this is no way to finish a tale of Aja's brief but beautiful life. She deserves so much more. I should be talking about how great she was. About how much I loved her. About how much she loved everyone. But that's the problem with trying to describe a girl who kept saying she was no one.

In Advaita, the system of yoga that Janet believed best described Aja's internal state, they often call the Big Person the Brahman. And they say the Brahman cannot be described by words, only by negation. "It's not this. It's not that." I don't know, maybe it's just me, but I'd have trouble hanging out with a master or teacher who answered every question I asked by saying, "That's a good question, Fred. Unfortunately, there's no answer to it."

It's time, I think, to throw negation out the window.

Granted, Aja was shrouded in mystery, but despite what I said earlier, I do believe she gave me and my friends a glimpse into the Big Person by the life she led. She was the only person I ever met who was a hundred percent genuine, absolutely sincere. She never once said something that didn't sound true; and somehow, no matter what the situation, she always said the right thing. And she was the most humble human being I ever met.

The most caring, the most loving, simply the most. . . .

What guided her from behind the scenes may have been too vast for anyone to comprehend, but at least I got to enjoy her as a normal girlfriend. When I kissed her lips, I felt cherished. When we touched, I got aroused. And when we made love I felt as if I had died and gone to heaven. Yeah, sure, she may have been sent to earth by the angels but she was the most passionate female I ever met.

I was lucky she was my first love. Lucky and cursed. I mean, I was just looking for a girlfriend to have sex with and fate handed me a goddess with galaxies inside her. Talk about scoring. But the flip side is how do I replace her? As a one-man band traveling the fifty states, I've met all kinds of women. Occasionally, if she's kind enough, cute enough, I may even feel a crush coming on. But then I wake up in the morning, after dreaming of you know who, I roll over in bed and open my eyes and reality hits home. And I'm back on the road again.

Only one in three hundred million people are struck by lightning twice in one life. I read that somewhere. Those are slim odds, and I know the chances of finding another Aja are just as remote. But I don't worry about it, not like Janet, Mike, and Dale worry about me finding someone else to love.

They're still my best friends. The passing years haven't changed that. They care about me and I still care about them. And they fear I wander the country lost, always searching to heal the hole in my heart that Aja's death caused. They don't understand what her death meant. Back then, I was in such pain, even I didn't understand. When she touched me, all I felt was an unlooked-for moment of relief. I hadn't a clue that I was witnessing the last of her miracles.

I'd like to go step by step and explain exactly what happened.

Unfortunately, I don't know what happened.

That's what's wrong with miracles. They make for great bedtime stories if you're religious and they can still be impressive to watch even if you're an atheist and can't believe what your eyes are seeing. Just don't try putting them under a microscope.

I should just say what happened that night.

Looking back on it from ten years later . . .

When Aja was dying and she touched my heart and said, *"It's okay. You will be okay. I will be with you here. I will always be with you. I promise . . ."* I was never the same afterward.

I'm not saying she gave me a dose of universal bliss. I was in agony when she died and months later I was still in pain. But a part of me changed with her final touch—permanently, deep inside—and I think it was because she put a piece of herself inside of me.

If you don't believe me I can't say I blame you.

But what I can say is that as my grief passed I became more and more aware that Fred was not who I was; or rather, that Fred was not *all* I was. To put it another way—in the center of my heart a diamond that I never knew existed began to shine. English has no words for the gem but I've no doubt that one day her final gift will lead me to the Big Person.

That said, I know most people will think Aja changed me into a "believer." That's not true—what she did was much more sublime. She erased my "disbelief."

It took me ten years but I finally felt it was time I wrote

about Aja and fulfilled my purpose for being on earth. I say that as a joke, of course, but not totally. I've never forgotten that night she told me I was an angel and that I'd come to this world for a reason. Meeting her, falling in love with her, telling her story—these things have given my life more meaning than anything else, even my music.

To write Aja's story, I finally came home to Elder. And I've written about her while sitting in just one spot—on the ground where the Carter Mansion used to stand, before Bart and I burned it down. I assumed before coming home that the area would still show signs of scorching. But such was not the case.

Now, either the ash from the mansion acted as some kind of superfertilizer or else Aja's ashes had fairy dust in them. It's hard to believe but the plot of land where the house stood is now covered with a surprising variety of trees: birch, oak, maple, elm, fir. None are fully matured but they're still fairly tall, especially when you consider they're only ten years old.

While writing this book, their leaves and branches were wide enough to provide me with plenty of shade from the hot sun. And I should mention a flower that's growing wild over the plot of land. Daisies, there are daisies everywhere. Romantic fool that I am, I often think they're just waiting for Aja to return to pluck them.

It's interesting to contemplate that what remains of Aja's physical body is here on this land. Perhaps that's why, occasionally, when my mind is still, I'll draw in a deep breath and feel I can smell her again. Not as she lay silent on her deathbed but as she smelled when she was alive in my arms. For an instant I imagine I hear her voice, a word or two, spoken in my ear. It's then I realize how lucky I was that I knew her and that she was my girlfriend.

I know most will see these final words as the sentiments of a guy who continues to grieve over a long-lost love. I can't lie, I still miss her. Yet I've finally realized that what she tried to tell me at the start, and at the end, is true. She really was beyond this changing world. She was forever. And even though I still long to hold her again, I know she is always with me.

Check Out Christoper Pike's *Red Queen*

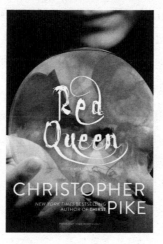

ONCE I BELIEVED THAT I WANTED NOTHING MORE THAN love. Someone who would care for me more than he cared for himself. A guy who would never betray me, never lie to me, and most of all never leave me. Yeah, that was what I desired most, what people usually call true love.

I don't know if that has really changed.

Yet I have to wonder now if I want something else just as badly. What is it? You must wonder . . .

Magic. I want my life filled with the mystery of magic.

Silly, huh? Most people would say there's no such thing.

Then again, most people are not witches.

Not like me.

I discovered what I was when I was eighteen years old, two days after I graduated high school. Before then I was your typical teenager. I got up in the morning, went to school, stared at my ex-boyfriend across the campus courtyard and imagined what it would be like to have him back in my life, went to the local library and sorted books for four hours, went home, watched TV, read a little, lay in bed and thought some more about Jimmy Kelter, then fell asleep and dreamed.

But I feel, somewhere in my dreams, I sensed I was different from other girls my age. Often it seemed, as I wandered the twilight realms of my unconscious, that I existed in another world, a world like our own and yet different, too. A place where I had powers my normal, everyday self could hardly imagine.

I believe it was these dreams that made me crave that elusive thing that is as great as true love. It's hard to be sure, I only know that I seldom awakened without feeling a terrible sense of loss. As though my very soul had been chopped into pieces and tossed back into the world. The sensation of being on the "outside" is difficult to describe. All I can say is that, deep inside, a part of me always hurt.

I used to tell myself it was because of Jimmy. He had dumped me, all of a sudden, for no reason. He had broken my heart, dug it out of my chest, and squashed it when he said I really like you, Jessie, we can still be friends, but I've got to go now. I blamed him for the pain. Yet it had been there before I had fallen in love with him, so there had to be another reason why it existed.

Now I know Jimmy was only a part of the equation.

But I get ahead of myself. Let me begin, somewhere near the beginning.

Like I said, I first became aware I was a witch the same weekend I graduated high school. At the time I lived in Apple Valley, which is off Interstate 15 between Los Angeles and Las Vegas. How that hick town got that name was beyond me. Apple Valley was smack in the middle of the desert. I wouldn't be exaggerating if I said it's easier to believe in witches than in apple trees growing in that godforsaken place.

Still, it was home, the only home I had known since I was six. That was when my father the doctor had decided that Nurse Betty—that was what my mom called her—was more sympathetic to his needs than my mother. From birth to six I lived in a mansion overlooking the Pacific, in a Malibu enclave loaded with movie stars and the studio executives who had made them famous. My mom, she must have had a lousy divorce lawyer, because even though she had worked her butt off to put my father through medical school and a six-year residency that trained him to be one of the finest heart surgeons on the West Coast, she was kicked out of the marriage with barely enough money to buy a two-bedroom home in Apple Valley. And with summer temperatures averaging above a hundred, real estate was never a hot item in our town.

I was lucky I had skin that gladly suffered the sun. It was soft, and I tanned deeply without peeling. My coloring probably helped. My family tree is mostly European, but there was an American Indian in the mix back before the Civil War.

Chief Proud Feather. You might wonder how I know his name, and that's good—wonder away, you'll find out, it's part of my story. He was 100 percent Hopi, but since he was sort of a distant relative, he gave me only a small portion of my features. My hair is brown with a hint of red. At dawn and sunset it is more maroon than anything else. I have freckles and green eyes, but not the green of a true redhead. My freckles are few, often lost in my tan, and my eyes are so dark the green seems to come and go, depending on my mood.

There wasn't much green where I grew up. The starved branches on the trees on our campus looked as if they were always reaching for the sky, praying for rain.

I was pretty; for that matter, I still am pretty. Understand, I turned eighteen a long time ago. Yet I still look much the same. I'm not immortal, I'm just very hard to kill. Of course, I could die tonight, who's to say.

It was odd, as a bright and attractive senior in high school, I wasn't especially popular. Apple Valley High was small—our graduating class barely topped two hundred. I knew all the seniors. I had memorized the first and last name of every cute boy in my class, but I was seldom asked out. I used to puzzle over that fact. I especially wondered why James Kelter had dumped me after only ten weeks of what, to me, had felt like the greatest relationship in the world. I was to find out when our class took that ill-fated trip to Las Vegas.

Our weekend in Sin City was supposed to be the equivalent of our Senior All-Night Party. I know, on the surface that sounds silly. A party usually lasts one night, and our parents believed we were spending the night at the local Hilton. However, the plan was for all two hundred of us to privately call our parents in the morning and say we had just been invited by friends to go camping in the mountains that separated our desert from the LA Basin.

The scheme was pitifully weak. Before the weekend was over, most of our parents would know we'd been nowhere near the mountains. That didn't matter. In fact, that was the whole point of the trip. We had decided, as a class, to throw all caution to the wind and break all the rules.

The reason such a large group was able to come to such a wild decision was easy to understand if you considered our unusual location. Apple Valley was nothing more than a road stop stuck between the second largest city in the nation— LA—and its most fun city—Las Vegas. For most of our lives, especially on Friday and Saturday evenings, we watched as thousands of cars flew northeast along Interstate 15 toward good times, while we remained trapped in a fruit town that didn't even have fruit trees.

So when the question arose of where we wanted to celebrate

our graduation, all our years of frustration exploded. No one cared that you had to be twenty-one to gamble in the casinos. Not all of us were into gambling and those who were simply paid Ted Pollack to make them fake IDs.

Ted made my ID for free. He was an old friend. He lived a block over from my house. He had a terrible crush on me, one I wasn't supposed to know about. Poor Ted, he confided everything in his heart to his sister, Pam, who kept secrets about as well as the fifty-year-old gray parrot that lived in their kitchen. It was dangerous to talk in front of that bird, just as it was the height of foolishness to confide in Pam.

I wasn't sure why Ted cared so deeply about me. Of course, I didn't understand why I cared so much about Jimmy. At eighteen I understood very little about love, and it's a shame I wasn't given a chance to know more about it before I was changed. That's something I'll always regret.

That particular Friday ended up being a wasteland of regrets. After a two-hour graduation ceremony that set a dismal record for scorching heat and crippling boredom, I learned from my best friend, Alex Simms, that both Ted and Jimmy would be driving with us to Las Vegas. Alex told me precisely ten seconds after I collected my blue-and-gold cap off the football field—after our class collectively threw them in the air—and exactly one minute after our school principal had pronounced us full-fledged graduates.

"You're joking, right?" I said.

Alex brushed her short blond hair from her bright blues. She wasn't as pretty as me but that didn't stop her from acting like she was. The weird thing is, it worked for her. Even though she didn't have a steady boyfriend, she dated plenty, and there wasn't a guy in school who would have said no to her if she'd so much as said hi. A natural flirt, she could touch a guy's hand and make him feel like his fingers were caressing her breasts.

Alex was a rare specimen, a compulsive talker who knew when to shut up and listen. She had a quick wit—some would say it was biting—and her self-confidence was legendary. She had applied to UCLA with a B-plus average and a slightly above-average SAT score and they had accepted her—supposedly—on the strength of her interview. While Debbie Pernal, a close friend of ours, had been turned down by the same school despite a straight-A average and a very high SAT score.

It was Debbie's belief that Alex had seduced one of the interviewing deans. In Debbie's mind, there was no other explanation for how Alex had gotten accepted. Debbie said as much to anyone who would listen, which just happened to be the entire student body. Her remarks started a tidal wave of a rumor: "ALEX IS A TOTAL SLUT!" Of course, the fact that Alex never bothered to deny the slur didn't help matters. If anything, she took great delight in it.

And these two were friends.

Debbie was also driving with us to Las Vegas.

"There was a mix-up," Alex said without much conviction,

trying to explain why Jimmy was going to ride in the car with us. "We didn't plan for both of them to come."

"Why would anyone in their right mind put Jimmy and me together in the same car?" I demanded.

Alex dropped all pretense. "Could it be that I'm sick and tired of you whining about how he dumped you when everything was going so perfect between you two?"

I glared at her. "We're best friends! You're required to listen to my whining. It doesn't give you the right to invite the one person in the whole world who ripped my heart out to go on a road trip with us."

"What road trip? We're just giving him a three-hour ride. You don't have to talk to him if you don't want to."

"Right. The five of us are going to be crammed into your car half the afternoon and it will be perfectly normal if I don't say a word to the first and last guy I ever had sex with."

Alex was suddenly interested. "I didn't know Jimmy was your first. You always acted like you slept with Clyde Barker."

Clyde Barker was our football quarterback and so good-looking that none of the girls who went to the games—myself included—cared that he couldn't throw a pass to save his ass. He had the IQ of a cracked helmet. "It was just an act," I said with a sigh.

"Look, it might work out better than you think. My sources tell me Jimmy has hardly been seeing Kari at all. They may even be broken up."

Kari Rider had been Jimmy's girlfriend before me, and after me, which gave me plenty of reason to hate the bitch.

"Why don't we be absolutely sure and invite Kari as well," I said. "She can sit on my lap."

Alex laughed. "Admit it, you're a tiny bit happy I did all this behind your back."

"I'm a tiny bit considering not going at all."

"Don't you dare. Ted would be devastated."

"Ted's going to be devastated when he sees Jimmy get in your car!"

Alex frowned. "You have a point. Debbie invited him, not me."

On top of everything else, Debbie had a crush on Ted, the same Ted who had a crush on me. It was going to be a long three hours to Las Vegas.

"Did Debbie think it was a good idea for Jimmy to ride with us?" I asked.

"Sure."

I was aghast. "I can't believe it. That bitch."

"Well, actually, she didn't think there was a chance in hell he'd come."

That hurt. "Love the vote of confidence. What you mean is Debbie didn't think there was a chance in hell Jimmy was still interested in me."

"I didn't say that."

"No. But you both thought it."

"Come on, Jessie. It's obvious Jimmy's coming with us so he can spend time with you." Alex patted me on the back. "Be happy."

"Why did you wait until now to tell me this?"

"Because now it's too late to change my devious plan."

I dusted off my blue-and-gold cap and put it back on. "I suppose this is your graduation present to me?" I asked.

"Sure. Where's mine?"

"You'll get it when we get to Las Vegas."

"Really?"

"Yeah. You'll see." I already had a feeling I was going to pay her back, I just didn't know how.

CHRISTOPHER PIKE

is a bestselling author of young adult novels. The Thirst series, *The Secret of Ka*, and the Remember Me and Alosha trilogies are some of his favorite titles. He is also the author of several adult novels, including *Sati* and *The Season of Passage*. Thirst and Alosha are slated to be released as feature films. Pike currently lives in Santa Barbara, where it is rumored he never leaves his house. But he can be found online at www.Facebook.com/ChristopherPikeBooks.

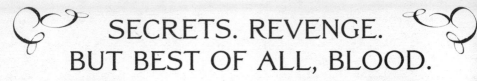